bishop

EDEN SUMMERS

Copyright © 2023 by Eden Summers

All rights reserved.

No part of this book may be reproduced in any form or by any electronic or mechanical means, including information storage and retrieval systems, without written permission from the author, except for the use of brief quotations in a book review.

This book is a work of fiction. The names, characters, places, and incidents are products of the writer's imagination or have been used fictitiously and are not to be construed as real. Any resemblance to persons, living or dead, actual events, locales or organizations is entirely coincidental.

The author acknowledges the trademarked status and trademark owners of various products referenced in this work of fiction, which have been used without permission. The publication/use of these trademarks is not authorized, associated with, or sponsored by the trademark owners.

*To the readers who grew up fantasizing
about the dark prince instead of the white knight,
you are my people.*

Enjoy all the red flags.

1

BISHOP

I'M GOING TO KILL THE WOMAN I WAS SENT TO PROTECT.

Call me psychic. Or maybe it's intuition. Who the fuck knows? But something inside me vibrates with a level of homicidal certainty. My palms itch to wrap around Abri's delicate throat as she schmoozes with the Denver elite in this seductively lit hotel ballroom with its pompous decorations and endless supply of expensive liquor.

I've called her fifty goddamn times today without answer.

I've left innumerable messages. Sent endless texts. Not once did she respond.

I explained to her voicemail how I'd been sent halfway across the country by her brothers because she—*she*—called them this morning *begging* for someone to watch her back after her dad made changes to her security detail.

But she seems more than fucking peachy now.

She's charming every man in a three-piece, her shiny golden gown dazzling, a matching sheer scarf covering the front of her neck like a choker, the long length of material draped down her back as her temptress smile hides whatever sinister intent she has lurking inside.

She's the queen of this smorgasbord of upper-class snobbery. She laughs with politicians. Rubs shoulders with those I assume are tech billionaires. Bats her lashes at old money in expensive tailored suits.

She's in her element, lapping up their attention without a care in the world while I remain by the bar at the back of the ballroom, my presence unknown to her.

For now.

The lights dim and a middle-aged guy in a tux walks onto the stage, introduces himself as some successful asshole from who-the-fuck-cares, and directs everyone to find their seats.

The herd of blue bloods comply, a grey-haired guy placing a hand on the curve of Abri's back to escort her to a table in the middle of the room then taking the chair beside her.

The formalities drag on, the unending speeches harder to endure than a root canal. Some slick asshole receives a gold star for donating what I assume is his pocket change to an Ethiopian orphanage. Another gets recognition for starting a charity with no mention that it was obviously launched as a tax dodge.

An hour into this ego masturbation, Abri silently rises from her seat with her gold sparkling clutch in hand and discreetly maneuvers her way around the mass of circular tables, smiling at those who make eye contact as she saunters to a side hall leading to the bathrooms. To isolation.

I scrutinize the members of security stationed around the room, waiting for the dogs on her detail to follow—the ones she doesn't trust. Because *that* was her issue this morning. She doesn't have faith in the guys in charge of her safety.

Funnily enough, those concerns appear valid. Nobody pays her attention, at least not in a professional way. There's no protective concern from the men I scan—only sexual interest.

I throw back the last of my scotch, slide the glass onto the bar, and stalk after her as the MC encourages yet another jerk-off to approach the stage to receive his participation award.

I reach the start of the hall as she disappears around the corner toward the ladies room. I follow, making sure nobody trails me while I take the same path and pause at the open archway into the female bathroom.

It's quiet inside. Barely a shuffle of noise until a violent retch breaks the silence.

I frown, tempted to storm in there to find out what the hell has caused the picture-perfect princess to start throwing her guts up. Instead, I lean back against the wall separating us and listen to the splash of her stomach contents against the bowl.

She looked flawless in the ballroom. Exuberant. Downright fucking sprightly.

So what's with the violent heaving?

Food poisoning? Bulimia?

The toilet flushes. The gentle bang of a closing stall follows. Heels tap against tile. A faucet turns on with a haphazard splash of water before being shut off. Then nothing.

No sound. No movement.

I chance a glance around the wall, catching her staring at her reflection in the mirror, her hands clutching the counter.

She stills for a moment, blinking back at herself, breathing slow and deep.

Then with a sigh, she straightens her bare shoulders and stands tall, her mask of charm shimmering back into place. Confidence curves her lips. Her eyes sparkle.

What the hell is she up to? Or, more accurately, what the fuck are her and her piece-of-shit father trying to achieve tonight?

She unclasps her clutch to remove a tube of lipstick and I inch back against the wall, not needing to watch her prep the moneymaker. I attempt to distinguish the shifting sounds, the popping of her lips, the rummaging through her clutch, then an unmistakable fast and hard sniff.

Once…

Twice…

Great. I signed up for junkie detail, too.

Isn't she just the most delightful goodie bag of surprises?

Fucking hell, Langston.

I knew my best friend's sister had issues when I offered to keep an eye on her. But this shitshow of downfalls is growing beyond my tolerance. I'm tempted to storm in there and snatch whatever stupid shit she's snorting up that pretty nose of hers. That's what Langston would want. Yet when he's MIA and copying his estranged sister's habit of dodging my calls it's only natural I take the opposite path to his preferences.

This should be *his* job. *His* annoyance.

I was only meant to watch out for her during the day. Langston was supposed to be here by now. He was meant to make the cross-country journey as soon as his meeting finished with my boss, who also happens to be his Uncle Lorenzo. But I guess the conversation of murdering your own father takes longer than I'd anticipated, because neither of those fuckers are keen to communicate.

Either that or they're both dead, which I refuse to contemplate.

There's another sniff. Another poke at my annoyance.

I shouldn't give a shit that Abri's dabbling in dangerous territory. Not my circus. Not my fucking monkey. But this shit irks me. Big time.

Langston will have to address her extracurriculars. He needs to tell the mistress of manipulation the most fundamental rule in this line of business—if you sell drugs, you never *do* drugs.

Unfortunately, that gem of advice is something most learn the hard way. I guess I was the lucky son of a bitch with a past that made me immune to those types of adult mistakes.

There's more rummaging in her clutch. A click of the clasp. Then the tap of approaching heels.

I time my push from the wall, making sure to step into the path of the bathroom archway the moment she exits.

Right on cue, she collides into my chest with a thud and a gasp.

Her hands snap up to grab my arms for stability. Her clutch falls to the floor. "I'm so sorry. I didn't…" Her frantic gaze raises to mine, the shocked, faux Bambi look blinking away in an instant as sheer loathing takes its place. "*You.*"

"*Me.*" I glower.

Sadly, this isn't our first fairytale meet-cute.

I've been right beside Langston as he spied on his family for years. Yet it wasn't until recently that we actually met—when I was in charge of looking after Langston's woman and this witch helped her escape.

Abri didn't score brownie points with me then. And she sure as shit hasn't now after ignoring me all goddamn day.

But I've never been this close to her. Not where I can see the differing shades of blue in her eyes. The smooth flawlessness of her skin.

She truly is beautiful. An exquisitely mesmerizing dick trap.

"Why are you here?" She shoves at my chest in a pitiful attempt that makes her stumble backward.

"You wouldn't have to ask if you answered your fucking phone." I bend to grab her clutch and hand it over. "You wanted more security for tonight. So here I am."

She snatches my offering. "No. I wanted Remy and Salvatore."

"Well, lucky you. You got an upgrade."

"I doubt it." She shoves the clutch under her arm, holding it against her ribs. "Where are they?"

"Currently indisposed."

Her eyes flash, in fear or ferocity I'm not sure. "What did you do to them?" she snaps.

Okay, it's definitely ferocity. "Calm down. They're with Langston. Safe and sound."

Except for a bruise or two. But she doesn't need to know about the injuries I took pleasure inflicting. This whole working-together bullshit is new to all of us. Last week, Langston and I were ready to choke out his younger brothers. And apparently now we're on the same side.

Fucking awesome.

"You need to leave." She makes to walk around me. "I don't want you here."

I counter with a sidestep. "I don't want to be here either, belladonna. But that's the job description."

She pauses. Straightens. Slowly regains her composure. Or maybe the speed ball is kicking in. But instead of her fury increasing, her seductive mask glistens back into place like a spell has been cast.

Her expression gentles, those sapphire eyes blinking with manipulative beauty. "I guess it's safe to assume Remy told you I called this morning with concerns."

I incline my head.

I overheard the conversation, from her pleading for Remy and Salvo to return home to protect her to her aggressive emotional onslaught once she found out they were in the midst of a plan to take down their father.

She turned livid, laying down the law, forbidding their intentions.

She made it known she wouldn't forgive and forget if action was taken against Emmanuel Costa.

Not that they listened.

Hence why I'm here and they're probably still in Virginia Beach, throwing back whiskey and discussing strategy with Lorenzo like the motherfuckers they are.

She drags in a long breath and waves an errant hand in my direction. "I apologize over how you've been caught up in this. I overreacted when I spoke to Remy. I assure you it isn't necessary for you to be here."

I wish I was born yesterday because then I could accept this act of blatant bullshit and be on my merry fucking way. *Toodaloo, Viper Barbie. I'm outta here.* "There was mention of you having an issue with the guards your father assigned to look after you. Are you telling me that's no longer a concern?"

She inclines her head. "That's correct."

"Great. Then you won't mind pointing me in their direction. We need to have a chat."

"No you don't. If my father finds out you're here, he'll—"

"It's not up for negotiation. Especially since I walked into the hotel through the kitchen, without ID, while strapped." I mimic her synthetic smile. "I've come across better security at Starbucks. Your men need a good dressing down for putting you in your current precarious situation."

"I wasn't aware I was in a precarious situation?"

I step closer, getting in her personal space, her neck craning in her attempt to maintain eye contact. "You could be. If I was someone else—"

"Someone other than a murderous member of the Italian mafia?" She breathes a laugh. "I can handle myself."

She's delusional. Careless. Or maybe just plain fucking stupid.

"I could haul you over my shoulder and drag you out the fire exit." I take another step, forcing her to retreat, backing her against the wall. Her perfume infiltrates my lungs, the exotic sweetness increasing with every breath. "Where are they, Abri?"

Her hands fumble around her clutch. The clasp clicks. Then it all falls to the floor as I inch closer. But despite her flustering, she doesn't break our gaze. "Get out of my face."

"Just as soon as you tell me who's meant to be ensuring your safety." *So I can teach them a lesson in customer service.*

"I won't ask again," she purrs.

"Neither will I."

"Then I guess we're at a fork in the road." Her smile increases as something nudges my crotch. Something hard. My dick responds with interest despite the blatant threat to my manhood. "Have you ever been tasered in the balls, Bishop?" She raises a haughty brow. "That is your name, right?"

My nostrils flare. My pulse fucking surges.

"It sure is." I inch harder against the threat. "And no, nobody has ever dared to taser me. *Anywhere*. Let alone the crown jewels. So just to make the repercussions perfectly clear, if you decide to make that move, you'd want to hope it kills me."

She chuckles, sickeningly self-assured. "And why is that?"

"You break it, you bought it, belladonna."

Her laughter continues, the sound deceptively innocent despite the underlying venom. "Move."

"I will once you tell me how it was possible to get this close to you." I plant my hands on the wall on either side of that gorgeous face. "How I can *continue* to remain a fucking dick length away without interference?"

She stares at me, the seconds ticking by without response. But that condescending brow of hers wavers slightly. The smile, too.

I edge closer, a breath from those venomous lips. "Dear ol' daddy took away your regular detail and left you with chumps, didn't he? They couldn't protect you if their lives depended on it, could they?"

She raises her chin in defiance. "I'm sure they could."

There's something about her words. That tone.

"Where are they?" I glide a strand of hair behind her ear, appreciating the strength it must take for her not to flinch. "You're not going anywhere until I get an answer."

"Or until I fry your little swimmers." She pokes my dick with the measly stun gun.

I grin. "Fuck around with my private parts and I'll do the same with yours."

She rolls her eyes. "You think I'm scared of you? I eat men of your caliber on a weekly basis."

"You have no clue of my caliber." I'm tempted to push this further just so she can have a first-hand account of the type of man she's dealing with. But fuck that. Fuck her. I'm tired of this shit. And so unbelievably fucking tired in general. When was the last time I slept? "Just tell me where the hell they are so I don't have to walk into that ballroom and start asking people one by one."

She falls silent. Unresponsive.

What is she hiding?

I retreat an inch, removing myself from her heavenly scented poison cloud. "Are they even here?"

The quiet remains. There's nothing but the droll tone of the MC carrying from the ballroom while her stun gun remains poised near my favorite asset.

Her delicate swallow gives her away.

"That's it, isn't it?" I retreat farther, giving her space to wallow in whatever shame is brimming to the surface. "It's not that they're shit at their job—they're nonexistent, aren't they?"

She bends down to retrieve her clutch, ignoring the question.

"Answer me," I growl. "Are they unreliable or nonexistent?"

"My safety isn't your concern." She straightens, her attention moving to the hall leading to the ballroom. "*Leave*. If I see you again I'll ensure security removes you from the building."

"All you'd be doing is scheduling them a lengthy stay at the nearest hospital."

"Such big, tough words from a big, tough guy," she drawls. "But one of us is bluffing, Bishop, and I'll give you a free piece of intel—it sure as hell ain't me."

2
ABRI

I stride from the bathroom alcove and into the hall without looking back, the long length of my scarf swishing against my shoulders as I make my way to the ballroom to reclaim my seat next to Gordon.

"Did I miss anything?" I place my clutch on the table, my dress perfectly positioned to exude a tease of cleavage without being blatant.

"Not at all." He leans close, his expensive, old-school cologne clogging my lungs. "All freshened up?"

"Mm-hmm." My eyes shift to the bathroom hall searching for tousled, dirty blond hair and a formidable frown while I grab my glass of champagne.

Bishop hasn't followed.

Good.

As if I didn't have enough reason to stab Remy and Salvatore after they decided to have a secret rendezvous with our estranged brother. But then they had the audacity to send my long-lost brother's partner as my protection? The other half of the Butcher Boys of Baltimore?

All three of my siblings can go to hell. Remy, Salvatore, *and* Dante…or Matthew Langston, as he now prefers to call himself.

I'll fucking kill them.

Gordon's hand disappears beneath the table, his palm finding my thigh. "These events are incredibly boring. Each speech more nauseating than the last."

I watch the stage, my lips cocked in a gentle smile that usually tempts men to kiss it right off my face. "I agree."

I've already won him over. My job is practically done.

But this task of mine is a fine art.

A delicate dance.

I was sent here for business. For strategy. To grease the wheels with the shipping magnate at my side so my family can use the distribution channels for whatever illegal product my parents decide to invest in next.

I take a sip of champagne and subtly lick the expensive liquid from my bottom lip, always drawing attention where it needs to be. Constantly tempting the man at my side.

At the moment, we're merely strangers brought together through promises by a third party. Gordon is unsure if what he's been offered is real, so it's only natural he's testing the waters. And I'm well aware what I have to give is best served to vultures in tiny morsels.

I need to leave him guessing. Questioning. Salivating.

I chance another casual glance around the room, making sure we're not being watched by a bulky brute of a man who shouldn't be anywhere near here.

"We should go to the hotel bar for a drink." Gordon's hand creeps higher, approaching my panties.

I slowly glide my gaze to his, pinning him with a stare. Impassive but authoritative. Staking control without chastising.

The ascent of his touch stops as he holds my attention, his apprehension showing in the tight tilt of his chin.

"Lead the way." I take another sip of champagne then place the flute on the table and grab my clutch.

He stands, guiding my chair backward as I follow to my feet.

With a hand palming my hip, he directs me around tables filled with wealthy guests, not stopping until we're a few feet from the massive double doors.

Two men walk toward us from the shadows, both in suits and exuding a security vibe.

For a second, I wonder if they were sent by my father. Maybe he didn't leave me high and dry. But both men focus on Gordon.

"We're going to the bar," my handsy companion informs them.

Why Gordon needs protection is beyond me. Sure, he's rich and dabbles in illegal territory, but I've been led to believe he's an outlier. Someone who remains on the edge of danger, never creating enemies.

The taller blond strides to the doors, opening one side of the thick wood.

"Abri, this is Finch." Gordon guides me forward, leading me into another hall. "And Boomer." He indicates the shorter, dark-haired guard with a jerk of his chin.

I raise a brow at the nicknames, acting coy despite the unwanted niggle in my gut. They're striving for anonymity when this is meant to be about forging connection.

Interesting.

"It's nice to meet you both." I flash my billion-dollar smile.

"Likewise." Boomer rakes his gaze over me from the corner of his eye, the attention overtly lecherous before he glances away in dismissal.

Finch doesn't acknowledge me at all.

I don't like them already.

They lead the way into the lobby, across the gleaming chandelier-lit marble floor to the entrance of the hotel bar where we're stopped by a bubbly hostess.

"I'm sorry. We've already reached capacity." She glances behind her to the packed crowd, every table in sight bustling with rowdy drinkers while more stand in line waiting for booze.

"Are you sure you can't fit us in?" Gordon reaches for her hand, subtly slipping her a wad of cash as he clutches her fingers in a fatherly gesture. "It's a special night."

The woman pauses a moment before inclining her head, obviously accustomed to bribes. She gains the attention of a male waiter who escorts us through the loudly talking patrons to a table that has miraculously become available in the back corner of the room.

Seats are taken. Drinks are ordered and delivered. Then I'm left to sit beside a salivating silver fox while his feral cubs watch us from the edge of the throng a few yards away.

"So, Abri." Gordon takes a gulp of gin. "Your father tells me you're an integral part of the family business. He says you're quite —" His mouth twitches "—*skilled* at obtaining what you want."

"He didn't lie."

Gordon chuckles, the sound barely heard over the growing noise in the room. He cradles his crystal tumbler, his other hand sitting against the table, his thumb tapping the wood in a rampant beat.

He's excited.

Impatient.

He wants me, yet he's too pathetic to voice his dirty fantasies.

"Tell me more about yourself." I raise my champagne flute, pausing it an inch from my lips. "Who is Gordon Myers? Apart from an exceptionally successful businessman."

He grins over the bare minimum compliment.

If this was about entrapment I'd already have him—hook, line and sinker. He's putty in my hands. Pathetic, malleable clay. But tonight isn't about extortion.

My father's rules were strict and simple—win Gordon over. Do whatever it takes.

"I've had a great deal of good fortune." He scoots his chair closer until we're side by side, looking across the crowded bar. "And I have a feeling that's only going to increase."

"And what about your wife?" I blink innocently. "What about her good fortune?"

He stiffens slightly, his hand tightening against my flesh for the briefest second before he relaxes. "She is also very fortunate. And understanding of the lengths I go to in an effort to form the strongest bonds with my clients."

"Is that what I am?" I purr. "A client? I was of the understanding this would become more of a partnership. A mutually beneficial arrangement."

"That, too." His palm continues its upward climb. "But we need to take baby steps, my dear."

My dear? What a delightfully nauseating endearment for someone he's currently trying to sleep with.

"Baby steps are for the fearful and inexperienced." I turn into him, ignoring the inevitable nudge of his fingertips against my crotch. "I'm neither of those things. My family wants access to your shipping routes, and I'm here to convince you to give them to us."

"And how do you plan on doing that?" His voice lowers.

"You know exactly what I have in mind."

He planned it, after all.

My father suggested a night to reclaim his misspent youth. To flaunt his masculinity. To dominate in the bedroom for once instead of merely the boardroom.

"I plan to let you fuck me, Gordon." I hold his gaze. "I intend to allow you to do whatever your wicked mind has been dreaming about since the first moment you laid eyes on me. And I anticipate making you so goddamn satisfied that you'll not only agree to go into partnership with my family, but you'll beg for the privilege."

He grins while my stomach instigates another round of Olympic gymnastics. I must have eaten something that doesn't agree with me. *Again.* Or maybe I just need another bump.

Is it too soon for one more bathroom break?

"You know I've heard a lot about you, Abri." His fingers rub against my crotch.

I ignore the touch, which isn't hard given the cocaine numbing my system. "All good, I hope."

"All incredibly scandalous. I heard a rumor you're a siren, luring unsuspecting wealthy businessmen to their demise."

"Demise?" I scoff a laugh. "To their knees maybe."

"That, too." His fingertips circle my mons.

"I can assure you my intent has nothing to do with your demise, Gordon. My family is only trying to build a partnership. Our time together is meant to forge a lasting business relationship."

"I'm not concerned." He adds more pressure to his touch. "Although getting caught taking advantage of your loose morals would be an inconvenience, my wife knows her place."

I don't flinch at the insult. At this point, it's water off a duck's back. "Then why are we wasting time? Why don't I freshen up so we can take this upstairs?"

Filth oozes from his smug smile. "That sounds perfect."

"I'll be back in a minute." I push from my seat, grab my clutch, and raise my gaze over the crowd to find a long line in front of the female bathroom. "On second thought, I'm going to use the restrooms in the lobby."

"I'll be waiting."

I stride through the drunken customers while my nausea increases, demanding to be acknowledged.

Why now?

I clench my hands around my clutch, my skin turning clammy as I fight to suppress the churn of bile in my gut. But every person I nudge past ruffles my tightly wound composure. I hustle into the reception area, my spine straight and smile brittle as I follow the signs to the amenities.

The closer I get to the sanctuary of isolation, the more my stomach roils, turbulent and painful. I'm going to throw up again, there's no stopping it.

I shove against the bathroom door, finding the polished-tiled room empty as I gasp for air. I scamper for the closest stall, shove the door open, and buckle to my knees, my clutch falling to the floor. Bile-infested champagne sears up my throat in an instant, escaping my lips in heaves.

Shit. Shit. Shit.

I can't mess this up. Tonight is too important.

I gag. Retch. Purge. Over and over, the deluge leaves me, the taste sickening, the stomach convulsions agonizing.

Goddammit.

My face breaks out in a cold sweat, my entire body chilled. Why is this happening?

I heave another round of champagne-infused filth and then concentrate on my breathing. Big inhale. Long exhale.

You're fine. It's something you ate.

My pulse runs rampant, the high pace of my heart pumping blood through my system like a freight train. I squeeze my eyes shut, ignoring the anxiety flooding my veins.

I'm not stressed. I'm chill as fuck.

Pull yourself together.

I dab at my mouth with the back of my hand and glare at the bowl.

I will *not* vomit again. I refuse.

I grab my clutch, flush the toilet, and stagger to my feet to walk from the stall.

This business of throwing up has to stop. I'm losing weight, and the first place it disappears is my chest. The last thing I need is my father encouraging a trip to the plastic surgeon.

I force my head high with each step toward the basins. I don't have the luxury of wallowing in illness. I have a job to do. One that has to run smoothly.

I stare at my reflection and turn on the water, refusing to be anything other than confident and composed.

I've got this.

I'm Abri Costa. A manipulator of men. A force to be reckoned with. Nausea will not *be my downfall.*

I wash my hands, fix my lipstick, finger comb my hair, then scavenge through my clutch for the intricately etched silver vial filled with powdered relief. I unscrew the lid, remove the tiny spoon, and raise it to my nose to sniff the numbing goodness into my system.

The coke will get me through. It always does.

It's the powdery pick-me-up I use like medicine. A temporary yet necessary measure that speeds up time and nails my persona in place.

I inhale another bump and sniff until my nose quits tingling and the euphoric wave hits.

There. Perfect. Bliss.

I smile at myself, the nausea retreating, and drop the vial into my clutch before grabbing a breath mint.

In a few hours, this will all be over. Another job complete. One more notch in my belt to make my father proud.

And he *will* be proud. I'll do everything necessary to ensure that outcome and ease some of the tension between us.

I readjust my breasts, plumping them through the cleavage-baring neckline, and reposition my scarf at the base of my throat.

Game on, bitch.

I escape the bathroom with my beaming confidence in place only to have a rough hand grab my wrist, yanking me to a stop.

"What the fuck is going on?" Bishop snarls.

He spins me toward him. My skin erupts in a mass of goose bumps beneath his touch as I meet his deadly blue eyes.

"Get your hands off me." I attempt to drag my arm away, but his grip is like a steel shackle.

"Where's your security?" he demands. "You were adamant they were necessary this morning, yet all I can see is the geriatric and his watch dogs. Those men aren't here for you."

Panic chips at my veneer.

"Are you fucking crazy?" I yank my arm harder, finally dislodging his fingers. "Leave me alone." I storm away, making it two steps before his hands imprison my hips from behind.

He spins me, my stiletto heels skittering across the marble floor as he turns me back toward the alcove leading into the restrooms. "I told you I'm not going anywhere. Not until I know what you're up to." He looms over me, his bulking frame intimidating me against the wall. "*Talk.*"

"I'm in the middle of a business meeting," I growl. "Leave me the fuck alone."

He leans close enough for me to taste the scotch on his breath, to smell the faint hint of cigarettes on his suit. "Well, that's some sort of interesting business model you've got there, belladonna."

I glare, daring him to continue offending me.

He doesn't. He simply stands there, scowling with cold sterility. "I didn't take you for the dramatic type."

"Meaning?"

"Meaning—you called Remy this morning with your panties in a bunch over your safety. Now, suddenly, it doesn't matter? Was it all a ploy for attention?"

No, it was a major mistake.

I'd been in the throes of a panic attack. It isn't the first time I've slipped, but it will be the last. My position doesn't allow for weakness.

"Remy didn't tell you I'm a drama queen?" I bat my lashes. "I guess he took the opportunity to get rid of you while he had an excuse."

Bishop straightens, granting me a few extra inches of space.

"I know it's hard to understand with your low IQ," I drawl, "but I don't want you here. All you're doing—"

"Is there a problem?" a familiar voice asks.

I battle against the instinct to snap rigid and turn to Gordon and his men. "Not at all."

"Is this a friend of yours?" Gordon eyes Bishop with disinterest while I hope to hell the asshole keeps his mouth shut.

"No." I give an apologetic smile. "I wasn't watching where I was going when I left the bathroom. We stumbled into each other."

"I don't blame him." Gordon offers me a hand. "If I weren't

about to take you upstairs, I'd be *accidentally* bumping into you myself."

Bishop stiffens. Every inch on the unfathomably rigid man hardens, including his eyes.

"You're incorrigible." I move around him to take Gordon's hand.

"My dear, you're going to have a far more explicit descriptor in the near future."

My pulse stutters. I tell myself it's an effect of the cocaine. I make myself believe it as Gordon leads me toward the elevators.

Bishop's gaze stalks the back of my neck as I walk away. I can sense his predatory intent. Can feel his anger.

"Ma'am," Bishop calls out.

I glance over my shoulder, not stopping my progression across the lobby. But the man standing behind me isn't the same as the one who grabbed me minutes earlier. This version of Bishop is suave. His smirk arrogant. His ocean eyes playful. It's as if he's mimicking me. Playing his own role.

"It was a pleasure bumping into you." He winks and casually slides his hands into his pockets. "I plan on doing it again real soon."

3

ABRI

I measure my breathing as I'm led into the elevator, the threat of Bishop's interference triggering more of my apprehension.

This is usually when the protection detail call it a night. But Finch and Boomer seem at home as the doors close us into the tight space, their thoughts unreadable behind expressionless faces.

Nobody speaks as we ascend, the elevator stopping at level eighteen.

"Room 1803, my dear." Gordon's hand stalks the curve of my back, the gentle pressure leading me into the hall and to the left. "I have to admit I'm rather excited about the continuation of our meeting. It's been a while since I've shared the company of such a beautiful young woman."

"I'm flattered," I coo.

"There's no need for lies." He chuckles. "I'm well aware I'm far too old for someone your age. You're younger than my daughter. But I'll take advantage while I can."

There's no shame in his blatant moralistic disregard.

We're two peas in a pod, both leeching what we can from the other while the opportunity lasts.

"This is business, Gordon. A partnership. If I'm generous to you, I'm sure you'll return the favor."

"You know I will." He pauses before his room, his arm curling around my waist to pull me to a stop. He nuzzles his face against my neck, a delicate lick gliding across the skin above my scarf. "So very generous."

I itch for another bump. Just one more numbing hit to quieten the growing voices in my head threatening to shatter my tightly woven composure as he pulls a room card from his jacket pocket and releases the lock with a definitive click.

If Gordon finds out I know Bishop…

If my father hears that he was here…

I strengthen my sinful smile, locking it in tight.

Gordon leads me into the suite, past the short entry hall and into the main area. The curtains are closed, but the dim light from the freestanding lamp in the corner illuminates the king-size bed with its pristine white covers and matching pillows.

The room is untouched. There's no luggage. No personal belongings.

Gordon doesn't plan on spending the night.

These four walls only have one use, and once that's over, he'll go home to his wife and rest peacefully in his own bed.

The suite door closes with a bang, and I glance over my shoulder to confirm our privacy only to find Gordon's guards have followed us inside.

I ignore the hairs bristling on my nape and turn into my mark, my palms coming to rest on his chest. "I think your men have earned an early night, don't you?" I slide my hands around his neck. "I'm ready to talk business."

"I'm ready, too." He walks backward to the armchair in the corner, then takes the seat, dragging me down to his lap.

But the men don't leave.

Instead, they creep farther into the room watching us intently. Finch moves around the bed to the waist-high window and cocks his hip against the sill while Boomer remains closer to the entry hall.

"You're such a pretty little thing." Gordon runs his fingers over my scarf, beginning to drag it back over my shoulder.

I place a gentle hand atop his. "It stays on." I learned years ago that men don't like to know when their *pretty little things* are scarred. They prefer perfection. Innocence.

"I like the way you smell." He nuzzles his face into my hair.

I close my eyes, drifting somewhere far, far away.

"I'm going to have fun with you," he murmurs. "So much wickedly sinful fun."

I squeeze my eyes tighter, searching for the deeper bliss that usually comes from my drug high.

"You should make yourself comfortable on the bed." Gordon pulls back to loosen his tie. "I have a checklist to get through."

My pulse stammers, the edge of unease slithering closer. Why hasn't he dismissed his guards? Is it so he can feel like more of a man? For bragging rights?

"A checklist?" I purr, pushing off his lap. "That's a first."

I saunter to the window side of the bed, ignoring Finch as I pass, then crawl atop the covers.

I ignore the lecherous way Gordon's men stare at me. I ignore the niggling sense of danger too.

This is my stage. My show.

I call the shots. I just have to make sure they're done tactfully.

I seat myself close to the pillows, my heels still on, my stomach a roiling ocean beneath my calm exterior.

"I was under the impression I wouldn't have to give a woman with your experience a play-by-play." Gordon's voice gains a sharp note of annoyance. "Take your clothes off."

"I'd prefer to wait until we're alone to unwrap your prize."

He raises a brow. "My dear, we won't be getting more alone than this."

Trepidation shoots through me, but I quickly shut it down with a confident raise of my chin.

He's pushing boundaries. That's all. I've never been with a man who hasn't attempted to take something I'm not willing to give. It comes with the territory. That's why contingencies are always in place.

Gordon knows this needs to remain within the guidelines of his agreement with my father otherwise enemies will be made.

I smile sweetly, almost tauntingly. "I don't discuss business in front of an audience."

"But they're not an audience, Abri. As negotiated with Emmanuel, they're the participants."

My blood turns cold.

"Participants?" I attempt to keep my voice strong, my bravado in place.

My father wouldn't do that. Not three men. Not alone without someone to protect me in case things get out of hand.

Finch removes his suit jacket. Boomer kicks off his shoes.

They're both confident this *business meeting* is going ahead even though it's not what I signed up for.

"Emmanuel didn't tell you?" Gordon raises a brow, one side of his lips peeked in a sickeningly sinister smirk.

"He seems to have left a few things out." I slowly slide from the bed, pacing my retreat so my actions don't scream as loud as the fear ringing in my ears.

"Well, let me make it clear." Gordon undoes the top button of his shirt. "Finch and Boomer are part of our meeting. I outlined those stipulations to your father on numerous occasions. I would never have agreed to this otherwise."

Well those stipulations were definitely kept from me, and I think I know why.

My father predicted my mutiny and decided to forgo the confrontation. He knew I'd eventually agree. That there would be no choice.

Winning over the shipping magnate is far too important for all of us.

"Sometimes he leaves out certain particulars to keep me on my toes." I control my tone, making sure the seductive lilt remains in place. "I will admit that *open* meetings are new to me, though. This is something I haven't prepared for. Maybe rescheduling so we can take full advantage of the situation would be in everyone's best interests."

"My men know what I like." Gordon waves me away with an errant hand and undoes his belt. "Don't you, boys?"

Finch throws his jacket to the windowsill and starts toward me. Boomer closes in from the other side of the mattress.

"And what do you like?" I ask.

Gordon lowers his pants zipper. "To watch."

A surprised breath escapes me, crazed yet oddly freeing.

Two is better than three, right? It's not much of a windfall, but I'll take it.

"I guess that makes us the perfect business partners." I look at each man in turn, showing my strength, defying their underlying hint of aggression. "Because I like to perform."

"So I'm told." Gordon's snickers. "But I haven't finished relaying my preferences."

"No?" I cling to my clutch, wondering how incredibly bad form it would be to take another bump in front of them.

"No." He gives a smug smile. "I'm a voyeur, my dear. And all those dirty things I like to watch are graphic and violent in nature."

The narcotic numbness in my veins turns against me. All the euphoric undertones blaze into angry wildfire. Panic-infused terror. "I'm not a masochist, Gordon. I don't do violence."

Finch stops a few feet in front of me. "You do tonight."

Shit.

The stun gun weighs heavy in my clutch yet there's no way I can use it. I have to figure this out without offending him.

"I need specifics." I hold a hand up to stop Finch's approach. "What do you mean by violence?"

Maybe it's nothing more than BDSM. A slap here and there. A harsh grip. Strong hands.

"Get back on the bed, Abri." Gordon strokes his dick through his briefs.

"I will once you clarify terms."

Finch steps closer.

I'm forced to retreat. "Gordon, I'm serious."

Finch reaches out, grabbing the long lengths of my scarf in both hands.

"Stop." I drop my clutch to the bed and grasp for the material around my neck. "It remains on."

"I had no plan to remove it." He grins, then yanks both ends, cinching the material tight around my throat.

Pain lances my neck as I claw at the restriction, fighting for breath.

I choke. Cough. Attempt to scream.

He pulls tighter, my throat a ring of fire, my face burning as I tug and pull before the material suddenly loosens.

What the fuck?

I stumble backward and hunch over, heaving for air, my hands clutching my knees in an attempt to remain upright.

Finch follows, leaning in, his mouth near my ear. "He said get on the bed, bitch."

4

BISHOP

I watch the numbers increase above the elevator Abri took upstairs.

Five. Six. Seven.

What deep fucking shit has she got herself into?

Eight. Nine. Ten.

I pull out my cell and dial Langston's number for the hundredth time.

Eleven. Twelve. Thirteen.

His voicemail cuts in like goddamn clockwork.

Fourteen. Fifteen. Sixteen.

"Where the fuck are you?" I snap. "Your sister is hanging with a kiddie fiddler and if he doesn't kill her, I will."

The numbers stop moving at eighteen.

"You were meant to be here hours ago. Fucking call me, asshole." I disconnect and shove the cell back into my pocket as the elevator numbers start their descent.

Abri hasn't given me much time, but I did some digging on the old man she's with. Shipping magnate. Republican donor. Wife with three adult kids who I guess are all older than the woman he's trying to fuck. And he's got no known association to underworld crime...yet.

I assume that's about to change.

I slam my hand against the elevator call button. Wait a few

seconds for my carriage to arrive. Then I climb in and press the number for her floor.

I didn't sign up for this shit.

Well, actually, I did. I put my hand up to leave Langston with his brothers in Virginia Beach because all they had to do was talk to Lorenzo. Fucking talk.

It may have been a temperamental conversation where Langston planned to ask permission from the head of the East Coast mafia to kill his own father—Lorenzo's brother-in-law—but that's all it was. A conversation. A plan. Then the three fucking brotherly amigos were meant to follow me to Denver.

So where the hell are they?

The itch under my skin is an inescapable reminder that Langston has never left me high and dry before. After years side by side, not once has he let me down.

What the fuck happened?

The elevator doors open on level eighteen and I've got no strategy for how to approach Abri.

I step into the hall, expecting to see the two guards waiting in front of a suite door, ready to hammer me with questions. But when I glance down either side of the expansive thoroughfare, nobody is there.

I wipe a rough hand over my mouth, gliding my gaze over all those doors. All those fucking potential hiding places.

I should smash the fire alarm and make my job easy. It'd provide plausible motivation for me to haul that woman over my shoulder and carry her from the building.

Instead, I take the right side of the hall and start on door 1840, hovering close to listen for voices, checking the peephole for movement.

There's none. Not a hint of life from inside.

I move to the next room, then the next, making my way down the numbers.

I don't hear a voice until 1826.

Female. Old. Not Abri.

I keep moving, marching my way back along the left-hand side. I don't even know what I'll do once I find her.

It's not my job to stop her giving blow jobs to the elderly if that's her goal in life. But three men entered that elevator and none remain in the hall. Even if this is an arranged situation, what happens if those pricks take more than she bargained for?

I stop beside yet another door and cock my ear against the wood.

Nothing. Nada. Not even a fucking whisper.

Where the hell are you?

I start for the next suite, the slight murmur of voices carrying from nearby. I pause. Listen. I trudge farther in search of the sound, passing one room then another.

The voices get louder. Clearer.

I stop before room 1803.

"Take your fucking underwear off," a guy demands.

It's not Gordon. The voice is unfamiliar. But my anger spikes regardless.

A female replies, the murmur too subtle for me to determine if it's Abri or not. But I know. I can sense her inside that room.

A coddled choke emanates from the other side of the door. Then male laughter.

"*Stop. Don't*," the female cries.

This time there's no mistaking who owns those pleas.

The panicked cadence is unrecognizable, but the tone is unmistakable. It's her.

"*Stop*," she screams.

I retrieve my gun from the back of my waistband and square up with the door, slamming my foot near the handle.

It holds.

"*Fuck*." I do it again. One more booted kick that sends splinters of wood flying and the heavy weight of the door to swing back and thwack against the wall. "Abri?"

I aim my gun at Gordon seated in a chair straight ahead, his pants undone, his cock tenting his briefs like a perve at a peek show. "Don't move. Keep your hands where I can see 'em."

He slides his palms to the arms of the chair as I continue inside to get the full view of my best friend's sister on the bed.

Jesus Christ.

She's sits atop the covers in her underwear, the deep red lace matching the color of her face as one of the guards fists her hair, holding her neck at an odd angle.

"You've got two seconds to let her go." I aim at his skull while the shorter guard raises his palms in surrender from the end of the bed.

"Do it," Gordon grates. "Release her."

The blond guard complies, his eyes angry slits as he slides off the mattress toward me, following suit with raised palms.

Abri scrambles to the head of the bed, panting as she pulls a pillow to her chest. "What the hell are you doing?"

What the hell am *I* doing?

"Get out of here." She glares, her hands white-knuckling the pillow, her breathing rampant as that scarf remains draped around her neck.

"You heard her," the hair puller snarls. "Get out." He eyes me off. Inching closer. Measuring me up.

It's no surprise when he charges, his shoulder lowered to barge into my chest.

I sidestep before impact, grab his wrist, and yank him forward, sending him off-balance, then coldcock that fucker in the back of the head as he passes.

He face-plants on the floor. Arms splayed. Motionless.

Abri gasps.

"Anyone else feel like taking a nap?" I ask.

The old guy stands, regal and poised as he raises his zipper. "What we're doing here was prearranged," he says slowly, "and consensual."

"Consensual?" I look to Abri with a hiked brow. "Is that true, belladonna?"

She nods despite the shock written all over her face. "It was. It *is*. You need to go."

Like fuck.

Langston would kill me for leaving her here, and I'd begrudgingly let him.

"*Leave*, Bishop." She throws the pillow at me, the projectile not getting within a few feet before it falls to the floor. "*Now*."

Panic is potent in her eyes as she raises her chin, defying her fear or maybe just defying me.

"How do you two know each other?" the old guy asks. "Did Emmanuel send you? Has he gone back on our agreement? Because I don't take kindly to bait."

"I'm not bait." Abri shakes her head, frantic. "That's not what this is."

"My instructions come from someone far more unaccepting of these types of situations." I shuck my jacket and throw it at her. "Put it on and start walking for the elevator."

She shoves my offering away and pushes to her knees. "No. This is none of your business."

God, how I wish that were true. How her safety wasn't currently mine to ensure.

"Put on the fucking jacket and get your ass off the bed." I scoop her dress off the floor and her clutch from the nightstand, then throw both in her direction while my gun remains on the standing guard. "Before I haul you over my fucking shoulder."

"You're making a big mistake," the old guy warns.

"Good. They're my favorite kind." I point my gun at his forehead and take a threatening step in his direction.

He stumbles back into the chair and quickly rights himself. "I mean you're making a mistake about her. She wanted this. She agreed."

I don't give a shit if Abri signed herself up to be a pincushion. It's not happening on my watch. "Give me a reason to pull the trigger, old man. All I need is one. It's been a few days since I had the taste of blood."

He stands taller. "I don't want trouble."

"It's a bit late for that." I keep my barrel poised in his direction and glare at Abri. "Move."

She doesn't.

I stalk for her, my blood searing with rage as I grab her arm and bend forward to haul her over my shoulder.

"Stop." Her words protest but her body doesn't. There's no hitting. No kicking.

"If anyone follows before we get in the elevator you'll be tasting bullets." I pivot the aim of my gun between the two conscious men. "Understood?"

Their only acknowledgement is continued eye contact.

I step over the piece of shit on the floor and back into the hall, expecting defiance.

"Please, Bishop," Abri begs. "Put me down. I have to stay."

"Shut your goddamn mouth." I stalk to the elevator, press the call button, and wait a beat before measuring quieter steps toward the fire escape.

I keep her over my shoulder as I inch open the thick metal door, then slip inside. I place her on her feet, closing in against her as I shove my gun back into my waistband, and spy through the tiny crack I leave open between the door and the jamb.

"Please," she repeats. "I know I was screaming but—"

I raise a hand to her face, placing a lone finger over her lips.

The elevator doors open with a clunk, painful seconds later, they close with a swoosh. Then there's silence.

I wait for Gordon to follow. To attack.

Nothing happens.

A few heartbeats later, the doors close again.

"Stay quiet," I whisper. "Not a fucking word."

Footsteps carry into the hall. Fast. Heavy. The guard jogs into view and slams his hand against the elevator call button.

"This is unacceptable." Gordon casually strolls up behind him. "Emmanuel will learn I don't appreciate surprises."

Abri whimpers.

I clamp my palm over her mouth, leaning harder against her. "If they hear you, they're dead. Is that what you want?"

Her eyes implore me, the deep ocean depths pleading.

The elevator arrives again as breaths heave from her nose, her body trembling against mine. I keep peering through the crack as Gordon and his guard walk inside, the doors closing a few moments later.

"You're fucking lucky that ended the way it did." I drop my hold from her mouth. "What the hell were you thinking going into a room alone with them?"

I'm hungry for all the secrets she's got hidden behind that deceitful face of hers. Fucking starved. Yet she shakes her head at me.

"You have no idea what you've done," she whispers.

That's not the answer I was looking for. And I'm too fucking pissed to ask again. At least not while we're in a public stairwell and she's all but naked.

I let the door fall shut, then haul her back over my shoulder.

"Put me down." She whacks my spine.

"Hit me one more time, Abri, and we're going to have a

problem." I carry her down the stairs, thankful she's smart enough not to test me further.

There's nothing but her huffy breaths to keep me on the edge of rage as I descend one flight after another until we reach the thirteenth floor.

I shove the door open into the hall, trek to the room I booked this afternoon in the hopes of getting some peaceful fucking sleep for the first time in days, and retrieve the key card from my pants pocket.

Once inside, I flop her backward onto the bed, my suit jacket parting across her chest to expose a wealth of plumped cleavage beneath all that sinful red lace.

"Start talking," I growl.

She pushes onto her elbows with a glare.

"And do it without the attitude." I match those evil eyes, spite for spite. "I think we're past beating around the bush, don't you?"

She dumps her dress and clutch on the mattress and sits tall, dragging the lapels of my jacket together to cover herself. "I didn't need your help." She scoots to the edge of the bed. "I knew what I was getting into."

"Oh yeah?" I raise a condemning brow. "And was that a spit roast with Father Time providing the glaze?"

"Fuck you."

"No, thanks. I've got kinks of my own, but they don't hold a candle to your daddy issues. How old was that guy anyway? Sixty? Seventy?"

She shoves to her feet, a storm of violence brewing in her eyes. "Are you done?"

Barely. I want to rail on her. To yell. To shake.

This princess of perversion could've done so much more with her life. And I'd know. I've spied on her enough over the years to understand she's smart. Capable. Determined.

We stare for long seconds, her rigid animosity ebbing from the harsh sharpness of her shoulders until I can almost glimpse a sign of vulnerability.

Almost.

I jerk my chin at the golden material pooled on the bed. "Put your dress on."

"I prefer your jacket."

Is she fucking kidding? Is this another seduction tactic? Am I her victim now?

Sorry, belladonna. You're the last place I'd want to get my dick wet.

"I said, put it on," I sneer.

"I can't." She glances away, the sharpness of her posture fading a little more. "It's ruined. The dress is torn."

Anger clenches a tight fist around my gut. I should've killed those fuckers. I should've fucking tortured them.

"Did they hurt you?" I scan her body—the toned legs, the pretty face, the delicate neck still draped in that fucking scarf.

She sighs. "Why are you here, Bishop?"

"I already goddamn told you your brothers sent me, so stop fucking asking."

"But why you?" She directs her question to the opposite side of the room, refusing to look at me.

"Because I offered."

Her gaze snaps back to mine. "Why? Is this retaliation for our last encounter? Did you come here to humiliate me?"

"No." I bare my teeth, still annoyed at how she made me look foolish when she let Layla escape under my watch. "Although I'm yet to thank you for making me look incompetent."

"I had a duty to help Cole's sister."

"And I have a duty to keep you safe. So don't think about running."

She raises her chin. "I need to set things right with Gordon."

"It can wait."

"No, it can't. That meeting was important."

"Meeting?" I scoff and turn away from her, dragging my cell from my pocket to dial. It's no surprise when message bank cuts in. "You'd better be dead, my friend. Fucking call me." I lock the home screen and shove the device back into my pants.

When I turn around to Abri, her hands are in my jacket pockets, her nose crinkled as she pulls cable ties from the left side, then a small plastic baggie filled with white powder from the right.

"Tools of the trade?" She raises a brow.

"They come in handy."

She throws the cable ties to the bed and inspects the powder. "What's this?"

"Not coke, little miss sniffles, so keep your nose out of it. That shit will put you to sleep."

Her scowl returns. "Was this for me? The cable ties. The sedatives. Had you planned on drugging me?"

"It's too early to be talking in past tense."

Her scowl deepens. "Funny."

"That's me, belladonna. I'm a barrel of fucking laughs." I slump onto the corner of the bed. "Now start talking. Tell me why you were shacking up with Gordon Myers."

She ignores the question and saunters to the alcove with the minibar, her back to me as she snaps the cap on a bottle, pours the contents into a glass, then throws down a generous mouthful of auburn liquid.

"Abri?" I warn.

"Give me a second, okay?" She rests her forearms against the counter, her head hung.

I don't like this. Something about the situation sits like lead in my gut and I don't know why.

Maybe exhaustion is the culprit. Or maybe it's getting a front-row view of what Emmanuel Costa has made of this woman. How he created a sexual commodity out of his daughter. A piece of fucking merchandise.

I look away, needing a reprieve from my stifling anger.

More liquid is poured. Glasses clink. Her feet shuffle.

She moves to stand in front of me, handing over a scotch glass with a finger of amber liquid swimming inside.

I take the offering, forcing my attention to her eyes instead of all that toned, smooth skin visible through the opening of my gaping jacket. "I've already been told about the type of work you do for your father. So I guess it's safe to say tonight was about extortion."

She swirls what I assume is vodka in her glass. "You know nothing about me."

"Then do me the honors." I throw back the scotch in one gulp, thankful for the burn that acts as a distraction from wanting to shake the answers from her.

"Like Gordon said, it was entirely consensual," she grates.

Bullshit.

That scream wasn't the sound of a woman who'd given consent.

The fear in her eyes when I stormed the room wasn't a reflection of her willingness to participate either.

"I'm growing impatient, Abri."

"And I'm getting bored. How about we make this mutually beneficial? I'll give you an honest answer if you give one in return." She raises her gaze from the glass, staring at me from under dark lashes.

It isn't hard to understand how she easily entraps men. She's perfectly choreographed. Exquisitely deceptive.

I place my empty glass on the floor at my feet. "What information could I possibly give?"

She shrugs. "Tell me what Remy and Salvatore are currently doing with Matthew."

"I wish I could. But I'm just as clueless as you." It's not a lie. I have no idea where those fuckers *currently* are or what they're *currently* doing.

She smiles, the curve of lips fraudulent but so fucking sinful. "Well, if you're not going to play, then neither am I." She finishes her drink, turns, and places the glass back in the alcove. "I need to go fix the mess you created."

"Don't pretend you didn't want to get out of there. I fucking saved you."

"You *shocked* me," she clarifies. "I didn't expect my estranged brother's right-hand man to break down the fucking door on an extremely private meeting."

"Stop calling it a meeting. It doesn't make what you were doing seem classy."

She blows out what I assume is a calming breath, but that woman is far from Zen. "I'm leaving. And you're not going to stop me."

"You bet your trouble-making ass I will. You're staying with me until I can hand you over to your brothers."

She pivots back to me with a barely audible laugh. "Like I'm an asset to be transferred? How misogynistic of you."

"I don't hate women, Abri. Just mankind in general."

"Nice to know. But unless you plan on telling me what my brothers are doing together I have no use for you."

Now *that* I can technically answer, yet for some reason I'm tempted to deny her again. I itch to see what she'll do. How she'll retaliate.

"Bishop?" She raises a brow. "Are we doing this? Or am I leaving?"

"They went to see your Uncle Lorenzo."

She grows an inch with the straightening of her posture. "Why?"

I cluck my tongue. "My turn, belladonna. What's with you and the old guy? Have you got a taste for rigor mortis or were you planning on blackmailing him with the affair?"

She crosses her arms over her chest, the plump of her breasts taunting my periphery. "I was strengthening a business relationship," she states, matter-of-fact. "What are my brothers doing with my uncle?"

"Langston went to get permission to kill your father," I reply, equally bland.

Her face falls, every single part of her mask of seduction shattering to the floor. "You can't be serious."

I hold her stare. Unblinking.

"Have they already spoken? What happened? Where are they now?" Her arms fall to her sides with her sharpening breaths.

"If we're being fair, I believe it's my turn to ask a question."

"Don't fuck with me, Bishop." She pivots to the alcove, grabs her clutch and fumbles inside, then turns back wielding that fucking stun gun. "Where are they?"

"I don't know."

She stalks forward, fire and fury in her eyes as she stops before me. Self-preservation doesn't kick in. Only lust.

She's such a pretty slip of a thing, bolstered by a weapon I could easily disarm from her, my jacket gaping over her chest, her exquisite legs stretching for miles.

"Tell me." She shoves the weapon under my chin.

I grin, letting her know my level of fear.

Her nostrils flare.

It's cute. A little too cute because I'm all caught up watching the anger travel across her face when she swings her arm and clocks me in the jaw with her weapon.

"*Fuck*." I reel back.

The viper shoves me into the mattress and mounts my waist.

"You think I won't use this?" She towers over me, jamming the stun gun harder under my chin. "Don't kid yourself."

"What I think is that you've wrongfully predicted my reaction to violence." I smirk. "If this is the reward I get for keeping information from you, I'm not sure you're going to be successful with your interrogation."

"I'd quit making jokes if I were you. I'm not an enemy you want to have."

"And I suggest you quit riding my lap before you wake my friend." I glance down between us, aiming my attention toward my dick, but all I see are those luscious tits. "It's not a big secret that I have a preference for whores."

She sucks in an aghast breath.

I snatch her wrists before she can zap me, the ticking electrical current penetrating the air as I buck my hips to the side and send her toppling to the bed beside me.

I follow, my body weight about to crash on top of hers when she bucks her hips and shoots her legs toward my head. She performs some crazy-ass jujitsu move that has her thighs wrapping around my neck. Tight.

"Your actions are still having the opposite effect, darlin'." I palm the bed to keep upright and grab at her leg with my other hand. "This kinda seems like an invitation with how close my face is to your—"

She wrenches those thighs tighter, her lips set in a catty grin.

Shit. Blood pools in my face as breathing becomes harder. I wrench at her legs, digging my fingers into her flesh.

"Okay, belladonna," I choke out. "You've proven your point."

She doesn't budge. If anything she squeezes harder, shortening my hold on consciousness.

Goddamnit. She's cutting off my blood circulation.

"Stop," I bite out. "Fucking stop."

The pressure vanishes, my wish granted in an instant.

I heave breaths as her legs slither out from around my neck, then with one mighty kick to my chest, she sends me toppling from the mattress.

I hit the floor. Hard.

"Call me a whore again, asshole." She slides from the bed and saunters back to the alcove, this time retrieving her cell from her clutch. "See where it gets you."

I remain on the carpet, equally stunned, pissed, and impressed. I try to regain my equilibrium, to suck in air to clear my head, but my brain is foggy. Exhaustion has me by the balls. That's probably how she got me down so easily.

I need a fucking nap.

She connects call after unanswered call while I fail to pull my shit together.

"Why aren't Remy and Salvo answering?" She dials again, the subdued trill ringing in the background. This time, an answering service kicks in.

"You've reached Emmanuel Costa. Please leave—"

I shove to my feet and lunge, snatching the cell. My brain protests the sudden movement by momentarily short-circuiting my vision. "What the fuck are you doing?" I stumble, holding the phone high above my head.

She scrambles for the device, her perfectly manicured nails scratching my arms through my shirt. "I need to talk to my father."

"Like hell you do." I shut off the phone.

"Give it back." She yanks at my sleeve. "Bishop, *please*, this is important."

"Why?" I tower over her, my dominance now an act because it feels like a bag of feathers could knock me down.

"Goddamnit. What is your problem with having to know *everything*?" She shoves a rough hand through her hair, raking the tangled strands. "I need another drink... Do you want one?" She starts for the alcove.

"No." I'm already living on an unsustainable concoction of adrenaline, insomnia, and the after-effects of her choking thighs. My sight is a mess, my vision blurry, my skull heavy. I can't sustain this level of animosity. It takes too much fucking energy. "I need to take a piss." I lob the cell to the bed. "If you attempt to call your dad again, the punishment will be my own version of that kung fu, boa constrictor, neck-crushing bullshit you pulled on me. And we both know my crotch isn't as pretty as yours." I walk for the bathroom, stopping behind her as I pass. "If you leave, I follow. And whoever I find you with will end up dead. Do you hear me?"

She glances at me over her shoulder and bats her lashes. Still incredibly beautiful despite the underlying venom. "Loud and clear."

"I'm not joking, Abri. If you leave, we'll both end up in prison."

"I heard you."

Good.

I need a fucking breather from her toxicity. This woman is an energy vulture and I'm her latest victim.

I enter the bathroom, flick on the light, and close myself into the sparkling white room. The blinding glow stings my eyes and skewers my brain.

Christ. How long has it been since I slept for more than a solid two hours? Three days? Four?

I postpone the bladder relief and walk for the sink to splash water on my face in the hopes of delaying the inevitable crash and burn. I need to get Abri out of here first. She can't be trusted to stay inside this room, let alone the hotel.

The safe house outside the city limits is where we need to be. But the thought of the ninety-minute drive is a killer.

I splash more water, scrubbing my skin, scouring my two-day stubble in the hopes of reviving some of my lost energy.

When I straighten to meet my gaze in the mirror, the world spins on its axis like a motherfucking Tilt-A-Whirl.

Shit. I clutch the counter, my legs heavy with fatigue, my chest thudding with pummeling arrhythmia. What the hell is going on?

I'm dead on my feet. Entirely wiped.

This isn't lethargy. It's something far more sinister.

"*Abri,*" I roar, stumbling for the door.

That fucking bitch drugged me.

5

ABRI

As soon as the door closes behind him, I run for the coffee table and carefully carry it back to the bathroom. I wait for noise—any sort of possible sound to disguise my actions. The distraction comes in the form of running water.

I lodge the rectangular tabletop under the handle, wedging the opposite end tight against the floor.

If I'm lucky, it will hold long enough for me to get out of here. All I need is enough time to get downstairs, find Gordon, and beg forgiveness before news of this gets back to my father.

I hustle to grab my cell from the bed then stride for the entry.

"*Abri*," Bishop bellows from the bathroom.

I escape into the hall, letting the door bang shut behind me as I continue to the elevators, my confident persona in place for anyone who might be watching through peepholes or surveillance cameras.

The numbers ascend, creeping closer as my pulse thrums through heavy limbs.

I eye the suite door, expecting it to fling open with Bishop in Hulk form storming out.

He's such a big guy. Broad. Muscled. He'd have to be almost twice my weight and could've easily flung me off of him when I'd had him in a choke hold. But he didn't.

The elevator doors open and I exhale in relief as I move inside.

I dial Gordon's number on the descent, the call jumping in and out of cell range. Yet there's no answer.

As soon as the elevator reaches the lobby, I clutch the lapels of Bishop's jacket together, hiding the scant underwear beneath, and saunter to the bar. I scan the crowd from the hostess's stand, the same drunken, rowdy chatter as before filling the air.

"Have you seen the man I came in with earlier?" I ask the woman. "The older guy. Grey hair. Expensive suit."

Her gaze rakes over me with disgust. "Ma'am, we have a dress code."

I scowl. The jacket is a million sizes too big. How does she know I don't have a short dress hidden beneath? Well, apart from already seeing me earlier I suppose. "Have you seen him or not?"

"No." She turns up her nose at me. "He hasn't come back here."

I pivot on the tips of my shoes and continue to the ballroom. My stomach fills with bile as I scan the still seated guests with mine and Gordon's seats remaining empty.

Shit. Shit. Shit.

I slink back into the hall and redial his number.

Did he go home? To his wife? To the place I'd be persecuted for invading?

I kick off my shoes and hustle into the lobby, trying his number one more time.

I must look a real treat, barefoot, disheveled, and wearing nothing but an oversized jacket and a long golden scarf.

My family's designer clothing label will be dragged through the mud if my picture is taken. Not that it would affect our actual family business. The label is little more than a front for laundering money. Always has been. But my father will be pissed.

Problem is, he'll go nuclear if news of Gordon gets back to him.

I can't let that happen. Not before I fix the situation.

I pass the concierge and continue outside to order an Uber, ignoring the gawking stares from street and foot traffic who make it clear my current fashion sense is far from subtle.

Fifteen minutes. I can't get a car out of here for fifteen fucking minutes.

"Goddamnit." I want to scream. To tear at my hair. To throw up.

I never should've let Bishop drag me out of Gordon's room. I could've handled the situation. At the very least, I could've gotten over it.

But I'd been in shock. Finch had choked me and thrown me on

the bed. My throat and neck were burning from the onslaught. Then the door smashed open and it felt like a lifeline had walked in. I'd been riddled with misplaced relief.

For a split second, I'd wanted Bishop to save me, and I'll be paying for that weakness for years to come.

I'm six blocks closer to Gordon's neighborhood, my feet protesting the power walk, by the time the Uber catches up to me. I keep trying to call Gordon throughout the drive, my impatience turning me into a sweating mess as the car pulls up in front of a massive Georgian-style home.

"Is this it?" the driver asks.

"Yeah." I've been past once before while doing recon for tonight. I wanted to get insight into the man I'd be sleeping with. To determine as much as I could about him from his surroundings. "Thank you."

I climb out and walk up the path to the locked gate of the wrought-iron fence with its brick pillars and bordered shrubbery.

The car drives away. I'm left alone. Just me, my stun gun, and the little silver bullet of coke that calls my name from the clutch gripped in my hand.

I take another bump to reignite calm as I stare at the house glowing with warm yellow light, the glass entry illuminated by a massive chandelier.

He has to be home.

I don't know where else to find him otherwise.

I walk to the call button on the pillar beside the gate, the grated beep loud through the silent night. Then I wait, my stomach growing heavier the longer the quiet stretches.

What if he's already on his way to see my father? What if he got hold of Emmanuel and demanded a meeting to discuss my betrayal?

I press the button again and contemplate another bump.

The drugs aren't helping this time. My hands shake. My stomach twists with curdling nausea.

"Who's there?" Gordon's voice crackles over the speaker.

Thank God. I press the talk button. "It's Abri."

Silence is my only response.

"I'm so sorry for the misunderstanding," I beg. "I had no idea that was going to happen."

"You dare to come to my home?" he seethes.

"I had no choice; you haven't answered my calls. All I need is a few minutes to explain. Let me clear this up." I infuse my voice with sultry confidence. "I can fix our business arrangement. We can make this work."

I'm not sure how, but I will. I'll do whatever it takes.

Gordon opens the front door, still dressed in his tuxedo, and strides down the drive toward me. His tie is gone. His top button undone. The casual disarray of his clothing makes him appear laidback and sophisticated. It's the callous narrowed slits of his eyes that don't match as he takes in my appearance.

He wants to tear me to shreds, and given my mistakes, someday soon he'll likely get his chance.

Once he's a few yards away, he slides a hand into his pants pocket and the gates grumble and whir as they part two feet before stopping.

"Your father is going to hear exactly how disappointed I am in tonight's events." He walks through the gap to stand in front of me. "I've never been more humiliated in my life."

"I understand. And I apologize." I paste on the most sincere puppy-dog expression. "I'm so incredibly sorry, Gordon. I had no idea my brothers had sent someone to watch over me. It was all a terrible misunderstanding."

"It was a waste of my time," he grates. "One that ruined any trust I may have had for your family."

"Please don't let tonight tarnish what could be a lucrative relationship." I step closer. "I'll make it up to you. I'll fix this."

He crinkles his nose in distaste. "You think pathetic groveling will help your cause? I have no time for a spineless tramp. My agreement with your father was to indulge in the 'temptress of high society.' Yet the woman before me is a coked-up disappointment."

I take the chastisement with the raise of my chin, attempting to reclaim the title I hadn't known I'd earned.

"Go home, Abri. You've done enough for one night."

Tires screech in the distance, the far-off traffic reminding me civilization exists outside my own little world.

"I can't. Not until you promise to give me one more chance." I reach out, gently touching his fingers. Bishop's jacket parts with my movement, revealing my half-naked body. I do nothing to rectify the exposure. "I'm exactly the woman you thought I was. I can give you the experience you dreamed of." I inch closer as more tires screech. "And now that I know your preferences, I'll be far more prepared to help you indulge."

"My men aren't happy," he sneers.

"And they have every right to feel that way."

There's another screech, closer this time, followed by an unhealthy rev of an engine.

"If we were to reschedule, my men would be sure to right the wrongs of tonight with far more enthusiasm." He holds my gaze, the twinkle of revenge burning in his eyes.

"Of course." I fight against the need to swallow. I don't want to know what he means. I'll deal with the repercussions later.

A fourth screech of tires squeals from nearby, an engine being gunned.

I glance over my shoulder, my eyes blinded by beaming headlights that have turned the nearby corner to hit me head-on.

"What in damnation…" Gordon grumbles.

I squint through the glare as the car careens our way at high speed.

"What's going on?" I retreat toward the fence, my pulse fluttering.

The SUV mounts the curb, heading straight for us.

"Get out of the way." Gordon grabs my arm, yanking me into him as I scream.

The driver slams on the brakes, the tires skidding through pristine lawn to come to a violent stop a few yards before mowing me down.

The old man flings me to the grass, my clutch falling from my hand as the driver's door opens and a bulking frame stumbles out from behind the wheel.

"Oh, shit." The whispered words escape me without consent.

Bishop stares at me with animalistic fury, his lip curled, his steps lumbered. He staggers toward Gordon, his business shirt untucked, the faint outline of a gun visible through the light material while I pull myself to my feet.

"What are you doing here?" I scramble after him.

His eyes are heavy lidded, his blinks slow and lethargic. The little baggie of sedatives I'd given him had a noxious effect… Just not noxious enough.

"Get in the car," he spits through clenched teeth and points a menacing finger at Gordon. "Stay the fuck away from her."

"Bishop, *no*," I plead. He's destroying the slight momentum I'd made and making this situation a million times worse.

"I swear if I see you near her again, I'll fucking kill you." He stops within feet of Gordon. "And if Langston finds out, you'll wish I'd done it sooner."

He cocks a fist and I gasp even though he's not within contact range. The swing leaves me silent. It's wildly off course, with way too much follow through.

His entire body continues the trajectory of that punch, his feet stumbling. He spins, losing balance to land on the cement drive with a grunt.

Oh, God, I'm done for.

There's no going back from this. No hiding it from my father.

Gordon retreats behind the safety of the gates as they grind and whir closed. "You've got two minutes before I call the police."

"Come back here you fucking pussy." Bishop climbs onto all fours. "Let me have a crack at those chalky bones."

"You already had a crack, you idiot." I scour the lawn, searching for my clutch so I can get the hell out of here. "You're making this worse."

"It don't get much worse than what you've done, belladonna." He stands to his full height, swaying, his eyes half-mast yet still promising retribution. "Now get in the fucking car."

"I'm not going anywhere with you." I snatch my clutch out from beneath a manicured hedge and retrieve my cell. "You need to leave before the police arrive."

"No, *you* need to get in the car before I wring your fucking neck."

"Could you even find my neck, though?" I raise a brow. "Because you sure as hell had the wrong coordinates for Gordon's face."

"Very funny." He huffs a murderous chuckle. "Get in the fucking car."

"Bishop, I wouldn't get in your passenger seat if you were

completely lucid and acting the gentleman, let alone this drug-addled mess of a man you are now."

"Who made me this way?" He storms forward, getting in my face, his lips snarled, his teeth bared. "Who fucking drugged me, Abri?"

I stand my ground. Unflinching. "I'm getting an Uber."

"You're getting in that car. Dead or alive. I don't care which." He grabs my arm and drags me toward the vehicle.

"*Stop. Don't.*" I pummel his chest, struggling not to fall to the ground as my heels sink into the lawn. "You're in no shape to drive. You'll kill us both."

He scoffs. "*Now* you're worried about your safety?" He pauses, digging into his pocket to pull out a key fob. "Here. You take the wheel." He smacks the key into my palm. "Start driving out of town. I'll put the location in the GPS."

Like hell. I have to go home. I need to see my father. To explain in person...

But maybe I could do that in Bishop's car. He can barely keep his eyes open. He's on the verge of unconsciousness.

"Now, Abri." He tugs me again, hauling me to the driver's door.

"Okay. *Fine*." I yank my arm from his grip. "I'll drive."

He stops. Stares. Scrutinizes.

He knows I can't be trusted.

"Hurry up and get in before I leave you behind." I yank open the door. "Or worse, the cops arrive."

His jaw ticks. "If this is a—"

"Just get in the goddamn car." I climb behind the wheel as he stumbles around the hood.

I should take off. Leave him stranded while I skedaddle my sorry ass out of here. I'm not sure why I don't.

I reposition my seat while he slides into the passenger side, then reverse off Gordon's nature strip, and drive away at speed.

Bishop fumbles with the GPS, his finger missing buttons over and over again. "For fuck's sake."

"Forget it." I keep my eyes on the road but my head is already at home with my father, trying to figure a way out of this mess. "I know where I'm going."

Bishop gives a dismissive grunt, clearly fighting against the sedative's effects. He taps the screen again and again, finally bringing up a location. "You need to go here."

I glance at the map with its directions outlining a one-hundred-and-forty-five-minute journey.

No, thank you.

"Don't fuck me around again, belladonna. Tomorrow is going to be bad enough between us without adding more transgressions to your list." He slumps into his seat. "Get to this location and maybe all will be forgiven."

I have to make it to tomorrow first, which, considering the disastrous outcome of tonight, isn't a given.

He has no idea what I've lost due to my failure.

But I follow the navigation momentarily, my hands clinging to the steering wheel while I chance glances at Bishop every thirty seconds.

He fights slumber, his head lulling before snapping upright. Once. Twice. It takes three minutes for him to pass out, his neck crooked sideways, his face somewhat handsome now that he's not wishing me dead with those cold eyes.

I cancel the navigation and do a U-turn at the next intersection to head home.

I'm well aware my father will shoot Bishop on sight. Or at least have someone do it for him. He's been murderous toward anyone that's contributed to my oldest brother's estrangement, which puts Bishop at the head of the list along with my Uncle Lorenzo, who took Matthew in.

I'll have to dump the car down the darkened farm road and walk through the property gates to keep air in Bishop's lungs. I'll also have to hope like hell that my entrance goes undetected so I can put some clothes on before I have to face my own firing squad.

But as I reach the desolate road on the far outskirts of the city to approach my home, something doesn't feel right.

The glow of lights that usually carries miles from my house isn't there.

There's only silvery moonlight to bathe the open fields.

I ease on the brakes, driving past the towering brick perimeter, scanning the road for potential threats before stopping at the gates.

Where is everyone? My parents? The sentries?

There isn't a single light to illuminate the two-story mansion or the yard. Not one spark of bright through the dark.

In all my years, I've never seen my home this lifeless. Completely abandoned.

Something is wrong.

Even if my father had joined the security team he'd sent out of town, he would've left someone here to guard the house. To guard *me* if I returned.

I scrummage through my clutch for the gate remote and open the massive steel barriers.

Bishop doesn't budge from his fairytale slumber fest, his head nestled against one shoulder, his lips slightly parted.

"I'm sorry, big guy, but you're coming inside with me."

If this is a trap, I'm not going in alone.

I scour the road again, squinting into the moonlit shadows, watching for movement.

There's nothing. No cars. No sign of life.

I attempt to call my father again, but he doesn't answer.

What if the house slipped his mind? Could this be an innocuous mistake I don't need to fret about? If my father left town in a hurry with all our guards, he might have forgotten to ask someone to watch the property. And if he's that distracted, maybe he's also forgotten the job I had tonight. I might have more time to work out a plan.

I inch the car past the gates and close them behind me. I slowly continue around the back of the house, scanning the garden, squinting at every shadow to check for movement.

I pull into the darkened garage without a peep from sleeping Satan, cut the engine, then close the door quickly behind me.

Normally a sentry would greet me. But nobody walks out from inside the house.

I unclasp my belt, turn to Bishop, and poke him in the shoulder. "Wake up."

He groans without batting one of those heavily closed lids.

"You're on your own if you don't get your ass moving." I give him another poke and get the same response. "Well, you can't say I didn't try."

I climb out, the headlights guiding the way toward the shelving units lining the wall. I grab a picnic blanket from the middle shelf, then return to the passenger side of the car, recline Bishop's seat all the way back, and throw the thick material over his entire body. Face included.

If my parents return, I can only hope they stalk straight inside to ask me about the unfamiliar car. If they don't, and decide to snoop instead… Well, Bishop's a big boy. I'm sure he'll bluff his way back through those gates.

I lean over him to place the key fob on the center console for good measure and grab my clutch. I'm sure he thought about the risks before he decided to get caught up in my business. And if he didn't, that's his problem, not mine.

I close the door behind me. The headlights turn off, plunging the garage into darkness. I walk inside, the *beep*, *beep*, *beep* of the alarm announcing I have a few seconds to enter the pin before sirens wail.

I hustle in the dark to the security panel and turn off the system. Both levels of the house had been alarmed.

I double check the panel to make sure the security for the doors and windows remain engaged, then flick on the light, illuminating the empty hall.

It's eerie. Desolate.

The hair prickles on the back of my neck as I continue to the heart of the home, my heels *tap*, *tap*, *tapping* on the tiled floor.

I've never been here alone before and the dead lump in the passenger seat of the random SUV in my garage doesn't count as company.

I enter the living room and flick another switch, then do the same in the kitchen and the dining room.

I walk through every inch of the sprawling house, turning on each light, hoping to find a placating clue to the reason behind this apocalyptic scene. But after a full search of both floors, I find nothing and no one.

I'm completely alone.

I call my father as I enter my bedroom, closing the door behind me to kick off my shoes, letting them scatter haphazardly on the floor.

…leave a message after the tone.

"Dad, please call me. It's urgent." I place a hand on my stomach, trying to appease the nausea rearing its ugly head again. "I have to explain some things... I, um..." My nose tingles with the awakening of emotions I can't afford. "I need you to trust me. Okay?... *Please.*"

My eyes burn, the frailty I've kept hidden for so long threatening to make a resurgence.

Tears won't fix anything. They won't fade my scars or fill the gaping holes carved into my soul. All they do is make me weak, and I lost the luxury of softness long ago.

6

BISHOP

I startle awake, an adamant buzz vibrating against my thigh while something smothers my face. "*What the—*"

I yank at the suffocating material, preparing to fight my way out of whatever death trap I've landed in, and find myself in darkness.

I'm alone. Still in the rental car.

I snap upright, taking in the dimly lit garage, the only glimpse of illumination coming from the moonlight streaming in through a small window three luxury cars away, and the slight gleam seeping around the edges of the closed door to my right.

I pull out my cell, the device continuing to vibrate as the screen blinds me through the darkness. The name highlighted through that searing glow punches my gut with relief.

Langston.

I swipe to connect and shove the cell to my ear. "Where the hell have you been, motherfucker?" I hiss under my breath and snatch at my belt, reefing it off as I take in my surroundings. Shelves line the wall in front of me, holding a stack of leisure items. Golf clubs. Tennis rackets. Gardening supplies. This is a family home. And the thing smothering me was a goddamn picnic blanket.

"I'm still with Lorenzo. We ran into a complication."

He sounds like shit. *Real shit*. Not every day run-of-the-mill fatigue, but bone-chilling, life-altering exhaustion. "What happened?"

"You first. From your messages it sounds like my sister has given you a run for your money."

My annoyance reignites at the mere mention of that seductive belladonna. "She's fucking crazy."

He chuckles, half-hearted and weak.

"No, I mean it. That bitch doesn't ride the crazy train—she fucking drives it. As it stands, I just woke up in the passenger seat of my rental, covered in a goddamn picnic blanket she must have thrown over my head, while I'm in some random garage. And all this is after she fucking sedated me."

"Sedated? How the hell did she do that?"

I should've kept that part to myself. Being drugged by my own bag of goodies isn't something I want made common knowledge. "The *how* doesn't matter. It's why the hell you weren't here to deal with her yourself that had me calling every ten minutes. Tell me about the complication."

"I'm not in the best shape to go into detail, but the short version is that the people we came to discuss were already here when we arrived."

Emmanuel and Adena. Fuck.

I wipe a rough hand over my mouth. "And?"

"They weren't alone."

"Keep going," I mutter.

"There was an exchange. Both parties sustained...*inconveniences*."

I grind my teeth over the cryptic, non-incriminating lingo. "You specifically?"

"Me and the person I came to visit."

Motherfucker. Lorenzo is hurt, too.

This never would've happened if I'd been there. "What type of inconveniences are we talking?" I keep wiping my palm over my face. Scrubbing. Punishing.

"Serious but temporary."

Were they beaten? Stabbed? Shot? *Goddamnit.* I need to know.

I clench a fist, my fury increasing the dull throb in my skull. "Did your brothers set you—"

"They didn't know," he cuts me off.

"That's seems awfully convenient, don't you think?"

"They were just as blindsided as I was. I trust them. You need to do the same."

No, I don't. I'll reserve my judgment for when they've earned it.

I grab my gun from the back of my waistband and slowly climb from the car, keeping my voice low. "Tell me more about these inconveniences."

He falls quiet.

"Langston?" I hiss. "Don't hold out on me."

"That's the last thing I want to do, but discretion is necessary. The situation resulted in permanent inconveniences for many."

"And was any of this permanence directed toward the other party?" I creep toward the internal door.

"Yes," he murmurs.

"Top tier?"

"The very top."

Holy shit. "Male or female?"

There's a sigh, one born of emotional upheaval. "Male."

Emmanuel Costa is dead? That lying, manipulative sack of spiteful shit is finally gone?

"Are you okay with that outcome?" I ask, knowing full well that killing a parent isn't easy, even when you despise them.

"We both know it's been a long time coming."

"Yeah, it has, but that doesn't make it any more palatable. Has everything been tidied up?" I grab the handle and slowly turn it, pulling the door open a crack to check if the coast is clear.

"Yeah. There's nothing to worry about. The discussion I came here for has happened, and the strategy I had planned for my siblings will come to fruition. My brothers will be on their way to get Abri soon. I gather you're still with her."

I pull the door wider, staking out the lavish interior of a familiar house.

"Apparently I am," I drawl, pointing my gun in front of me as I slowly trek the brightly lit hall. "It looks like I'm in your childhood home?"

"What?" Concern enters his voice. "What the fuck are you doing there?"

Good question.

"I told you your sister is crazy. When I passed out she must have driven here." Right into the heart of the fucking lion's den.

"Where are the sentries?"

I stalk every room, not hearing a damn peep other than Langston's voice, the soft sweep of my shoes, and my measured breathing. "Asleep?"

"They don't sleep. At least, they're not meant to. You need to get out of there."

"I will," I whisper. "As soon as I strangle your sister."

He laughs, faint and pained.

That *inconvenience* of his must be severe to have him sounding the way he does.

"As far as I'm aware, Remy and Salvo haven't broken the news to her yet," he adds. "I told them not to mention it over the phone. So if you're going to fill her in, do it gently."

"I'm not sure *gently* is an avenue I can take after the shit she's pulled." I walk past the kitchen and head toward the staircase leading to the upper level. "I assume you're staying put for a while?"

"I'm going to need a few days. I'll reassess after that."

I nod, my gun still trained on the path ahead as I enter the upstairs hall. "I'll make my way to you as soon as your brothers get here."

"You should escort them back. They're going to be rattled for a while."

"Hard pass, my friend. I'd rather be fucked by a cactus."

He may have chosen to forget the shit that went down with Remy and Salvatore recently, but my memory remains clear.

"One of them will be stepping into Lorenzo's role," he murmurs. "You might want to curb the hatred toward a potential new boss."

"Like hell. When Lorenzo steps down, so do I. I won't be doing shit for your brothers." I approach the only closed door down a hall of empty bedrooms. "I've gotta go. Keep your fucking phone on."

"I will."

I disconnect and slide the cell back into my pocket as I edge up to the door. There's no sound. Not that I expected any when the entire house is choked by silence.

I gradually twist the handle, push the door open an inch, and peer inside.

The scent of her hits me. The perfumed sweetness. The misleading purity.

The light from the hall creeps over the end of a ruffled pink bed, the outline of a body hidden beneath the covers.

She doesn't move. Doesn't even stir.

I edge my way inside, my shadow creeping across her still form in sinister shades of grey as I spy my jacket dumped in a messy pile on the carpet. I close the door behind me, returning the room to darkness, and measure my steps closer, not stopping until I'm peering down at the devil trapped in an angel's body.

Her cheek rests against the pillow, her hair splayed behind her while her fingers clutch the covers held close to her chin. Those long lashes lay against flawless creamy skin, her pouty lips slightly parted.

I haven't seen her without makeup before, yet funnily enough, this version of her is more mesmerizing. When she's stripped back. Without all those fraudulent layers.

Like this I could almost be fool enough to think she's normal. Not a viper. Not a vixen. Not a venomous dick trap of a woman who's witless enough to drug a man like me.

I should grab those covers and plaster them over her head, returning all those thoughtful smothering vibes she gave me.

Instead, I grab my jacket, putting it on as I retreat to the wall and sink down to the floor.

The clock on the bedside table glows a bright 4:21. I can still catch a few hours rest and dissolve the remaining trace of sedatives in my system.

Only I don't sleep.

I find myself staring at her shadowed form, trying to align all the beauty with the overwhelming treachery.

She should've asked Matthew for help years ago. Despite the estrangement, he would've done anything for her. He still would. Only now she'll have to live with all the shit she's done.

I yawn and lean my head back against the wall, dozing.

I wake every time her breathing hitches. Every time she shifts. Until those breaths and movements become a waking sequence, and the sunlight of a new morning squeezes past the edge of her curtains.

She groans then kicks off her covers, exposing a whole heap of smooth thigh.

I clear my throat.

She gasps and jackknifes to a seated position grabbing the bedsheet to clutch it at her chin as her eyes meet mine. Why she's suddenly modest I have no idea, but I enjoy the contrast from the way she gave zero fucks last night.

"Morning." I spread my legs out in front of me, calm and cocky. "Sleep well?"

"What are you doing in my room?" She glares. "Besides enjoying the view."

"I'm enjoying the view as much as the killer headache, thanks to your pharmaceutical interference. Did you know your parents weren't home before you drove me into enemy territory?"

"I covered you."

"So that wasn't a failed suffocation attempt?"

She rolls those pretty eyes. "If I wanted you dead you'd be dancing with the devil."

It kinda feels like I already am. If not the devil, then one of his pretty little minions.

"If you're worried about my father, why are you still here?" She scoots to the edge of the mattress, the covers still held to her chin as she snatches a scarf from the bedside table. "He could turn up at any minute."

"I doubt that."

"Why?" She grips the sheet with one hand, wraps the scarf around her neck with the other, then slides from the bed in a tiny slip of satin fabric that delicately rests against her subtle curves.

She pads to the dresser in the corner, the lengths of last night's scarf trailing over her tits. What the fuck is that about? She had no problem crossing the city in her underwear, yet can't walk a few steps to her dresser without a swath of material around her neck?

She retrieves a robe from the top drawer and slides her arms into the sleeves, cinching the tie around her waist. "Why aren't you worried?"

I hold on to the information a little longer, building the anticipation, imagining what her shock will look like. How the relief will weaken the venom in her eyes.

"Did that powdered concoction mess with your head?" She turns to me. "Or are you always this slow?"

I push to my feet. "I'm not worried about your father, belladonna, because he's dead."

I wait for the explosion of emotion. Will she be happy? Will the reality of freedom from Emmanuel's dictator-like ways enable me to catch an unscripted smile?

But her expression doesn't change. Neither does her posture.

"Excuse me?" she says.

"He's dead. Snuffed. Worm food."

The slightest furrow mars her brows. "If that poor excuse for a joke is retaliation for last night, I have no time for it. I'm taking a shower." She saunters into her private bathroom and closes the door behind her. "I left the key to your car in the center console," she calls out. "You can see yourself out."

The shower turns on in a rush of pattering water.

Is she that confident Emmanuel can't be touched?

I walk for the curtains, wanting a bright and sunny view once round two of the revelations begin. I bide my time while she's in the bathroom, checking out the knickknacks on top of her dresser—the photo of a sunrise over tree-covered mountains set in a polished silver frame, the cliched porcelain mother and daughter statue—then I open her drawers to peek inside.

The woman has enough lingerie to open her own Victoria's Secret. Every color of the rainbow stares back at me in padded lace or see-through slips of tiny material.

The scent of flowers filters from the bathroom, along with the sound of clattering plastic bottles.

I grab her shoes from the floor, giving myself the excuse to walk into her closet. The expansive room is filled with enough clothing to cover a small country, all of them neatly folded or hung in perfect alignment.

I place her shoes in the spot available amongst the shelves of designer pumps. She's got boots, flats, and a million tiny, sexy heels.

She might have had a strict cash allowance, but by the looks of it, Daddy let her spend whatever she liked on the tricks of her trade.

After ten minutes snooping around her clothes, I return to her bedroom, my impatience growing until I catch sight of the golden clutch from last night resting on the floor beside her bed.

I snatch it off the carpet, unclasp the latch, and peer inside.

Stun gun. Cell. Garage remote. Credit card. Lipstick. Mints. And that little silver vial of nose candy.

I pocket the narcotics and reclasp the clutch, placing it on the bedside table as the shower turns off. She isn't snorting any more of that shit on my watch. She's going to have to wait until I'm gone to continue ruining her life.

I return to my position near the door, waiting out the final minutes until she saunters from the bathroom with a cream fluffy towel wrapped around her body, another piled atop her head, and that fucking scarf around her neck.

"You're still here." She shoots me a two-second scowl and stops in front of her dresser.

"Aren't you little miss observant?" I lean my ass against the wall, my feet crossed at the ankles.

"More so than you." She pulls out a matching set of white lace underwear. "I thought I'd made it clear you're not welcome here."

"I was hoping you were playing hard to get."

She steps into the leg holes of her panties, unabashed as she shimmies them up her legs and underneath the towel. "I'm extremely hard to get."

"Gordon Myers would disagree."

She glares, those pretty blue eyes scathing in their fury. "*Leave.*" She turns her back to me and drops the towel.

Every inch of her is exposed except for those ass-hugging panties. All that smooth, tanned skin is on display, the picture-perfect hips, the lean, lightly muscled thighs as she pulls on her bra.

I don't look away.

The few gentlemanly qualities I had died when she drove me into enemy territory and attempted to keep me *safe* with a fucking picnic blanket.

If she's willing to put on a show, I'm more than happy to take the free tickets.

She grabs a white cotton T-shirt from the third drawer and pulls it on *over* the top of the scarf.

What the fuck is she hiding?

I push from the wall and stalk toward her, holding out a hand. "Give me the scarf."

She keeps me at arm's length as she pads to her robe, pulling the long material from beneath the neck hole to sit on top of her shirt. "Get out of my house."

I follow, coming to stand in the doorway as she grabs a pair of white pants from a shelf and drags them on.

I watch her jiggle, shimmy, and tug the tight clothing to her waist, then yank up the zipper.

"What are you hiding?" I square my shoulders, standing at my full height in the doorway.

"Love bites from last night," she drawls sarcastically, dragging a white blazer from a hanger to pull it on. "Do you mind?" She jerks her chin toward her bedroom. "I'm getting dressed."

"You're already dressed." Not to mention she hasn't given a single fuck about modesty up until this point apart from two inches of her neck.

She saunters to the far end of the expansive robe and slithers a navy scarf from a hook on the wall. "You're acting like a predator."

"I'm glad you finally understand the situation."

She rolls her eyes. "Get the hell out, Bishop."

"Not until you show me what's beneath the scarf."

"Fine. *I'll* leave." She stalks toward me, her gaze adamantly focused on her bedroom over my left shoulder.

I hold my ground, blocking her path.

"Move," she growls.

"Take off the scarf."

"No." Her nose crinkles in disgust. "Who are you to dictate what I do? Do you think Matthew would approve of your heavy-handedness?"

"You haven't seen heavy-handedness, belladonna." I lash out, grabbing the scarf. "But you will."

Her eyes bug, her hands gripping the material woven around her neck. "Stop. *Wait*."

"I don't like repeating myself."

"I have a scar. I've had it for years." She grabs my wrist, her nails digging into my skin. "I always cover it."

I think back on all the times I've spied on her. All the places she's been. All the things she's worn.

It's true she does tend to wear collared blouses and blazers. But there have been times when that bear trap of a body has been draped in a cleavage-exposing dress. Has she always worn a scarf?

"Call Remy. He'll tell you the same thing." She slides her hand under mine, trying to unlatch my fingers one by one. "My neck was sliced open years ago. I hate the scar."

"You could've said that to begin with." I release the material.

"And you could've minded your own goddamn business." She pushes past me and into her bedroom, raising the collar of her blazer to hide her neck as she quickly changes the gold scarf for the navy.

"I thought one of your *colleagues* from last night's *meeting* might have hurt you."

"I know what you thought." She ties a knot in the navy scarf, throws the golden one to her bed, then lowers her collar back in place. "And even if they had, it's not your concern. I don't understand why you're still here."

I don't either.

I told myself I'd stick around until Matthew showed. Then after he called, I wanted to repay the favor for the sedatives and picnic blanket.

But I should've left hours ago.

"I wasn't kidding earlier," I say, breaking the lengthening silence.

"About?" She walks into the bathroom and out of view.

Yet again, I fucking follow. This witch has me on a leash.

I stand in the doorway as she grabs one of the numerous beauty products from the organizational unit on the counter, pours some sort of liquid onto her palm, then rubs it over her face.

"About your father's death."

She doesn't bat an eye as she places the product back where it came from and reaches for a tube of expensive-looking sunscreen.

"I'm serious, Abri. Emmanuel is dead. I spoke to Langston earlier."

She places the product back in its place, then meets my gaze through the reflection in the mirror. For long heartbeats, that's all there is—her eyes on mine, her expression curious. "How?"

"I don't have specifics. Your brother and I never chat shop over the phone."

"But somehow you know my father is dead?" she counters, unconvinced.

"Langston got the point across without being incriminating."

She raises her brows, then snatches for a tube of mascara. "And how did he do that?"

Jesus Christ. This woman is a pain in my ass.

"With fucking words. Call him if you want. Or don't." I shrug. "I don't give a shit. Remy and Salvo will be here to corroborate soon enough."

She flicks the mascara wand over her lashes, seeming disinterested in the conversation. "They're coming here?"

"That's what I said, didn't I?"

She pays both lashes equal attention, then discards the tube. "Fine. I'll make some calls." She swings around and walks toward me.

I step out of her way and let her stride across the room to swipe her clutch from the bedside table. She retrieves her cell from inside and starts pressing buttons.

"Who are you calling?" I ask.

"My dad." She holds the phone in front of her almost as if in defiance, the ringtone loud as it trills once. Twice. Three times. Then it cuts to voicemail. She tries again. One ring. Two. Three. Then voicemail.

"You can call him all you like, belladonna, but I'm pretty sure there's no cell reception in hell."

She shoots me a scathing look then taps the screen a few more times, connecting another call.

The same thing happens. *Ring. Ring. Ring.* Voicemail. This time Remy's voice kicks in with his scripted message before the obnoxious beep.

"Call me," she grates. "*Now.*"

She repeats the task over and over. Calling Salvatore. Langston. Adena.

Nobody answers.

"Mom, I need to speak to you. It's urgent." A slither of apprehension enters her voice. "I'm at home. Alone. None of the guards are here. They haven't been all night. I don't know what's going on. Please call me."

She drops the cell to the bed, still staring at the device as she places her fingertips to the scarf at the front of her neck. She's quiet. Deep in thought.

"Believe me now?" I shove my hands into my pants pockets, fighting the need to be smug.

"It's not unusual for everyone to be unreachable."

"Maybe. But it sounds like it's not the norm for you to be unmanned."

"My father told me yesterday that he was sending a team out of town. I shouldn't be surprised that nobody is here."

"But you are. You're surprised and maybe a little convinced that I'm right."

"No." She shakes her head, those ocean eyes meeting mine with defiance. "I know my brothers were up to something but they never would've made a move without me."

"From what I understand, they didn't have much choice. It sounds like the team your dad organized was used as an ambush."

"Where?" She swallows, her expression turning stricken. "How?"

"Like I said, I don't know the finer details. All I can tell you is that I was with all three of your brothers in Virginia Beach yesterday morning when you called. They had plans to speak to Lorenzo about gaining support to take down your father. But when they arrived, your parents were already there."

She keeps shaking her head. "Remy and Salvo wouldn't do that without me."

"They would and they did."

Her cell vibrates on the bed, Salvatore's name lighting the screen.

She snatches the device and connects the call. "Where are you?"

I step closer, trying, and failing, to hear his reply.

"I asked you to come home yesterday. Why didn't you?" She frowns as she listens to his response. "What sort of complications?... No. Tell me now. Tell me what the hell is going on."

I remain silent as her posture becomes rigid.

"Tell me our father is okay, Salvatore." She raises her voice. "Tell me you haven't been stupid enough to make a huge mistake."

I step closer, tilting my ear toward her until I can make out his voice.

"Abri, *listen*. This wasn't how we planned for things to happen. But we've got a safety net for the future. All those financial threats he held against us are only going to be a temporary issue. We'll be set for life. Trust me."

Her eyes turn to mine, those baby blues stark. There's no relief. No excitement. What stares back at me is fear.

"No." Her free hand clings to the scarf at her throat. "You couldn't have."

"We didn't do anything, Bree. Just try to remain calm until we get home. We aren't far—"

Her arm falls to her side, the cell toppling to the carpet.

Salvatore's mumbled words carry from the floor as she stares through me. Distraught. Shocked.

"It's not true," she murmurs. "They wouldn't do this to me."

"From what I'm told, they had little choice." I remain in place. On edge. Unsure where her unpredictable emotions will turn next.

I'd thought she'd be relieved. Potentially ecstatic. But I don't know what the hell this reaction is. Heartbreak? Or maybe just confusion. "This was Emmanuel's doing."

"He wouldn't have made a move against my brothers," she snaps, her voice cracking. "*They* did this. *They* made plans without telling me first. *Goddamnit.*" She shoves her hands into her hair. "They have no idea what they've done."

I keep my mouth shut as her cell darkens on the floor, the call disconnected.

"What about my mother?" she asks. "Where is she?"

"I don't know."

"But she's alive?"

I shrug. "I haven't been told otherwise."

Abri glances away, staring at a random spot on the wall over my shoulder. "I need to find her."

"Good luck. My guess is she'll lay low for a while. If it were me, I'd withdraw a stack of cash, lose my cell, then bunker down until I could figure out what was going on. But then again, I'd never have attempted to kill the head of the East Coast Italian mafia."

Her face pales as she continues staring at the wall, her teeth nibbling her lower lip.

"Langston was hurt," I add. "Your Uncle Lorenzo, too."

She flicks me a two-second glance, the shock registering for a moment, then she returns to wall gazing as if the information didn't truly sink in.

"Abri?" I inch closer. "Did you hear me? Langston and Lorenzo were hurt. I'm not sure if your father inflicted the injuries, but it was done under his command."

She picks at the quicks on her fingers, the movement becoming increasingly agitated, her teeth digging deeper into her lip.

What the fuck is going on with her? This chick is harder to read than Hebrew.

"Abri." I touch my fingers to the back of her arm, her skin warm beneath my touch.

She startles, then shoves at my chest. "Get out. Just get the hell out."

7

ABRI

My pulse thrums in my temples. My ears. My throat.

I storm for the door, each step an earthquake of upheaval.

He can't be dead.

I run through the hall, sprinting out the panic, passing bedroom after bedroom, then skitter down the stairs. I don't stop until I'm on the lower level on the farthest side of the house, staring into my father's empty office, my chest heaving.

Sunlight streams in through the floor-to-ceiling window, beaming down on the antique mahogany desk where I saw him last. He'd been sitting in his luxurious leather chair, his face set in concentration, his brow furrowed.

This isn't happening.

"Abri?" Bishop's voice carries from upstairs. "Where are you?"

God. Why the hell is he still here?

I step inside the room and close the door behind me.

I need to focus.

Now, more than ever, I have to be strategic. I've feared very few things more than my father's death, and I can't let the panic overwhelm me.

I stalk to the filing cabinet and open the top drawer, my heart dropping at the tightly compacted papers crammed into haphazard files. Not that I expected him to have a folder clearly marked 'leverage,' but I'd hoped for something more organized than this.

I grab a chunk of documents and dump them on his desk,

spreading out bills, employment records, and contracts. There's nothing of use. No contact information. No paper trail of the work I've done.

I return to the cabinet for another pile, dumping them on top of the last, scattering papers far and wide. I do a visual scan of letterheads, finding business logo after business logo. But nothing I need.

Shit. I grab another pile and another. Scattering. Searching. Panicking.

The door opens with Bishop on the other side. "What are you doing?"

I yank open the second drawer, finding another tightly compacted paper tornado. My father must have kept his important business elsewhere. There has to be another cabinet.

I rush to his desk drawers, removing the first from its tracks to tip the contents onto my growing trash pile. Pens, paperclips, and Post-its fall like rain. I do the same with the second drawer. Then I struggle to dislodge the larger third drawer.

I tug. Pull. Yank.

Every time I fail to lift the heavy weight from the tracks, it acts like a meaty stab into my flailing composure.

My face flames hot, my forehead growing slick with sweat.

Emmanuel blackmailed hundreds of powerful people. Where did he put all that leverage? Where is it kept if not in the office that was out of bounds to his own family?

"What are you looking for?" Bishop approaches.

I release the drawer, standing tall as I glare at him. "I'm looking for you to get the hell out of my house." My voice breaks, the outward fragility compounding my growing instability. I can't lose my shit. Not now… But my throat burns. My chest, too.

He stops at the opposite side of the desk, disregarding my request for the millionth time as he scrutinizes me. "Are you okay?"

"Of course I'm not okay. Apparently, my father is dead, my mother is MIA, and my brothers betrayed me."

Nobody understands what my father's death means.

I can't even think about it myself. I *won't*. Not when the threat of a panic attack nips at my heels. I refuse to fall victim in front of Bishop.

"Your brothers did what was necessary." He holds my gaze, unapologetic in his callousness. "Your father was a son of a bitch."

My throat burns hotter, the rampant beat inside my chest thrumming through every vein. I snatch the metal letter opener from beneath the pile of paperwork and picture myself stabbing it under his perfectly defined jaw. "*Necessary*?"

"Yes." His attention dips to my weapon for a second of dismissive appraisal. "Your brothers filled me in on your financial situation."

I snap rigid.

"I know Emmanuel treated you like slaves," he continues. "You were given a meagre cash allowance, and although the credit cards were more easily used, they were heavily monitored to make sure you didn't try to leave. He had you trapped." He guides a hand over the mess on the table, moving the top pages to look at those underneath. "So if you're searching for financial statements or certain bank details, tell me. I can help."

My palm aches from my tight grip around the letter opener.

He thinks I'm scavenging for money? That I have a one-track mind focused on how to bankroll my future after learning of my father's passing?

I'd laugh if I didn't think it would be the catalyst for a breakdown.

"I'm so glad you're well informed." I talk slow. Measured. "And that you've already got me pegged. Not only am I a drama queen, but yes, I'm exceptionally greedy. All I want is access to the riches I'm owed."

"I didn't say that," he grates. "I was only trying to let you know I understand."

"You, *and* my brothers, understand nothing. The relationship I had with my father wasn't the same as theirs."

"So you mourn his death?"

"*Yes*." In so many ways. I grieve what should have been and what I may never get back. My father was the cornerstone of our family. Everything we did, had, or were, was due to him.

"In that case, I apologize for not letting someone else break the news." He steps back from the desk, palms raised in flimsy apology. "But just so you understand, Langston has arranged a future for you. One within your Uncle Lorenzo's organization. You'll be taken care of."

I shouldn't be surprised, but I am. The hits keep coming.

"And I'm meant to be thankful?" Venom enters my voice. "I don't want anything to do with the Italian mafia, Bishop. You included."

"You'll be safe."

"With the *Italian mafia*," I reiterate. "That's not a flex. I know the type of things my uncle is known for. You, too, for that matter, *Butcher*."

His hands fall to his sides, his nostrils flaring. "Well, color me surprised, *belladonna*. Given your extracurriculars last night, I didn't pick you to have such stringent morals."

The simmering pot of my rage, fear, and self-loathing threatens to bubble over as we glare at each other.

He assumes to know me. He thinks I'm an open book.

Nothing could be further from the truth.

My life is an intricately tangled vine of mistakes and failures, the creepers growing and flourishing with the nourishment my father fed them.

Emmanuel always knew how to use a bad situation to its advantage. To twist the narrative. To divert to a different course.

In that, he was utterly brilliant. A manipulative mastermind. And I was his protege.

"Tell me what you're looking for," Bishop repeats.

I swallow, feeling the weight of my bad decisions pressing down on me. I'm not going to find what I need in here. I may never find it at all.

My breath catches in my throat, the air congealing in my lungs. I need a bump. Just one numbing hit to keep the panic at bay.

I stalk for the hall, my pulse increasing, my fear manifesting in rampant heartbeats. I don't know how to fix the mess piling around me. I don't even know how to think about it without anxiety cutting me down at the knees.

"Where are you going now?" Bishop yells after me.

My lungs tighten as I make my way up the stairs, the opening sequence to hysteria closing in. I have to get to my room. I have to calm down.

"*Abri*," Bishop shouts.

I pant my way along the upstairs hall, tugging at my scarf that makes it harder to breathe, yanking at the neck of my cotton shirt.

Secrets will die with me once I'm gone, dear daughter, and this will bring pleasure to many. But not you.

My stomach threatens to spill its contents over my father's words. He never ceased to remind me of the changes that would occur once he passed. To reiterate the consequences if anything were to happen to him.

I enter my room and scan the floor, searching for my clutch. It's not there. And neither are the heels I kicked off last night.

Did Bishop touch them?

His footsteps carry along the hall then his large frame engulfs my doorway.

"Did you move my stuff?" I turn to him, no longer able to hide my panic.

"What are you looking for?"

We are an unbreakable team, beautiful daughter. If I were to die, you know a part of you would too.

"My clutch." My throat restricts. Only the barest hint of oxygen filters into my system as I gasp for breath. "W-where is it?"

He raises a brow, and for one terrified moment I think he'll deny me, but he jerks his chin toward the bed. "On your bedside table."

Relief slightly eases my suffering as I spy my prize and rush toward it. I open the clasp, scavenge inside, and…nothing.

My fingers brush over lipstick. Breath mints. Stun gun. Credit card. But no vial.

"You won't find it," he grates.

My pulse spikes, the adamant beats of my heart thunderous.

"I confiscated the blow," he clarifies.

I drop my clutch to the floor and storm for him. "Where's my vial?" I suck in air, but nothing fills my lungs.

I *need* that coke. Not a lot. Just enough to mask the fears. To kill the demons.

"You're not getting it back, belladonna."

"Don't do this to me." I grab his jacket, my arms shaking, and shove my hand inside his pocket, searching for relief. "I'm serious."

"And you think I'm not?" He snatches my wrist, his grip threateningly tight. "Don't make it a challenge to get you sober, because once that switch is flipped you'll never see rails again."

"I'm not a junkie."

"Well, you're sure reading from the script."

"My father just died," I scream. "God forbid I want something to dull the edge."

"Then pick another vice, because you're done with drugs."

I stumble backward, sucking in breath after breath, my lungs on fire, my face aflame.

Life may be challenging with me, Abri, but it will be hell once I'm gone.

"No." I shake my head and hunch over. "I…I have panic attacks."

"Then you need to slow your pulse. Not put your heart under more pressure." He walks up to me and captures my arms to guide me backward.

"Don't." I fight against him, trying to punch. Thump. Strike. But he's too strong. "Bishop. I'm begging you."

He forces me into the bathroom where the panic increases. The soul-screaming, arrhythmia-inducing fear suffocates every inch of my body.

He takes me to the open-ended shower. "This will help."

I barely hear him over the deafening pulse in my ears, my arduous breaths gasping from my lips. I'm going to have a heart attack.

He releases one of my arms and leans into the shower to turn on the water.

I use the slight freedom to yank at the neck of my shirt. To tug at the scarf.

I need air.

"You'll be okay." Bishop grabs my chin, raising my face to meet his. "I'll help you."

I shake my head, my lungs heaving. Nobody can help me.

Nobody but my dead father and my missing mother.

I'm alone. Completely isolated. Trapped.

I hyperventilate. Wheeze. Sway.

I know what's best for you, Abri. I know what my daughter needs. And protection from your own mistakes is the gift I've given you.

8

BISHOP

Her breaths are manic.

"Don't pass out on me." I hold her upright against the glass shower wall and shuck my jacket, but her eyes start to roll.

Fuck. I haul her into the shower, not having time to ditch the rest of my clothes, and lead her backward under the heavy spray. The water hits her head in a rough onslaught, cascading over her hair and straight through her blazer.

She gasps, her eyes widening to saucers, her lips sputtering.

She claws at me, slicing at my face with flailing hands and scratching fingers.

"I've got you." I wrench her arms down to her sides and smother her to my chest as the cold water peppers my cheeks and soaks my clothes.

"Stop," she wails. "Let me go."

"This will help." I back her farther into the spray. "Just breathe."

She screams, her fight renewed, her strength enviable. But unlike last night when she planted my ass on the floor, I'm in control.

I lock my arms around her until she can barely move, the deluge hitting her face.

"The panic will subside." I close my eyes to the torrent. "Just breathe."

Water sinks into every inch of me while her hips twist, her shoulders banging into mine. Over and over she fights. Squeals. Wiggles. But second by agonizing second, her ferocity weakens.

The shouts and screams lose their venom. The jolt and hit of her shoulders no longer pack a punch.

I don't quit holding her as she shivers, her trembling body like breakable glass with the rapid rise and fall of her chest against mine.

"It's cold." Her teeth chatter.

It's fucking freezing. My balls are already hibernating in my abs. But I don't speak my agreement. Instead I keep holding her, tight, not deviating the strength of my grip.

It takes a minute for her to stop battling for freedom. Then another for her inhales to lose the manic edge as they saw from her lips.

"That's it." I open my eyes and chance releasing one arm to loosen the scarf around her neck. She doesn't fight me this time. Doesn't even move apart from the unrelenting tremble.

"You're doing good." I pull back, meeting her blank gaze under the waterfall, her mascara weeping down her cheeks.

She seems distant, her thoughts a million miles away.

She curls her arms in close, huddling them between our chests. "Please stop."

That's all there is. Two words. One heartfelt plea from a hardened witch.

"Just a few more seconds." I wipe the hair from her cheeks and pivot her to the left so the water quits pummeling her face. My shoes slush with the movement, every inch of my skin sodden with soaked clothes. But her breathing strengthens. Steadies. And the panic in her eyes fades, now replaced with exhaustion. "Feel better?"

She looks away. "Just cold."

"Do you think you're ready for warm water?"

She nods. "Please."

There's that word again, the delicate cadence almost making me regret the manhandling.

Humble sounds good on her. Too good.

I reach behind her and turn on the hot tap, my other arm still holding her tight. I'm not ready to trust she won't buckle to the floor.

Lukewarm water pours between us, taking away the bitter chill.

I cradle her back, measuring the slowing rise and fall of her breaths as her scarf slides from her neck to slap hard against the tile.

She's out of the woods—at least for now. But who knows what delightful surprises she'll challenge me with next?

"Does this happen often?" I reach around to increase the warmth a fraction. My shoes are drenched. My socks, pants, and shirt, too. Not to mention my fucking gun.

She doesn't answer.

"When was the last time you ate, belladonna?"

"Why do you call me that?" She gently pushes from my chest, her Bambi eyes finding mine. "Isn't belladonna a flower?"

"Yes," I murmur. "A poisonous one."

Pretty but toxic. Just like her.

She winces, her attention lowering to my shirt.

She can't be hurt by my description. I'm sure she's been labelled far worse without the barbs penetrating her Teflon coating.

She inches farther away, creating a small ravine between us, my arms still cinched around her back. But the space isn't my concern—it's the abnormality in my periphery that steals my attention.

I lower my gaze to her throat, seeing the scar she spoke of, the jagged line an inch above her clavicle and roughly a finger long. But it's not the puckered skin that turns my blood to acid. It's the bruise that circles her neck in vibrant shades of blue, purple, and pink.

Rage infuses my blood, the fury increasing the longer I scrutinize her injury.

Not only did she lie last night, she protected the assholes responsible.

"Which one of them did this?" My tone is lethal as I raise a hand, dragging a thumb over the abuse.

She stays silent. Unresponsive.

Her skin is like velvet under my fingertips, creamy and smooth. How someone can be so soft yet incredibly thorny at the same time is beyond me. But she does it well. Yields to my touch yet remains silently unruly. Fragile in the aftermath of her panic attack and also infuriatingly hardened.

I drag my touch over the darkest purple patch on the right side of her neck, fury creating havoc in my veins at whoever dared to hurt her.

She flinches.

"Who, Abri?" Steam billows between us from the shower.

She shakes her head. "It doesn't matter."

"It does when it means the difference between one death or three." I keep my tone calm despite the murderous intent. "Do you want them all to die?"

She raises her chin, defiant. "It's not your score to settle."

I lean down to her eye level. "Like hell it isn't. It happened on my watch, which means it's my mistake to correct. No niece under Lorenzo's protection should ever be touched."

I anticipate her defiance. Her retaliation.

But all she does is stare at me while my thumb continues to take liberties with her neck, the waterfall cascading over her shoulder, every inch of her exposed skin moist and dewy, including those lips.

"Tell me a name, Abri."

She shakes her head. "A lot has changed since last night. I don't want to look back."

"That's not how this works."

Whether she likes it or not, she's now a figurehead in Lorenzo's organization. I can't let this shit slide.

"I'm tired." She drags in a deep breath, the water dripping over her mouth. "Let me get through today without having to deal with unnecessary complications."

I can't tell if her bleak demeanor is an act.

I'm sure the different masks she wears have made many men fall to their knees. Cheat on their wives. Betray their children. Risk scandal. Has she assumed her softer side will get me to brush my duties under the rug?

Her brows knit. "Please, Bishop."

There's that word again. The one that sounds foreign from her deceptive mouth.

"Fine." I need more time to work her out. To unravel what the fuck is going on. "Have it your way." *For now.*

She smiles, weak and unfathomably beautiful with her soaked hair and matted lashes. Most women would resemble Medusa under the circumstances. But not Abri. She knows how to wield those deep eyes and venomous lips like an enchantress. "Thank you."

I reach around her waist to shut off the water, then backtrack to the farthest corner of the open-ended shower, giving her space to leave as I start undoing my shirt.

She doesn't move.

Instead, she watches as I work my buttons. "I'm not sure I'll be able to find you something to change into." Her gaze treks my chest, then my stomach. "You're as tall as Salvo but…broader."

I tug my arms from the clinging fabric, exposing the switch blade attached to my left wrist by a now-drenched leather cuff, and let my shirt fall to the shower floor with a heavy slap.

"*Far* broader." She eyes the weapon. "And more battle ready."

"I wouldn't be caught dead in your brother's clothes." I kick off my shoes and discard my socks. "Have you got a drier?"

"Yes. But I've never used it. We have staff who usually take care of the laundry." She discards her blazer, then pulls the cotton shirt over her head. Her skin is pebbled with goose bumps, the purple bruising a thick collar around her neck.

I don't look away when she bends to shimmy out of her white pants, but I sure as shit keep mine on. I've risked enough proximity to this woman without exposing her to my package. Especially when my dick gives a throbbing reminder that it's been a while since it had any action.

"*Abri?*" A man's voice carries from somewhere in the house.

Her head snaps toward the doorway.

"Is that Remy?" I ask.

"Yes." She leans over to snatch the only dry clothing from the floor—my fucking jacket—and shoves her arms in the sleeves. "I suggest you stay in here."

She storms for the door, her spine ramrod straight as if she's prepared for war.

"Wait," I warn.

She doesn't listen, disappearing into the bedroom.

"Fuck." I stride after her, my soaked pants leaving a wet trail along the carpet while my gun sticks to my back.

"*Abri?*" Remy calls again, his voice carrying from the lower level.

I'm halfway down the staircase, peering at her brothers bruised faces in the foyer below by the time she reaches the bottom in a whirlwind of pumping legs and drenched hair.

Salvo takes in our appearance with narrowing eyes, apparently not appreciating how we're both half-dressed and dripping if his clenching fists are any indication.

"Morning," I taunt as I stop on the bottom step, Abri still continuing toward them.

Remy's lip curls. "What the fuck is thi—"

She lunges the final foot toward him with a raised hand, cutting off his reprimand with a brutal slap across his cheek.

His head wrenches to the side, the savage clap ringing off the walls.

"How could you?" She slaps him again and again, battering his face. "You fucking bastard."

Remy retreats, raising his arms to defend against the blows without retaliating while I remain still, gorging on her exquisite violence.

"Ease up." Salvatore grabs her wrist with a yank.

"Fuck you." She elbows her older brother in the gut, then swings around with a cocked fist.

"I'll hit you back, Bree," he warns. "You know I will."

She launches anyway, the crack landing on his jaw.

She doesn't flinch with the bone-crunching impact. Neither does he.

"You were warned." His nostrils flare as he raises a hand.

"Hit her and we're going to have issues." I pull my gun from the back of my pants, the weapon dripping water on the fucking floor as I aim at his head.

With my current luck, if I shoot, this motherfucker will backfire. But I'm willing to risk it if Salvatore gives me the excuse to finally make him eat lead.

He snarls, his eyes hard on mine as she strikes him again, this time with an open palm.

I lunge the final step toward her, wrap my free arm around her waist and haul her off the ground. She kicks, swipes, and swings, but the fury isn't directed at me. Even while contained, she tries to attack her brothers.

"*How could you be so stupid?*" she screams. "*So selfish?*"

Both men straighten, standing to their full height, ignoring her as they pin me with incredulity.

"Are you responsible for what happened to her neck?" Remy ignores her, thumbing a swollen spot on his lip.

"No." My denial is barely heard over her continued outrage.

"*How could you kill him?*" she screeches. "*What did you do to our mother?*"

I backtrack, carrying her toward the stairs.

"Mom took off," Salvatore sneers. "She ran."

"And Dad?" She quits swinging and wiggles instead, her ass rubbing against my crotch as she attempts to escape my hold. It's not the most opportune time for a hard-on, but if she doesn't stop that's exactly what she's going to get. "What did you do with him?"

"Lorenzo's men took care of it." Remy keeps touching his lip, poking it with his tongue.

"*It?*" she accuses. "Are you referring to our dead father?"

"Calm yourself, belladonna," I grate in her ear. "Hysterics will get you nowhere."

She elbows my side, my arms momentarily weakened.

She shoves from my hold and jabs a menacing finger at her brothers. "Fuck you both." She turns on her heels and scrambles up the stairs.

Jesus Christ.

I wipe a hand down my face as she disappears into the upper level.

She's fucking exhausting. A whirlwind of emotional upheaval. I don't know where she gets the strength to be such a nightmare.

She slams a door. Something smashes.

All three of us ignore the commotion.

"How did she get the bruises?" Salvatore's tone is spiteful, laced with authority.

Does he think he's already the head of the East Coast mafia? Is he expecting me to show allegiance?

"Ask her yourself. I only found out about the injury a few minutes before you did."

Remy bares his teeth. "Was that while you two were getting naked?"

I open my mouth to correct him, then think better of it and smirk instead. *Fuck him.* Two days ago, these assholes sucker-punched me and tied me to a goddamn chair. I don't owe them shit—least of all the truth.

His nostrils flare. "You're a real piece of work, Bishop."

I incline my head. "And even so, you still wish you were me."

"A butcher?" Salvatore returns my smug taunt. "No, thanks."

"You'll need to be far worse than that if you plan on taking Lorenzo's position."

"I'm sure I'll be able to dictate the dirty work to a worthless offsider, just like my uncle did with you."

I grin, my smile widening the longer the insult digs under my skin. "If it wasn't a legacy I helped build, I'd be excited to see you burn it to the ground. But we can save the talk of your demise for later. I want to know what the fuck happened yesterday."

Remy huffs a deep breath. The defiant stiffness in both their shoulders loosens.

"Our parents were already at Lorenzo's when we arrived." Salvatore drags a hand through his dark hair. "They must have known we were coming."

"How?" I don't hide the accusatory contempt from my tone.

"I don't fucking know. But he came with a plan. And as soon as he caught wind that Remy and I were out to take him down, his men stormed the property. Guns blazing." He looks past me, falling into memories that steal the color from his skin. "It was a goddamn bloodbath."

"Did you hide and let Langston and Lorenzo do the dirty work? Is that why they were both injured and you two came back unscathed?"

Salvatore's lip curls.

"We did the best we could with limited resources," Remy sneers. "It didn't help that Matthew walked in there without a gun."

That stupid motherfucker. I knew his stance on carrying would come back to bite him.

"Was he shot?" I ask, hoping for a less significant injury.

"They both were. Along with Lorenzo's housekeeper and numerous—"

"Extremities or vital organs?" Dread solidifies in my gut. I don't give a shit about anyone else. Lorenzo and Langston are all that matter.

"Lorenzo took a hit to the leg. Our brother wasn't as lucky."

I stiffen, every inch of me coiled tight. "Meaning?"

"He was hit in the abdomen."

Fuck. I step back, shoving a hand through my hair.

"He's okay," Salvatore adds. "He's a lucky son of a bitch. Mainly soft tissue and muscle damage. Blood loss, too. And the risk of infection is high. Yet somehow the bullet only grazed organs. There was no penetration."

"Kinda like your sex life?" I mutter, but the humor doesn't stick.

Langston was shot in the gut. Gunned down while I didn't have his back. Almost killed while he wasn't carrying because I never demanded that motherfucker be strapped.

"Lorenzo said he'll be fine despite a doc cutting him open in the fucking basement." Salvatore's gaze lifts to the top of the staircase where footsteps carry down the hall.

Seconds later, Abri comes into view wearing tight denim jeans, a white T-shirt and blazer, with a different navy scarf. She descends the stairs, carrying a small suitcase, her face stony, her lips a thin line.

Her Converse Chucks-covered feet hit the foyer, then she wordlessly continues forward.

"Where are you going?" I ask as she passes.

"Away from here." She stops before her brothers. "As far as you're concerned, consider me estranged like Matthew. I'm done with you both."

Remy winces. "Abri…"

Salvatore quietens him with a raised hand. "You'll understand our actions once the shock wears off. Then we'll be waiting here for your return."

"Please hold your breath." She stalks to the hall leading toward the garage.

They do nothing.

"You're not going to chase after her?" I seethe.

Salvatore starts for the kitchen. "I've already been bashed and stabbed this week. So excuse me if I don't feel like being bludgeoned by my sister."

"She's not in a state to drive." Not when she's flooded with adrenaline and emotion. *Shit*. Did she find the vial of coke in my jacket?

"She needs space." Remy makes for the stairs. "She'll calm down and realize we're not at fault."

"Have you met your sister? She doesn't seem the type to backtrack."

He shrugs. "There's nothing anyone can do but give her time."

They're just going to let her go? One mentally unhinged junkie behind the wheel of a luxury vehicle?

"Fuck you both." I stalk after her, my wet feet slapping against the tile, my drenched suit pants hanging heavy from my hips.

I reach the garage door and fling it open to an excessive rev of an engine. Tires screech as she reverses an Aston Martin onto the pebbled drive.

"Abri, wait." I run after her, catching up to the car she stops to shift out of reverse.

I plant my hands against the hood, staring down those crazed eyes.

"Move." She white-knuckles the steering wheel. "Or I'll mow you down."

"Believe me, belladonna, I hate chasing after your crazy ass as much as you despise me doing it. But if you're not going to let those assholes look after you it means I'm still on the clock, so let me get you out of here."

"I don't need to be taken care of," says the wild-eyed, brother-slapping, coke-sniffing daughter who's grieving for her psychopathic father.

"Humor me."

The engine revs again, the threat mediocre in comparison to what she's previously launched in my direction.

"I've got a place you can go." I raise my palms, patient on the outside, itching to strangle her on the inside. "Climb into the passenger seat and I'll take you there."

9
ABRI

I cling to the steering wheel, my sweat-slicked palms aching from my grip, but the discomfort is nothing in comparison to the agony in my chest.

"Abri, listen to me. As soon as word hits that your father is dead, all your family bank accounts will be frozen. You'll have access to nothing. Which means no food. No gas. No fancy hotels. No ability to go where you want. Let me take you somewhere safe. Somewhere it's quiet where you can work out a plan."

That's the problem—it doesn't matter how quiet his safe haven is, I still won't have the ability to figure out how to fix this disaster.

"Abri." My name is a warning this time.

"I don't want to see them again." I raise my voice. "Wherever you take me, my brothers can't know about it."

"I hate seeing their pretty-boy faces more than you do."

He's placating me. But it's all I have to rely on until I can manipulate my way under the skin of someone else who can help.

I unclasp my belt and climb over the center console.

Bishop stalks around the hood to open the driver's door and sinks into the car. His chest is still on full display, his pants wet against the leather seat as he shifts into first.

"Get comfortable," he mutters. "This will take a while."

I stare through my side window, watching the only home I've ever known pass me by, praying I never have to return. I don't breathe a word when we drive out the gates or take the back roads away from the city. I burrow farther into my seat, trying to mentally scream back at the voices in my head that tell me my future is beyond bleak.

"There's a place about an hour from here." Bishop turns on the radio, the low murmur of pop music doing little to distract me. "It's out by the—"

"I know where it is."

"You do?" He shoots me a glance, one brow raised in mocking disbelief.

"You don't remember putting it into my car GPS last night?" I raise a superior brow of my own. "It was a few minutes after you took an air swing at Gordon and landed flat on your ass."

He glowers, returning his attention to the road.

The silence eats at me, allowing the shadows of another panic attack to prowl into the outer edges of my consciousness. How will I get through this nightmare? Will my soul survive the repercussions?

"You don't remember that either?" I ask, grasping for something to occupy my mind. "We were out the front of his property after you almost hit us in your car."

"I remember."

"Fighting isn't really your strong suit, is it?" I focus on those memories, refusing to let the nightmares back in. "If you ever find yourself in a boxing ring, I suggest you play dead."

A low rumble carries over the barely heard radio. Is he growling at me?

"You're lucky I only used half that little baggie of sedatives," I add, wishing he'd respond, silently begging for him to step between me and the monsters clawing at my thoughts.

His jaw ticks.

Pressure builds inside my chest as he ignores me, my fear, anxiety, heartache, and exhaustion mixing in a recipe of impending disaster. Will my brothers come after me? Will I be held accountable for their actions?

I can't break down again. I can't allow my demons to take control.

I swallow over the desert in my throat. "I'll know better next time and utilize the full stash."

"There won't be a next time." He glares at the road ahead.

"I'm sure there will be if you keep tagging along after me like a pitiful little puppy."

He huffs a snide laugh. "I'm well aware you taunt me to distract yourself from your suffering, belladonna, but tread lightly. There's a limit to how much bullshit I can take and you're coming close to the threshold."

My eyes burn at how easily he sees through me. At how pathetic I am when my life's role has been to disguise the truth. "You're the one who begged to come with me."

"I'm the one whose job it is to protect you, despite the stupidity of volunteering for the role." He turns his gaze to mine. "I'm good at what I do, Abri. But if you cross me again, I vow you'll regret it."

I drag my gaze back to my side window, hugging my arms around my chest in the hopes of stopping the agony from spreading further.

I don't speak another word as we travel away from Denver, driving for thirty minutes that slowly drag into forty. Thoughts plague me. Mistakes haunt me. I pick at the quicks of my thumbs with my forefingers. I work my bottom lip against my teeth.

My entire world has tilted, the contents now scattered and disheveled.

The cloudless sky mocks me, the beauty and peace a taunting contrast to the surging storm of my life falling apart.

Bishop was right about my financial situation. There's no money. At least none that's not left under the control of a ghost. I have no accounts of my own. No assets. No freedom. And the credit cards will be nothing more than worthless plastic soon enough.

We turn onto a dirt road, my car kicking up dust as it shudders over the uneven ground.

I don't recognize our surroundings. The stretching fields. The sloping hills. I've never been out this way before, so far from the busy highways, and lack of human influence it's clear not many others have either. There hasn't been another car or house in miles.

"How much farther?" My voice is raspy, the aftermath of the last twenty hours making my throat sore.

"A few more minutes."

I eye him from my periphery. The quiet authority. The calm menace.

I'm embarrassed of the sides he's seen of me. Of the things he's witnessed. Nobody has ever glimpsed so far behind the curtain.

How long will it take for him to hold it against me? To use my secrets to his advantage?

We drive for another ten minutes of oscillating road, then pull onto a weed-covered dirt drive before a rusted gate almost hidden by tall grass.

There's nothing out here. Only a field, a hill, some trees, and the barest overgrown track on the other side of the fence.

Bishop retrieves his cell from his pocket, taps the screen a few times, then the metal gate opens with surprising ease.

Not just a rusted-out gate, but an automated one with Wi-Fi?

"There's a house somewhere out here, right?" My gaze follows the track until it crests the hill, disappearing into the unknown.

"Are you worried I've led you into isolation for sinister reasons?" He looks at me with incredulity. "Yet again, it's a little late for self-preservation, don't you think?"

"You're no threat to me."

He huffs a breath of a laugh as if correctly assuming my underlying insult—even if he wanted to hurt me, I could handle him. I landed him on the hotel suite floor last night after all.

"I'm glad I don't get you." He drives us into the field, then presses another button on his cell, closing the gate behind us. "Understanding how you tick would do my head in."

Good. The less he comprehends, the better.

I don't want anyone understanding me—least of all a man like him. One who comes from a background where enemy weaknesses are exploited. "I'm an acquired taste."

"And I'm someone who doesn't have a palate for bullshit."

I stifle a wince. I'm not used to men dismissing me so easily, even when my behavior demands it. I have to remember I need him. At least for now.

He accelerates slowly along the bumpy trail, my poor Aston Martin unaccustomed to the rough terrain. Long grass scratches at the side of the vehicle. Twigs snap and break beneath the tires.

We reach the top of the hill in silence, the summit giving view to a valley with a ranch-style house roughly a mile ahead. The building is relatively small, bordered with a scattering of towering trees and overgrown shrubs. The lawn is unruly and long.

"What is this place?" I lower my window, letting the light breeze calm me.

"Your home for however long you need it." His words lack the spite I deserve. "It's safe and comfortable. But it hasn't been visited in a while, so it might be a little dusty."

"This is your house?" I turn toward him, noticing the increased shadows of fatigue under his eyes.

"Mine and Langston's." He meets my stare with a hardening gaze. "Nobody else knows this exists and it's going to stay that way."

A safe house.

A secret hiding place I've been entrusted to keep.

Gratitude seeps into my anxiety, giving me a slight breather from the potent mania.

I nod, trying to piece together more of the puzzle of my estranged brother's life. There's so much I don't know about Matthew—like pretty much his entire existence since he ran away at eighteen.

Why would he have a safe house in Denver when he escaped our parents to live on the other side of the country? Why here? Why now?

We drive over a grate and into the wire-fenced house yard, the garden beds framing the wraparound porch spattered with unruly flowers that dance alongside weeds in the breeze. But the home looks fresh. The paint on everything from the tin roof to the porch rails is bright and clean. The windows are wide with contemporary curtains pulled closed on the inside.

Bishop stops in front of the closed garage and cuts the engine. "It might not be the fairytale dream house you're used to, but it should do until you pull your shit together."

"Thanks for the heartfelt sensitivity," I murmur.

He unclasps his belt. "I've given you my protection, patience, and restraint. Expecting anything more from me would be a mistake." He shoves from the car and slams the door behind him.

He's right. Expecting *anything* from him is a bad idea when his actions thus far have been unpredictable.

I remain in place as he stalks barefoot up the few steps to the porch, yanks open the screen door, then sets to work on the small keypad locking the main entry. It isn't until he's inside that I follow, taking my time to retrieve my suitcase from the trunk before climbing the few steps onto the porch.

Security cameras point at me from both ends of the house, the round white domes with their black lenses seeming entirely out of place amongst the dust and cobwebs.

The clink of a belt carries from inside. A rustle of movement. Then Bishop's footsteps as his silhouette moves into the hall.

"If you're waiting for an invitation you'll be standing out there a while," he calls.

"You're not going to welcome me inside with mojitos and a friendly smile?" I open the screen door, finding him waiting at the threshold to what I assume is a bedroom.

He's changed clothes, now straightening the collar of a black business shirt that rests beneath a matching suit, his feet covered in leather business shoes.

"If you ever catch me smiling I suggest you run. The things I enjoy aren't for the faint of heart." He jerks his chin at the room. "You can dump your stuff in here, but everything you need should already be in the wardrobe."

"What do you mean?" I approach, my brows knitted.

"Langston always hoped you'd reach out to ask for help to escape your parents. So he stocked this place with all the shit you and your brothers would need in an emergency—clothes, food, girlie shit."

"Excuse me?" The question whispers from my lips as I peer inside.

The furniture is simple. A four-poster queen bed with a ruffled white quilt cover and numerous pillows. There's a dresser along the wall. An armchair in the corner.

"Don't get excited. There's no designer gowns or Gucci labels in there." He leads the way inside as I stop at the threshold. "And we both took a wild stab at sizing years ago." He yanks open the curtains, sending a wave of dust bunnies bouncing through the sunlight. "There's one bathroom and we run on tank water, so keep that in mind if we hang around long enough to use the shower."

His eyes harden. His jaw, too.

Is his mind like mine, assailing him with unwanted memories of the last time he was stuck under the water's spray? When his strong hands held me in an unflinching grip? When I trembled against his chest like a goddamn fool?

"I promise not to be a diva when it comes to water usage." I glance away, dumping my suitcase on the floor before walking for the cupboards to pull the doors wide.

Cotton shirts are folded and stacked on the shelves, both male and female.

There are jeans. Sweatpants.

The hanging side of the closet contains a few blouses and business shirts, and numerous styles of jackets. On the floor is an array of shoes. Chucks. Vans. Sneakers.

"I don't remember any scarfs being amongst the shit your brother ordered," he mutters. "But everything else should be there."

My hand instinctively moves to my throat, my fingers touching the material covering my bruises.

"If you need anything I'll be in the kitchen making coffee." He stalks for the hall with a curve to his shoulders. A slight hunch to his usually pin-straight back. He's exhausted and I'm to blame.

Why does that fill me with guilt?

"Bishop?" My stomach squeezes as he stops at the threshold and turns to face me.

"What?"

"I know I've asked before, but can you explain again why you're helping me?"

"Because you're Langston's sister, and he wants to make sure you're safe."

"That's it? He wants something so you provide it."

"Yes," he states simply. "This is what loyalty looks like, belladonna. He might be your brother by blood, but he's mine by choice. If he needs help, I give it. And he does the same in return."

My heart clenches. I'd give anything to have that allegiance. From anyone. Yet this hardened, murderous man got what I've always wanted from my own brother. The devotion. The kinship. The trust.

"Do you want coffee or not?" He pivots back toward the hall, the soles of his shoes squeaking against the floorboards. "We've only got long-life milk."

"Coffee sounds great, thanks. But do you mind if I stay in here a while? I've got calls to make."

He shoots me a glance over his shoulder, his brows raised as if the sudden appearance of my manners is surprising. He continues into the hall, disappearing from view. "I don't care what you do as long as you're not causing me trouble."

10

BISHOP

I ENTER THE OPEN LIVING AREA THAT'S COVERED IN A THIN LAYER OF dust and head straight for the coffee machine in the kitchen, my jaw locked tight, my muscles tense.

I shouldn't have brought her here. Not alone. Not while she's desperate and I'm too tired to think straight.

Last night was bad enough. When she'd been forthright and stubborn. Tempestuous and explosive. But today is worse.

One minute she's fractured glass, threatening to break. The next she's a clawing wildcat, fighting as if her life depends on it.

The woman is a ticking time bomb, and I'm not equipped to dismantle this level of unhinged.

I also don't appreciate how I itch to figure out the rhyme and reason behind all the crazy.

I want answers. To make sense out of the tangled mess of her.

Instead, I make coffee, the memories of the last twenty-four hours running through my head as the machine sputters and gurgles. I recall the sight of her half-naked and terrified on Gordon's bed. How she mounted me with spite-filled audacity in my own suite moments later. Or the show of goddamn brutal vulnerability in the shower a mere hour ago.

She's under my skin. Stuck there. Like a fucking parasite.

I deliver the coffee to her room where she stands staring out the window, her cell held to her ear, her forehead pinched.

"I understand what you're saying, Jenna, but it's urgent that I speak to him." A strangled edge of authority enters Abri's voice. "I can stay on hold all day if I have to."

I place her mug on the dresser, getting a fake smile of thanks for my troubles, then return to the kitchen in search of food.

I keep my distance, staying away from her insanity in the hopes it dissipates without the need for forced pharmaceutical intervention.

For hours, all I do is drink more caffeine, message Langston with an update, and dabble in a little calculated eavesdropping.

I overhear Abri leave numerous messages for her mother. Then the less interesting calls where she talks about material swatches and sales figures. Jenna is addressed numerous times throughout the day, each utterance of her name made with increasing desperation.

From what I understand, the other woman is gatekeeping Abri from speaking to some guy of importance—whether it's regarding the family fashion label or Emmanuel's death I'm not sure. But the building panic in Abri's tone has me invested.

Occasionally she escapes the confines of her bedroom to grab another coffee or a granola bar, her cell still attached to her ear.

Lunch consists of the mozzarella sticks and chicken strips I find in the freezer.

She doesn't eat much. She says even less.

Then it's back to her room for more disgruntled conversations with Jenna and innumerable messages left on her mother's voicemail.

It isn't until the sun begins to set that she comes in search of me on the back porch, her hair loose around her shoulders as she takes in the view. The hours haven't been kind to her. Her features are drawn and weary, her skin no longer glowing with its usual radiance. She's still manipulatively beautiful, though. Only now she's human. A real woman with real problems instead of the synthetic Barbie doll.

She walks to the few steps leading down to the backyard, her attention casting over the rolling hills. "Do we have to leave for dinner?"

"We've got enough food for now." I take a drag of my cigarette and lean against the far corner of the porch railing, exhaling the smoke away from her. "I found some ground beef in the freezer along with spaghetti sauce and pasta in the cupboards. It won't be fine dining, but it'll be edible."

She nods, wrapping her arms around her middle.

It's quiet, nothing but the far-off caw of a bird trying to get home before dark and the lightest rustle of the wind through the trees. But I hear her. Her grief toward an unworthy piece of shit remains loud between us. The upheaval she keeps hidden rings like static in my ears.

"I wish I'd known about this place years ago," she says quietly. "It would've been nice to think I had options."

I take another drag, hating that the scenic view no longer holds the peace it did moments ago. It only took a second for my body to become finely attuned to hers. The slow movements. The way her scarf dances in the breeze. I notice her more than I need to. More than I *want* to. It's a sickening compulsion. "Would you have asked Langston for help?"

"No."

"Because Emmanuel had you trapped?"

She turns to me, her dark eyes heavy with exhaustion. "Because I realized the brother I thought I knew was only an illusion after he left me behind. And that reality only became more apparent the longer time stretched between us." She moves closer, stopping a few feet away to cock her hip against the railing. "Can you imagine my shock when I heard the rumors that my sweet, overprotective older brother had become one half of the Butcher Boys of Baltimore?"

Is she baiting me? Trying to get a reaction? To start another fight?

I hold her gaze, unflinching as I take another inhale of smoke-riddled death. I keep my expression unreadable. No remorse. No anger.

"How does one go about getting that sort of moniker?" she asks.

I raise a sardonic brow, wordlessly asking if she's naive enough not to assume the broad strokes of violence.

"You've killed a lot of people," she murmurs.

I take another drag, unapologetic and calm, silently blowing the smoke out one side of my mouth. I let her imagination run wild with the carnage. I'm sure the quiet paints a vivid picture.

"Did you mutilate them?" She cocks her head to the side, scrutinizing me. "Is that where the butcher reference comes from?"

"Hardly."

"Then why? How did the two of you earn such a sickening reputation?"

I keep staring at her, unblinking, unfazed, wanting her to know her presence has no hold on me even though the facts paint a different picture. "Because a blade makes less noise than a gun, belladonna."

"That's it?" She frowns. "That's the only reason?"

No. Not the *only* reason, but the one that's most palatable. "There was a time or two where we needed to make an example of those who went against your uncle. Where fear needed to be created and a lasting impression left on anyone who dared to cross him. But don't worry—Langston never took point on those jobs."

She stands taller, hearing the words I don't speak. Understanding that those atrocities fell on my shoulders.

That I'm the brutality. The horror behind the moniker.

I wait for revulsion to morph her pretty face. For terror to stare back at me from those ocean eyes. That's what I want. Her fear. Her disgust. Something to sever my curiosity in her.

Instead, she turns to the railing, gripping the wood in both hands.

The quiet stretches, the darkness of night creeping closer with each passing second.

"Do you always smoke?" Her voice is low, the confidence in her tone diminished despite how she attempts to make a smooth transition from a conversation about murder to something as menial as my nicotine habit.

"Only when the circumstances demand it."

She nods again. "And I'm that circumstance?"

"One of many. You women have an impressive way of complicating life."

"*You women*?" She shoots me a tired look. "Does that mean you have a girlfriend?"

"Give me more credit." I take the last puff of my smoke, then put it out in the ashtray at my feet. "Unlike your brother, I make smart choices where females are concerned."

Her mouth twitches, the barest hint of a smile breaking free.

I find myself itching to see it in full form. To glimpse what amusement looks like on her when unbridled and carefree.

Get your fucking head straight, asshole.

"Until now," she muses. "It must be hell on Earth to be stuck here with me."

"True. It's not the most fun I've ever had."

The humor fades from her profile, her gaze lowering to the lawn a few feet ahead. "I owe you an apology for my behavior." She flicks another glance my way, this one tinged with regret.

"An explanation would be preferred." I want to know the reasons behind every stupid decision she's made since I reached Denver. Why was she fucking around with Gordon? Why rail on me after I saved her when she'd clearly been screaming for help? And who the fuck is Jenna?

There are so many things about Abri that don't make sense, and I won't stop until I find the answer.

She swallows, the faint hint of her throat working against the top of her scarf as her focus returns to the yard. "You already know why I act the way I do. I'm a money-hungry drama queen, remember?" She backtracks and turns for the house. "I'm going to make a start on the spaghetti."

I don't protest. If she wants to hide from me, that's fine. I'll figure out her secrets another way. I watch her, though.

While she occupies her time in the kitchen I remain in the growing darkness of the porch, peering through the floor-to-ceiling glass as she cooks our dinner.

Money-hungry drama queen or not, she's keeping her cards close to her chest. Trying to bluff her way around a man who is becoming increasingly more invested in learning her nuances.

There's more to her temperamental state than grief. It stretches beyond financial issues, too.

Be cautious with her. Langston had messaged earlier. *I don't want her running when I'm not in a position to search for her. I'm relying on you to keep her safe while I'm down for the count.*

I didn't need the reminder.

Not about how she's likely to run or that he's recovering from wounds I could've prevented if only I'd been around.

"*Bishop?*" She calls out half an hour later, beckoning me inside with two bowls of spaghetti.

We sit on opposite sides of the dining table, neither one of us breaking the silence.

She holds her scarf as she leans over to eat a few bites, her gaze affixed to her cell phone as it lays silent beside her bowl.

"Have you heard from your mother yet?" I don't know what she added to the basic spaghetti sauce to give it less of a production-line flavor, but it's good. *Real* good.

"No, and I'm wondering whether or not I should file a missing person's report. I don't know what's going to make me look less guilty once the police start to investigate."

She doesn't need to worry about the authorities. Lorenzo has the cops in Virginia in his pocket, and those in Denver are firmly placed in mine.

"Give it a few days. Then we can call your brothers and discuss a plan."

"No." She meets my gaze, her eyes hard. "My future doesn't involve them."

I shove a forkful of spaghetti into my mouth to stop an annoyed response, opting for a more placating repeat of, "Just wait a few days," after I swallow.

She nods, picking her meal to pieces, barely eating half her serving before she stands and disposes of the mangled wreckage in the trash.

"Leave the cleanup for me," I mutter over my shoulder. "The cook doesn't do the dishes."

"Thank you." She returns to her room, closes the door and makes additional calls, leaving unending messages, begging for her mother to answer her pleas.

The worst part is that she doesn't sleep. Which means I can't either.

Even though I hid the car fob, I wouldn't be surprised if she has another stashed in her suitcase. I won't risk her deciding to hightail it while I'm out for the count. So I'm left to nap on the sofa, my senses on high alert for her every move.

The midnight hours are marked by her journey back and forth to the coffee machine, the silence of night constantly broken by her frantic messages that grow in despair the closer the hour moves toward daylight.

Even though my eyes are closed, I see her.

I fantasize about getting into her personal space, placing a cloth over her mouth, feeling those sweet lips part over the material doused in chloroform. She'd turn limp in my arms, her grief no longer a thorn in my side as she finally fell fucking quiet.

By the time the sun rises, I'm one grumpy son of a bitch.

I update Langston with a text—

ME

No change here.

He doesn't respond.

I'm tempted to call. To get my own update on his health and make sure he's still breathing. But Lorenzo would be blowing up my phone if his favorite nephew was knocking on death's door.

And besides, Langston needs to focus on his recovery and not his manic sister.

The day follows a similar routine to the one prior. Breakfast consists of toast thanks to the bread in the freezer. Lunch is ramen noodles. Abri remains glued to her phone in the bedroom, pleading with a mother who has successfully fallen off the face of the Earth.

"Mom, *please* stop ignoring me. It's urgent that I speak to you."

Later it's, "At least tell me you're okay. Where are you?"

Followed by, "I can't do this much longer. We have to talk, Mom. *Please*. I'm begging you."

But it's the conversations surrounding Jenna and the mystery man Abri is trying to speak to that have me inching closer to the hall to overhear.

"I don't care that he doesn't want to speak to me. Either he does it on the phone or I come to his office. Which would he prefer? *No*, don't put me on hold—*son of a fucking bitch.*"

A few minutes later. "Give me his cell number, Jenna."

Half an hour after that. "If you won't put me through, then make sure he's prepared for me to pay him a visit." Her voice turns viperous. "Or maybe I'll go to his home instead. Do you think the senator's wife will be around tomorrow?"

The senator? My, how her twisted plot thickens.

I do my research, scouring the internet for local married senators in the state with anyone named Jenna on their staff. Joe Hillier fits the bill.

Married.
Thirty-five.
No kids.

Republican.

His priorities include the agriculture sector, education, and upholding the second amendment. His website boasts an image of him in a crisp suit with a gleaming shmuck of a smile.

I shouldn't fixate on why this fucker is important to her. But I do. All afternoon and into the evening.

I retrieve the laptop I have stashed in the kitchen pantry and do a deep dive on the blond senator with the demeaning smirk.

I find his address. Then do a more exhaustive search for any dirt this motherfucker might have on his coattails. By the time dinner rolls around again, I'm no closer in discovering his connection to Abri than she seems to be in getting past his secretary to be able to chat to him.

"Have you had any luck on the phone today?" I place her meal in front of her—marinated chicken wings atop a bed of packet-made fried rice. "Has your mom reached out?"

"No." Abri grabs her fork and pokes at a pea, the slightest tremble visible in her hand.

The lack of sleep is etched into every inch of her—the pale tinge of her skin, the tired slump of her shoulders. At least she had the energy to change out of her pajamas this morning, but the light grey suit pants and sheer white blouse are a little too tight for my liking. The sight of her white lace bra beneath isn't appreciated either.

"She's radio silent. I can only assume she thinks I'm to blame for what happened." She shrugs. "Or maybe she's dead, too."

I take the seat across from her. "If that's the case, you'll know soon enough."

She nods, then scoops a measly forkful of rice into her mouth.

"Who else have you spoken to?" I ask.

"Business associates." She sips on a glass of water, her attention downcast on her meal. "Although the staff at Alleya run autonomously, they'll start asking questions if they don't hear from my parents. I'm trying to keep them distracted as long as possible."

Right—the family fashion label. The one that's a front for all their illegal dealings.

"And what about the senator?" I grab a chicken wing and bite into the flesh.

She keeps her head pointed toward her food, but those eyes raise to meet mine through dark lashes. "What about him?"

"You've been calling for more than twenty-four hours, and from what I've heard, you still haven't got past his secretary. Is there something I can help with?"

"No." She raises her chin, looking at me head on. "My issues with the senator are private and I'd like to keep it that way."

I take another bite of meat. "I could get you a conversation with him."

She places her fork down on the table. "How? Do you know him?"

"I don't need to. I can get it done."

Her eyes widen, as if correctly assuming I'm referring to violent means. "That isn't necessary. Your type of help isn't required."

"Is that because you're trying to forge a relationship with a government official in case the cops come calling?"

"No." The adamant denial paints a picture of defense and panic. "Please just drop it."

I wish I could, but curiosity has me by the balls. "Are you looking for money? Does he have ties to your father? Are you and the senator having an affair?"

"Stop it." She shoves to her feet, her chair scraping loud against the tile. "I said it's none of your business." Her chest rises and falls, labored and frantic. Is she having another panic attack?

She may be bold enough to raise her voice to a murderer, but fear stares back at me. The question is—why? What makes this senator so important?

"Sit, Abri." I finish my chicken wing and grab another. "You need to eat."

Her breathing continues to labor, her fragility increasing my pulse. Is she going to crumple again? Will I need to rescue her from the brink? Is that fucking excitement thrumming through my veins?

"Eat," I repeat. "You need something in your system other than caffeine, otherwise that tremble in your hands will only increase."

She cringes and clasps her fingers together, tempering the tremor.

"*Now*." My tone carries a demand as I take another bite of chicken. "I promise to quit talking about him."

She doesn't move.

"I said I'd drop the conversation," I grate. "Now sit."

Her shoulders slump but finally she obeys, slowly lowering to her seat to scoot it back in under the table.

"You should have a glass of wine." I jerk my chin toward the kitchen. "There's a bottle of red in the pantry."

"No, thanks. I have to stay awake."

"What you need is sleep."

She ignores me and attempts to eat a chicken wing with a knife and fork, painstakingly carving strips of meat. It's basically threads of shredded protein as she holds her scarf to her chest in one hand and forks the food into her mouth with the other.

"You don't need to wear that around me." I dump another cleaned bone on my plate.

"Hmm?" She keeps intricately slicing, not meeting my gaze.

"The scarf. You should take it off." I don't want her to hide her scars. I prefer the reminder of her imperfection.

She forks another shred of chicken, barely enough to feed a mouse, and places it between her flawless lips.

I keep eating. Keep watching. Keep waiting for her to obey me.

She chews. Swallows. Runs her tongue over her bottom lip. Then finally, she places her fork to her plate and removes the material around her throat to lay it on the table.

My pulse increases. It's a temperamental mix of triumph over her acquiescence with a volatile kick of animosity as she exposes the bruising now darker than it was in the shower yesterday.

I should've taken Gordon's life in that hotel room.

I should've killed them all.

Slowly.

Methodically.

Ruthlessly.

"Are you ready to have the conversation about who hurt you?" I drag my gaze from her marred skin and grab another wing.

"I've told you before, it doesn't—"

"I'm obligated to right the wrongs, Abri." And even if obligation played no role, I'd still punish those responsible, if not due to my loyalty to Lorenzo, then out of respect to Langston. "Was it Gordon?"

"No." She dumps her fork atop the bed of rice and pushes her plate away, the food barely eaten.

"Do you know the names of the other two?"

She sighs. "Bishop—"

"I'm stuck out here with nothing to occupy my violent mind, belladonna. It's best if you give me something to focus on."

Her eyes meet mine. She stares for a moment, her silent thoughts making me itch to find out whether she's smart enough to fear me yet.

"The names, Abri."

"Only one was responsible." She crosses her arms over her chest. "And his nickname is all I have."

Adrenaline seeps into my veins. "Give it to me."

"What will happen if I do?"

"He'll get what he deserves."

She sits straighter. "Will you tell me before you take action?"

I push my plate away, my appetite vanishing with the build of bloodlust. "If that's what you need."

"It is." She nods. "I want to know what you plan on doing and when you plan on doing it."

"Then give me the name, belladonna, and I promise to keep you updated."

She raises a brow. "You're promising me?"

"Yes. You'll know before I take action."

Her eyes narrow, her scrutiny intense for a few short seconds before she unlocks her arms from around her chest and stands. "Gordon called him Finch. That's all I know."

11

BISHOP

She enters the kitchen, scrapes her food in the bin, then fills the sink with water. She does the dishes while I finish my meal alone.

I don't stand and follow until I hear the coffee machine, the slow gurgle of a new brew dripping to life.

"No more coffee." I stalk toward her, dumping my plate on the counter before reaching around her to switch off the machine.

She stiffens and turns to face me as my arm grazes her waist.

"You need sleep." I ignore her wild eyes, her parted lips, the scent of her floral shampoo. "Go and get ready for an early night." I return to my plate and shove the chicken bones in the trash as I wait for her to protest. To lash out with words or claws.

Neither happen.

She simply stands there, staring at my profile as if too battered to fight.

"You heard me." I dunk my plate into the bubbled water in the sink and give it a once-over with a dish cloth. "I can't sleep unless you do, and I'll be one nasty motherfucker tomorrow if I'm kept awake again."

"Coffee or not, I won't be able to sleep," she murmurs.

"Maybe not, but you'll have even less chance with more caffeine in your system."

"But I have calls—"

"They can wait until morning." I shoot her a hard look over my shoulder, almost regretting my severity when she peers back at me with crestfallen defeat.

This woman isn't the same one who flung me from the hotel bed. She's not the one who drove me into the viper's den and covered my unconscious ass with a picnic blanket either.

This Abri Costa is brimming with hopelessness, like she's subconsciously screaming for help. She's weak. Pathetic. And I hate how I itch to save her.

"Go." I jerk my chin at her and return my attention to the bubble water.

I don't expect her to silently leave the room like she does. To shower without protest.

Maybe she has redeeming qualities after all.

Maybe she has too many.

While she's in the bathroom I make her an alternate drink, leaving the mug of hot chocolate on her bedside table. I'm about to walk from her room when she pads in from the hall, a towel heaped upon her head, her modesty barely covered by a ruby satin chemise.

Thin straps hug her shoulders, the deep neckline exposing a fuck-ton of lush cleavage along with a completely unrestricted view of the injuries along her neck—the bruising, the aging scar.

"Did you decide to go through my things again?" She continues toward me, stopping a few feet away at the end of the bed. She removes the towel from her head, her hair disheveled and damp as it topples to her shoulders, the ends brushing the curves of her tits.

This moment shouldn't resemble the start of a porno, but it does, and my brain isn't the only organ to take notice.

She's too attractive for her own good. Too tempting despite the shadows of exhaustion under her eyes.

"Hot chocolate," I mutter, moving around her to stalk for the door. "I thought the least I could do is meet you halfway."

"Is it safe to drink?"

I pause at the threshold, despising the birth of her self-preservation when it's barely existed before. "It'll help you sleep."

"That doesn't answer my question."

No, it doesn't. And for good reason.

I continue into the hall without another word.

I shower, jerking off like an old perve to the image of ruby satin fabric, dark bruises, and tangled hair. It's not that I'm into her. Hell no. I need the fucking increase in my pulse to keep me awake, the gratification more of an exercise in punishment than pleasure.

The sooner Abri pulls her shit together and gets out of here, the better. I helped her because no one else could, but surely my shift is up.

I'll give her one more day. Maybe two. Then she's her brothers' problem.

I need to get back to Virginia Beach. To Langston. I have my own businesses to manage. My own crazy shit to contend with due to Salvatore taking over from Lorenzo.

I dress in a fresh suit. Re-strap my throwing knives to my ankles and the switch blade to my wrist. Shove my gun into the holster at my back—a *new* gun from my bedroom closet safe. One that isn't waterlogged thanks to Abri's theatrics yesterday morning. Then I leave the bathroom, planning to casually pass her bedroom on the way to mine. But her closed door gives me pause.

No sound comes from the other side, and after thirty-plus hours listening to her on the phone, the silence is eerie. There's no glow of light under her door either.

I should keep walking.

I *should*.

But my palm finds the door handle and slowly turns it.

I push inside, the light from the living area filtering down the hall and onto her bed to gently illuminate her sleeping under the sheet.

"Abri?" I keep my voice low.

She makes a faint noise, a whimpered acknowledgement, as I enter her room.

Her cell rests on the pillow beside her head. One hand is protectively placed over the damage to her neck. But she doesn't wake. She's out cold.

She drank the hot chocolate even though she had to have assumed it was spiked.

Does that mean she trusts me? Or were the sedatives what she wanted to quiet her frantic mind?

I walk to her side of the bed to peer down at her, the quiet beauty of her slumber spoiled by the violent bruising tattooed to her smooth skin.

Finch needs to suffer.

No matter Abri's intent the night of the gala, the marks he left are unforgivable, the brutality inexcusable to someone of her lineage.

I kneel on the carpet, oddly humbled by the sight of her.

It's been years since I've been this close to a sleeping woman. Since I've heard the soothing cadence of another lost in slumber. And it's the first time I've witnessed it with someone as beautiful as Abri.

Her lips are gently parted. Her inhales a calm, rhythmic dance.

But it's those bruises that continue to draw my attention and steal the tranquility, making my temples pound.

I reach out, sweeping a stray strand of hair from her left cheek, my fingers brushing the pure softness of her skin. "Abri."

She whimpers, faintly coherent.

"I need you to wake up." Slowly, I rub my knuckles along her jaw, earning another whimper, gaining a faint bat of her lashes. "Just for a minute."

"Bishop?" She opens her eyes, the deepest blue staring back at me in confusion as she struggles to rouse. "What's wrong?"

"Nothing's wrong." I don't stop touching her. I can't. I take liberties with my fingers, trailing them lower until I'm skirting the edge of the damage Finch left behind.

She moans, her eyes falling closed. It almost sounds sexual—pleasurable—but I'm smart enough to understand that perception is only due to the lingering effects of my most recent shower activities.

There's no love lost between us.

I don't want her and she doesn't want me.

But I can admit the pretty package she comes in is far more tempting when all her crazy is locked away.

"I need you to hear me, belladonna."

She gives another whimper. Struggles again to open those ocean depths and blink back at me.

"I gave you a vow I had every intention to keep." I hold her gaze as her glazed eyes fight to remain open.

"Mmm?" She raises her brows in question.

"This is me keeping my promise." I change the path of my fingers, giving in to temptation with a slow swipe of my thumb along her bottom lip.

A delicate sound emanates from her throat, one I picture

capturing with my mouth. I could smash my lips to hers and maybe she'd never remember. Maybe she'd never know. But I would. Her poison would forever taint me.

She's my belladonna for a reason.

I drag my hand away and stand. "I'm leaving to take care of Finch. By the time you wake, the man who hurt you will be dead."

12

ABRI

I wake up slow and warm, the comforting edges of a good night's sleep still cuddling my consciousness.

I keep my eyes closed. Stretch. Then pause at the unfamiliar fabric of the pillow.

In a heartbeat, solace slips away and reality floods in—where I am, why I'm here.

I sit up, swallowing back the panic that wants to drag me down, fighting against it like I have for two days.

The morning sun beams heavily against the thin curtains, announcing it's far later than my usual five-thirty wake-up call. *Jesus.* I've wasted too much time.

Faint noise filters from the other side of the closed bedroom door, the barest scent of bacon singing to my empty stomach. If only going out to the kitchen didn't mean I had to face Bishop in all his authoritative glory.

I'd known he'd dosed my drink last night, and it had been a struggle to decide whether or not to take it. But having him dictate rules had felt different to when my father did it.

I'd needed sleep. Bishop was pushing me toward what was right.

That insight had never been clear to me with my father.

Now I feel all the better for what must have been more than ten hours rest. Exhaustion doesn't have me by the throat. Today will be the day I pull this shitshow together and take charge, no matter how impossible that seems.

My stomach turns at the thought and I clench my muscles, refusing to let dread bubble back to the surface.

Breathe. Focus.

I reach for my cell on the bedside table and pause as my fingers brush the device, struck with a sudden wave of hazy déjà vu.

Did Bishop come into my room last night?

Did he stand over me in the darkness?

I wouldn't be surprised if he did. But I must have dreamt it.

I snatch my cell, my attention skimming past the 8:25 time in the top corner of the screen before I focus on the notifications.

Two missed calls from Salvatore.

One text from Remy—

> REMY
>
> I know you're with Bishop, but at least tell me you're all right.

I swipe away the notices, allowing another to jump into view—a Google alert with a link to a news website.

Since our family fashion label became an international success, I've had notifications set to inform me of online articles that could affect the running of the business. In more recent years, I've set those alerts for my targets as well. The men I've extorted and those they hold dear. This morning, Gordon Myers' name is in the short preview.

I click the link, my blood running cold at the headline—*Shipping Magnate Attacked by Home Intruder.*

I skim the article, all the blood draining from my face.

Masked assailant.

Strangled with belt.

Survived but remains in hospital.

Police are also investigating the death of his bodyguard, Graham Finch, found dead in his apartment from a suspected suicide.

My heart changes gears from the calm of slumber to something panic-riddled as clattering pans and clinking cutlery carry into my room.

Bishop.

I scowl, forcing my thoughts back to last night. The hot

chocolate. The steep dive into slumber. Then him. In my dreams. Standing over my bed.

I faintly recall his face through the darkness. His quiet murmured words that still held such strong conviction. *By the time you wake, the man who hurt you will be dead.*

"*Shit.*"

I fling back the covers and slide from the bed, then pad to the door and yank it open. I'm wearing nothing but my satin chemise and I don't care. I don't care about anything except answers until I reach the open living area and stop dead in my tracks.

Bishop stares down at a sizzling pan on the stove, dressed in a black business suit, his back to me as he holds a pair of tongs.

Grocery bags line the counter. Fresh bananas, apples, and oranges now sit on the dining table along with a carton of juice and two clean glasses. Did he go grocery shopping after committing murder?

"Did you sleep well?" he asks without looking over his shoulder.

I stiffen, disturbed by his keen senses. Even more baffled by his calm demeanor.

"Yes." I walk farther into the room and stop near the start of the kitchen. "You?"

"Sleep is a luxury I haven't been afforded in a while."

Maybe because he was awake all night doing the Grim Reaper's work and complicating my already hellacious existence. "You've been busy."

"Not really." He grabs the pan handle and gives it a shake. "It's only bacon. I'll crack you a few eggs in a minute."

"I don't want any. And I think you know I wasn't talking about the food."

He doesn't react. I would've expected him to flinch. To look at me. To deny the underlying accusation. Yet he continues to stare at the pan, quiet, the pop and sizzle of the meat growing deafening.

Seconds pass, his silent peace confusing the hell out of me, almost tempting me to fall into the same calm. To ignore that the murder occurred. But he killed a man. Hospitalized another. How can he stand there, immaculately dressed and profoundly refined, without a care in the world?

"Are you going to pretend it didn't happen?" I continue toward him, stopping a few feet away to hold up my cell, the online article illuminated on the screen. "It's all here in black and white."

He peers over his shoulder, shoots my phone a quick glance, then returns his attention to the bacon without batting an eye. "It needed to be done."

Adrenaline floods my veins. "What, exactly, needed to be done?"

He sighs and turns to me, taking in my sleepwear with a quick onceover then clenching his jaw. "I told you last night I was leaving to kill Finch."

"You told me while I was messed up on sedatives."

He inclines his head and points his tongs at me. "But I told you nonetheless, just like I promised."

Son of a bitch.

"I was barely conscious," I grate.

"Conscious enough to fulfil my end of the deal." He reverts his attention to the pan, pretending he's Chef Ramsey instead of Ted Bundy.

"Do you even realize Gordon is still alive?" I want to push him. *Slap* him. God, how is he so composed? "He's in hospital."

"I'm not incompetent, Abri. I know exactly what state he's in. I can't kill him when I don't know why he's important to you, which means he lives. For now."

My lips part, but shock leaves me speechless.

Do not *be thankful, you dumb bitch.*

As much as Gordon deserved a lesson in manners and Finch's death was justified, both are complications that can only bring more problems for me. And besides, Bishop didn't do this for my benefit. It was a job requirement. A *mafia* thing.

"Aren't you worried about being caught?" I whisper.

"How will the cops figure it out?" He uses the tongs to flip over a piece of bacon. "Are you going to tell them?"

"Of course not. But Gordon might."

"I've spent more than a decade honing the skill of keeping people quiet. Rest assured, he won't say a word."

"What about DNA? Surveillance? Your alibi?"

He grabs one of the clean plates waiting on the counter, places a few strips of bacon on it, then turns and hands it to me. "I know what I'm doing."

I take the offering. I'm too stunned to do much else.

He has no remorse. Not one inkling of concern or baggage over the crimes he's committed.

"Start eating." He jerks his head toward the table. "We can talk shop once I'm finished cooking."

I blink, slowly, unable to drag my gaze from him, finding it hard to function.

I don't know what this new state of events means for me. Gordon shouldn't mean anything at all now that my father is dead, but the weight of potential catastrophe bears heavier on my soul.

Nobody knows the problems I'm caught up in. They don't know how long I've been drowning.

I force my feet toward the table, take my usual seat, and wade through the tangled mess of my mind while Bishop cracks eggs into the pan.

I need my mother. Why the hell won't she call me back?

It's true I wasn't her favorite. Never was. That pedestal was reserved for the son who got away. The one who was smart enough to run.

But the least she could do is call. Right? Even if she suspected I was involved in my father's death, even if she thought I was the mastermind, wouldn't a mother need confirmation before giving up on her child?

I know I would.

I'd want crystal clarity before I destroyed my own flesh and blood in retaliation. And that's exactly what she'll do. Destroy me.

I pick up the piece of crispy bacon with my fingers and take a bite of salty goodness, momentarily distracted by how the meat practically disintegrates on my tongue.

At least Bishop knows how to cook—a fact I wish held more of a punch than the lengths he went to in the name of avenging the wrongs done to me… But it doesn't. Even though I knew he was a murderer, I'd expected more emotion over the act. A little stress maybe. Or a glimpse of fear.

Yet there's only confidence. Poise. Perfectly sculpted self-assurance.

Is he still dressed in his slaughter suit or did he change?

I swallow my first bite, the lingering discomfort from the injuries Finch inflicted following the bacon's journey all the way down my throat.

I don't feel sorry for the asshole. I don't care that he's dead. But I can admit murder doesn't feel good when it rests on my shoulders. If I hadn't fallen prey to the panic attack in the shower, my bruises never would've been exposed, and Finch would still be alive.

If my mom finds out I had anything to do with this...

I suck in a deep breath, filling my lungs to the brink before I let it out.

I'm not going to let anxiety ensnare me today.

I take another bite, my gaze covertly stuck on Bishop. He hasn't shaved. The stubble along his jaw is almost long enough to claim beard status. He can't have slept for at least two days.

How is he functioning?

He grabs a spatula from a drawer, shovels his eggs onto a plate along with the bacon, then turns off the stove and makes his way to the chair across from me.

Sitting face-to-face seems more intimate this morning. He's closer somehow now that fresh blood is on his hands.

"Can you please tell me what happened?" I ask.

He uses a knife and fork to tear his breakfast into bite-sized pieces. "Do you really want to know?"

I'm not sure.

My mental state has been balanced on a tightrope for days. One wrong move could push me back into meltdown. But the more I look at him, the more I want to know what he's capable of. I need more than just the assumptions that come with his moniker.

I nod. "I want all the details...while lucid this time."

He gives a subtle smirk as he forks a mouthful of eggs into his mouth. He chews. Swallows. Licks his bottom lip. "There's not a lot to tell. I paid Gordon a visit first. Extracted the necessary information, then—"

"What information?"

He scoops another forkful, eyeing me through his lashes. "Why he was with you at the gala. What his plans were in that hotel room."

I fight not to break our gaze, but shame niggles me. I glance down at my plate, my stomach twisting in knots.

"That shit won't happen again." He takes another bite. "You won't be used or manipulated."

He says it so simply, flinging the words around with a careless disregard that strips me bare and leaves me exposed.

"*I* wasn't the one being manipulated," I correct. "Gordon is a powerful man. I was—"

"Call it whatever the fuck you like, just know you won't be put in that position in the future. That shit won't fly with Lorenzo."

To hell with Lorenzo.

I don't even know my uncle, let alone have faith in him changing my life into sunsets and rainbows. I'm too far gone for that.

"So something like sedation is okay in the eyes of the almighty Lorenzo Cappelletti," I muse. "But what Finch did to me cost him his life?"

Wait a minute.

More memories from last night seep into my consciousness, foggy and dark. Did Bishop touch me? Had his fingers trailed along my jaw?

Heat floods my chest as hazy flashbacks assail my mind. The gentle brush of contact. The lingering hold.

"And the way you came into my room before you left—the way you laid hands on me?" I ask. "What was that all about?" I raise my gaze in time to see his jaw tick.

"I didn't have much choice when I needed to keep you awake long enough to hear me fulfil my promise."

Bullshit.

The shadowed memories paint a gentle picture. One with delicate brushes of fingertips and softly spoken words.

He could've shouted at me if he'd wanted to. Unless my recollection has been warped by the sedatives and all the tenderness is merely a figment of my imagination…

Did his thumb brush my lips?

There's no way in hell.

The sedatives have messed with my recall.

"Did Gordon know it was you?" I ask.

He scoffs a half-hearted laugh and stabs a piece of bacon. "I rarely work anonymously, belladonna. I prefer when my targets know who owns them. But rest assured, Gordon won't talk. The threats I hand out don't leave much room for disobedience. People tend to listen when they know exactly how you're going to torture everyone they love if they so much as breathe in the wrong direction."

Unfortunately, I know exactly what he means.

"And as far as the cops are concerned," he continues, "Finch was a disgruntled employee who attempted to kill his boss before ending his own life. It's an open-and-shut case."

"But wouldn't there be defense wounds on his body?"

"Don't insult me. Murder is an art, and as far as the authorities are concerned, they don't even know this Michelangelo exists." He points his fork to his chest. "Now, are there any other questions before I can start tending to my wounded pride?"

I shake my head. I don't want to know anymore.

It's hard to fathom how he can exude abundant dignity for his underhanded career while I struggle to hide the shame over mine.

We eat in silence, his appetite that of a Goliath while I nibble around my constant thoughts.

"Obviously I went grocery shopping while I was out," he says once his plate is empty. "I wasn't sure how long you wanted to stay, but I can't live another day without red meat. There's a lot of food options now. I also bought you some wine, and there's chocolate in the fridge."

"Thank you, but I won't impose much longer."

"No? You're ready to go home to your brothers?"

I fight a scoff as the icy tendrils of betrayal crystallize in my chest. "I've already told you I don't want anything to do with them."

He pushes to his feet and takes his plate to the kitchen. "I agree that they're assholes, but they were ambushed. You can't blame them for something that was out of their control."

"I'm not arguing about this again. All you need to know is that I'll be out of your hair soon."

"Not if you're on your own. You don't get to run unless someone has your back."

I bite my tongue, wanting to snap yet withholding for some reason.

There's something about his protection that brings a warped sense of companionship. Nobody has cared for me like this before. Not me as a person. Only as an asset. My value has only ever been measured by my manipulation, and here's Bishop, promising I'll never use those skills again.

"I appreciate the concern." I finish my bacon and push to my feet. "Really, I do. But you won't stop me." I follow to the kitchen, my chin high, my shoulders straight despite my limited clothing.

He needs to know I'm not daunted by him. I'm *not*. My pulse flutters for other reasons.

Bishop triggers so many parts of me—my intrigue, my aggression, my confusion—but I don't fear him.

The sooner I get away from him, the more chance I'll have to settle my skittish pulse.

"It's my turn to do the dishes." I sidle up beside him at the sink, giving him a soft nudge with my hip.

He grunts and steps away, but instead of leaving the kitchen, he grabs a dish towel and returns to my side.

"You don't have to dry." I turn on the faucet, grab the dishwashing liquid from the cupboard, then squirt some into the running water. "I can handle it on my own."

"You keep making it clear you can handle shit. Hopefully soon you'll catch on that it's better to share the burden."

I raise a brow. "You want to fix my problems, Butcher?"

He shrugs, his gaze on the mound of bubbles growing in the sink. "Would it be such a bad thing if I could?"

The hairs raise on my arms, the subtle sound of alarm bells ringing in my ears.

I learned years ago that relying on anyone is dangerous. Everyone is a backstabber for the right price.

"I appreciate the sentiment, but I'll be okay." I cut the water and begin scrubbing the dirty dishes and piling them on the drainer.

I feel his eyes on me, sense his meticulous mind trying to align my puzzle pieces. I can't let him figure me out. Not when I've succeeded in hiding the worst of my mistakes from the world for this long.

"While I was out, I made another house call we haven't discussed." His voice is suspiciously devoid of emotion as I hand him a bubbled plate.

"Let me guess—you caught up with my brothers."

"No. I paid Senator Joe Hillier a visit."

I turn to stone, all my limbs rigid.

"He wasn't happy to see me, but not many people are." He keeps looking at me, the weight of his stare relentless in my periphery.

"Why would you do that?" I keep my tone light even though fear infuses me with pulse-raising adrenaline.

"He kept refusing to take your calls. I thought my intervention might help."

"You didn't think to ask first?" The bacon curdles in my gut, threatening to make a resurgence. "You need to quit eavesdropping."

"I've gotta get insight somehow. You aren't really a fountain of forthcoming information."

My throat dries, the tightrope I'm treading growing thinner. I should've been more cautious about being overheard. I should've known he'd use the insight against me.

"Don't worry, I didn't touch him," he mutters. "*Or* his wife. I didn't even force my way inside his house. All I did was pretend I was a local searching for a lost dog to get my foot inside the door."

I swallow, forcing myself not to show the panic that has its tight grip around my neck. I clean another plate and hand it over. "Then?"

"Then I kindly asked why he wouldn't return your calls."

I hold my breath, my teeth digging into my bottom lip. *Fuck.*

"He said he wasn't going to give you any more money, Abri."

I stare at the bubbles, my heart thudding.

"Is that what you were after?" he asks. "Because I already told you Matthew and Lorenzo will take care of your finances. All you have to do is reach out to them."

I shake my head, playing along. My calls to the Senator weren't about money, but I'll take the diversion over the truth any day. "I don't want help from either of them."

"Then you should've asked me. I'll give you anything you need until you get on your feet."

My gaze snaps to his, tugged by an emotion I'm yet to name. Is this a trap? A strategic way to lead me into a false sense of security?

I don't understand him. I can't tell if he's genuine.

"That's a generous offer." I return my attention to the water, scooping his knife and fork from the bottom of the sink. "But I'll make do."

"How much money do you need?"

I dump the cutlery on the drainer, keeping my gaze averted, needing shelter from his scrutiny. The worst part is that he didn't ask *what* I need money for. Only how much.

It's strange after having my father micromanage my expenses for so long. He was paranoid I'd run just like Matthew, even though there was no way I could.

"It was more of a safety net." I finish the dishes and step back, wiping my wet hands on the hips of my chemise. "Don't worry. I'll figure it out."

"I know you will. But that help won't come from the senator. He made it clear he wants nothing to do with you."

I meet Bishop's eyes and fake a smile. "Then I'll stop calling."

My skin itches with the need to know what else was said between them. To learn all the details. But I press my lips shut. Clench my teeth. If he knew the worst of it he would've said something by now. Wouldn't he?

Bishop dumps his drying towel on the counter and cocks a hip against the cupboards, laidback despite the growing curiosity in his stare. "Have you known him long?"

I walk for the table to grab the orange juice. "A few years."

"Did you get close to him for your father's sake?"

I straighten, hearing what he doesn't say—did you extort him? Manipulate him?

"My relationship with the senator was mutually beneficial. He needed campaign money and we wanted a government official up our sleeve if any hardship were to arise." I pad back to the fridge and place the juice inside.

"Do your brothers know you fucked him?"

My stomach bottoms. My grip on composure splatters at my feet.

I hate that he's privy to the type of things I've done. Where my power comes from. But worst of all, I loathe the edge in his tone. The judgement.

This guy just killed a man for laying hands on me, yet I'm disgraceful for using pleasure instead of pain to get what I want?

I glower through the shame. "This conversation is over."

"I wasn't trying to piss you off." He raises his hands in surrender.

"Then what *were* you trying to do?"

"Make conversation." He shrugs. "Get you to open up. Hell, just having you take a few bricks off that wall you've got built around you would be nice."

"You're a smart guy, Bishop. You should know walls are built for a reason. If I wanted them down they would be."

What the hell am I doing?

I should be working him. *Manipulating* him. A few bats of my lashes, a flash of a sultry smile, and a subtle increase to my cleavage and I'm sure I could have him wrapped around my little finger. Why have I waited this long?

"You're right." He pushes from the cupboard and straightens. "It's none of my business. The problem is, I have one more question I need to have answered before I can drop this subject."

I hold my breath, praying he doesn't know, silently begging for one saving grace from the universe. "And what question is that?"

He holds my gaze, the calm confidence taunting me. "Does anyone else know you and the senator had a kid together?"

13

BISHOP

I inched toward the question as slowly as I could. Patiently crept into it with stealth because I had a feeling the child has been the reason behind her emotional state since Emmanuel's death.

An assumption that seems accurate if the horrified shock frozen across her features is any indication.

"Do your brothers know?" I move closer, conscious of the increased pace of her breaths.

She's freaking out again, the color draining from her face.

"It's okay." I keep my hands raised, palms up, non-threatening. "Whatever the problem, you're going to be fine."

She stumbles backward. "What else did he tell you?"

"What else is there to know?"

"Don't fuck with me, Bishop." Her eyes are stark with panic. "Tell me what he said."

"Nothing." It's the truth, laid bare and given too easily. Her suffering does strange things to me.

I've killed many and tortured more without feeling the faintest whisper of humanity, yet the suffering before me screams through my skull. "All I know is you have a kid, and the senator has been giving you money in what I assume is some sort of extortion-driven child support."

She winces, her nose crinkling through the rapid pace of her breaths.

I don't know why she does this to me, but the more I learn about her, the more secrets I crave to reveal.

"It's okay." I chance another inch toward her. "Whatever you need you'll get. Your kid will be taken care of."

"Stop." She hyperventilates, those perfect tits rising and falling faster and faster.

"It's true. Money isn't an issue. And safety doesn't need to be either." I reach out, touching her arm.

My actions are foreign. As if I'm watching myself through a lens.

I don't do comfort. Or kindness. Still, I'm driven toward that ledge without my consent. Just like last night, the compulsion to place my hands on her takes over.

"Lorenzo loves children. He's always petitioning his kids to have more grandbabies. Your child will want for nothing under his protection."

"Stop," she begs. "*Stop.*" She shakes her head. "*Just stop.*"

Over and over she pleads, the word becoming fractured, her inhales sawing like a serrated blade through turmoil I don't understand.

She hunches, clutching for the counter.

"Abri, you need to calm down."

She doesn't listen. Her fight for oxygen increases, the front of her chemise gaping to expose excessive cleavage that should *not* be on my radar.

"Tell me what's going on," I grate, pissed off by the sordid distraction.

She keeps shaking her head. Keeps clinging to that fucking counter.

"Abri," I warn.

She sways. *Shit.* She's going to pass out.

I close in behind her, my chest to her back, my fingers over hers on the counter. "Do I need to drag you to the shower again?"

"No." She pushes backward, her ass rubbing my crotch.

If I wasn't already going to hell for my sins, I'd be fast-tracked to the front of the line for the way my dick reacts.

"Let me fucking help you." I grab her hips and turn her to face me, the terror in those mesmerizing eyes punching hard into my sternum.

She blinks back the weakness, scrunches her nose as if hating the emotion she can't control, each ragged breath waging war against her fragility.

"You can't help." She shakes her head, this tenacious, venomous woman a quivering mess in my hands. "I need my mom. I have to find her."

"She doesn't want to be found, belladonna, and she doesn't deserve your loyalty. You're better off without her."

She heaves a sardonic laugh. Gulping. Gasping.

"I know it's been hard." I press closer, keeping her upright. "You lost your dad and now your mom is MIA, but you'll learn to live without them."

"No, I won't." She shoves at my chest. "I need to find her."

"Abri, you—"

"I have to, Bishop." Those eyes pin me, the ocean blue fathomless in their stricken depths. "She's the only one who might know the location of my daughter."

I straighten, my blood running cold. "Why? What does that mean?"

She continues to push me away, heaving, wheezing.

"Listen to me." I step into her, my shoe between her bare feet, my knee between hers. Hip to hip. Face to face. "You've gotta calm down."

I know she can't. She's too far gone.

Fuck my life.

I grab her, hauling her off the ground. She doesn't fight. If anything, she willingly complies, flowing with my movements as if she's part of me. I stalk the few feet of space to the fridge, place her on the counter beside it, then yank open the freezer for a fistful of ice.

"Keep talking to me." I slam the door shut and give her my undivided attention, my stomach against her knees, the lower half of her legs trailing down the top half of mine. I feel her everywhere, no place more potent than my chest as her suffering burrows under my ribs. "Tell me about your daughter. Why don't you know where she is?"

I grab her hand, turn it palm up, then place the ice to her wrist.

She gasps, the cold a clear shock to her system. But not enough to stop those heaving breaths. She keeps panting, struggling for air, those heaving tits goddamn bait in my periphery.

"Talk to me, belladonna." I run the ice back and forth, drips of water falling to the tile. "I'm going to help you."

"No." She wheezes.

"I vow it." I get in her face as I trail the ice higher, over her forearm to her elbow. "You can trust me."

She winces.

"I've got you." I rub the ice along her bicep, across her collarbone. "Tell me what's going on."

The moisture glistens on her skin, forming rivulets that disappear into her cleavage.

I shouldn't notice that either. But I fucking do. I notice everything. The softness of her body. The puckered length of her scar. The way her neck bruising has changed in color, from bright purples and pinks to duller edges tinged with browns and yellows.

Her nipples pucker beneath her chemise and I salivate like a perverted fuck.

"Deep breaths," I demand, trailing the melting ice up her neck, along her delicate jaw.

Her eyes close. Her shoulders loosen. She sways.

"Abri. Look at me." I shake her.

Her eyes flash open, all that deep blue sucking me in like a whirlpool.

"Don't tap out on me, belladonna."

She sucks in a breath, but this time it's longer. Deeper.

"That's it." I glide the ice over her cheek, her chin. I'm fucking tempted to place it on her lips. Instead, I clench my teeth and trail it back down her neck, along the bruising.

I shouldn't have let her out of my sight the night of the gala. I should've fucking been there.

I failed her. Her brother, too. And Lorenzo.

But I won't fail in this. Whatever she needs, I'll provide. I'll get the fucking job done until Langston is back on his feet to take over.

She takes another long breath in between gulps for oxygen. Five fast, one deep. Four fast, one deep. Three fast…

The ice is working.

"I'll get more." I reach for the freezer.

"No, don't." Her hand latches around my wrist. "I'll be okay." She's still panting, but I believe her.

I continue to slide the last vestiges of the ice over her shoulder, back down her arm.

I listen to those breaths, my own panic dissipating as her inhales continue to lengthen.

"How do you know how to fix me?" she finally whispers. "To stop the anxiety attacks?"

I scowl.

I haven't needed to delve into my past in years. And I sure as shit don't do story time. But as she stares at me, skin moistened, soul shaken, I find my own weaknesses clawing their way out of the graves I've dug them.

My nightmares want to dance with hers.

"I spent a lot of time at my aunt and uncle's when I was a kid." I focus on the facts. Nothing else. "She used to suffer from the same attacks."

"Did you help her, too?"

"No. I was too young. But I'll never forget how my uncle would rush to care for her. Most of the time he would drag her into the shower, fully clothed, where he would hold her under the water, whispering words I couldn't hear. Other times he used ice." I lower my attention to where my hands cradle her fingers, the melting cubes creating a puddle in her palm. "Don't ask me how it works. I'm only replicating what I saw."

"I don't care how it works—just that it does."

The fragile sweetness in her voice gets to me. *She* gets to me.

I look away, lobbing the remaining shrunken cubes into the sink before releasing her hand.

"Thank you," she whispers.

"Don't mention it." I itch to drag a hand through my hair. To wipe a steadying palm over my face. She's got her hooks in me and I fucking hate it. "You good to talk now?"

She inhales a long breath through her nose, then heaves the exhale. "There's nothing to tell. I just need to find my mother." She palms the counter, making to scoot to her feet.

"That's not how this works." I grab her hips, holding her in place, my possessive grip a warning. "You don't fall apart in my arms—*twice*—then expect me to forget. We're getting this out in the open, you hear me? Unless you'd prefer I call your brothers and have them take care of this for you."

Her face falls.

"Do they know you have a daughter with the senator?" I ask.

She lowers her stare to my chest. "Nobody does. Nobody but my parents."

"How is that possible?"

She turns quiet, the answer trapped behind tempting lips.

"Abri…" I raise a hand to her chin, inclining her face until she's forced to meet my gaze. "How do they not know?"

Her brows knit as she silently begs me not to push. But I can't stop myself.

I can't fix what I don't know. And I *will* fix this. Whatever the fuck it is.

"How do they not know?" I repeat, this time slower, as gentle as a man like me can possibly articulate.

She swallows. Licks her lips. "Because my father had me sent away during the pregnancy. Before I started to show."

I scowl, trying to remember something Remy relayed a few days ago. Something about how Abri used to be the most vocal sibling against her father's dictatorship. Only to vanish for months on end.

"One minute you were fighting over family dinner," I paraphrase his explanation, "the next you were gone. Emmanuel sent you away, and when you returned you weren't the same. He somehow made you compliant."

Her nose scrunches, the pain potently evident. "I didn't want her." Her voice breaks. "I planned to have an abortion. But my father figured out how much a baby could earn him. What the secret would cost Joe."

Rage runs hot through my veins. "Emmanuel forced you to have a child?"

She lowers her gaze again.

"Look at me, belladonna." I hitch her chin, rubbing my thumb back and forth along her jaw. "I'm going to fix this for you. I'm going to make it right. But I need you to help me. You have to tell me everything."

Waves of grief swim in her pretty eyes. She squares her shoulders and sits taller. "I didn't want her…not to begin with. But then he sent me away and it was just me and her. Alone in a cabin in the mountains. A nurse and guard the only human interaction for months."

Son of a goddamn fucking bitch.

"He trapped me there," she continues, "out in the middle of nowhere. But in those six months, the only thing I had was my daughter." Her lips curve in a tortured smile. "I sang to her. Cried to her. Fell in love with every flutter of her feet against my belly. I hated myself for thinking I could live without her and begged my keepers to tell my father about my change of heart. I even started to believe he'd done me a favor. That he'd saved me from making the biggest mistake of my life."

"But?" I growl.

"But I never saw or spoke to him again until the morning Tilly was born." Her tone pitches, the high notes exposing emotion she struggles to trap inside.

"What did he do, belladonna?" I drop my hold on her chin, cautious my building rage had tightened my grip.

She straightens her shoulders, seeming to take the pain head on. "As soon as I gave birth, he took her from me. I haven't seen her since."

14

ABRI

He stares at me, eyes fixed, nostrils flaring. He's angry, and I don't know if the turbulent emotion is directed at my father's actions or the shameful way I've led my life.

Both are reprehensible.

"Do you know if she's still alive?" he asks.

I nod, swallowing over the painful restriction of my throat. "It's how he got me to do his bidding. He'd ask me to extort someone, and in return I was promised a photo. Or a video. Sometimes he'd give me one of her drawings etched in crayon. But I never receive anything without earning it first."

His fists clench, the fury ebbing off of him.

"Are you angry at me?" I shuffle close to the edge of the counter, about to scoot to my feet to gain much-needed distance.

"No," he snarls.

I don't know why he bothers lying when revulsion is etched into every tight line of his face. The broad stiffness of his posture.

This is why I couldn't tell my brothers. I couldn't bear their judgement.

So I kept Tilly's existence to myself.

The pain.

The torment.

The shame.

It's not like anyone could help me anyway. Not against my

father's control. So I let it eat away at me until I became exactly how Bishop describes me. A belladonna. A poisonous work of nature.

"There's no need to lie." I push from the counter, hating how I have to stabilize myself against his chest as my feet hit the floor.

"I'm not." The same tone is sneered at me as he reaches out, stopping me from fleeing with a tight grip around my chin.

He forces my face to his, his hard stare weighing down on me. "My rage is *for* you, not against."

My heart squeezes, the vehement sincerity in his tone, touch, and gaze fracturing me further.

"I wish your father was still alive." His voice is menacing. "So I could kill him myself."

They're brutal words cut from the darkest depths of humanity. But I cling to them, cherishing each syllable because they feel like the only support I've ever had.

My eyes burn, the moisture blurring my vision.

I *will not* cry.

He watches me as if entranced, the seconds ticking by through thunderous heartbeats, then abruptly he looks away, his rough fingers falling from my face.

He stands in the middle of the kitchen, focused on the counter, his thoughts unreadable.

I should leave him alone to contemplate the new state of events. I need to wash the sleep from my face. Get changed. Pull myself together.

Only I can't move.

I stand there, silent, patiently waiting for a glimmer of insight.

One minute passes… Two.

"Tell me what you're thinking," I ask, pitiful and weak.

"I'm trying to piece it all together." He wipes a hand over his stubble. "I've misjudged you. But it all makes sense now. Why you fought to stay in Gordon's hotel suite. Why you were even there in the first place." He turns to face me. "You're an exceptional actress, Abri, and an even better manipulator. I just didn't know those skills hid sexual slavery."

I wince.

I'm not a slave. Not really.

"How could your brothers let this happen?" he growls.

My throat dries. I'm so incredibly angry with Remy and

Salvatore. Matthew, too. But they aren't responsible for this. I'm the only one accountable for the steps I took into so-called slavery. "They didn't know."

"Bullshit."

"No." In this I can't blame them. "They couldn't have. Working for my father started a lifetime ago, and I was complicit in the beginning."

His eyes narrow on me, but he doesn't voice the questions plaguing him.

"My father has had me exploiting powerful men since I hit puberty." I huff a sardonic laugh. "After a childhood of him ignoring my existence, he finally seemed to see me…I didn't realize until years later that it wasn't me he saw, just the benefits my appearance and innocence could provide."

"This started when you were a teen?"

"Thirteen."

"Son of a fucking bitch," he mutters under his breath.

"It wasn't like it is now. It began with small favors. He would ask me to flirt with a wealthy colleague. To bat my lashes and pretend I was infatuated. And I liked it. The men would lavish me with compliments. Wealthy, successful men. They made me feel beautiful… Special."

I'd been such a pathetic fool. I guess I still am—I just learned to hide it through a flawlessly arrogant facade.

"Then the years passed and the stakes increased. *'Seduce Justin Gardner into kissing you.'*" I mimic my father's voice. "*'Start texting Malcolm Miller. Send photos. Don't stop until he sends some back.'*"

I still remember the first dick pic I received. How it had made me sick, even scared, yet oddly empowered.

"Emmanuel taught me how to manipulate these men. He'd take me out for dinner and we'd people watch for hours. He'd point out the women who had the upper hand in a relationship on sight alone and tell me how to mimic them. He outlined how most men valued very few things over power and pleasure. He made it seem simple. That if I could be their pleasure, I could steal their power." I shrug. "So I did."

Bishop's jaw ticks.

"I wanted it," I reiterate, turning that anger on myself, bearing the punishment of my stupidity.

"You didn't know any better," he snarls.

"Maybe at first. But I figured it out."

"And?"

My lungs tighten, the ability to breathe becoming harder all over again. "And I didn't do anything about it. I still wanted the attention. I loved bringing powerful men to their knees. And I enjoyed making my father proud."

"When did you start fucking men for him?"

I flinch. "A few days before I turned eighteen."

Bishop shakes his head, disgusted. "Your brothers have a lot to answer for."

"I told you, they had no clue. Nothing ever happened in public. Apart from flirting. And that night was hectic. My father threw an early birthday party at our house. People were everywhere. Mainly business associates. Wealthy men and their trophy wives. Remy and Salvatore have always done their best to show their faces as little as possible at those types of events while I did the opposite."

I still remember the reflection that stared back at me from my bedroom mirror. The subtle makeup. The thick braid of my hair that hung over one shoulder. And the pristine white lace dress with a high neckline and a thick ribbon that acted like a belt around my waist with its large bow tied at my middle.

I was innocence personified.

Ripe for the picking.

"I'm certain my dad auctioned off my virginity." I add steel to my tone, owning my mistakes. "I slept with a twenty-eight-year-old stockbroker, unaware that my father was recording the festivities until weeks later when I overheard my parents talking about how they could use the footage to their benefit."

Bishop turns away, his posture stiff. "I want names. Places. Dates." Vehemence drips from his tone. "I need information on every asshole who's laid hands on you since this started."

I give a pained smile.

God, what would my life have been like if I'd had Bishop by my side all those years ago?

"I was willing," I repeat. "Those men were the victims of my manipulations as much as I was of my father's."

"You were a fucking child."

"I was of legal age." I breathe in his disgust, the noxious air thickening in my already tortured lungs. He might think his rage is aimed at my father, but neither of us can deny part of it should be directed toward me.

My naivety.

My pathetic, shameful hunger for attention.

"I'm not spending any more time in the past." The future is hard enough to face. "Thank you for all you've done for me. For the food and shelter. And also for guiding me out of the panic attacks and not using the weakness against me. But it's time I go. I can't stay here any longer."

He stiffens, yet still keeps staring out the windows toward the sweeping hills.

"Can I have my car fob?" I step closer, hoping he has it in his pocket. "I can drop you off somewhere if—"

"We're not done here," he grates under his breath. "You need to tell me about your daughter."

My gut does a sweeping roll, this roller coaster taking another dive. It's hard enough thinking about her. Dreaming about her. "There's not much to tell. I don't know where she is or who has her. The most recent photo I have is months old and she changes so fast."

"You have no clue who's raising her?"

"No. And my mother is the only person I can think of that might know where she is. The only solace I have is that Emmanuel always told me she's with loving parents. The photos and videos have been proof of that. She's a happy child. Healthy and bright."

"Fuck your mother." He swings around to face me, his expression drawn with exhaustion. He looks like he's aged five years in the last ten minutes. "I won't let you leave. I don't care where you want to be or what your plans are, you're not doing this alone."

My eyes burn, but I refuse to tear up. Not again. "Please give me the key to my car."

"And have Langston kill me for letting you disappear? Fuck no. He thought you were in deep enough shit already. He's going to be homicidal once he hears about this."

"No. He's not going to hear anything. It's none of his business."

"Like hell it's not."

The panic returns, one spark igniting wildfire. "Bishop, you can't tell him." I rush the few steps toward him. "*Please*."

He peers down at me, brows pinched. "Why?"

Because I'm ashamed. Guilt-ridden. But that's not the worst of it. "I need to tread carefully. I don't know what my mother will do to her."

"You think she'd hurt her own grandchild?"

"When she's despised my daughter's existence from the moment of conception?" I nod. "Yes. She never wanted me to go through with the pregnancy. It was always a point of contention between my parents. She hates that my carelessness led to an illegitimate child and has never once spoken Tilly's name. She pretends she doesn't exist. She even takes pleasure in nagging me to settle down and have children in front of her friends because she knows how much playing along hurts me."

Bishop stands taller, his gaze narrowing.

I know what that reaction means. I understand it because the same silent thoughts I hear loud between us always haunt me when I'm at my lowest.

"Tilly's alive." My voice breaks. "My father didn't give me fake photos."

I'd recognize her face anywhere. Even in a room full of little children, I'd be able to pick her from the crowd. I'd know her despite her having no clue who I am. That I'm her mother. That I love her more than anything in this world.

"You sure?" He rubs a hand over the back of his neck. "It sounds like Emmanuel's MO to tell you she's fighting fit and loving life, but in reality she's probably—"

"She's alive," I repeat, refusing to believe otherwise. "The only thing that's up for debate is my mother's agenda. And if Matthew finds out and starts meddling—after what he already did to my father—" I scrunch my nose. "I don't trust her, Bishop. If she has the right incentive, I'm scared she'll kill Tilly."

He falls silent.

"Please," I plead. "You can't share this with anyone."

He refuses to respond, his gaze unforgiving.

"*Please*. Promise me."

"I can't do that."

"Bishop…" I grab his lapels and yank. I must catch him off-guard because he staggers forward, bumping into me with a growl. "I'm begging."

"I can hear you, belladonna. But you're asking me to break the trust of one of the only people I give a shit about."

He's not going to keep quiet.

He'll tell my brothers. Inform Lorenzo and the fucking Italian mafia bloodline my mother comes from. What happens if they side with her and decide Tilly is a liability?

"Oh, God." I suck in a ragged breath, my hands falling from his suit as I retreat.

"Hey." He grabs my upper arms and drags me back into him. "We're not doing this again."

What am I going to do? I need to figure this out. To calm my pulse and think without trepidation.

But I can't trust anyone.

I can't risk Tilly's safety in that way.

Especially not with my brothers who were selfish enough to take action against my father without sparing a thought for me first. What if she dies? What if my decisions kill her?

"Breathe, belladonna." Bishop pulls me closer, placing his forehead to mine. "Just breathe."

His tone is abrasive, yet for some reason his concern wraps around me, smoothing the harsh edges of my resurgent panic.

"I won't say a word," he mutters. "Not yet. But they're going to need to know."

I have to find Tilly before that happens.

He pulls away, meeting my gaze. "I'll get her back for you. I won't stop until it's done."

I fight a wince. He doesn't understand. I can't expect him to.

"Thank you," I whisper, my guilt renewed because he looks exactly how I feel—like hell warmed up. "You must be exhausted."

He inclines his head. "I am."

I huff a faint laugh. "Is that the Butcher finally showing weakness?"

"It ain't hard when I haven't slept in a week. I'm running on fumes here."

"In that case, I'm surprised you haven't killed me by now with all the stunts I've pulled." I ache to touch him again. To graze my fingers over his beard.

"Believe me, so am I."

I grin, halfhearted, yet my humor quickly fades. "Then sleep. Go to bed."

"I can't do that when you're going to run as soon as I'm horizontal."

"I'll stay. I promise."

He mimics my whisper of a laugh. "I'd love to believe you, Abri, but I'm sure your promises carry the same underhanded tactics as mine. And I'm too tired to figure out your strategies. I won't risk failing you again."

I frown. *Failing me?*

His gaze lowers to my neck as he raises a hand. I stiffen with the gentle trail of his thumb over my bruises. "I should've got to you sooner. For that I apologize."

"I've suffered through worse."

Anger wrinkles his forehead. "Was that when this happened?" His touch moves to my scar. The puckered flesh close to my carotid is just another reminder of what my father put me through.

"No. That was due to a run-in with Cole Torian the night Layla's husband died."

His attention raises to mine, his eyes narrow, spiteful slits. "Torian did this."

I shake my head. "It was self-inflicted."

"Explain."

"It's a long story. One I can share after you get some rest."

"I'm not sleep—"

I grab his wrist in both hands, and although I despise myself for what I'm about to do, I use the skills my father taught me, peering up at Bishop with pleading innocence, my tongue meekly swiping my lower lip.

Remorse floods my veins. Disgust, too.

But he falls under my spell like so many men in my past, his attention lowering to my mouth, his anger dissipating.

"How 'bout I do you a deal?" I drag his arm down to his side, then release my hold. "Panic attacks always wipe me out. So I'll lay in bed with you, then you won't have to worry that I'll run."

15

BISHOP

"That's a bad idea, belladonna." I school my expression as the visual of her suggestion rams my frontal lobe. Her body lax. Her hair splayed on the pillow next to mine.

Fuck that. I'm already too close to her.

"Why not?" Her nose crinkles. "Are you worried you'll become traumatized by sharing a bed with a poisonous flower?"

No. I'm worried I'll enjoy it.

"Look, Bishop, you're dead on your feet, and after my second embarrassing breakdown, I really do need the extra rest. We both have to be clearheaded if we're going to find Tilly, right?"

I understand her logic but all my surging testosterone can focus on is that chemise. The way it hangs low at the front. The generous show of cleavage. How it glides over her smooth curves.

"I'm not going to try and have sex with you." She gives a half-hearted smile—one that doesn't reach her eyes. "I'm a working girl, remember? I'm not going to give that stuff out for free."

I should've known her seductive side was nothing more than a role. A fucking charade. I see through it now to the tormented woman beneath. Why didn't Salvatore and Remy do the same?

"Okay, this is depressing." She sighs. "You know your worth has to be in the gutter when the Butcher of Baltimore, who not only killed a man hours ago but also strangled another, won't even lie in the same vicinity as you to get the rest he clearly needs."

Jesus Christ. Does she ever let up?

I start for the hall, done with this conversation. "Hurry up and get in my fucking bed, Abri." I march to my room. Drag closed the curtains. Kick off my shoes.

I keep my gaze away from her as I pull my gun from the back of my waistband and shove it under my pillow, then climb into bed.

I don't remove my jacket. I don't even loosen my fucking belt.

I remain on top of the duvet. Close my eyes. And don't open my fucking peepers for nothing.

I don't watch her climb in beside me. I don't even blink to confirm she's crawled under the covers, because thankfully they rustle as she slides beneath them. But the downside to the darkness is how my imagination creates its own damn display.

I picture her facing me. Watching me. Those lips close enough to plunder.

I roll away. Turn my back to her. Hear her defeated sigh.

Did she expect me to fucking snuggle?

The silence stretches, the seconds ticking by with my entire body tense. I can't sleep like this. Not with Langston's sister in my bed. Not with the vision of every inch of her tattooed into my grey matter.

But she sure as shit doesn't have the same problem.

Within ten minutes her breathing deepens, the steady rhythm of slumber slowly coaxing me to relax.

I roll onto my back. Then fucking despise myself for watching her from the corner of my eye. Breathing in the beauty that hid a tormented life.

I'm pissed I was wrong.

That I had her pegged as a conniving, manipulative bitch. And yeah, she's still conniving and manipulative, but the bitch part was off base.

She was an exploited child.

Now she's a frantic mother.

Her father should've suffered. Long and hard. I would've made him beg for the peace of death.

I stare at her for what feels like an hour, rewriting history with my new understanding to see those events played by the woman she is and not the viper she portrays.

She was going to willingly be beaten and raped by Gordon and his men. For what? A video of her daughter? A finger painting?

I wouldn't have a kid if I had the last dick on Earth and civilization depended on me impregnating a harem of supermodels, and here she is, selling her soul for proof of life.

I watch the flutter of her long curved lashes. Discover the barely visible freckles across her nose. She holds the covers to her chin like always, and it seems fucking strange that I even know that's her thing.

I'm sure she does it because of the scar on her neck. She's self-conscious. Or maybe it's due to instinctual protection. Does she shield her throat so history doesn't repeat itself?

Fuck Cole Torian. I'm going to get to the bottom of that story, too, and if he's responsible for her injury I'll—

What, asshole? What the fuck are you going to do? Why do you even care?

This is a job. A duty. One that revolves around current events, not those in the past.

If Torian did wrong by her, Langston has to deal with it. Lorenzo can go to war if he wants. My nose needs to stay well away from that shit.

I close my eyes. Breathe deep. Force my body to relax.

I do *not* think of her. I'm somewhere else. Alone. Undisturbed.

And that's the way it needs to stay.

I WAKE WITH A HARD DICK, my breathing ragged, the flashbacks of an illicit dream still palpable in my mind.

Abri. Naked. Sweaty. Panting.

Fuck.

The room is pitch black. The quiet deafening. The door closed.

I reach across the bed. She's not there. The sheets are cold.

I snap upright, my pulse slamming into fourth gear. "*Abri.*"

"In the kitchen," she calls back.

Her voice shouldn't be a balm, but it fucking disintegrates my aggression.

I slump back onto my pillow, my cock deflating as the occasional clink and scuffle of noise carries through the house.

I slept all day, which is great when it comes to getting away from the temptress, yet not so stellar when I should've been keeping my promise to find her daughter.

I retrieve my gun, climb from the bed, then find my shoes through the darkness to slip my feet inside. I walk down the hall, annoyed at myself. At her. At her father and mother. At Langston for getting shot. Pretty much at life in general.

I pause in the doorway to the open living area, and there she is in the kitchen, chopping vegetables at the island counter, her hair pulled back into a loose pony, her jeans snug around her ass, her neck injuries bare above the collar to her tight T-shirt.

She doesn't turn to me. Does she even know I'm here?

When our positions had been switched this morning at breakfast, I'd known the moment her eyes were on me.

I'd thrummed under her attention, my pulse pounding, my dick beginning to stir.

It does the same now, boosting my annoyance.

She glances over her shoulder and smiles. "Did you sleep well?"

I grunt.

That curve of lips increases and God, it's stunning. I don't know if it's because I'm now aware of what type of woman truly lies behind her expression or if it's due to the perfection of her lips. Either way, it only continues to poke my bad attitude into more dangerous territory.

"I thought you'd never wake up." She returns her attention to the chopping board and continues cutting. "Did you know you make this deep, low grumbling sound when you sleep? Kinda like a grizzly bear."

An unfamiliar heat creeps into my face, like I'm catching a fucking cold or something. "It's strategic. To keep my enemies at bay."

She shoots me another glance and laughs, light and cheerful, showing a side of her I haven't seen before. "Are you blushing?"

"I don't fucking blush, woman." I stalk into the room, heading for the fridge and the beer I bought earlier.

"Are you sure?" She turns and watches my movements, her humor-filled smirk shadowing me. "Because it looks really cute."

She's taunting me now? Does she also know she's tugging at my fucking libido like a goddamn church-bell ringer?

After having to sit through breakfast with her in nothing but a sinful chemise, then all that sleeping-in-my-bed bullshit, along with the goddamn illicit dreams… This hell has to stop.

"It sure looks like a blush to me," she coos.

I change my trajectory, forgetting the beer to stalk up to her, not stopping until we're foot to foot. She doesn't flinch as I get in her face, and that only annoys me more. She should be scared of me. Fucking petrified.

"Do you think a man like me blushes, belladonna?" I inch closer, staring her in the eye. "Do you need a reminder of what I do for a living? And why you shouldn't mock me?"

She leans back, her hands finding the counter behind her. "No." Her voice is an alluring whisper. "But with your close proximity, do I need to ask if you've forgotten *my* career choice and what I'm profoundly good at?"

She bites her bottom lip, dragging her teeth across the puffy flesh. Slow. Overtly sexual.

I sink deeper under her spell despite the deliberate provocation.

Jesus Christ, you pathetic motherfucker.

"You're definitely good at your job." I edge closer, trying to prove she has no effect on me despite the hardening of my dick. "But not good enough. I haven't fucked a woman in years, and that's not going to change now. Nice try though."

Surprise slackens her features. "Are you serious?"

I step back and return to my path toward heavenly beer. "About not fucking you? You better believe it." I yank open the fridge, grab a bottle of boutique beer, then chug that shit like a man dying of thirst.

"About not having sex in years."

"Does it sound like something I'd joke about?" I hide in the fridge, not wanting to witness her reaction. "It's also the reason your wicked wiles don't work on me. So you can give it a rest." I grab another beer and slam the door shut with my foot. "I need to make some calls. How long until dinner?"

"Not long." Confusion lingers in her tone. "It's only Thai beef salad. I can hold off cooking the steak until you're ready."

My steak? *Oh, hell no.*

I yank the fridge door back open, praying to the Gods that she found a piece of meat in the freezer and didn't use the Wagyu I purchased earlier. But there it sits, the grade-A, top cut of bovine goodness now chopped into pieces and resting in a bowl, ready to be crucified.

I slap the door shut and take another chug of beer.

At least the woman knows how to kill a hard-on as fast as she creates one.

Fucking Thai beef salad.

"I'll make my calls outside." I finish the first beer and dump the empty bottle in the trash. "I won't be long."

I don't look at her as I pass, but my traitorous eyes find her reflection in the glass windows.

She watches me, still flawless in her shock.

Goddamn her.

I walk onto the porch, down the few steps, and into the dark of night. My shoes crunch through the dry lawn, crackling along with my self-restraint. I don't stop until I reach the wire fence of the house yard.

I have to get her out of here. Away from me. Under someone else's supervision. After dinner, I'll make the necessary calls to set the wheels in motion to find her daughter. I'm not diving into that minefield without more strategic thinking. I sure as shit won't be responsible for the kid's death.

For now though, I drink beer and return business calls.

I need to extinguish one spot fire at a time, and with Langston being the face of the clubs we own together, I have to pick up the slack and take on his leadership role while he's laid flat.

I chat with management. I get updates. I yawn my ass off through boring-as-fuck conversations about temperamental DJs and a junkie being caught shooting up in one of our public bathrooms.

I make sure everything is running smoothly so no corporate bullshit is on Langston's plate while he tries to recover. But once those calls are done, there's no escaping the irritating feeling that eats at my gut.

I stand in the darkness, the gentle breeze rustling through the trees as I stare at Abri in the kitchen.

Langston needs to know about her. About his mother and the fucking kid. Keeping the depth of her suffering from him is a low act. I'd kill someone over a lesser betrayal.

Not that I have anyone else in my life to give a shit about. But if I did, he'd do whatever it took to keep me informed.

But what about her?

The hairs raise on the back of my neck. I've got some sick, twisted sense that I owe her something. Loyalty? Trust?

It's not like she's earned my allegiance. She only has a modicum of my commitment because of her bloodline.

I dump the empty beer bottle at my feet and grab my cigarette case and lighter from my jacket pocket, torch the end of a cancer stick, then breathe that shit deep into my lungs. The smoke burns my throat, the heat adding to the sparks that still linger in my veins from a woman who should be nothing more than another feminine name instead of a hundred enticing body parts.

I unlock my cell screen, press Langston's contact details, then wait as the dial tone rings.

"How is she?" he says in greeting.

"Painful," I grate. "The more time I spend with her, the easier it is to determine all the annoying traits the two of you have in common."

He huffs a laugh, but unlike our last call there's actual energy in his voice, not the frailty of impending death. "Did she drug you again?"

It feels like it. Like somehow, she's plunged a needle in my vein and hijacked me with an aphrodisiac.

"I'm going to pretend I don't regret telling that story." I glare into the darkness. "You feelin' any better?"

"Yeah. Can't complain. Remy and Salvo still haven't heard a word from Abri though."

"Well, she did try to gouge their eyes out a few days ago. I assume it will take a while to get her back in civil territory."

He pauses, the silence thick as I take another puff. "How is she really?"

I exhale the smoke, the toxic white tendrils disappearing into the night. "Not great. That's why I'm calling. I found out she's mixed up in some pretty heavy shit."

"Mixed up how?"

I take another puff, despising the tightening of my chest that I refuse to believe is guilt. "You need to hear it from her."

"Then put her on the phone."

"I can't. She doesn't know I'm talking to you about this. If she did, she'd run." I rake my hand over my mouth, annoyed at myself for bringing up her secrets, but also angry that I have no goddamn choice. Lord knows what his crazy bitch of a mother has planned for Abri's daughter. Maybe it's already too late. "You need to get your ass here. This is the type of conversation that needs to take place in person."

"He can't travel." Layla's voice cuts in. "He's on strict bed rest."

I balk as rage blindsides me, white hot and explosive. "You've got your girl listening in on our conversations now?"

"She hasn't left my fucking side since I was shot." There's a warning in his tone. "I have no plans for her to start."

"You've turned into a little bitch, Langston."

"Says the asshole who got sedated by my baby sister."

I snarl, my teeth bared, my fingers digging into the cell.

"It's okay," Layla murmurs. "I'll give you some privacy. I'll be back soon."

"It's not like it's too much to fucking ask." I take another drag, holding the smoke in my lungs, letting it poison me longer.

Neither of us speak for drawn-out moments. One minute. Maybe two.

"She's gone, okay?" Langston's animosity filters through the speaker. "You fucking happy now?"

"Goddamn delighted."

More silence. More tense, palpitated anger from both ends of the call.

Then he sighs. "I need you to tell me what's going on with Abri."

"I already told you I can't."

He doesn't answer.

"Langston? Did you hear me?"

"I heard," he mutters. "I'm just trying to determine why you've become loyal to my sister overnight, and if the reason demands castration."

"I haven't touched your goddamn sister." *Yet*. "In fact, she's currently inside making me a salad for dinner. Does that sound like the type of woman I'd want to fuck?" My gaze finds her through the windows as she places cutlery on the dining table, her attention turning to the yard as if she senses me watching.

"I've only ever known your type to be those who seek payment for their services. But that doesn't mean things can't change."

"I haven't fucked her." I've thought about it. Dreamt about it. Goddamn salivated over it.

"But suddenly you're team Abri instead of dead against the woman who drives the crazy train?"

"She put the crazy into perspective." I turn my back to the house and stare at the darkened hills. "Her behavior is justified."

"Jesus Christ, Bishop. You're starting to worry me. But that was the intent, right?"

"Like I said, this shit is serious."

"You can't bring her to me? Tell her there's a threat and you need to change location. Get her on a jet and head this way. I'll have some of Lorenzo's men waiting at the airport."

It's not like the thought hadn't crossed my mind. I could sedate her again. Could force her against her will.

He huffs a tired breath. "You're not going to do that either, are you?"

He knows me. Knows what I'm capable of. Denying him says too fucking much, but I can't bring myself to add to her trauma.

I take one last inhale of my cigarette, burning the paper to the filter, then flick it to the ground. "She's been through enough."

"*Fuck*... Fine... Give me a few days. I'll fly there as soon as I'm upright."

"It might be an idea to bring Lorenzo, too. It's time she got to know the benefits of having him as her uncle."

"I'll get it organized. Just make sure you keep her close until then."

I clench my teeth. Proximity is the last thing I want to commit to. But the call disconnects and I return the cell to my pocket.

I stamp the smoldering cigarette butt with my shoe and grab the beer bottle at my feet before walking for the house.

Her eyes meet mine as soon as I step inside the open living area. I look away, not having any patience for her shit, playful or otherwise.

"Everything okay?" she asks.

"Yeah." I leave my empty bottle on the table as I pass, then continue toward the hall. "I need to take a piss."

"Charming." There's humor in her voice. "Dinner will be in five."

I keep walking, not needing the bathroom break. The only thing necessary at the moment is distance.

I hide in the bathroom.

I *hide*. In *the fucking bathroom*.

Me—a man with a moniker that strikes fear into the hearts of grown men.

I need to pull my shit together.

It's her job to be flawless. To seduce. To manipulate.

I'm not a schmuck who should be caught dead falling victim.

I yank open the door and trudge back to the open living area where she's already lowering bowls onto the place settings across from each other at one end of the table.

"Perfect timing." She beams at me.

I glower. "You're in a happy mood tonight."

"I am." Her smile falters as she pads back into the kitchen. "Due to this." She grabs a glass of wine from the counter and raises it in my direction. "But also because of you."

I stiffen. "Me?"

Her brows furrow, yet her smile remains in place. Confusion and happiness. It's a weird combination, but fuck it looks pretty on her.

"You've done a lot for me over the last few days. Just having someone know the truth feels like the weight of my burden has been lessened. I've never had that before."

"Great, now I'm a saint," I mutter under my breath.

She raises her chin. "You seem to be in a mood yourself." She places her wineglass in front of her table setting and takes a seat. "One that grates."

I ignore her and pull out the opposite chair, the legs scraping against the tile as I drag myself toward the table.

"Did something happen while you were on the phone?" she asks.

"No."

"Who did you call?"

I contemplate lying. Hell, even denying her a response would be better than the truth I confess. "Langston."

Her chin hitches, but whatever she's feeling remains locked tight behind an amiable expression as she takes her fork and punctures a piece of lettuce. "I hope you didn't tell him my business."

"I kept your secrets, belladonna." I stab a piece of steak. "For now."

She eats some cucumber, a chunk of carrot, and more lettuce, letting the conversation die.

Good. I prefer the silence.

"I've been meaning to ask you," she starts two minutes later. "It's been a few days now. Is it time to report my father missing?"

"No." I claim another piece of meat and shove it in my mouth. "I don't know why you'd want to draw the attention of the cops."

"Maybe because I spent twenty-four hours leaving message after message on his phone, then suddenly stopped. Won't that make me look guilty when police investigate his disappearance?"

"His body will show up in Virginia soon enough. An autopsy will figure out his time of death. And you were at a public event in Denver when it happened. It's not going to be an issue."

"But what about conspiracy? What if they think I was involved?"

"They won't." I stab again. Chew. Swallow.

She pauses, staring at me a moment. "I'm not trying to be painful, but this is my future, and I have no idea how you're so calm."

"Because cops don't get paid enough to give a shit. They work for bonuses and those don't come in-house. Their gravy train is from outsiders like me."

"But what if it becomes a federal case? What if I'm up against someone who can't be bribed?"

"Then that's when my special set of skills comes in handy."

She reaches for her wine and takes a sip. "I wish the confidence you have in murdering people was comforting. The whole situation just seems too easy."

"It *is* too easy. Money trumps morality. And when it doesn't I get my hands dirty."

She lowers her attention to her meal. "What about my mother?"

"What about her?"

"Do you know how I can find her? She still won't answer my calls."

"I've got contacts, but not enough. That's why you're going to have to tell your brothers—"

"*No.*"

I huff a breath. "Abri, you can't—"

"Quit bringing it up." She looks at me from under dark lashes, the deep blue of her eyes a brewing storm.

I'm not fighting with her. I'd much prefer to go back to not talking at all.

I pierce another piece of meat, then eat as I scrounge around the bowl full of chicken food in the hopes of more protein.

"You don't like the salad?" she asks.

"It's fine." My tone says otherwise.

"Are you lying to me?" She quirks a haughty brow. "I thought you said I could trust you."

"It wasn't a lie." I place down my fork and look her dead in those sparkling eyes. "Did the meat taste okay? Yes. Would it have been better left the way God intended and cooked whole on a chargrill? You bet your sweet ass. But you created the meal, and I'm not going to be a dick about it."

"Maybe not out loud. But you're definitely thinking dick-ish thoughts." She reads my mind. Effortlessly. With precise precision. "I can just imagine what's going through your head as you pick around your bowl, fearful a piece of lettuce will touch your fork."

"Men eat protein."

"Too much protein can cause cancer."

I scoff a laugh. "Even if that were true, I'm not going to live long enough for cancer to get me, salad queen. So let's leave the vegetables to the farm animals, okay?"

She forks something green and slides it between her teeth, slowly, her lips kicking in a subtle grin. "A celibate carnivore. What a strange combination."

"I never said I was celibate."

"Then what did you say?" She takes another sip of wine.

"That I don't *fuck* women."

"So you swipe right, take a girl out for dinner, then ask if she wants to follow you home to what? Fiddle around third base?"

She's making fun of me. I don't like how my pulse increases in response. That I'm fueled by her sass.

"There's no dinner." I grab my bowl of grass and stand. "I pay for what I want without the threat of unnecessary complications."

"Sex workers?"

I walk to the kitchen and dump my garden scraps in the trash.

She follows, carrying her empty bowl and wineglass. "And you've done this for how long?"

"Since I became fortunate enough to have the finances to fund a no-bullshit policy."

She places her bowl in the sink while I hang back near the fridge, waiting for her to move so there's no risk of her breeching my personal space. "Be more specific. Are we talking in months or years?"

I shrug. "Your uncle has always paid well."

"And I guess your skill set doesn't come cheap." She steps in my direction.

I jerk out of the way, maybe a little too fast because she shoots me a questioning glance before pulling the bottle of wine from the fridge to fill her glass.

"So I'm assuming you've spent a long time reaching third base with sex workers." She closes the fridge and turns to me. "Don't you crave more?"

"What's with all the questions?"

"I'm curious. Your choices are interesting."

No. She thinks I'm a puzzle in need of completion. Fuck that shit. I'm nobody's mystery to solve.

"If you've done the same thing for a decade," she continues, "I'd also assume you have regulars, right?"

"Do you mind moving your ass away from the fridge so I can get myself a beer?"

Her eyes flash as she gives a sinful smile. "Are you scared to get close to me, Bishop?"

"Excuse me?"

"You need me to move? You stepped away when I came within two feet. And you've barely looked at me since you woke up."

"No, belladonna. I'm not scared."

She steps closer.

I fucking stiffen.

She raises a brow in victory.

Jesus Christ.

I laugh it off. I have to. Otherwise my dick will tap into this game, then she'll end up getting an insider's guide to my sex life. "You've taken me to the floor once before, Abri. It's only natural I prepare for another attack."

"Mmm." She nods, her eyes on mine as she takes another sip of wine. "But I don't think you're worried about me taking you to the floor. My guess is that you're concerned I'll take you to my bed."

"Don't flatter yourself."

"Then what is it?"

"Manners," I growl. "I'm trying to stay out of your space."

She takes a step closer. "You didn't care about manners when you walked in here earlier, trying to remind me of your job."

"I've since learned the error of my ways."

"Hmm." She takes another casual sip, her gaze taunting mine. "So tell me, Bishop, do you get to know these regulars? Is there any emotional connection? Do you like them?"

"No," I grate

"Do you kiss them?" She creeps closer.

"No." I fight against the instinct to back away, my dick thrumming on a hair trigger.

"Do you satisfy them?"

I glare, hoping to intimidate her into a topic change. "Only because it satisfies *me*."

Her brows rise. I can't tell if it's in interest or condemnation.

"You don't approve of my exploits, belladonna?" I scoff. "That's rich."

"I didn't say that. You can get lucky however you want. I was actually going to say that I think it's sad."

"In that case, you might need to dial your imagination up a notch because there's nothing remotely sad about sliding my dick between the lips of some of the highest paid escorts in the industry. Maybe next time I could record it for you." I wink, the gesture far from friendly. "Just to set your mind at ease."

"That's not necessary. What you do with your dick isn't what I was referring to." She takes another step, moving within reach as my pulse runs rampant in my throat. "What I think is sad is the lack of intimacy. No kissing. No connection. How long have you lived without love?"

"You ask as if it's a bad thing," I sneer. "Let me assure you, it's not."

"Why?"

"Love is a weakness. So is attraction, to a lesser extent."

"But you've taken care of me at my lowest, with kindness and compassion. Don't you hunger for the same in return?"

"I've taken care of you out of duty and with respect."

"I know that." She raises her chin as if I've wounded her. "But don't you miss being touched? Not even a little?" She places her glass on the counter near my side and inches in front of me. "Don't you crave contact for reasons other than sexual gratification?"

"You can't miss something you've never had."

She flinches, acknowledging the insight I didn't want to give. "Then can I also assume you won't mind if I show you what you're missing?"

My muscles turn rigid, each limb tightening to the point of pain. "You're playing games, belladonna. They won't end well for you."

"It's not a game." She reaches out, gliding her palm over my jaw. Gentle. Excruciating in its softness. "You're missing out on the best of what life has to give."

Her gaze follows her hand while mine follows her face, my eyes eating up the dash of pink in her cheeks, the light sweep of her lashes.

I ignore the swell of my dick. The increased burn in my veins.

I shut it all down. Become sterile. A void. Nothing but breath and thunderous heartbeats.

There's no lust. No attraction. No craving. Only existence as I clamp my jaw and clench every muscle.

"How would you know?" I ask with cruelty, hoping to gain some emotional space. "Your sex life is as toxic as mine."

"I know what my heart craves." Her fingertips whisper along my stubble down to my mouth, her thumb trailing over my bottom lip. "Have you never felt that way?"

"I feel nothing."

Her hand travels to my ear and descends my neck like cascading water as my skin acts like it's breaking out in a heated rash.

She's so close I can taste the sweet wine on her breath, can feel each exhale against my mouth.

My dick throbs. Lengthens. I ignore it, feigning impatience with an aggressive huff as her palms glide over my chest. "You done yet?"

Her lips lift in a warm smile. "I could do this for hours."

Like fuck she could.

She's been at rock bottom for days. Straddling panic over her missing daughter. Why the hell would she want to pause the hysterics to finger fuck my goddamn face?

Reality hits like a freight train, the disgust punching me in the gut.

I snatch her wrists. Hard. "You think I don't know what you're doing?"

She gasps. Her eyes flare.

"That I don't know you're currently using all the skills in your arsenal against the only person who's on your fucking side?" I shove her arms away. "Not a smart move. I'm not a goddamn target you can manipulate."

Her face falls, her shame staring back at me in merciless technicolor.

"Stay the fuck away from me, belladonna," I snarl. "Before I decide your daughter isn't worth the goddamn effort."

16

ABRI

He storms away.

"Bishop, wait." I reach for him, but he yanks his arm from my grip and continues across the room. "I'm sorry." I follow him into the darkened hall.

He doesn't stop. *Goddammit.* He barely pauses once he reaches the front door, flings it open, then stalks outside.

"Let me explain." I step onto the porch, not sure what I'll say if he does decide to listen.

He jogs down the front steps and marches toward my car.

I chase after him to the overgrown lawn. "Where are you going?"

He shoves a hand into his pocket and my car indicators flash as he continues to the back of the vehicle, pops the trunk, then leans forward, disappearing out of view.

"Talk to me," I beg.

I walk to the trunk, finding him hauling out a jack and a lug wrench.

"What are you doing?"

He ignores me and moves to the left back wheel throwing the wrench to the dirt drive before shoving the jack under my car.

"Are you removing the tire?" I frown.

"What I'm doing is making sure I get enough notice if you're stupid enough to try and leave." He winds the jack, raising my car.

"I'm not leaving." I throw my hands out at my sides. "I stayed while you were sleeping, didn't I?"

He keeps winding, his face stony.

"Bishop, I'm sorry, okay? I—"

"I don't give a shit. Go back to the house."

No, he needs to listen. "I didn't know how else to get you to help me."

His gaze snaps to mine, his narrowed eyes predatory. "*Get me to help you?*" He shoves to his feet and squares up to me. "I already said I would. I'm here aren't I? I didn't tell Langston what the hell is going on even though I fucking owe it to him. What more do you want from me?"

"You're right. And I'm sorry. I just… I don't know how to do this." The words tumble from my mouth. "I don't know how to be reliant on someone. And I hate it. Especially when everyone I've trusted to help me has…" I sigh, not wanting to repeat the sordid details we've already hashed out.

He still glares at me, though.

It's not the first time a man has looked at me that way. It's the first time I've felt this dirty though. This worthless.

"Nobody has helped me before. Not without getting something in return." My admission stings, yet it's the truth. "And to have someone I barely know promise to find my daughter…" I shake my head. "It's too good to be true."

"So you've been waiting for me to take advantage?" His nostrils flare. "This whole fucking time?"

My heart squeezes. "It's all I know."

The revulsion beaming down on me increases.

He doesn't understand what it's like to be me. He has no clue. Nobody does. Which makes my life all the more isolating.

"I come from a rich family, Bishop, but my father ensured that I have no money. No value. The only thing I can offer is—"

"Stop." He gets in my face, eyes narrowed. "I'm done getting to know your messed-up life story. But do us both a favor and quit believing the shit Emmanuel put in your head. You're worth more than what lies between your fucking thighs so start acting like it."

I stand tall against the reprimand, loathing how pitiful I've become. "I will."

"And don't try that siren shit on me again. Next time I won't be so nice."

I steel myself against his anger with the squaring of my shoulders.

"Now get the fuck out of my sight. I'm not ready to calm down yet."

I do as he says, returning to the house with my tail between my legs, my self-respect in the gutter.

He stays outside for more than twenty minutes, returning with my car tire balanced on his shoulder before shutting himself in his room.

I don't know what this means for me. Or my daughter. Is he still helping? Is he going to delay any assistance because of what I did?

The unknown is brutal, especially when I have absolutely nobody else to rely on.

I pace the living area for an hour. Then move to the window and stare at the crescent moon. I sit on the sofa for a while, too.

There's nothing but silence in the house until late at night, when the indecipherable murmur of Bishop's voice filters toward me.

I rush to the hall, tiptoeing to his door to listen.

"I'm out of town," he says. "The clubs can run themselves. But I require your skills with a problem I'm working on. You need to start looking for someone for me. Discretion is key."

I exhale on a heave, the relief that he's making good on his promise so potent it's painful.

"The name is Adena Costa. Married to Emmanuel. Birth names of their kids are Dante, Salvatore, Remy, and Abri. Current residential address is on the outskirts of Denver, Colorado. Last known location, Virginia Beach." He falls quiet a moment. "No, there's no expense spared. I want you to dig into bank account transactions. Hack phone records. Do whatever it takes and do it fast."

I press my forehead against the wall, my chest tightening with gratitude.

"Nobody can know you're doing this. Most of all Adena herself." There's a warning in his voice. "I won't take kindly to anyone triggering her suspicions. Do you understand?"

My heart flutters, sickeningly warmed by the threats he's laying for my daughter. For me.

"Good," he grunts. "Keep me posted."

The house returns to silence as I remain in the hall, wishing I could do something. Anything.

He makes more calls, some where he's menacing and demanding, others where he's smooth and charming.

"I know it's late, but I need you to do me another favor, sweetheart." He huffs a chuckle. "Yeah, I'll make sure it's worth your while. All you need to do is keep an eye on incoming flights. Shoot me a text with the details of any private planes hitting the runway over the next few days."

I sink to the floor beside his closed door, eating up every word.

A few minutes later. "Hey Najeeb. It's Bishop... I need your special set of skills. Do you still have access to the face recognition software you used to track down Ben McCarthy?... That's exactly what I'm after. I'm going to shoot you through a photo of a woman. I need you to find her. There's a substantial bonus in it for you if you're successful."

Bishop's door swings open and I gasp, shoving to my feet as light floods the hall.

He glowers at me paused in his doorway. "I need a photo of Adena. Air-drop it to me." Then he slams the door in my face without warning, plunging me back into darkness.

I do as he requests and within minutes I've returned to the floor, my back pressed to the wall, my eyes closed as I listen to him chat with one person after another.

He calls in a stack of favors. Most in English. Some in Italian. I hate how easily I hang off the foreign language, the dreamy, confident words sinking under my skin.

He's still at it after midnight. "Yasmin, it's Bishop... Hey Martin, it's me... Diego? Yeah, man, it's been a while. Can you do me a solid and look into someone for me?"

It's one in the morning when I grab a sofa cushion from the living room and make myself more comfortable on the floor beside his door.

I'm not sure what time I fall asleep, but when I wake, I'm not in the hall. I'm in my bed, the covers pulled up to my chin, my curtains closed around the beaming sun.

I rush to my feet, anxious for an update, but Bishop barely looks at me from his seat at the dining table as he announces my mother hasn't been found.

He doesn't talk to me again.

I stay out of his way all day. Either walking in the fields or lying in my bed.

Salvatore texts, demanding my location. Remy does the same a few hours later with much more finesse. I ignore them both while my hope for finding Tilly fades with the passing hours.

I grow tired, and it's not the sleepy kind. Exhaustion turns my limbs to lead. A bone-weary lethargy that's filled with sorrow and so much agonizing self-pity.

I should be doing something. Anything. But I've fought this battle for my daughter for two years without victory, and defeat nips at my heels.

I've begged. Pleaded. Negotiated. Argued.

Emmanuel promised she was safe. Loved. In need of nothing.

Was it wrong to believe him? To take the photos and videos and trust they weren't doctored?

I sit on my bed and fixate on the cocaine vial resting in my palm as pans clatter in the kitchen. I assume Bishop is making dinner when all I crave is a bump.

I need something to take away the ache in my chest. Yet I haven't loosened the cap since I took it from his jacket back at the house. It remains screwed tight, the powder locked inside, taunting me with its ability to numb my sorrow even if momentarily.

I won't succumb.

I refuse to push Bishop farther away no matter how bad the pain increases.

His footsteps carry down the hall while I keep staring, continue craving, hating the existence of the white powder while I yearn for it in the same breath.

He enters my periphery, his large suit-covered frame standing in the doorway. He's silent, his animosity thickening the air between us.

"Are you high?" he asks without emotion, as if he's given up on me.

I shake my head.

"Do you plan on being that way in the future?"

I tilt my hand, letting the vial roll down to my fingertips. "I'm tempted. But no, I don't need it. I told you I'm not an addict."

I came close once. Close enough that each day blurred into the next, my intake increasing along with the jobs my father demanded of me. I rode the wave too long, too hard, but it was so much easier to live like that… Until I realized I'd been mindless enough to forget taking my contraception pill.

My drug use was the reason I fell pregnant. The reason a little girl may now be living through hell because of my mistakes. Or maybe she's no longer living at all.

"Dinner is ready," he mutters.

I nod, hating the silence that follows, the bitter taste of my manipulation yesterday still lingering.

"I don't have any more news yet," he adds, as if trying to console in some sort of gruff, sterile way. "But it's only a matter of time. Once we pin down what state or city she's in, things will move faster."

I nod again. Hollow. Tormented.

Bishop mumbles something under his breath. A curse or a prayer, I'm not sure. But he finally enters the room, cautiously moving to the foot of my bed.

I feel his attention on me as I remain focused on the vial, his gaze sending a skitter down the back of my neck.

"I hate that I can't work you out, Abri. I don't know which side of you is real—the confident crazy bitch or this emotional fuckin' wreck."

"Then imagine what it's like to be me. I have no idea who I am outside what my father made me." I keep rolling the vial around my palm. "But it's safe to assume I'm the pathetic emotional wreck."

I can't seem to find the strength I once had. That flawless actress is on hiatus. "Even if we find Tilly, I don't know how to live without my father dictating my every move," I admit.

"You can do whatever the hell you like."

I huff a laugh. "Just as long as it fits my uncle's agenda, right? Isn't that how the mafia works?"

"He's not going to do you wrong."

"That's hard to believe when every single family member has betrayed me." I clasp my palms, holding the vial tight between them. "You don't understand what it's like when the deepest knives in your back come from those closest to you."

"Don't I?"

My gaze snaps to his again.

He stares down at me, tight-lipped.

"You're right to despise me for how I treated you yesterday." I swallow over the guilt that dries my throat. "But you never should've expected my trust after what I've been through. You need to understand that—"

"I understand," he mutters.

Is he placating me? Or merely attempting to stop the conversation before it starts? "The only control I know is when I—"

"I said I understand," he cuts me off again. "I know exactly why you tried to manipulate me. And I don't despise you for it. Maybe I did at the time but—" He shrugs. "—it's my fault for forgetting who you're trained to be."

I hang my head, the weight of regret heavy on my shoulders.

"You're a master at your craft, belladonna. Don't be ashamed of that. I understand you're desperate to save your daughter. Hell, I probably would've done the same thing. But it's in the past, and I'm not going to hold it against you."

Relief sparks a tiny flame inside my chest. Normally it would be due to the turning tables, the knowledge that I'm winning him back and gaining an advantage I can manipulate. But this time it's different.

I don't want to deceive him. I never did.

It had been instinctual. Self-preservation.

Being a deceitful whore is all I know, and *God*, I hate myself for it.

I don't deserve his forgiveness. Not even his understanding.

It's enough to make my eyes burn, my nose crinkle.

I sniff, hating the years of built-up emotion that scream to be set free.

He should run. Get as far away as he can. Because even I don't know if I'll attempt to betray him again. When habit will take over and I'll reach for the part of myself that my father created.

"Don't cry, belladonna. I'm not good with that shit."

I nod and rub my nose.

I need to do whatever he says as long as it means forward

progression toward Tilly. I'll stay in my lane. I'll attempt to be someone I'm not—someone who doesn't manipulate or deceive. I'll adhere to his terms because if I don't I'm on my own, with no money, no leads, and no hope.

"Come on. Get up." He steps back from the bed. "It's time to eat."

I sigh and scoot from the mattress, too drained for food yet well aware I've barely eaten all day.

"Want to get rid of the temptation?" He holds out a hand as I pass.

I pause, the vial of coke warm in my palm. "I can take care of it."

"Fair enough. But the offer stands if you change your mind." His voice lowers to a calm, controlled timbre, so confidently smooth and authoritative. "I won't ask you to trust me again either, but I will tell you I know you're strong enough to get through this without that shit clouding your judgement."

I lock down my expression, not showing how hard his faith hits me square in the chest.

He's nobody to me. Yet he's also so many things nobody else has ever been—a savior, a protector.

I stand there, stripped bare, thankful yet scared someone is finally seeing me. The *real* me. Not only the viper who revels in seduction and exploitation, but also the battered puppet, strung into action by threads of cruelty and malice, who desperately wants to pull her life together.

My eyes blaze with the fight to keep my emotions in check. The heat in my tingling nose increases.

I lower my gaze to the carpet, my throat drying with each beat of my pulse.

He doesn't move from his place a few feet in front of me. He doesn't walk away like he should. He remains quiet as I struggle to hide the slightly ragged hitches of my breathing, the ache in my chest growing unbearable.

"What do you need from me?" he murmurs so quietly I almost think I'm imagining it. The care. The concern.

Part of me is convinced it's a trick. Some sort of cruel tactic to get me to weaken further. Yet another more grueling part of me scrambles to cling to the lifeline.

"It's okay," he says. "Whatever it is you need just tell me. I'm not going anywhere. I might as well help while I'm here."

The torment grows inside me, tearing at my heart, threatening to turn me into a puddle of pathetic frailty.

"I need to know she's safe." I blink faster, the carpet blurring before me. "That's all."

"I already know that part, and I'm working on it. What else can I do?"

Each word claws at my defenses, battering my shields. "I don't know."

"Figure it out, belladonna."

I raise my chin to look at him.

He stands tall before me. An emotionless wall. Strong, sturdy, and too goddamn reliable.

I don't get how his sterile strength is appealing. How he can be cold and consoling at the same time.

All I want is to lean into that strength. To siphon it. Devour it.

"Tell me, Abri."

I can't. He'll think I'm trying to seduce him again, and I won't risk earning more of his wrath.

"Say it." There's a demand in his tone, one I desperately want to adhere to.

"I don't need anything else." I start for the door, the threat of tears heating my eyes.

"Bullshit." His hand latches around my wrist and I'm tugged backward. "Why can't you just fucking ask?"

I gasp as I'm swirled to face him, dragged roughly into his chest, his arms wrapping around me.

I turn to stone, not sure what to do now that he's giving me exactly what I need—comfort. Compassion.

He's doing something I'm sure he despises. Holding me against him, even though his body is as tightly coiled with unease as mine.

Why? Why would anyone, let alone him—a murderer, a man committed to a cold existence—console me like this?

My mouth turns to ash, my throat clogged with emotion.

I sink into him, my cheek to his shoulder, my nose to his neck, but my arms remain at my sides, awkward and dismissive as a lifetime of mistakes batters me from the inside out.

I don't know what to do. How to fight my surging emotions.

How to ease my suffering. I'm just as foreign to this type of contact as he is. I've never been held. Never been afforded the luxury of breaking down.

My throat threatens to close over, the searing tightness of my airway making it harder to breathe.

I didn't realize how much it hurts to be this vulnerable. To allow myself to be at the mercy of his judgment. The frailty wraps its thorny vines around me, squeezing, wringing the remaining strength from my limbs. And Bishop is right there to hold me up against the onslaught.

I suck in a shuddering breath. It only makes him hug me closer.

He swaddles me with silent assurance, chasing away the sorrow even though I'm aware the reprieve is temporary.

"Thank you," I murmur in fractured tones.

I don't know what else to say as the first tear spills free, its heated trail cascading down my cheek.

I haven't cried in years. Not since I watched my daughter being taken away before I could hold her. Soothe her cries. Fill her tiny belly.

A sob escapes.

I bury my head in Bishop's neck, my ragged breaths against his skin, my fingers creeping up between us to cling to his jacket.

I know he'd prefer to be anywhere but here. Doing anything else as long as it doesn't involve holding me. And still, I can't stop myself from being a burden.

After a lifetime of emotional isolation, I'm a slave to his arms. To the gentle way he comforts me. I'm too weak to let go.

"You'll be okay," he murmurs into my hair.

More heavy tears fall, the moisture landing on his shoulder to dampen the material.

"You're going to get through this."

I shake my head. "I don't know how. I'm not used to being like this. The panic attacks—" I hiccup. "The tears. I don't cry, Bishop."

"I know." He remains steady against me. An unwavering force. "It's temporary. There's no avoiding rock bottom after what you've been through. You'll bounce back once this blows over."

I close my eyes, sending another wave of moisture down my cheeks. "What if I break instead?"

"I won't let that happen."

The tears come harder, the ragged breaths exhaled into a man who shouldn't have all the right words. But that's the way they feel—right. Real. True. How can he be such a brutal, murderous force one minute, then a considerate shelter from the storm the next?

It's not normal. Not natural.

He's everything I need him to be exactly when I need it. First with Gordon. Then with my attacks. Now this.

"You keep saving me," I whisper against his neck.

"It's my job to look after you."

I sniff away the tears and scrunch my nose, fighting like the devil to regain some semblance of composure as I pull back to meet his gaze. "I bet you're sick of that job."

"I've definitely had assignments I'm better suited for." His eyes scan mine, stoic and calm. "I'm going to need you to stop crying now, belladonna. It's not good to rely on someone like me for comfort. I don't know what the hell I'm doing."

"You're doing just fine." I force a somber smile. "Then again, this whole comfort thing is new to me, so maybe you're really bad at it and I just don't know any better."

One side of his lips kicks in a smirk, the sight pausing my pulse.

The expression is transformative, changing him from sterile to sinful in a blink, before it vanishes just as fast.

"Do you really not have a frame of reference?" he asks.

"No." I drag in a breath and distract myself by playing with his lapels. "My role within the family has never allowed for a romantic relationship. And even paternal comfort wasn't a thing when both my parents lack nurturing instincts."

He keeps his arms around me, showing no sign of letting go. "So all that shit you tried to manipulate me with last night in the kitchen rings true to you, too."

It's not a question. It's clear my life lacks the intimacy I taunted him with. All I've ever known is sexual exploitation, both giving and receiving.

"As sad as it might sound," I say to his chest, "I think the only compassion I've been given from a man came from Cole Torian the night I received the scar on my throat."

His muscles tense beneath my palms. "Is he the one who cut you?"

"No, but he should've. Instead, I did it to myself as a cover after he staged a hostage situation where he told my brothers he'd cut me. Cole had sliced his hand instead and held it against my throat, claiming his blood was mine. It would've been safer for him to make it real."

"So why didn't he?"

I shrug. "I don't know."

"Was it because he'd already taken what he wanted from you?"

I give a somber shake of my head. "No."

Bishop grips my chin and forces my gaze to his. "Don't lie to me."

"I'm not." I bask under the weight of his ferocity, wishing his response was due to jealousy and not just some threat of a tarnished reputation to my uncle. "I never slept with Cole. He was in love with someone else and wanted nothing to do with me."

"He's lucky then," he mutters.

"I'm glad you approve."

"I'm not that asshole's biggest fan."

"I can see that."

He releases my chin, his hand returning to my lower back.

We fall quiet, his hard eyes fixed on mine through the silence.

It's far more intimate than anything I've experience before. I feel vulnerable and exposed. But in a non-threatening way.

I stand there, learning the intricacies of his expression. Seeing the different shades of blond in his growing stubble. Capturing how the dark blue of his irises are bordered with thick black. And how his forehead bears the faintest frown lines.

"You don't usually have a beard, do you?" I reach out, unabashed as I trail my fingertips along his jaw.

His shoulders tense. "Not like this, no."

"It looks good on you."

"Everything looks good on me," he mutters with such understated confidence I can't help but grin. "Now are there any more compliments you want to share before we call this quits? Dinner is getting cold."

I ignore his question, not ready for this to end. I keep dragging my touch down to his chin. Slow. Lethargic.

He doesn't react. But I'm sure emotions bubble under his tough exterior. Frustration maybe. Impatience, too.

My gaze falls to his mouth. To the lips that seem unfathomably soft for such an incredibly hard man.

What would it be like to kiss him? To lean forward and bridge the space between us? Would his harsh personality bleed into the contact? Would he be rough? Or would his lack of experience make the connection awkward?

"Don't even think about it, belladonna," he warns under his breath.

My fingertips pause at his cheek as I wait for him to storm away. He doesn't.

Why? Why does he continue to hold me? To remain close when he already knows what's running through my mind? But that's not all I think about. The faintest memories haunt me, dark and almost out of reach. When I'd been battling sedation and his hands were on me, his touch gentle.

"Did you run a thumb over my mouth the night you sedated me?" I whisper.

His mouth snaps shut, his lips forming a tight line.

"I'll take that as a yes." I return the favor, trailing the pad of my thumb over the outer edge of his bottom lip, grazing the stubble beneath.

His nostrils flare. "Belladonna…"

I wait for more. A demand to stop. An insult to cause injury.

Nothing comes.

He falls silent, watching me with narrowed eyes.

"What would happen?" I murmur.

His jaw ticks. He doesn't need specifics to understand I'm talking about a kiss. But he doesn't respond, and my body warms as if he's given approval.

I glide my thumb back to his cheek, my gaze trekking the path. "Why does it feel like kissing you would deafen my screaming mind?"

"Because you're in pain and any distraction, no matter how toxic, feels like it would be a reprieve."

A lump forms in my throat.

I'm sure he's right. That doesn't mean I'm any less curious.

"You'd regret it," he grates.

"I've regretted a lot of things in my life." I meet his eyes, dragging my fingertips to the sensitive spot below his ear, his skin awakening with goose bumps beneath my touch. "None have been as modest as this."

I place my free hand to his chest, feeling the heavy beat of his heart under my palm, the thudding tempo matching my own.

I still can't read his emotions. Can't figure out what lurks beneath that cold blue stare.

I swallow and inch closer, the slight hint of cigarette smoke brushing my senses, the whisper of his breath caressing my lips. Adrenaline floods my body, sending warmth between my thighs. My pain and sorrow are pushed to the back of my mind as curiosity and attraction thrive.

"Don't do it," he warns.

I can't help it. I keep touching, returning my thumb to his lower lip to drag more adamantly over the tempting flesh.

"Enough." His hand snaps up between us, his palm curling around my wrist.

I gasp even though it's not a harsh touch.

The gentleness of his fingers leaves me frozen. The contact is delicate yet merciless in an exquisite mix, as if loyalty to my uncle fuels him but desire calls in equal measure.

"You need to think before you act, Abri." He tightens his grip. "We both know you shouldn't be fucking around with a man whose most valuable skill is murder."

17

BISHOP

She stiffens.

Good.

She's playing a dangerous game. We both are. And I'm the pitiful fuck who can't walk away. I'm caught here. Trapped in those eyes.

She swallows again, and this time her tongue snakes out and moistens her bottom lip. It's more than enough to make my dick stir.

"Do you warn all the women you're with?" she asks.

"I don't need to." I drag her arm down to her side and release it. "I've told you I don't kiss any of them."

"How long has it been?"

"A while," I grate.

Her gaze searches mine. "Tell me how long."

"I was seventeen, Abri. I haven't wanted that sort of contact since." Until she walked into my life, her beauty mind-fucking me while her sweet scent poisoned my lungs.

"Seventeen?" The whisper of her voice is my undoing. "Now it makes sense why you're so cold and abrupt."

"Being a murderous son of a bitch isn't a good enough reason?"

"I guess it is, but—" She shrugs.

"But what?"

Her brow forms the cutest furrow. "Nothing. It doesn't matter."

She stares at my mouth, her gaze holding the power of a caress.

She's in my head. Pulsing through my goddamn veins, the tainted blood pooling in my groin.

I need to walk away, but my legs won't move. I want to taste her. To steal her breath.

"Will you hate me if I kiss you?" she asks softly.

No, worse—I'll hate myself.

Fucking loathe and detest.

She's a job. One I've already messed up on numerous levels.

She's also Langston's sister. Lorenzo's niece.

She inches toward me, her exhales becoming my inhales. Those mesmerizing eyes blink up at me, cautious and inquisitive, while my limbs turn rigid.

"Don't fucking do it." My palms sweat with the need to grab her again, this time ruthlessly.

After years abstaining, I want to fuck this woman. To sink into her so fast and hard she screams for me to stop.

"Why don't you back away?" she whispers.

She knows I'm stuck here, tethered to her beauty like a dying man nailed to a cross.

"*Abri*," I warn.

She leans closer, her lips almost dancing over mine. "Just back away."

Fuck this. Fuck her. Fuck every moment that's led me here and the memories that will haunt me once she's gone.

"Kiss me, Bishop."

I should.

I should shut her up with the most awkward contact of her life. One without expertise or finesse.

Too bad humiliation isn't one of my kinks.

"That's not going to happen." I grab her chin, my fingertips digging into the most delicate skin.

She stiffens, seeming timid, almost goddamn skittish despite the tally of men that lay in her wake. It triggers something inside me, flicking a switch that never should've been discovered, let alone activated.

I itch to give her what she wants. To build her back up to the victorious viper I could've strangled the night of the gala. To not only strengthen who she once was, but to ensure she exceeds the power she previously had. To make her a goddess among lust-drunk men.

"Why not?" She blinks back at me, her innocence seeming pure, but who the fuck knows if it's an act? Do I even care anymore? "I want you."

Jesus Christ.

"What you want is a reprieve." My cock thickens, pressing against my zipper. "You're looking for respite from the pain."

She lowers her gaze, in disappointment or agreement, I'm not sure. Either way, denying her is torture.

I force myself to release her chin. To stop touching. To quit fixating. But she's so fucking beautiful.

"The best I can do is give you a distraction." I ignore the regret already pounding through my temples. "As long as you don't get caught up thinking this is something it's not."

She meets my gaze. "I won't."

"This means nothing," I reiterate.

"I understand." She licks her bottom lip. Subtle. Sweet.

"And no kissing."

Her brows pull tight, but she nods. "Okay."

God, I hate how gorgeous she is. How everything else about her is a contradiction. The strength that can quickly turn to fragility. The heartlessness that transforms into compassion. The fierce determination which changes to broken despair in the blink of an eye.

But that beauty always remains.

It's a constant.

A torturously unwavering truth.

I grab the waistband of her jeans and tug her into me. "I'll make you feel good."

Her palms plant against my chest, her nails scratching through my shirt.

"You're going to come around my fingers, belladonna." I release the button on her pants. Lower the zipper.

She whimpers. "You can at least try."

I lean close to her ear, releasing a menacing chuckle. "You think I can't get you off?"

"No." She shakes her head, her hands latching onto my

shoulders while I walk into her, forcing her backward, taking her to the wall beside the door. "That's not what I meant."

I place a palm against the plaster, caging her while my other hand slides down her abdomen and under the elastic of her panties. "Explain."

Her siren song has me by the balls, the floral scent of her shampoo carving itself into my lungs.

"I meant that nobody else has before," she murmurs.

My hand freezes beneath her underwear. My entire body follows suit.

Shit.

This hole I'm digging is getting deeper, drawing close to the earth's crust where the devil lays in wait.

"You're telling me no man has ever made you come?" I sneer.

As if this could get any worse. The temptation. The need.

Now livid rage is added to the mix, along with the sharp hook of ownership that waits to dig its metallic length under my skin.

"Once we're done here, you're going to write me a list," I grate against her neck. "I want the names of every son of a bitch who took from you without giving in return."

"And what will you do with the names on that list?" Her hips arch into my touch as if to spur my fingers back into movement.

I slide my hand lower, each inch of smooth skin fueling my stupidity. "I'll kill them all."

She shudders, her grip on my shoulders increasing. "That shouldn't be a turn-on."

It shouldn't be something I crave either. Avenging her honor isn't my business. The motivation should be kept strictly to rewriting the insults made against *Lorenzo*. Against *Langston's* reputation.

But that's not why my instincts are frazzled.

I want to feel the beating hearts of those men in my hands while they regret what they did to her. To hear them wish with their dying breaths that they'd never touched this woman. Never played with what's mine.

Fuck.

I grind my teeth. Close my eyes.

"Don't tease me." She grabs my wrist, attempting to guide my touch. "I need this."

I fucking need it too. Like a goddamn hole in the head.

She's warping my mind. Making me fall under her spell, whether intentional or not.

I clench my knuckles against the wall and descend farther.

She drags in a ragged gasp, her clasp on my arm tightening. But those inhales stop.

"Breathe, belladonna." I succumb to temptation, skimming my teeth along the perfectly sculpted line of her jaw. "Let me hear how much you want me."

She groans. "Of course you're going to be an arrogant bastard at a time like this."

"If I could change my personality to get you off, I would. But this is me." My fingers glide to the crevice of her pussy, her hips bucking when I graze her clit.

She's sensitive. Attuned to the slightest touch.

I go farther. Lower. I part her sex with my fingers and slide to her entrance.

She's wet. Lush. So fucking ready for me it's excruciating.

"Are you always like this?" I growl. "Soaked and fucking perfect."

"The perfection is a smokescreen." She tilts her head back against the wall, panting as I swirl my fingertips around her opening, drowning my skin in her pleasure, spreading it over her clit. Back and forth. A precious little groan follows each brush of that tiny bundle of nerves, the sound sinking beneath my ribs to wreak havoc on my pulse. "What you see is nothing but a mirage."

"You're no mirage." She's real. Her flawlessness is undeniable. "You're a fucking goddess."

She moans. "A poisonous one."

"True." I nuzzle her neck. "But your venom is delicious." I keep swirling my touch around her sex, along her folds, until she's drenched from front to back. "Do you want my fingers inside you?"

She clings tighter to my wrist. "Please."

I smirk against her ear. "There's no greater sound than hearing you beg."

"Then consider yourself lucky." Her words are guttural. "You're the only man who can make me do it."

Goddamn, this woman works psychological magic like it's her bitch.

She taunts me. Angers me. Then stokes my ego with the barest compliment that has my dick seeping.

I draw back, needing to see her. To *watch* her.

Those lust-drunk eyes stare at me half-lidded. Shallow breaths escape the most captivating lips.

I swirl my fingers, circling her opening, tormenting, punishing, just like she's done to me for days.

"You want me to keep begging, don't you?" she pants. "I bet you need the power play."

What I need is to bend her over the bed and sink my cock inside her. To feel that sweet pussy milking me as she screams my name.

"No. The fact it comes naturally when you're with me is more than enough."

She cringes, but those hips keep rolling into my touch. "Then what do you need to quit teasing me? This is agony."

"I need nothing." I plunge two fingers inside her. Fast. Deep.

She gasps, her eyes closing, her pussy clamping around me.

So. Fucking. Perfect.

I picture what it would be like to have my dick where my fingers are. I can't get the imagery out of my head, the sordid thoughts exquisitely painful torture that increase the throb along my shaft.

She rolls her hips with the curl of my fingers, her body dancing with my hand as she clings to me. Her breathing quickens, greedy, rapid inhales that come from parted, glistening lips.

I want to devour her. Fucking gorge.

Jesus. If this woman makes me finish in my pants, I'll never live it down.

"How's that feel?" I ask an inch from her mouth.

"Incredible," she whimpers. "So good."

"Yeah?" I raise a taunting brow, pretending like fuck that I'm unfazed by her when the reality is that I don't know how I'm going to maintain my control when she comes. "How much do you wish it was my dick?"

Her eyes roll and she groans, rocking those hips harder, faster. "Unless you're going to deliver, don't tease."

I'd never fuck her. Not in a million years. And not only because it would break the decade-long drought, or how Langston and Lorenzo would castrate me, but because I refuse to become another name on the list of men who've mistreated her.

I won't be a fucked up memory she has to forget.

Not any more than I already am, anyway.

"You're killing me," she whispers.

"You don't like to be teased, *la mia sirena ammaliatrice*?"

She moans.

"You don't like to think about how much better this would be if you were riding my cock?" I fist her hair, pulling her head back to lick my way up her neck. "I'd make you scream, Abri."

"Too bad you've pigeon-holed yourself at third base. That doesn't leave you much to work with."

"You need to give your imagination a pep talk." I graze my teeth along her jaw, my mouth dry with the need to show her all the things I could do. "Because the unruly shit I could inflict upon you runs a mile long."

She shudders. "Tell me."

"Are you sure?" I speak against her skin. "Do you really want to know what I'd do if you weren't you and I wasn't me?"

"Yes." The word is a breathy plea.

I fight a groan, my cock demanding I show instead of tell. "I would taste you. Spread you out on that bed like a fucking feast and drench my face between your thighs." I tense my stomach against the visual onslaught. "My thumb would be in this sweet pussy while I sucked on your clit. Lapped at your slit. And that fucking perfect ass would be filled with as many fingers as you could take."

She groans, bearing down on me as I continue to simulate sex with my hand.

"And if my mouth wasn't enough to get you off, then I'd show you what it's like to be fisted. To stretch you out slowly, the pleasure so close to pain you'd be mindless. I'd make you gush, belladonna. Every inch of your thighs would be drenched."

"Dear Lord," she whispers.

"No, my sweet villain. The heavens wouldn't save you from me. Nobody could if I decided you were mine."

"I wouldn't want to be saved." She releases my wrist, wrapping both hands around my neck, her nails digging into skin. "I just want to be lost."

"You would be. So fucking lost you couldn't find yourself again." I can't help but grind my dick against her thigh, the friction dragging a groan from my throat. "I'd tie you up and edge you for so long you'd pray for me to let you finish."

"And what about you? How would you come?"

"Simply by watching you. I'd fist my dick at every opportunity. I'd teach you how I like to be jerked off. I'd stare down at you as you took me to the back of your throat. Then I'd spill my seed all over those beautiful lips."

She pants. Fast. Sharp. "But you'd never fuck me?"

"No."

"Why?"

Yeah, why, Bishop?

I steel myself against the reasons. "That's not a conversation we need to have." I place my thumb over her clit, adding pressure, and smother her body with mine. Chest to chest. Thigh to thigh. "My focus is on the here and now. On how your needy pussy is flooding my fingers." I skim my other hand down her back, beneath the waistband of her loosened jeans, past her stretched underwear. "And how that ass calls my name." I slide my fingers between her cheeks, skimming another entrance I'm itching to plunder.

"Fuck." She jolts. "I hate that you feel so good," she murmurs to the ceiling. "Why can't you be like the rest of them?"

The reminder of her past stabs through me, leaving me livid. "You'll never be touched like that again," I snarl. "Your time being used is over. Do you understand?"

She mewls, the erotic sound nothing but a placation.

I curl my fingers into the flesh of her ass as I pump her pussy faster, harder, my mouth moving to her ear. "I said, do you understand?"

She trembles. Claws. Hyperventilates.

"I don't like to be ignored, belladonna. Answer me or this is going to get hectic."

"It isn't already?" she gasps.

"Barely. You're not even naked yet. Imagine what I could do with a blank canvas."

"That sounds like an incentive to remain quiet."

"Are you sure?" I sink my teeth into her shoulder, hard enough to make her squeal.

"*Okay*," she cries. "*Yes.* I understand."

"Good girl."

"Oh, God."

And there it is—the fucking orgasm I wring from her in exquisitely feminine whimpers. The one that will haunt my dreams. The one I already regret with every thunderous beat of my pulse.

Her pussy flutters around my fingers, her head pulled back as her tits rise and fall with her rapid breaths.

I itch to fist her hair, to force her gaze to the first man to make her come. To cement the memory in her mind. But I don't need that potency fucking with my head later.

Jerking off in the shower tonight will be quick enough without the recollection of staring into her lust-drunk baby blues, making the time trial pitiful.

Instead, I let her finish in silence, the controlled movement of my fingers matching the rhythm of her hips, over and over, until she finally begins to recede from the peak.

I'm a fucking prick for touching her. For pretending it was okay to indulge in Lorenzo's niece because she needed a distraction.

But that's all it was. Pretend. Make-believe.

I'm no better than every other fucker who's been tempted by her. I couldn't keep my hands off when she was clearly suffering.

She relaxes against the wall, her lips curving in a dreamy smile, her hands sliding from my neck to drift down my chest while I wallow in self-loathing.

My fingers remain inside her, soaked as I stand rigid, a captured beast entirely ensnared in the bear trap I'd willingly walked into.

She lifts my shirt at the hem, her soft knuckles brushing my stomach. I clench my teeth so fucking tight I might crack a molar. And still I can't back away.

I'm thrumming.

Drowning in lust.

She grabs my belt, tugging at the clasp.

"What are you doing?" I growl.

"Returning the favor."

I yank my hands from her pants and clasp her wrist. "No. We're done here."

She freezes, all that blissed-out lust vanishing with a hard blink. "But—"

"You wanted a distraction and I gave you one." I step back, my limbs tense, my dick aching for relief. "Now, go eat your dinner."

18

ABRI

The house is deathly quiet as we eat.

Bishop hasn't spoken a word since he marched from my bedroom fifteen minutes ago. Hasn't even dared to raise his scowl in my direction.

Obviously it's not the first time a man has regretted touching me. But somehow that reaction from Bishop stings.

I've never been pleasured before. Not selflessly or any other way. All I've ever been is a tool of pleasure for others.

What Bishop and I shared was different.

Monumental.

And it's clear he despises the memory.

"I'm having an early night." He shoves back in his chair, grabbing his empty plate and glass of water and heading to the sink. "I'll see you in the morning."

I bite my tongue, refusing to say something I can't take back. Something angry to purge my humiliation. Or worse, something pitiful.

I hate feeling like this. Powerless. Not only toward my daughter, but toward *him*—the only man strong enough to resist my manipulation. And the worst part is that our moment in the bedroom hadn't been manipulation at all. I'd been plummeting toward rock bottom and he'd caught me mid-air, saving me from impact. At least temporarily, anyway.

Now I'm falling again. Nosediving toward hysteria.

Too many emotions compete for my attention. Anger. Regret. Humiliation. Panic. Fear. All of them potent and toxic in my veins.

I want to scream at my mother. To wrap my hands around my brothers' necks. To snort coke and drown in liquor. But when it comes to Bishop, all I want to do is simply understand.

His thoughts.

His actions.

His tightly held emotions.

I want to decipher him. To crawl behind those callous eyes and discover how he sees the world. How he sees me.

He leaves for the hall, the bathroom door closing with a definitive thud seconds later.

Goddammit.

I shove my plate away, the few bites of his homemade burger curdling in my gut. I don't want to fight with him. On the other hand, it's all I want to do. To taunt, yell, lash out.

He's turned me into a tangled mess of irrational thoughts, which makes my actions equally volatile.

Before I know what I'm doing, I'm on my feet and padding after him to stand in wait outside the bathroom door.

Still, there's no sound.

He doesn't use the facilities. Not the shower or the toilet. There's nothing. No movement. The silence is nerve-wracking.

"Bishop?" I ask quietly.

There's a shift of noise. A slight rustle of fabric. But no answer.

I sigh and tap on the door. "Bishop?"

"What is it?" he snaps.

I wince. "Can we talk?"

He doesn't answer.

"Please?" I test the handle, my heart thudding hard when I find it unlocked.

I slide the door open and there he is, hunched over the basin, shirtless, his hands clutching the vanity in a white-knuckled grip, the gun and knives usually hidden beneath his clothes now laid out before him.

The scars on his back claim my attention. The long thick slash on his left shoulder. The two round, reddened circles above his right hip. Then the myriad of smaller faded lines.

His body is a timeline of violence, tattooed in marred flesh instead of ink.

"What do you want?" he grates, not looking at me.

I swallow and lick my drying lips. "How much do you regret touching me?"

"Regrets are a waste of time."

"Then I assume you're angry with me."

His jaw ticks, his scowl hardening as he glares at the faucet. "Everything is fine, Abri. Go to bed."

No, it isn't. Not with us. Not with my daughter. Or my brothers. Or my life.

Everything is falling apart, and I just need something to be okay. Just one thing to make this nightmare a little less hellish.

"I wasn't trying to manipulate you." I swallow over the ache in my throat. "None of what we shared was an act."

"I know." He hangs his head, loose strands of his tousled hair falling to shroud his face.

"Then what's wrong? Why can't you look at me?"

His hands squeak against the counter, his fingers tense in their clawed grip.

"Bishop?"

"*Jesus fucking Christ.*" He glares at me over his shoulder. "I'm looking at you. Is that better?"

Each bitter syllable slices me like a paper cut, sharp and refined.

He knows it's not any better. Not with the fury in his eyes or the hatred ebbing off him.

I raise my chin to the hostility. Breathe deep over the ache in my chest. "What did I do wrong?"

He winces and drags his focus back to the faucet. "Damn it to hell, woman. I'm trying to do right by you, but you're making it fucking difficult." He shuffles on his feet, shifting his hips, still hunched over the basin.

That's when I see the formidable bulge against his zipper.

I swallow again, but it does nothing to alleviate the desert taking over my throat.

He's hard. *Really* hard.

He rocks on his heels, the muscles in his arms tense, his Hulk grip on the counter seeming like he might rip it from the wall at any second. "Leave, Abri. My temper is threadbare."

"And what about your lust?"

He scoffs, his lips thinning. "My dick ain't hard for you, if that's what you think."

I'm well aware. It's merely circumstance after what happened in the bedroom. But that doesn't mean I can't help him like he helped me. "Don't worry. You've made it clear you're not attracted to me." The house returns to its pained silence, the air thick with tension. "I've never touched a man without incentive," I whisper. "It's always been a job."

His jaw ticks. "Then it's a good thing you no longer have to do it, isn't it?"

"Yes." I inch into the room with timid steps to match my equally timid emotions. I've never felt like this before—wary and worried over the possibility of rejection.

He reduces me to feeble reluctance. All my self-assurance clasped in his palms to squash at will.

"I no longer have to." I stop behind him, hating how he tenses. "The thing is…I want to."

He straightens and swings to face me, shoulders broad, height towering, and blatantly meaning to intimidate. "Get the fuck out."

My pulse kicks into top gear, the pounding of my heart felt through every limb as those hard eyes glare at me.

"I've never been drawn to touch a man because I wanted to, Bishop." I hold his gaze. "Never once have I craved it like I do now."

"You crave punishment," he snarls. "You crave chaos and pain."

"No, I crave *you*." I reach out, my hand trembling as I palm the bulge in his pants.

He sucks in a hiss, his nostrils flaring.

"This means nothing." I repeat his declaration from earlier. "We can forget it as soon as it's over."

"And if I decide to punish you for daring to touch me, will you forget that too?"

My heart thunders, the tempestuous storm deafening in my ears. "Yes. I've already done it a million times before."

Something flickers in his eyes. Something fast and fleeting. Disgust? Pity?

"Tell me what you want, Bishop."

"I want you to walk the fuck out of here before I betray your brother and uncle all over again."

That's why he's angry? Due to loyalty?

"They'll never know." I squeeze his length, earning a groan.

"*I'll* know." He grips my wrist. "I'm not using you, Abri."

Can he hear himself? Does he know how chivalrous he sounds?

He may be a bloodthirsty killer, but he doesn't come close to being in the vile catalogue of perverted assholes I've previously been with.

"I wouldn't let you use me. This is for my benefit." I glide my free hand over his chest, my palm sliding over the plains of muscle, the fine dusting of hairs. "It's purely selfish. I'm dying to know what you look like when you come."

"If you don't release your hold on my dick, you'll soon find out."

I smile, my belly tumbling in a way I've never felt before. Excitement? Adrenaline? Maybe it's just the thrill of giving pleasure without underhanded obligation. Either way, I like the sensation. "Good. Now release my wrist, *macellaio*."

His eyes widen for a split second of surprise before returning to narrowed slits. "You can call me a butcher in whatever language you like, belladonna, just as long as you remember that's exactly what I am."

"I'll remember." I inch closer, our thighs brushing. "I promise."

His grip loosens on my wrist, the tiniest breath of reprieve that allows me to unclasp his belt and lower his zipper.

My pulse beats like crazy as I drag his suit pants and boxer briefs down to his knees, our eyes locked.

I'm dying to look at him. To see the generous length that rests in my palm. To examine the ridges and veins I can feel in my hold. But I want to maintain our heated gaze more.

I can't fathom how he remains refined and restrained while I slowly stroke him. How he seems entirely controlled even though his cock jerks in my hand. "Teach me the way you like to be touched."

"At this point, I'm a few short strokes away from coming. I don't need to give you pointers to make it any more pitiful."

I don't believe him. He's too disciplined.

I release him and lick my palm, lubricating it the best I can. "Is that right?" I grip him again, my heart skittering behind my ribs when his shoulders tense, a low rumble emanating from his chest.

"Are you looking for praise, *la mia sirena ammaliatrice*?"

Yes. But even more than that, I want to know what he just called me.

My Italian doesn't stretch beyond the basics no matter how adamant my mother was that I learn and now I'm left hungrily curious, yet too stubborn to ask.

"Haven't I already given you enough?" He grips my chin, his hips slowly rocking into my hold. "Do you want more examples of what I'd do to you if given different circumstances?"

My blood heats, no place more punishing than between my thighs.

I nod, stroking faster. "Tell me."

Another sound emanates from his chest. Hungry. Animalistic.

"I'd hurt you," he purrs. "If unleashed, I'd have you on your back so often and for so long that your pretty pussy would be swollen and sore. You'd beg for respite. And maybe I'd oblige. Maybe I'd give that sweet cunt a time-out while I fucked your hands or your mouth or your feet. But you'd never find peace with me. I'd never let you catch your breath."

I clench my thighs, my panties damp enough that I'm sure the wet patch will soon be seen through my jeans. "I'm not sure I believe you."

He smirks menacingly as he starts to truly fuck my hand. "Yeah you do. You know I'd destroy you. And I'd enjoy every minute of it."

I shudder, my inhales outpacing his own.

Is it wrong to crave what he describes? Because I do.

I want him to consume me. To mark me. To taint me in a way that has nothing to do with exploitation and everything to do with hedonistic pleasure.

I clench him tighter, my pussy begging for the release I'm about to give him as he continues to hold my chin.

My mouth aches for his kiss. Every inch of me does right down to my toes.

"You confuse me, Bishop." I stroke faster, his cold stare growing more icy with his increased pleasure. "I don't know what it is, but no matter how hard I try to hate you, I can't."

"I want to hate you too, belladonna."

"But you don't?" My pulse skitters over its frantic beats.

"I don't usually finger-fuck women I hate," he growls. "Or allow them to dictate my actions through my dick."

His admission steals my common sense. I have as much ability to dictate his actions as I do with the moon and stars. I'm powerless. Entirely paralyzed with incompetence.

But something in his gaze makes me want to believe him. To drown in the confidence that comes with affecting a man as disciplined and calculated as him.

I increase the pace of my strokes, concentrating on the head of his shaft, squeezing the tip.

A low groan grates from his throat, the sound delicious for a few short seconds before he releases my chin and grasps my wrist in a punishing grip. "We're done."

I frown. Panic.

"I'll take it from here." His hold tightens. His jaw clenches.

I shake my head. "Why?"

"Because you're about to make me come, belladonna, and I don't want to ruin those pretty clothes."

19

BISHOP

She blinks at me in disappointment.

Goddamn-fucking-disappointment.

Under any other circumstance I'd laugh, but that grip around my dick has me shook. I'm a chump already poised to come after a few greedy strokes, pre-cum seeping from my slit.

"Abri," I grate.

"You won't ruin my clothes." She uses her free hand to grab the hem of her shirt and yanks it over her head, exposing lush tits in a pretty pink bra. "I want to feel you on me."

My nostrils flare as I turn my head away, my balls tight as fuck.

She's destroying me. Slowly. Painfully.

I've never been so easily bested. So agonizingly fucking hard. And by what? A fine rack and a fuckable mouth?

She moves to lean her ass on the vanity, dragging me along with her by my goddamn dick.

When she starts stroking me again, I have no control to stop a groan from escaping. To quit fucking her fist. It takes all my energy to fight against groping her. But that's exactly what I do. Fight against the need to squeeze her breasts in my hands. To embed my fingers in that fine ass.

She reaches her free hand behind her back, I assume to unclasp her bra.

"Don't," I bark. "Keep it on."

This shit is bad enough without having to look Langston in the eye with his sister's perfect tits burned into my retinas.

She bristles but complies, dropping her hand to my waist, digging her nails into my side. I hiss in a breath, the bite of pain a potent aphrodisiac as she gently drags a palm along my shaft.

"I'll take it from here." I clamp my jaw. Tense all my muscles against the pleasure. Clench her wrist.

"*Please*," she begs.

That's all it takes. One word. One beseeching syllable from an otherwise calculating viper and my dick loses its mind.

I glare at her as pleasure blinds me, my balls heavy, my knees threatening to buckle.

I come with the next glide of her palm, hating how much I can't deny her as I shoot my load on her belly, each warm jet of seed painting her like a fucking canvas.

She pants, those gorgeous lips parted as if my release is her own. As if I'm mind-fucking her as hard as she's fucking me. And the whole time she stares at me, meeting my vehemence head-on with mesmerizing eyes that blink with blazing heat.

"That's enough," I growl, my chest heaving as I struggle to regain level breathing.

She releases me, her other hand sliding from my waist. She looks down at herself, at the taint I've marred on her skin, and trails a finger through the cum on her belly. "Do you feel any better?"

Fuck no.

The release only compounds this messed up situation. And the fact my cock is having a hard time softening is a glaring red flag.

"We're done here."

She nods. "Right after we get cleaned up."

She grabs my hand, slides out between me and the vanity, and leads my pleasure-drunk ass the few steps to the open-ended shower.

Don't do it, asshole. Don't fucking get in there with her.

She leans forward to turn on the water, her fingers gently gripping mine when she pivots back to me. "Don't look so worried. I'll leave my underwear on." She unclasps the button on her jeans. Lowers the zipper. Shucks the pants.

My eyes remain on hers—I'm determined not to fall victim all over again. Intent on keeping some fucking distance between us as she pads into the shower to make that remarkable body of hers all the more tempting as it glistens under the water spray.

My resolve lasts a whole five seconds before I'm powerless to stop my gaze trekking over her. I'm a slave to all her dips and curves. I drag my attention across her tits plastered in the pretty pink bra, along her stomach where my seed dribbles toward that cute belly button, to the matching lace panties, my intent narrowing on the dark circular marks on the inside of her right thigh.

My anger spikes. "Are those bruises?"

She doesn't need to answer. It's fucking obvious. Yet her silence enrages me.

She moves to the far side of the spray, grabbing the soap before resting her back against the tile. She creates a lather in her palms, the bubbles flowing over her fingers.

"Abri, who hurt you?"

"Get in the shower and we can discuss it."

She wants to continue playing games?

Fuck her and the way she strings me along.

I kick off my shoes. Yank off my socks. Then shuck my pants and boxer briefs to stand fully naked. "Who?" I stalk into the shower.

"Why does it matter?"

"You know exactly why."

"You're not murdering another man for me, Bishop."

Yes, I am. And this time I'll make the asshole suffer. "Do you understand how pathetic it is to protect someone who hurts you?"

"He's a good man."

"Great," I snarl. "I can't wait to meet him."

She huffs a laugh. "If I wanted him dead I would've done it myself."

I disagree. She's got too much heart hidden behind all the faux layers of malice.

"His name." I get in her face, my pulse pounding with the need to right the wrongs made against Lorenzo's family. "Who was it?"

She meets my gaze, her eyes solemn. "Why do you care so much?"

"I don't. This is my job."

"It's a few bruises."

"*Any* bruise, unless given in pleasure, is something I'm going to rectify. Any cut or bump or graze. No injury will go unpunished under my watch."

She shakes her head. Subtle. Barely moving.

"Who?" Adrenaline floods my veins. "Tell me a fucking name."

She swallows. Licks her lips. "No."

I slap my palm against the tile. "Do you really want to push our already temperamental civility?"

"No. Just drop it."

"Can't and won't, *la mia sirena ammaliatrice*."

"What does that even mean?"

I grin, the curve of lips feral. "Tell me and I'll tell you."

She rolls her eyes and turns her head away. Fed up looks good on her. *Everything* looks so fucking good.

I grab her chin and press my nose to her cheek, speaking against her skin. "Who do I get to punish, *belladonna*?" I'm alive with the need to avenge. Somehow absolved of my elicit behavior with the promise of retribution.

She shudders, my pulse pounding through her silence until finally she whispers, "It was you, Bishop. You're responsible for those bruises."

I stiffen.

"In the hotel room," she murmurs. "On the bed."

The flashback hits—her thighs around my neck, my fingers digging into her flesh to stop her from choking me.

My anger grows tenfold. At myself. At her forgiveness. At this whole ridiculously messed up situation.

I'm always so fucking angry around her. Clouded, yet undeniably livid.

I release her chin and straighten, glaring down at her. "I'm responsible, yet you ignorantly still consider me a good guy? What the fuck is wrong with you?"

"You *are* a good guy."

I bare my teeth. "Do you want to know—"

"No." She cuts me off, her chin raised in defiance. "I don't want to know. Whatever you plan to say, I suggest you quit wasting your time. I've spent years reading men. Learning their intricacies. Understanding the way their minds work for the sake of underhanded manipulation but also for my safety. And I know enough about you to draw the right conclusions."

"Obviously not."

"You're a good man," she repeats. "You got behind the wheel, while drugged, to save me from Gordon. You ended the life of someone who hurt me. You even held your tongue when I destroyed your steak." Her lips quirk in a subtle smile that quickly fades. "I could've killed you. You were only defending yourself. No harm. No foul."

"I have kids," I snarl.

She balks, her brows pinching.

"That's the last words Finch said before I killed him—*I have kids*." I lean closer, our noses almost touching. "I did not give a shit. I still don't. I have no remorse. No guilt. I've ended the lives of more people than you can imagine, in ways that would haunt you, and I sleep like a fucking baby."

"A bear," she whispers. "You sleep like a bear."

She still doesn't get it.

I turn on my heel, needing to get out of here before I detonate.

"Don't you dare." She grabs my arm. "Don't walk away from me."

I scowl over my shoulder, one quick heartbeat away from making her regret how fucking stupid she's being.

"If those bruises are such a monumental crime, then make up for it." She raises a defiant brow. "Get on your knees, *macellaio*."

My nostrils flare. "Get on my fucking knees?"

How dare she? And how dare my cock harden all over again?

I picture myself there. At her feet. Between her thighs. But it's not remorse that would guide my mouth to her pussy. It's all the pent up rage I need to get out of my system.

She lowers her gaze, taking in the sight of my resurging dick with the slightest hint of superiority. "Be a good little *macellaio* and give me what I want."

This is a game to her, *fun*, while I'm on the precipice of losing my ever-loving mind over a woman I shouldn't look at, let alone touch.

I grin angrily at the taunt, so full of malicious intent I'm almost scared for her. *Almost*. "You still want to believe I'm a good guy?" I eat up the space between us, getting in her face. "You're committed to playing these games?"

"I'm not—"

I clamp a hand over her mouth, the sound of her gasp shooting through the cracks between my fingers. "You want me on my knees, belladonna?"

She stares at me. Wide-eyed. Breaths heaving.

Say no. Say fucking no, Abri. For your safety. For my sanity.

She nods.

I feel the movement through every inch of my skin, my pulse ratcheting to higher levels with each dip of her chin.

I want her. Want *this*.

I can already taste her. Can imagine just how sweet that poisonous pussy will be on my tongue.

"Be careful what you wish for." I palm the back of her thigh with a rough hand, violently yanking her foot off the ground, earning another gasp as I guide her leg around my hip, then grab the crotch of those panties. "I don't appreciate misconceptions."

That's all I'm doing. Dissolving an illusion. Abolishing this *good guy* fallacy.

I tug at the lace. Yank. Her hips jerk with the rough handling as the material tears.

She needs to be scared of me. Fearful of my capabilities.

She'll have more marks tomorrow. More bruises to convince her I'm not the man she mistakenly thinks I am.

I sink to the floor, hauling her thigh over my shoulder, the shower spray pummeling my back.

I face off with the trim patch of curls between her thighs, my dick stiff as stone. She's pretty and pink, her pussy glistening, the puffy flesh calling my fucking name.

I despise how my mouth salivates. The way my tongue throbs. Her soft fingers threading through my hair don't help either.

This needs to be a lesson for both of us.

A fucking circuit breaker.

I palm her stomach. Shove her back against the wall.

She gasps again, in shock or anticipation I'm not sure. I don't give a fuck because I'm already planting my face between those impeccable thighs.

I latch onto her clit and suck, *hard*, the scent of her arousal filling my lungs as I slide both hands to her ass, my fingertips digging into all that lush flesh.

She squeaks. This temptress—this goddamn destroyer of men —*squeaks* as she grips my hair, her hips bucking into me.

The sound is an aphrodisiac. A cast spell.

I want to hear it all over again. To evoke sounds that shame her.

I part her sex with my tongue. Lick her slit. Hold in a groan at the sweetness.

It isn't hard to understand how men get ensnared between these thighs. Every inch of her is perfect, right down to her taste. I can't hold myself back from lapping at her, digging my tongue into her entrance over and over before returning to her clit for a harsh suck.

I feast as she pants, my beard sure to leave a rash on her delicate skin with how far I bury my face into that pretty cunt.

She needs the painful reminder of this pathetic mistake.

"Right there," she whispers.

I should stop and focus elsewhere. Show her that I'm not a slave to her pleasure.

I should.

I. Fucking. Should.

Instead, her moans fuel me to lick faster, suck harder, my blood pounding with the need to hear her cries. She should feel disgusted by my touch. Tainted by what these hands have done to others. Yet when I slide my thumb inside her, she groans, her pleasure vibrating off the tiled walls.

"That feels good," she whimpers.

"You like feeding a butcher?" I stare up at her. "You enjoy the mouth of a murderer between your thighs?"

"I enjoy your mouth, Bishop. The only mouth that's ever been there."

Her words hit like a blow.

"You're shocked?" She raises a brow. "You think men willingly go out of their way to selflessly pleasure a sure thing?"

"I want that list, belladonna." I snarl against her pussy. "Every motherfucking name."

"It's yours." She nods, rocking into me, her core clamping around my thumb as I pump it inside her. "Just don't stop."

If only I could.

I flick her clit with my tongue, my cock throbbing for attention, my balls aching and tight. She tastes like heaven to this unworthy sinner.

"Holy shit." She bucks. "*Bishop.*"

"Keep saying my name," I growl. "Never forget who's between your thighs."

Her fingers tear at my hair. "*Bishop*." It's a plea this time. "*Macellaio*."

How did I end up here? Obsessed with her? Addicted?

This woman fucks with my head. With my lust. With my life.

I splay the rest of my pumping hand over her ass, sucking harder on her clit while my index finger slides between her crack to find its target.

She gasps. Her thighs squeeze.

"I want this ass," I growl against her pussy. "Give it to me."

"I…" She pants, her grip unrelenting in my hair, her leg tight around my neck. "I've never…"

Of course she hasn't. This woman, who's decimated empires with her body, has never orgasmed for another. Never been devoured. Never had her ass plundered. Never been with a man who's given a motherfucking shit about her.

My pulse rages with the injustice, the wildest storm raging inside me because I shouldn't be the man to steal so many of her firsts. But the need to claim ownership becomes a living, breathing thing in my veins.

"Relax." I circle my thumb inside her pussy, lapping her juices in between flicks of her clit. "Breathe."

Her panting increases—harsh, fast gasps that make her perfectly encased tits rise and fall in the soaked fabric. She's such a pretty sight. The damp hair. The pink cheeks. The wild eyes.

"Take what I give you." I press my fingertip against her ass. Slow. Edging it inside her. "*Sii la mia brava ragazza.*" I fight the need to groan at how she wiggles and jolts as I slowly sink a knuckle deep.

She whimpers. Mewls. Each sound makes my dick pulse as I work my thumb and finger in tandem, fucking her with my hand.

"*Oh, God*," she says in a rush. "Give me more."

"Such a greedy little belladonna." I pump faster. Harder. I want her as crazed and addicted as she's made me. Bitter and enraged.

Her gasps increase. Each breath is a hiss of surprise that makes my cock weep.

I can't deny myself any longer. I can't fight the ache.

I fist my length with my free hand, already poised to blow a second rapidly pitiful load as I continue to feast on her. Harsh, brutal sucks. Punishing repetition.

Her breathing grows frantic, her whimpers melodic as her nails dig into my scalp. "*Macellaio.*"

I jerk harder, the reminder of who I am seeming meaningless when pitted against the crime of succumbing to her.

"I'm close." She squeezes my face between her thighs. "So close."

I feel it before she takes her next breath. The flutter of her pussy around my thumb. Her ass tightly clenching my finger. She comes undone against my hand, her delirious sounds of pleasure shoving me over the edge.

I pump my cock, my orgasm painful in its potency, my cum spilling against the tile.

She gushes against my face, fucking flooding my mouth. I drown in her, hungry for every last drop, my pulse frantic, the high blinding.

But all too soon the pleasure fades, my dick taps out, and Abri slumps back on the wall.

I inch away to stare up at the temptation I should've ignored yet couldn't deny.

I may have lasted longer than her usual marks but I still became another pathetic fool to be notched into her bedpost.

She peers down at me, her eyes narrowed as if she's reading my mind. "This means nothing," she says softly.

It *should* mean nothing. *Less than* nothing.

Yet even my position on the tiled floor seems to be a sign of the exact opposite—me on my knees, her towering above me, my actions akin to worship.

You dumb prick.

Her leg slides off my shoulder, her grip falling from my hair. She watches me with caution, her chest still heaving with frantic breaths.

This whole lot of nothing is starting to feel a lot more like something.

Something I'm not familiar with. Something that festers without permission. A potent poison in my veins.

She's becoming more than a job.

More than a pain in the ass.

More than just my boss's niece. Or my best friend's sister.

Fuck.

I remove my hands from her body. Rest back on my haunches. Let the shower spray batter my shoulders as I hang my head, her taste clinging to my tongue.

I've fucked up—that much is clear. Yet the worst part is that even with the acknowledgement, I still crave more.

The hunger hasn't lessened.

What the hell has she done to me?

Slow fingers run through my hair, gently pulling the strands, dragging my head backward.

I could stop her. Could pull away. But I'm a fucking shmuck, starved with the need to look up at those eyes.

"It means nothing," she repeats, her cheeks flushed, her long blonde strands clinging to her shoulders as her breasts haunt my periphery. "*You* mean nothing, Bishop."

Her words are meant as a pardon. To appease the mistake of diving face-first between the thighs of forbidden fruit. But it only increases the severity of this shit show, her reasoning seeming to compound the fuck-up.

"You still mean jack-shit to me, too, belladonna." I yank my head away from her touch and wipe the back of my hand over my mouth as I shove to my feet. "We're done here."

Her chin raises as she stares at me through a mask of indifference. No words. No taunts. She denies me what I want. A fight. I need to snarl and bark and spew venom until she hates me as much as I hate myself.

Instead, those long lashes bat with gentle lethargy, her cheeks still flushed with the pleasure I provided. "You're vibrating."

Yeah, with fucking hostility. I thrum with it. My limbs tense with self-loathing.

"Your cell," she clarifies, glancing to the vanity. "You should get that. It could be about my mother."

Fucking hell.

I turn and stalk from the shower, yanking a towel off the rack to wrap around my waist before snatching my phone.

"Give me good news," I grate at Najeeb in greeting.

"Can do. I got a hit on your woman with the facial recognition software. She was on Interstate 64 just outside Louisville, Kentucky, roughly twenty-four hours ago."

What the fuck is Adena doing in Kentucky?

"So I went back and followed her path," he continues. "I've tracked her through every freeway checkpoint from Virginia Beach. It looks like she's making the car trip home."

I frown, turning my back to Abri as she quickly washes herself with soap and then shuts off the shower. "She mistakenly assumed the road would make her less detectable than an airport."

"Probably. She's in a rental. A black Dodge Durango. And she's not alone. There's a male driver. I haven't been able to get a clear image of him yet, but I'll run what I've got through my photo-editing software a few more times and send something over as soon as it's worthwhile."

"I also want details on any other cars that might be following her. I need to know if she's got a team."

"Already done. I haven't seen an entourage. It's just her and the guy."

"Good. Keep me updated and get me those images asap."

"Will do."

I disconnect the call, all too aware of Abri wrapping herself in a towel behind me.

"Was that about my mother?" she asks.

I grab my weapons off the vanity and my clothes from the floor. "She was sighted in Kentucky. If we're lucky, she's on her way back to Denver." I start for the door. "I'll see you in the morning."

"Wait. What happens now?"

She reaches for me and like motherfucking Spiderman, I swing away from contact at warp speed.

Her lips press tight, the edges twitching upward as she attempts to suppress a laugh.

"What?" I snap.

"Nothing." She raises her palms in placation. "It's just cute how you're scared of me, that's all."

How the fuck could I be scared of her when her taste still lingers on my goddamn tongue?

"That's the second time you've used *cute* to ignorantly describe me, let alone *scared*," I snarl. "I suggest it be your last."

Her lips press harder, her humor barely contained. "Okay.

Understood." She nods, still holding up those palms in surrender. "But can you please tell me what happens now?"

"Nothing. Not a fucking thing. You keep your hands to yourself and I'll do the same with mine."

She snaps her gaze to the tiled floor, her cheeks high with a bubbling smile.

She meant what happens with her *goddamn fucking mother*.

Jesus Christ, Bishop. You dense son of a bitch.

"We sit tight until we have more information," I grate through clenched teeth, continuing from the bathroom without a backward glance. "Goodnight."

"Night."

I march down the hall, my vision clouded with her fucking grin as I close myself into my darkened bedroom.

I slam my clothes and towel on the floor beside my bed. Dump my cell on the bedside table. Shove my weapons under my pillow. Fling back the covers. Then slide my naked ass across the mattress as my temper sizzles.

This bullshit with her is dangerous.

I'm no good for her. Even in small, sordid doses. No matter if it's for distraction, to ease anxiety, or merely for shits and giggles. And she sure as hell ain't good for me either. She's a certifiable, grade-A manipulator who enjoys fucking with the male mind.

I run a hand through my damp hair and listen to her brush her teeth. I stare at the ceiling a few minutes later when her feet pad down the hall. There's a squeak of hinges. Her bedroom door closes.

Good.

That's where she needs to stay. Preferably until her brother/s come to claim her ass.

I don't want to see her again. To hear her. To drag her sweet scent into my lungs.

I snatch my cell off the bedside table and tap out a message to Langston.

ME

Hurry up and get your ass to Denver. Got news on Adena. She's headed this way.

I shouldn't rush his recovery. Shouldn't push him when he almost died a few days ago. But this shit with Abri has to stop. I can't remain alone with her. Not when each taste of her has me craving more.

Sleep doesn't come.

Half an hour passes before I hear Abri call her mother and leave another pathetic, pleading message.

Soon after, she treks back down the hall, reigniting my annoyance at the thought of her opening my door. But she continues to the kitchen, the gurgle of the coffee machine poking at my anger.

I want to rail on her for focusing on caffeine instead of sleep. To get out of bed and in her face about the need for rest.

Instead, I keep my ass firmly planted under the covers, my imagination crystal clear as I picture her walking around the house in her sexy satin nightwear.

I don't even budge an inch hours later when it sounds as though she's camping outside my door again. I won't carry her back to her room tonight. Won't stare down at her through the darkness and think of all the things that perfect mouth could do while she rests peacefully.

I clench my fists. Thump my pillow. Turn onto my side. I'm so fucking exhausted because of her. Heavy with accumulated fatigue.

No more.

No more thoughts.

No more fantasies.

No more letting my dick run point on this fucked up situation.

I'm going to pass out, sleep like the dead, and wake up a new man—one that's entirely done with illicit thoughts of Abri Costa.

At least that's what I plan, but when I finally lose consciousness my hands are right back on that perfect body.

20

ABRI

I ATTEMPT TO SLEEP IN MY OWN BED.

Once I fail miserably, I try to occupy myself with caffeine.

That doesn't work either. The moment I take the last sip of liquid fuel, the sex high now well and truly faded, my mind reverts to attack mode, my thoughts flooding with anxieties I'm still not ready to face.

Being with Bishop had been the most exquisite distraction.

Which is why it isn't surprising that I now find myself in front of his bedroom, clueless at how I'm going to explain the late-night interruption when I whisper against the door, "Hey, are you awake?"

He doesn't answer. I'm not sure why I expect him to after he practically ran to get away from me earlier.

I grab the knob, quietly turning it until I can push the door open.

"Bishop?" I step inside, the far-off light from the kitchen drifting down the hall to cast a slight glow across the carpeted floor, his bed bathed in shadow. "Can we talk?"

I don't care what we chat about. He can yell at me for all he likes. The verbal sparring match will still be a reprieve from the mental onslaught that has me picturing my daughter in an unmarked grave as my mother shovels dirt on top.

"Are you asleep?" I ask.

I'm certain he's not. I know what his slumber sounds like and it isn't this calm, muted silence.

"I can't switch off." I close the door behind me and creep toward the end of his bed. "And although I'm well aware that's not your problem, I wondered if I could stay in here in case you get an update. That way I don't have to lie in my room wondering if I'll be alert enough to hear if you get another call."

Not only do I want a distraction and the ability to eavesdrop, I also need the opportunity to test the waters. To see how much he loathes me for forcing him to face his lust.

We both know he never wanted to touch me.

Not the first time. Or the second.

And the thought of him regretting the moments that are now woven around my libido like silken ribbons digs into me like a vine of spiky thorns.

"It can be like last time but in reverse." I head for the side of the bed I previously slept on. "It's my turn to stay on top of the covers."

Still there's no response.

No bark of protest. No hiss of dissent.

"Bishop?" I murmur.

He grunts and I'm not sure if it's an affirmative response, but I take it, gently easing myself on top of the duvet, my head hitting the pillow.

Before I can relax my shoulders, the mattress jolts. There's a snap of movement. A swish of sheets. Then hard, unyielding metal digs into my cheekbone, his gun cold against my flaming skin.

I don't move.

Barely even breathe.

"Bishop..." I force myself not to succumb to panic, to remain calm like my father taught me, but that training is hard to cling to under the threat of death. "I'm sorry. I shouldn't have—"

"*Abri?*" Confusion clings to his gruff tone. "What the fuck?"

The cold metal disappears. The bed bumps. His bedside lamp flicks on, blinding me.

I squeeze my eyes shut, thankful for a reason to turn my face away.

"Are you fucking crazy?" he snaps. "I could've killed you. You're lucky I grabbed my gun and not my goddamn knife."

I scrunch my nose and nod. "It was stupid."

So fucking stupid.

I hold the air in my lungs, swallowing back the bile that's

formed a whirlpool in my stomach. Obviously, it's not the first time I've been caught in a dangerous bedroom situation, but it's the only instance where I've willingly gone to a man with my guards lowered.

The violent snap back into defense mode has me reeling.

"I don't know what I was thinking." My voice breaks, betraying what little strength I'd hoped to display.

"Shit," he mutters. "Are you good?"

"Yeah." I nod. Wave him away. I'm well aware it must be unconvincing when my eyes remain clamped shut.

"Look at me," he demands.

"Just give me a second." I sink my teeth into my bottom lip, hoping the urge to vomit will suddenly disappear.

"*Now*, Abri. Fucking look at me."

So many times he's demanded my attention. So many instances when the moments following his order have brought me back from the brink of a panic attack.

I open my eyes, his fathomless blue depths staring back at me in furious anguish.

"You're safe," he states firmly.

I nod even though I feel more volatile than ever. More hollow. More alone.

I raise onto my elbows. "I, ah, really am sorry." I push from the bed, force a laugh. "That was a close call."

He watches me, his gaze fierce enough to heat my cheeks. "It was a dangerous fucking call, belladonna. You're lucky I didn't splatter that gorgeous face all over my pillows."

I wince. Nod again. Squeeze my fingers together in an attempt to stop the tremble.

His attention lowers to my clutched hands, his jaw ticking. "You're not okay."

The concern threatens to break me. "It's the adrenaline."

His scowl deepens. But he doesn't offer more concern. Instead, he rolls over, flicks off the light and plunges the room into darkness. "Get into bed, Abri."

I pause. "Yours or mine?"

He scoffs. "God forbid I deny a woman who risks her life to climb between my sheets."

The heat from my face lowers, carving a path through my chest.

The overwhelming sense of stupidity hasn't fled. It's still right there, pumping like a freight train through my veins. Yet comfort sings to me, pushing me to move forward.

I pull back the covers, my body remaining a slave to the tremble in my limbs, and slide in beside him.

For a few tense moments, there's nothing but the still of night. The heavy silence of mistakes.

Neither one of us moves. It's a painful stretch of time where I relive the memory of his gun pressed to my cheek, my heart remaining in my throat.

"Have you finally learned to be frightened of me, belladonna?"

Something about his question sends a shiver over my skin—one that isn't entirely unpleasant. "I'm not scared of you, Bishop. I am scared of guns, though."

"A gun is an object. It's the person wielding it that's the threat."

"I know. But..."

"There's no 'but.' You crept into my room while I was asleep. *I* could've killed you. *I* would've been the one responsible for your death. Not a goddamn piece of metal."

Bile continues to churn in my stomach, and the last thing I want to do is continue being a withering fool in front of him. He's already endured my tears and panic attacks. The pleas for help and the blubbering about my past.

"You're right." I throw back the covers, resigned to spending the night in my room, cuddled up with my demons.

"Stay." His hand latches around my arm.

The adrenaline lessens, but I'm left trembling for other reasons.

If I were a stronger woman, his touch wouldn't stop me from doing the right thing and walking out of here. Unfortunately, I'm still a pitiful fool, clinging for any form of comfort.

"We both know it's not a good idea for me to stay," I whisper.

"It's only to curb the panic." He tugs me down to the mattress, his strength guiding me to spoon against his chest. "To stop the shaking." His arm drapes over my waist, holding me tight. "I'm a son of a bitch, but it doesn't mean I want you spiraling into hysteria out there on your own."

I should tell him I'm not on the brink of an attack. That I tremble for different reasons. Only the words don't form. Not those ones, anyway.

"What a gentleman." I glide my hand over his, my heart skipping a beat when he opens his palm to mine, allowing me to thread our fingers together.

"I'm no gentleman, Abri. Never forget I'm a butcher."

"You forgot I was a siren," I counter.

"I didn't forget. I just fell victim."

I wince into the darkness, his palm warm against my chemise.

"I don't like being bait, belladonna." He trails his hand in circles along my belly, slow, almost romantic in the exquisite softness. "But denying you is impossible."

"You weren't bait. Tell me you know that." I dance my fingers between his, our fingertips waltzing between the sheets. It's such a simple touch. Basic. Yet the sensation sinks through to my nerve endings, tingling all the way to my bones.

"I know this is a mistake," he speaks against the back of my neck. "I can either help find your daughter. Or we can spend our days fooling around. There's no room for both."

"Why?" The needy question escapes without consent.

"Because I can't focus on what matters when all the blood in my brain has travelled to my dick."

I wish I could laugh through the pang in my chest.

He knows there's no choice. My craving for proximity doesn't stand a chance when pitted against Tilly's future.

"You fuck with my head," he adds. "I'm no use to you if all I'm doing is biding time, thinking about the ways I can make you come."

I swallow, my nipples beading painfully against my nightwear. "Then maybe I should go to my room."

"No." His hand becomes an adamant force against my belly. "Tonight you stay here. At least until the fear subsides."

"It wasn't—"

"Even if for a few moments, you feared me, belladonna. And although it pains me to admit, I didn't enjoy it as much as I would've liked."

"How much *did* you enjoy it?" I whisper into the darkness.

His mouth finds my shoulder blade, his lips pressing into my skin as he speaks. "I've never hated anything more."

I squeeze my eyes shut, hoping to kill temptation before it takes hold.

"Don't fear me, Abri. Not physically anyway. I could never intentionally hurt you like that."

"But you could hurt me in other ways?"

"I will. Without a doubt. Emotionally. Psychologically. I'm not a man built for companionship."

"Tell me why?" I ask. "Why don't you have sex? Why don't you kiss? Share your baggage with me. I already shared mine."

"You didn't willingly share anything. If given the choice, your vulnerabilities would've remained hidden."

"So it's vulnerability you hide?"

"Any information can be a vulnerability if used in the right way."

I sigh. "I guess that means you're not going to tell me. Is there no trust between us?"

"Why would there be?" His tone isn't cruel. Merely factual. Blatantly honest.

"I don't know." I shrug. "Maybe because you've had certain parts of your body in explicit parts of mine, and that news wouldn't be welcomed to my brothers or uncle. You must trust me enough not to snitch on you…because I definitely could."

He huffs a laugh, his fingers curling into claws against my stomach. "You blackmailing me?"

"Maybe," I add a playful lilt to my tone. "What would it get me?"

"A one-way ticket to the bottom of a six-foot hole."

I smile. It's just another form of stupidity, but his smug aggression does funny things to me. "I thought you said you'd never hurt me like that."

He nuzzles my shoulder blade, scraping his teeth against the bone. "There's always a caveat, and self-preservation is at the top of that list."

"Then maybe there's a caveat to us fooling around?" I roll toward him, keeping his fingers clutched between us, the outline of his shadowed silhouette staring back at me.

"No."

"Even though you want to?"

He raises my hand to his lips, kissing my knuckles. "Even though I'm dying to."

I always thought nothing would come close to the agonizing

yearning I feel for my daughter's safety. But the current way I ache for Bishop nudges toward that sensation, the wrenching squeeze decimating my insides.

"I can tear the skin off screaming men without remorse, Abri. Yet touching you feels like a crime worthy of damnation."

I shake my head. "I don't understand why."

"Neither do I." He kisses my knuckles again, then slides his hand to my hip, gently guiding me onto my back. "Roll over. It's time you got some sleep."

And that's exactly what I do—sleep—never feeling safer than while locked in the arms of a murderer.

I'm the first to wake, the sun bleeding through the curtains, his body still spooned against mine.

He'll reject me today. The bright light of morning will illuminate his regret and I'll be plastered with the same label every other man has given me after a heated affair.

I'll be a mistake. A massive error in judgment.

There's no doubt in my mind.

My stomach churns, dreading the moment history repeats itself for the millionth time. But I'll get over it. I have to for Tilly's sake.

I gently scoot out from beneath his arm and slide from the mattress.

He grumbles and rolls to his other side. "Don't think about touching that tire. If you run, I'll hunt you down."

I pause at the end of the bed, his threat not invoking the response he's looking for. It's not a deterrent to be chased. To have him consider my safety such a concern that I'm hunted for my own protection only brings a thrill.

"I won't." I walk for the door. "I'll be here when you wake."

I'm standing in the kitchen an hour later, showered, dressed, with a coffee mug cradled in my hands when he enters the room prepared for the day in another immaculate designer charcoal suit.

Given our isolation, I would've thought he'd give up the constrictive threads. But not Bishop. He seems to want to be one hundred percent business one hundred percent of the time.

"Morning," I murmur into my caffeine.

"Morning." He doesn't meet my eyes as he makes his way to the coffee machine behind me, his stride confident, his posture authoritative.

He grabs a mug from an overhead cupboard, and what I assume is a teaspoon from the cutlery drawer, my impatience too potent to withstand the silence.

"Can we ditch the morning-after awkwardness?" I ask. "I'm willing to pretend nothing happened."

He turns on the coffee machine, the gurgle and spit of liquid my only response.

I glance over my shoulder, his narrowed gaze pinning me from a foot away.

"Do I look like I feel awkward to you?" He grabs his filled mug and leans his hip against the counter. "Or were you referring to your own issues?"

"I don't have issues."

"Belladonna, you have many." He takes a sip of steaming liquid. "Daddy ones being at the top of the list."

I can't tell if he's attempting to be funny or malicious. All I know is that his appeal sings more to me than it did yesterday.

I'm left staring at him, taking in the longer lengths of his stubble, the blue of his eyes more piercing in the bright light of day.

He mustn't appreciate the scrutiny because his expression changes under my attention from confident to stern. Arrogant too annoyed.

He pushes from the counter to stand tall, his posture tight and commanding. "Don't look at me like that."

"Like what?"

Here it comes. The thin press of lips. The tight etch of his jaw. He sobers out of the confidence-fueled bravado he walked in here with, his eyes hardening as if I've reclaimed enemy status.

"Like you're—" He snaps his mouth shut.

"Like I'm...?" My stomach twists as I wait for the impending insult. "What? Trying to manipulate you again?"

He remains silent.

It's all the answer I need.

I dump the remainder of my coffee in the sink and leave the mug. "I'm going to take a shower."

I storm for the hall, but he grabs my shirt, yanking me backward.

I stumble into him, my ass to his groin, his hands clamping onto my hips to steady me with the most delicious heat.

"Don't ever assume to know what I'm thinking," he growls near my ear. "You'll be wrong every time."

My heart seizes. "Then tell me what you were going to say."

"Those words are best left unsaid."

I swallow, hating the deliciousness of his firm hands on me when I know his thoughts are unkind. What I feel for him is a sickness. A pathetic, irrational curse.

I turn to him. "Tell me."

I need the rejection. The bitch slap of reality.

I want to hear him say how I'm nothing but a puppet. My father's sinister little slut. I need to hate him so all those wonderfully comfortable feelings of the opposite nature quit haunting me.

"Say it." I hold his gaze. "Let me have your worst."

"You're feisty this morning," he mutters.

No, I'm emotional.

I've spent hours daydreaming about a reality that can't exist with the threat of his rejection waiting in the wings. Now I just want it over and done with. "Say it, Bishop. Tell me not to look at you like I'm my father's deceitful little whore."

His eyes narrow to slits, his chin raising slightly.

Did I hit a bullseye?

"Tell me," I snap. "Say how I look like a pathetic, worthless—"

He clamps a hand over my mouth, tight and painful, his fingers digging into my cheek as I gasp. He swoops closer till we're nose to nose, those harsh eyes glaring. "Speak about yourself like that again and I'll spank those words right out of your fucking mouth. You hear me?"

He pauses. Maybe he wants me to respond. But I have nothing. No words. Only a heated imagination.

"I was going to say, don't look at me like you want me, belladonna," he snarls in my face. "I'm not strong enough to deny you today."

My stomach bottoms, my heart frantically attempting to outrun the stampede of delirium barrelling down on me.

He drops his hand from my face, still glaring, still in my personal space.

I swallow. Drag my teeth over my bottom lip.

His gaze catches the movement, his eyes narrowing with enough intensity to make my mouth burn.

"Don't do that either," he warns. "I already jerked off while you were sleeping, then again in the shower. You're not out of my system yet despite how much I'd prefer otherwise."

Between my thighs, an ache forms. But the pleasure holds nowhere near the potency of the relief that rushes through me for being wrong about his cruelty.

"Don't tell me Abri Costa is speechless." He raises a condescending brow, retreating a step. "I guess that's better than the sass I've dealt with for days."

He walks for the fridge. "I'm more than happy to do what you suggested and forget what happened. I already planned on giving you a wide birth. I'll stay out of your space and you stay out of mine. I'll give you updates as I have them." He pulls open the fridge and all I can think about is how the heat from his touch still lingers on my face. Through my shirt.

I want to touch him like he touches me. Roughly. Without permission.

To take liberties and claim victory over his body as he's done to mine so many times.

My pulse races with the need to return his animalistic energy. To get in his face and demand things of him. To revel in the volatility of whatever this is.

To hell with holding back.

I bridge the space between us, not thinking about the consequences or the potential aftermath as I settle in close. "You prefer my silence to my sass?" My breath quickens as I wrap my arms around his back to his chest, his muscles tensing beneath my touch. "I know a way you can keep me quiet a little longer."

A deep rumble vibrates from his throat as he swings around to face me, kicking the fridge shut. "My preferences wouldn't keep you quiet, belladonna. You'd be left screaming until your throat ran dry."

"I can handle that."

His expression tightens. "I doubt it."

"Give me your worst."

His nostrils flare while he leans closer. "My worst isn't something you're capable of withstanding, Abri."

I smirk. "Chicken?"

"You really like playing with fire, don't you?"

No, I just like playing with him. Not as a game. Not because I see him as bait.

The sole reason is because he's the only human on this earth to have ever made me feel good. "Get me out of your system, Bishop. Let's get this over and done—"

His mouth swoops forward without warning, his lips descending toward mine.

I suck in a breath, so painfully ready for his kiss, but at the last second his path pivots, the contact I long for blistering along the scar at my neck.

I ignore the disappointment and focus on the savagery of his tongue against the sensitive skin, his mouth devouring the brutal memories of how I schemed with Cole Torian to betray my father.

My fingers scramble to undo Bishop's shirt, his kisses unending as he hauls me off my feet to plant my ass on the kitchen counter.

My pants are roughly undone, my waistband tugged down to my ankles.

Then he goes down on me again. It's the second time I've experienced the finer workings of a man's tongue on my sex and both instances have come from Bishop.

He jerks himself off as I orgasm, afterward grabbing a clean dishcloth to silently help mop up the mess.

I'm not surprised when he walks away without a word to close himself into his bedroom.

I try not to fixate on how much he must regret every time he succumbs to me as I busy myself responding to work emails. But once midday hits, he strides into the kitchen and gets in my face with a brief update on my mother's location, then spins me around to face the dining table before bending me over with a rough hand on my back. He pins my chest to the wood as he yanks down my pants, his fingers coaxing me to come all over again.

I orgasm so fast I laugh through the bliss, the shock of such easy euphoria confusing the hell out of me.

We eat lunch in silence. Then he escapes to the back porch to make calls while chain smoking.

I hate being the reason he's killing himself with those cancer sticks. That his inability to deny the chemistry between us is what drives him to the subtle punishment. And still I don't have the decency to look at him with anything other than wild hunger when he comes back inside hours later and we succumb all over again on the living room sofa.

After dinner we shower together, one of his hands in my hair to hold me hostage while the other delves between my thighs.

He glowers as his fingers pump inside me, the harshness of his expression doing nothing to stop me craving the kiss he withholds. But never do his lips brush mine. Never does his cock fill me where I need it most. And always, without fail, his brooding regret shadows the aftermath of every savage coupling.

When he finally retires to his bedroom for the night, I don't wait hours to intrude.

I'm at his door within minutes, silently pushing my way into the darkness, gently climbing into his bed without permission.

He growls his annoyance but his touch finds me under the covers, his strong arm pulling me backward to spoon into his body where I feel most at home.

"Are you close to getting me out of your system?" I whisper.

"It's only a matter of time, belladonna." He grinds his cock against my ass. "Who knows what the next twenty minutes will bring."

21

BISHOP

I wake to the single vibration of my cell on the bedside table and grab it while Abri remains asleep beside me.

> LANGSTON
>
> We're on our way.

Shit.

I slump back against the pillows and run a hand through my hair.

Of course he's coming now that I've succumbed to his sister enough times that her taste permanently lingers on my tongue.

I should've ended it last night.

Are you close to getting me out of your system? Her question was a blinding neon sign to quit this shit. An escape route.

Yes, Abri. Not only am I close, I'm done. Finished.

That's what I should have said, but it wasn't my response. I had to have her twice more, her greedy pleas only increasing the sexual soundtrack that now runs through my head on a loop.

Every time I touch her I want more. There's no relief after release —only increased need. Excessive hunger.

She's a vise, just like the vial she keeps in the top drawer of the nightstand in her room. A weakness I may not need, but fuck, I crave it.

I climb out of bed, careful not to wake her as I grab my gun from under the pillow.

I shower and dress in the bathroom, my suit no longer just hiding the weapons I carry but also the marks she's left on my body. The hickeys. The scratches.

I'm in the living room on the sofa when the squeak of mattress springs carry from my bed, followed by the pad of soft footfalls. And like a spineless prick, I march to the front porch for a cigarette, kidding myself that I'm not trying to hide from her.

She needs to be told Langston is coming. He could be hours. Or minutes. Not that it matters. She'll sharpen her claws as soon as she finds out I told him to get his ass here.

I breathe the nicotine in deep, the early morning sun bearing down on my face as the front door opens and she walks outside.

Her hair is damp around her shoulders, and even though she's showered, all that covers her is one of my button-downs, the swamping size making her seem smaller. More vulnerable.

She smiles, subtle and somehow timid. Like she's shy despite the wicked things she's done to my body and the sinful things I've done to hers.

"Hey," she murmurs.

I jerk my chin in greeting and take another drag.

She continues toward me, walking up to me. *Into* me.

Her arms wrap around my waist, her chest pressing against mine, her gentle curves somehow softening my hard edges.

Fuck she feels good. Smells good. Looks good.

I slink a loose arm around her back, casual and uncommitted, my slow retreat from idiocy already in full swing.

She rests her cheek to my shoulder and stares toward the dirt road leading to the house. "You shouldn't smoke."

I exhale the toxins high above her head. "You worried it's going to kill me, belladonna?"

"No. You should quit because I won't like the taste."

I tense. God knows why.

I've never come close to kissing her. Not physically anyway. Mentally is a different story. But her mouth won't get a chance to be on mine after I tell her what today brings.

Regardless, I find myself snuffing the cigarette against the porch railing like a chump and dumping it in the ashtray at my feet.

"We need to talk." I lean away, giving her the hint to do the same.

"Can I say something first?" She retreats a step, her arms falling to her sides. "I know this means nothing to you." She waves a hand between us. "And that's fine. I just…" She frowns. "I really wanted to say…"

Shit.

I wipe a rough hand over my mouth, unsure how to stop whatever carnage is about to spill from her lips. "I was clear on what—"

"Bishop, please." Those beautiful baby blues meet mine. "This is hard for me. I've never had anyone care about my safety before. Not me as a person. Only as an asset. And I just want you to know that I appreciate—"

"Abri. I get it. You don't have to—"

"But I do." She winces. "Not just because it's good for me to step out of my comfort zone and voice appreciation, but because I think someone like you needs to hear it."

Someone like me?

A criminal? A murderer? A cold, heartless son of a bitch?

"You've done a lot for me in a short space of time." She inches into me, making me stiffen when her fingers idly grip the bottom of my shirt. "And although it's clear the intimacy means nothing on a romantic level, it sure packs a punch that a guy actually cares about my enjoyment for once. You're the first to make me feel human instead of a mere object, as pathetic as that sounds."

It's not pathetic. Those men never should've had the ability to touch someone like her. I shouldn't have either. But I can't tell her that.

"I trust you," she murmurs.

I fight to hide a cringe.

"And you're obviously uncomfortable with the admission." She chuckles. "Which is okay. I didn't say any of this because I was looking for some form of reciprocated admiration."

The crunch of gravel carries in the distance, adding a lead weight to my gut. "Abri, listen, I'm—"

"No." She smiles. "Don't bother saying something awkward and completely out of character. Just let it be what it is—a few words of thanks that needed to be spoken and not necessarily acknowledged."

The rumble of the approaching vehicle grows, becoming more

than background noise. It's the sound of the inevitable end to this messy hookup.

She looks to the hill, her brow furrowing as she focuses on the dirt road. "Can you hear that?"

I itch to light another cigarette. "Yeah."

She glances at me in confusion. "Should we be worried? Is someone coming?"

I don't answer. Instead, I hold her gaze, memorizing the calmness of her gorgeous features as they slowly transform.

"You're expecting company?" She frowns.

I keep staring, keep letting reality sink in.

She stiffens, her hands dropping from my shirt. "My brothers?"

I incline my head, the confirmation subtle even though I get a front-row seat to the way it punches through her, parting her lips and widening her eyes.

A car enters my periphery. The same black Lincoln Langston drives whenever he lands in Denver. She turns to watch it crest the hill and travel toward us.

When her attention meets mine again, the gentle beauty of a woman I've learned to appreciate in such a short space of time has transformed back to the venomous viper I faced at the gala.

"*Who?*" she barks. "Matthew? Salvo? Remy?"

"Matthew."

"And you asked him to come." There's no question in her tone, only vicious aggression as her chin rises in disdain.

"I told you I'd hurt you."

Her eyes flare in outrage. "That's it? That's your apology?"

"I'm not going to apologize for doing the inevitable." I push from the railing and she backtracks, fleeing from me. "I haven't told him your secrets. I'll leave that up to you."

"How fucking thoughtful."

I shrug, pretending I don't care that I've betrayed her. That it's no biggie that I've become a fucking snitch. "It's the least I could do."

"No, the least would be not telling my brother to come here. The same brother who killed my father and put me in a position where I'm scrambling to get a sign of life from a daughter none of my siblings even cared to notice I had."

Okay, well, that jab feels like shit. Still... "You knew this was coming, Abri."

She scoffs, her hand raising to her neck, seeming to instinctively cover the scar she trusted to leave uncovered in front of me for days. "When did you tell him to come?"

"Does it matter?"

"Yes. I want to know if it was before you got what you wanted from me. Or after you used my body like everyone else."

My nostrils flare. "That's not how it was."

"Really?" She drops her arm to her side and straightens her shoulders. "So you contacted him *prior* to getting a piece of Emmanuel's little whore?"

The blood heats in my veins. "I've told you not to talk like that."

"Or what? Are you going to bend me over and spank the words out of me like you previously threatened? I'm sure my brother would love to see that."

I bite my tongue, refusing to give her the fight she wants when the result of our colliding aggression will set this house on fire.

"Put the tire back on my car, Bishop." She turns on her heel and starts for the house. "And stay out of my fucking way." The front screen slaps closed in her wake. Seconds later, another door slams inside, rattling the windows.

"Fucking perfect," I mutter.

I lean back against the railing and pull out my cigarettes, lighting a smoke as the Lincoln pulls up in front of the house. Lorenzo is in the front passenger seat, one of his men acting as chauffeur.

The driver cuts the engine and Layla gets out the far back door, giving me a cringing smile over the roof of the car.

Great. She saw enough to pull whatever the hell that pitiful expression is meant to be.

She strides around the trunk to the opposite side of the vehicle and helps Langston climb out, the sight of him dousing my self-loathing in a layer of guilt.

He's fucking frail, his movements slow and measured as he struggles to his feet.

If only I'd been there when Emmanuel attacked. If I'd stayed in Virginia Beach instead of coming here...

Then Abri would've been raped in that hotel room.

I take another drag, holding the smoke in my lungs.

Langston's hard eyes meet mine, making it clear he saw enough between me and his sister to determine I deserve his spite. Layla nestles close to his side, wrapping her arm around his back, slowly guiding him toward the house in short steps.

The chauffeur attempts to do the same with Lorenzo, exiting the car to open the passenger door only to be batted away with a walking stick.

"If you continue to fuss around me like I'm a newborn I'll make sure walking becomes a difficulty for you, too." Lorenzo's Italian accent is thick with frustration. "Stay in the car. Or outside the house. I don't care which. Just stay away from me."

"Yes, sir." The guy nods.

I could smirk at how green the driver is, how fucking pathetic and new, but the fact Lorenzo had to bring a novice to Denver shows the success of Emmanuel's onslaught. Many men must have been lost.

Langston reaches the bottom step and grabs the railing. "I can take it from here, *mia dea*."

Layla's lips part. She wants to protest. Instead, she closes her mouth and nods, remaining close as she watches him ascend the stairs as if he's a toddler learning to walk.

He climbs onto the porch to face me, animosity swimming in his eyes. "I thought you said you weren't fucking my sister."

"I'm not." I take a drag, exhaling the smoke slowly as he scoffs.

"Don't use your word games on me, Bishop. I know you." He continues to the door, Layla reaching the screen seconds before him to pull it open and allow him access.

She watches me as Langston moves inside, her gaze bright with enjoyment.

"You got something to say?" I sneer.

"It looks like you've got yourself in a pickle." She smirks. "It couldn't have happened to a nicer guy." She blows me a kiss and follows after Langston, the screen slapping shut behind her.

I deserve that after the shit I've given her recently. Doesn't stop me glaring though.

"I must admit, *figlio*—" Lorenzo hobbles his way up the stairs, favoring his left leg. "—this is not what I expected to find when Matthew told me Abri was in some sort of trouble."

"There's nothing going on." I butt my cigarette, too pissed off to even smoke anymore.

"I guess that depends on your definition of nothing." He indicates the door with the wave of a hand. "Are you coming inside?"

"No." I turn my back to him, resting my forearms on the railing to stare across the yard. "I'm not family. She can explain her situation to you on her own."

She wouldn't want me in there anyway. Probably already has a knife clutched, waiting for the moment I come within slashing distance.

"As you wish." His footsteps trek across the wooden porch boards, then the screen door squeaks open. "We will discuss this later."

"I can't fucking wait." I glare at the scenery. The birds, trees, and fucking clouds.

Lorenzo's guy rests against the hood of the car, drawing my attention. I glare at him too. Glare so fucking hard he snaps rigid and scampers to climb into the driver's seat.

Asshole.

If he's not careful, he'll turn into the punching bag I desperately need. Or better yet, target practice.

I breathe deep. Inwardly curse myself. Sulk like a motherfucker.

I should've made Remy and Salvatore chase Abri from their house. I should've hightailed it from that pretentious mansion as soon as my sedated ass became conscious.

I've never fucked up like this before. I don't appreciate the way it feels.

I stay there for more than half an hour. Just me and the goddamn birds in the trees, my usually nonexistent conscience now a yabbering, judgmental prick.

I can't stop picturing how Abri is retelling her story. If her anger toward me will keep the demons at bay as she relays the atrocities inflicted upon her.

Will Langston know what to do if the words become too much and she begins to panic? Will he be able to calm her like I did?

I shove from the railing and drag my feet to the lawn.

Will they come get me if she hyperventilates? Will they stop her descent into madness before she passes out?

I clench a fist, battling the unknown as I make my way around the side of the house.

I need to know what's going on. How she's handling reopening freshly cut scars.

I continue to the back of the building, planning to stay outside. Have another smoke. I don't want to be in the conversation, but being able to observe it will ease the knife that's tightly twisting between my ribs.

I take the steps onto the porch, subtly looking through to the kitchen from the corner of my eye to find Langston and Lorenzo at the dining table with Layla in the kitchen at the coffee machine.

Where's Abri?

I quit the pretense and scan the room without subtlety, waiting for my belladonna to scoot out of the pantry or pop up from beneath the counter.

But there's no popping or scooting.

She's not there.

Has she already quit story time to wallow in her room?

No. If Langston was in the know, he'd currently be sitting there in thinly veiled shock instead of continuing to scowl at me with volatile rage.

I raise my arms in question and mouth, "*What's going on?*"

"You tell me," he yells back.

Fuck this shit.

I stalk to the glass door, yank it open, and continue a foot inside.

"What did she tell you?" I demand.

Langston's eyes narrow. "We can't get her to show her face, let alone talk. Care to explain why?"

I glance to the hall as if she'll miraculously appear just because I've mentally demanded it of her. "Where is she?"

"Locked in one of the bedrooms," Lorenzo offers. "I think it's time you told us what's going on."

"I can step outside if you'd like." Layla approaches the table, two filled coffee mugs in hand, and places them down on the wood.

"I've already made it clear it's not my story to tell." I keep my gaze on the hall, willing Abri to show her face and let me know she's okay.

"But that's *all* you've made clear," Langston mutters. "I'm losing patience, my friend."

The endearment is far from friendly, and I'm getting pretty fucking sick of his holier-than-thou attitude. One more grate against my raw nerves and nobody is going to appreciate where this conversation goes.

"I'll get her." Every limb is tense as I march to the hall and straight past the empty room we've shared the past two nights. It's no surprise she's not in there. Not lingering in the scent of sex and sin.

I stop before the closed door of the second room, her subtle sniff of emotion carrying from the other side of the barrier.

She's crying?

Fuck. My chest grows uncomfortably tight. I'm not built for this shit.

I much prefer the sterile existence I had before this woman messed up my life.

"Abri?" I press my knuckles to the door. Attempt to knock softly. "Let me in."

I give her a beat to respond then test the lock, the handle unmoving. "Open the door, belladonna."

"Put the tire back on my car and I will, *Butcher*."

I grind my teeth, hating how every word we share is inevitably being scrutinized by those eavesdropping. "Open the door." I lower my voice. "Or I'll kick it down."

She ignores me.

"Abri," I warn.

The quiet continues.

Lorenzo, or maybe it's Langston, clears his throat from the living room. When I look down the hall Layla is standing at the opening.

"Want me to give it a try?" she asks.

I bare my teeth.

"Jesus." She raises her hands in surrender. "I was only trying to help."

"Don't," I snarl.

"Understood." She turns and walks out of view, muttering under her breath.

I wish I could do the same. Walk away. Get the fuck out of here.

Instead I turn to the door separating me from Abri and rest my forehead against the barrier between us. "Open the door, belladonna." The request is barely audible. "You have to tell them what's going on."

"No, thank you," she replies with a chipper tone. "I'd prefer to stay in here and self-medicate until you fix my fucking car."

Self-medicate? The sniffing was because of the coke?

Son of a goddamn bitch.

My temper explodes, all hope of resolving this peacefully disappearing in a blink as I step back, then plant my foot below the door handle with a heavy kick.

The jamb splinters, the flimsy barrier she'd hoped to keep between us swinging violently toward the wall.

She gives a bitter smile as she sits on the far side of her bed, now dressed in jeans and a blouse, her hair pulled back in a pony. She crosses her arms over her chest, a scarf covering the scar on her neck while that vial lays open and discarded on the carpeted floor.

"Big fucking mistake." I stalk inside, my rage ratcheting to notches I've never felt before.

She raises a haughty brow, but it's the mask she wears that pisses me off the most—the heartless ballbuster persona with her defenses high and her spite higher.

"What the fuck is going on?" Langston yells.

"Nothing," I snap back. "I'll have her out in a minute."

Abri rolls her eyes with a huffed laugh. "Will you?"

"Don't do that," I warn her.

"Do what?"

I continue to the end of the bed, nothing but a few feet of space between me and more mistakes. "Pretend you're a snake. I don't like that game."

"Oh, sweetie, that part was never the game." Her lips curve into a sly smile. "That's the real me. You got played by the fake tears and anxiety attacks."

A cold chill runs down my spine, my breath temporarily locked in my lungs.

She grins. "Surprise."

Bullshit.

Bull-fucking-shit.

She let down her walls for me. I know she did. This right here is the goddamn game.

"It was all an act?" I stalk to her side of the bed, aggression fueling each step.

"Mm-hmm." She nods.

It's a defense mechanism. A barrier to pain. Just like those fucking drugs. All because I dulled the picket fence around her heart. Now those pointy tips are sharp as knives.

"I didn't do this to hurt you, belladonna."

"But I knew you would. That's why I bought myself time with the theatrics. I needed you to find my mother." She shrugs, her malice so fucking pretty, her fire a potent aphrodisiac. "It's what I do."

"No, it's not," I growl. "At least not with me it isn't."

She cringes. "You're embarrassing yourself. Just fix my car so I can get out of here."

"Nobody is touching your car." I stop in front of her, sneering down my nose as she remains on the bed. "You're going to march your ass out to the kitchen and spill your guts to Langston and Lorenzo. In return, they're going to show you the support you never thought you had. How you're not alone. Then you'll see I did right by you."

"Aww." She pouts. "It's sweet that you think I'd actually care."

I clench my jaw, my impatience a ticking time bomb. "You want to keep playing this game? Fine. Go ahead. But if you're going to act like a petulant child then I'll treat you like one." I reach for her, prepared to throw her over my shoulder.

She scrambles out of reach. "Although I appreciate the kinky dominance from a born-again virgin, I'm done using you. I prefer men who know how to fuck."

"I didn't need to know how to fuck to be the first man to make you come though, did I?"

She laughs. "Oh, honey. Do you want to know how many men think they were the first?"

"*Enough*," I roar.

Her façade doesn't falter. My rage doesn't either.

Footsteps skitter down the hall, Layla's pale face entering the doorway. "Please stop fighting. Matthew is refusing to remain at the table, and it's not good for him to be moving so much."

"*Stay where the fuck you are, Langston*," I yell, then lower my tone to spew my ire at Layla. "You'll keep them out there until we're ready. You hear me?"

"I can't—"

"If they come down here, Layla, all hell will break loose, and I'll be the last man standing. Do you understand?"

She glances between me and Abri, her concern for Langston's sister obvious, yet not enough to risk the health of her lover. "We're worried."

"You're impatient," I correct. "Now, like I've already said—fuck off and give us some space."

She stands tall against the command, denying me for numerous heartbeats before she backtracks. "You're such an asshole."

"Yep," Abri mutters. "The biggest."

Layla looks at her with a wince. "Are you okay?"

"I'm fine. But I'd be better if you got my brother out of here."

The wince deepens. "I'm sorry, I—"

"*Leave*," I bark. "Now."

A string of barely intelligible curses flutter from Layla's mouth as she turns for the door. "You've got five minutes."

I wait until her steps fade down the hall, then lunge for Abri, grabbing her ankle to drag her along the bed toward me as she squeals. "Did you take note of that conversation, belladonna? Do you understand what I risk by threatening those men for you?"

"I don't care." She thumps my chest while I climb on top of her, my weight trapping her against the mattress.

"Such sweet fucking lies from the most beautiful lips." I lower my attention to her mouth, aching to kiss the deception out of her system. To leave her gasping and clawing to admit the truth. "You opened up to me. I understand how hard that must have been."

"Get off." She bucks her hips. Thumps my arms. "Or I'll—"

"You'll do nothing." I grab her pummeling hands, yanking them above her head. "It's time for you to listen."

"Get—"

I smash my mouth to hers, immediately drowning in the softness of her lips as she turns rigid beneath me.

It was meant to be a brief peck. A barely there brush of contact to shut her up. But it's been too fucking long. A damn lifetime. And she's become so undeniably pliant beneath me. A frigid little lamb.

I drag my tongue along her mouth in a silent request for access.

She concedes, opening up to me right before her teeth latch into my bottom lip.

She bites down. *Hard*.

"*Fuck*." I jerk back, tasting blood.

"You kiss me *now*, you piece of shit?" she whisper shouts, turning wild, legs kicking, hips jolting, wrists fighting against my hold. "Go to hell."

She knees me in the thigh, too damn close to the family jewels.

"Calm yourself." I release her wrists, giving her some semblance of freedom. "I only did it to get you to listen."

Her eyes flare, a brief glimpse of pain shining in those ocean depths before I'm blindsided by the hard slap that lands across the left side of my face.

"Goddamnit, Abri." I shove off of her and backtrack from the bed, my tongue prodding at the swelling on my bottom lip.

"Fuck you," she whispers, crawling across the mattress.

Yeah, fuck me.

For helping.

For caring.

For obsessing.

Crunching gravel carries from outside, the untimely sound of another car pulling up.

She scrunches her nose, her look of betrayal killing me. "Let me guess—Salvo and Remy are here, too."

22

ABRI

I sit at the head of the dining table. Lorenzo is at the opposite end. Matthew and Layla are to my right. Remy and Salvo on my left.

Bishop is the only one who remains standing, his frame tense near the glass doors, his back to us as he stares out at the hills.

I wish I'd taken that bump instead of throwing the open vial across the room in anger. Maybe then my lips wouldn't continue to burn from his kiss.

I sniff again, just to increase his rage over the misconception of my drug use and suppress my delight when his spine stiffens.

"Bishop said you were in trouble." Matthew gently breaks the silence. "Whatever it is, we're here to help."

I drag my focus to the coffee mug Layla placed in front of me a few minutes ago, the barely visible wisps of heat trailing into the air.

I swallow over the thick lump of my mistakes, trying to ignore the growing mass clogging my throat.

"What's going on?" he continues. "Are you in danger?"

"I think we're all in danger after what you did." I meet his gaze. "Mom will come after us."

"My sister will be handled." Lorenzo gives a sad smile. "There's no need to worry."

"There's no need to worry?" A vindictive chuckle escapes me. "Right... Okay."

"I don't know what's up your ass, Abri, but Dad attacked *us*." There's anger in Salvo's voice. "*He* made the first move."

"Maybe because you planned to kill him," I snap. "What did you expect? You knew he was always two steps ahead."

He raises his chin and relaxes back into his chair. "Well, he's not anymore."

I balk at his callousness. At the stupidity. "You're wrong. He had traps in place for the sole purpose of stopping us from taking him out."

"We'll figure out the money issues." Remy offers with a hint of compassion. "It's going to be fine."

"It's not just about money. That might have been the threat he used to keep you in line, but my relationship with him wasn't the same. He had different tactics. Ones that far outweighed yours."

"We all went through hell." Salvo screws his nose up at me. "Don't play the victim and think whatever you experienced was the worst of it. You weren't aware of our struggles either."

My heart thunders with ragged beats. "I've *never* played the victim."

"Have you looked in the mirror lately?" Salvo says.

I hide my shock, but the verbal backslap stings.

"You'd want to shut your fucking mouth," Bishop warns from across the room, still staring out at the yard. His cold threat washes over me with a glacial chill, stealing the conversation for brief seconds.

Salvo glances from me to Remy to Matthew. "I'm getting tired of his shit. He did his job. Why is he still here?"

"Tell him, Abri." Bishop looks imperious in his arrogant stance. A confounding force.

But I have no plans to do anything for him. Not when I'm still angry.

"I think it's safe to assume Dad dragged you into some sort of mess," Salvo continues. "We already know he had you extort wealthy businessmen. *Married* wealthy businessmen."

My cheeks heat, my heart struggling to pump through the shame.

"Tell him," Bishop sneers.

My throat tightens, making it impossible to speak even if I wanted to.

Bishop swings around to face me, his hard stare meeting mine. "Tell him before I kill him."

I don't waver under his attention. Don't soften to his command. I let his heavy-handedness fuel me, reigniting the strength that's been doused in ice.

"*Mia cara nipote.*" Lorenzo slides his hand across the table, the olive branch left stranded out of reach between us. "I'm not sure how familiar you are with Bishop, but he doesn't make idle threats. I respectfully ask you to consider sharing your struggles so blood isn't shed."

Salvo shoves to his feet. "That asshole has already taken swings at me. My own brother stabbed me in the arm. And my father tried to kill me. I will *not* take kindly to any more threats."

"Then maybe take the hint that nobody likes you." Bishop glares at him.

Salvo returns the visual venom while Lorenzo, Remy, Matthew, and Layla focus on me, waiting for a white flag I don't want to wave.

If I expose the truth, they'll never see me the same way again. I'll no longer get to play pretend and convince everyone I'm the confident, infallible femme fatale. I'll lose the cloak of strength. The mask of power.

I'll be cemented as the pathetic fool I've always been.

"Would you like me to wait outside?" Layla whispers. "I don't have to—"

"No." I shake my head. "I have as much connection to you as half the people in this room."

Matthew winces.

"That may be true." My uncle drags his hand back to the edge of the table. "But the distance between us isn't from lack of trying. I fought to be a part of your life for years. Your father was a stubborn man."

"My father was a monster," I correct.

Lorenzo inclines his head. "So I've learned. Will you tell me more?"

I struggle to align my uncle's reputation with the man seated before me, with his kind eyes and open heart. He's far more considerate than my father. Excessively more patient.

"Sit down," Matthew mutters to Salvo. "We're all tired and impatient. But we have no idea what she's been through."

Remy nods. "We need to stick together."

Salvo scowls but complies, his arms crossing over his chest.

"Please, Abri." Layla begs. "Share your story and let us help you."

I swallow, lowering my attention back to my coffee, my mind filling with flashbacks of all the things I've done.

I don't want to do this. Don't want to slice open my chest and let the filth spew out. But I have to share something. I have to move forward in my search for Tilly. "I have a child."

Layla gasps. That's all there is before the vacuum of silence.

I fixate on the liquid in my mug, my heart thudding in my ears, my palms sweating.

I want to scream. Run. The memory of my little girl's gorgeous face is all that keeps me seated.

"I don't get it." Remy murmurs. "How?"

"Well, brother." I meet his gaze from under my lashes. "When a man and a woman—"

"Don't do that." Bishop warns. "Don't downplay what you've been through."

I hate how easily he reprimands me. How he pretends to care. How I want more.

I drop my stare back to the glossy black mug. "As you all seem to be aware, I helped our father extort powerful men over the years." My pulse falters with the lowering of my guard. "I was careless, fell pregnant, and had a daughter."

"Where is she?" Salvatore asks. "How did you hide the pregnancy?"

"I went away for a few months." I withhold the parts of my story that show weakness. "I had her in secret."

"I remember." Remy speaks quietly, as if to himself. "It was a few years back. You and Dad were constantly fighting and when you returned, you were different. You started agreeing with a lot of his bullshit."

"My life changed during those months." It's a non-explanation I hope they don't notice through their shock. "Everything changed."

"Where is she now?" Layla speaks up. "Are you trying to get her back?"

"I'm trying to keep her safe. But I have no idea where she is. Dad placed her in the care of a loving family as soon as she was born. I get updates every now and then. But we've led separate lives."

"Abri." My name is a warning from Bishop—yet another reprimand.

I raise my chin, ignoring him as I meet my uncle's gaze. "I've never known her location—that's something my parents kept to themselves. And now that my brothers are responsible for our father's death, I fear my mother will do something to Tilly in retaliation."

"Tilly," Layla whispers. "That's such a beautiful name."

I shut out the commiseration in her tone. Block out the pitying glances from my siblings. And I sure as hell disregard the hard stare Bishop pins on me.

"You think she's capable of hurting a child?" Lorenzo asks.

"No." Salvo reaches for me. "She wouldn't do that, Bree."

I drag my hand away. "We both had very different relationships with our parents. Please don't assume to know how they would or wouldn't punish me for your actions."

His face falls. "You really think she'd hurt your daughter?"

"Our mother has hidden her hatred of me for as long as I can remember. I was Dad's favorite asset. She's been jealous of me for years. Catty and malicious behind closed doors. If I didn't believe she was capable of killing Tilly, I wouldn't have humored *him* for as long as I have." I jut my chin at Bishop, his jaw ticking before I quickly return my attention to my uncle. "I've called her non-stop for days. I've left a hundred messages. She won't talk to me. She won't tell me where my daughter is. Do you have the ability to find her?"

"You know I've already got men on it," Bishop grates. "She's driving across country. The last traffic surveillance checkpoint she passed was yesterday morning. She's already halfway through Missouri. And given her timeline from Virginia Beach, I predict she'll be back here in less than twenty-four hours unless she takes a major detour."

The timeframe comes as a surprise. But I don't respond. Don't quit waiting for an answer from the head of one of the most infamous factions of the Italian mafia who glances back at me with sympathy.

"Abri, alongside Matthew, I trust no man more than Bishop." Lorenzo speaks with solemn conviction. "If you'd come to me first, I would've turned to him to do the digging regardless because he's the most capable."

Bishop steps closer, moving to stand a few feet behind my uncle. "All I need is permission to use your contacts and resources to get this moving faster."

"Is there anyone else who can take over?" I ask.

"I'm handling it," Bishop growls. "And I suggest you don't ignore me again, *belladonna*, otherwise we're going to have more problems."

"Or maybe I could handle it myself." I smile at my uncle. "If I had access to your resources—"

Bishop storms to the table and slams his palm against the wood. "It's not a good idea to push me, Abri. Especially when I don't approve of this picture you've painted."

"My artistry isn't your concern." I sit taller as he attempts to stare me down.

"What the hell is going on between you two?" Matthew demands.

"Whatever it is, it's been going on for days." Salvatore glances between us. "They were already at it the day Rem and I got home."

"There's nothing going on." I shove to my feet. "He's just bitter that I bested him. More than once."

I hold my breath, waiting for Bishop to deny it. To tell our audience what really happened. The tears. The weakness. The panic.

All he does is stare, his lips set in a thin line, his chin defiantly high.

I hate that through his anger, he's keeping his word not to spill my secrets. I hate it because I goddamn appreciate it so much.

"Look, I need space from all this." I wave a lazy hand to indicate everyone as I stare at Lorenzo. "Can you help me get in contact with my mother or not?"

"Whatever you need I'll provide it, *dolce bambina*. Everything I have is at your disposal."

Good. Now I can do this my way. I just have to figure out what that way is… And if it involves the man who has my insides twisted in knots.

23

BISHOP

I sit in the driver's seat of Abri's car, the backrest reclined all the way so I lie staring at the ceiling.

This is the only place I've found peace from the house full of assholes who continued to bicker over Abri's situation for hours while the woman in question hid in her room.

Salvatore decided to go on a power trip, making demands and raising his voice.

Lorenzo has been on the phone, barking orders to soldiers.

Remy kept arguing with himself over how Abri could've wound up in her current situation without him knowing.

Layla periodically begged everyone to stop thinking about their feelings and consider what Abri is going through.

And Langston remained quiet, retreating inside himself like he usually does when he wants to start a war.

The squeak of the front screen door has me poking my head up to see Lorenzo hobble onto the porch, his gaze searching the yard.

I don't move. Don't budge. But he finds me, his wrinkled face softening when our eyes meet.

Great. I slump back into the seat. Just what I need.

My annoyance simmers as I wait for him to approach and round the hood.

He opens the passenger door and lowers himself into the seat with a barely audible groan. "I'm not sure where you plan on going, but I don't think you'll get far with three tires."

He's not usually one for humor unless he's trying to soften an approaching blow. This doesn't bode well.

He glances around the Aston Martin's interior as if fascinated by the luxury. "It's a nice car."

"Your niece has good taste."

"Does she?" He shoots me a pointed look.

I glower, unwilling to touch the insinuation as I return my chair to the upright position.

"How are you, *figlio*?" he asks.

"Fine. Najeeb got the location on Adena a few days ago. I've had him tracking her ever since. There's a—"

"That's not what I asked."

I clench my teeth and turn my attention out the side window to stare at the house.

"How are you?" he repeats. "I know it must've been difficult for you to remain here after you heard of the attack."

"I've been kept occupied," I mutter.

"So it seems. I'm surprised how protective you are of Abri."

"I'm not being any more protective than you would've demanded for your niece."

"I have eyes. It's clear she's under your skin."

"Yeah, like a fucking parasite. I've never known a woman to be more infuriating."

"Is that all she is?"

"Jesus Christ." I drag a rough hand down my face. "Not this shit again. I told you I haven't fucked her."

"I already assumed as much. You haven't slept with a woman for as long as I've known you."

I clench my fists through the punch to the gut. "I guess I'm a fool for assuming you'd given me privacy over the years."

"I keep an eye on all those I care about. And you've always been like a son to me. A son who is now clearly developing feelings for my niece."

"I'm doing my job. Nothing more."

He nods slowly. "Then I relieve you of your duty. You can return to D.C. and look after your business interests while Matthew is out of action."

I shut my mouth, letting the deliberate provocation coast by.

"Your presence upsets her," he adds. "It's better for all involved if you leave."

"You said it yourself—I'm the best man you have."

"I don't need the best for this. I already spoke to my sister the day after the shooting. Although hostile, communication has remained open. I'm certain she'll take another call from me, which will give Abri the opportunity she needs to talk to her mother." He grabs my wrist and gives it a fatherly squeeze. "Go back home and we can reconvene at a later date regarding Salvatore taking over my position."

"Adena won't appreciate you taking her daughter under your wing. She'll retaliate."

"Then we will handle it."

"*We?*" I shrug away his hold. "You mean the collection of invalids who have all either been beaten, stabbed, or shot in the past week? Those brothers are worthless in their current state. Even at full capacity, I suspect Salvatore is as useful as a concrete parachute."

"Your criticism speaks volumes, *figlio.*"

"You think I'm jealous," I snap. "Come on, old man. You know me better than that."

"Yes, I know you well." He retrieves his cell from his jacket pocket. "Enough to understand your work here is done. I'll call for the jet to be refueled so you can leave as soon as possible."

"No, you won't." I glare.

"Are you defying an order?"

"I'm staying to get the job done like I always do."

"You want to stay because you care for her."

I look away. If he was anyone else, I'd deny it. I'd shove from the car and refuse to acknowledge such a fucked up accusation. But Lorenzo earned my honesty a long time ago. I won't lie to him. It doesn't mean he needs full disclosure, though. "I'm concerned for her safety. And I believe there's a real threat toward her daughter. I haven't mentioned this to Abri, but it's possible Adena is driving across country to get the girl."

"It's more than that."

My fingers twitch on my thighs as I huff a laugh. "Is this where you warn me away from your niece? Where you tell me I'll never be good enough?"

"*Figlio*, there is no man more worthy." He places his cell back in his pocket. "Despite the things I've asked of you over the years, I know you're a good man. One I may not have fathered, yet I have always claimed as a son. But we both know you will hurt her."

I stare at the house, the tension in my shoulders creeping up my neck.

"You'll push her away, Bishop. Just like you've pushed everyone away all your life."

"I didn't push you away, did I?" I grate.

"You had no choice when you were sick and starving on the streets."

"I haven't been sick or starving for a long time."

"No, you haven't. Instead, you feel indebted and unable to turn your back. After all these years and the blood you shed in my name, you still think you owe me something."

I turn to him. "Have you lost your mind? You're the one who said I could never leave. You told me the only way I could get distance was to follow Langston when he walked. To be his shadow and ensure his safety."

He nods, solemn in his contemplation. "Because what would you do if I gave you freedom?"

Disappear.

Leave the state.

The country.

Preferably the planet.

His lips curve in a knowing smile. "That's right. You'd take off, and nobody would see or hear from you again. And isolation isn't good for souls like ours. Darkness grows in solitude. You need to remain around those who know you to ensure you remain grounded."

"I'm not as fucked up as you think I am." That's a lie—one that brings guilt.

I'm sure I'm far worse than the way he sees me. More temperamental. Overtly fucking hostile under all the layers of control.

"Then stay." He shrugs. "But if you do, you need to love her as she deserves to be loved."

I laugh, for real this time. He's riding rails harder than Abri if he thinks my concern for her has anything to do with love.

"You are my son," he continues. "A Cappelletti at heart. And Cappellettis treasure their women."

"She's not my woman."

"Well, she's no longer your job either. So make the decision—stay and claim her as your own. Or leave and let me take care of my niece."

I scowl at the house—scowl so hard my teeth ache.

He's not going to let this go.

"Fine," I mutter. "I'll fly out in the morning."

"Okay." He nods and opens his door. "If that's what you want, I'll make sure the jet is ready at first light."

It's not what I want and that fucker knows it, but I keep my mouth shut as he climbs from the car, closes the door behind him, then hobbles his way back into the house.

I should just leave now. Pack my shit and go.

And maybe I would if Abri didn't need me.

Lorenzo isn't as strategic as he was in his glory days. His mind is slower. The once sharp edge of his malice has dulled with fatigue.

Movement catches my periphery and I turn my attention to the right of the house, roughly half a mile into the field of thick grass as Abri walks toward a towering tree at the bottom of the rolling hills.

Once she reaches the thick trunk she disappears around the other side, denying me the sight of her.

It was a mistake to kiss her. To etch her deeper under my skin.

Not only is she an earworm now, with her voice constantly humming through my mind, but the feel of her lips is there, too. I'm haunted by the recollection of our bodies becoming too goddamn familiar with each other too fucking quickly. By the intricate details of her sexuality that I'm sure no other man has bothered to acknowledge.

I noticed how she prefers to come around three fingers, not two. How she responds to movement over her clit but prefers pressure. And how she breathes through her orgasms when some women tend to hold their breath.

Fuck, I worship her sounds. Her frantic gasps. The rushed frenzy.

I remain in the car, waiting for her to get whatever space she needs before returning to the house to sort her shit out with her family. But she doesn't come back into view.

Ten minutes pass without sight of her.

Twenty.

The longer I sit without a visual, the more impatient I become until I can't take it anymore.

I shove from the car and make my way across the yard. By the time I reach the middle of the field, my suit pants are prickled with burrs, my shoes dusty as fuck. The closer I get, the more my pulse increases, as if proximity to her is enough to rile my blood.

I round the tree, finding her seated on the ground, her back resting against the trunk as she picks the petals off a wildflower.

"Nice hiding spot," I mutter.

"Well, the driver's seat of my car was already taken so…" She shrugs.

"You could've sat in shotgun."

"Kinda defeats the purpose of hiding if you're sitting next to the person you want to get away from."

So she still wants to fight. How surprising.

"You're not worried about snakes?" I do a visual scan of the grass around us.

"Why would I be when I've been sharing a bed with one?" She throws another petal to the ground, her expression blank even though she has to be proud of all the right hooks she's landing.

"You done?" I shove my hands into my pockets.

"I'm a woman, Bishop." She throws another petal to the dirt. "Holding a grudge is a birthright. Get used to it."

Her facade isn't as perfect as it was days ago at the gala. Cracks form in the slump of her shoulders. The lack of energy in her posture.

"I need you to listen." I move closer, stopping a foot away to peer down at her. "When you get back to the house, Lorenzo is going to tell you he can facilitate a call between you and your mother."

Her hand pauses in the middle of picking another petal.

"I know it sounds like good news." I touch her sneaker with my shoe, trying to test her anger only to have her shift her feet away. "But if Adena is as temperamental as you say she is, you have to think before you act."

"I always think before I act," she snips.

"Well, when you do, I'm sure you'll come to the same conclusion

I did—that your mom isn't going to appreciate finding out her brother is helping you. I want you to give me more time to work out a better option."

"Thanks for the concern." She discards the flower to the dirt and pushes to her feet. "But I can figure out the best way to approach my mother on my own. I don't need your help."

"You *do* need it, belladonna. And I'd stake my life that you appreciate it, too."

"*Appreciated*. Past tense. That was when I was ignorant to the underhanded shit you were doing behind my back."

"You're smart, Abri. You knew it was coming."

"Yeah, I knew. I didn't foresee that crap you pulled in the bedroom, though." She stands tall in front of me, her eyes full of fire. "After all the protests you made, how could you kiss me, let alone like *that*?"

"How did you want me to do it?"

"You don't refuse to kiss a woman while giving her more orgasms than birthdays then finally lay one on her just to shut her up." She glares. "And I bet you thought you were better than every other piece of shit who's touched me."

My jaw aches with the pressure of my clenched teeth. I inch closer. "I'll ask again, how did you want me to kiss you?"

She raises her chin, her lips pressed in a tight line, those eyes narrowing to spiteful slits.

She wants a replay.

Fuck. I want it too. To get another taste of her spite. To drown in her venom.

"How, belladonna?"

Her jaw ticks.

Say it. Let down your fucking guard.

"I wish you never kissed me at all." She sidesteps, deliberately bumping my shoulder as she turns away. "I'm done with you, Bishop."

"Then you'll be pleased to know I'm leaving in the morning."

She stops in her tracks.

Is she happy? Angry? Does she think I'm taking the first opportunity to leave her in my rearview?

"It was under Lorenzo's order," I add. "But given what's

transpired today, I thought you'd want me on the first plane out of here."

Her chin remains defiantly high, her shoulders straight. "Why would he order you to leave?"

"He thinks something is going on between us."

"And why would he think that." She swings around to face me. "Do you usually treat women like garbage? Is that your tell?"

"I don't usually treat women like anything. But Lorenzo has assumed the way I'm acting toward you places your holiness in a different category."

"I'm sure you enjoyed telling him otherwise."

God, she infuriates me.

I want to grab that perfect face in my blood-stained hands and yell at her to quit the taunts. To stop having the last fucking word because it's driving me batshit fucking crazy. "Do you want me to stay, Abri? Is that it?"

"Hell no. I can't wait to see the back of you." Her smile is malicious before she turns on her heel. "Safe travels, Bishop."

Fuck... *Fine*.

Goodbye it is.

She starts for the house, the long grass brushing her thighs, the sway of her hips no doubt deliberately erotic. Even walking away, she taunts me.

"I'll find an alternative to Lorenzo's phone call before I leave," I yell after her, my own cell vibrating in my pocket. "It's a mistake to reach out to Adena through him. Give me a few hours to organize an alternate plan."

"I don't need your help."

"Yes, you do." I yank my phone from my pocket. Najeeb's name is written across the screen. "Give me more time, belladonna."

"Go fuck yourself, Bishop."

24

ABRI

I REFUSE TO ACKNOWLEDGE THE HEAT OF BISHOP'S ATTENTION ON THE back of my neck. I ignore his existence as I stride across the porch to pull open the glass door and enter the back of the house.

Remy and Salvatore turn to stare at me from the kitchen, while Matthew remains at the dining table, his face a sickening shade of grey as Layla begs him to lie down.

"Soon." He gives her a sad smile and meets my gaze. "We think we have a way for you to get in contact with Adena. Sit and we can talk."

I do as requested, reclaiming my seat at the head of the table as the thud of Lorenzo's walking stick approaches down the hall.

He enters the room with a warm smile and waves a hand at Remy and Salvo. "Come."

Everyone returns to their previous positions, the room exactly the same except for the void Bishop's absence has created.

"You have a decision to make, *mia cara*." Lorenzo hooks his walking stick onto the corner of the table. "After your father's passing, I spoke to your mother on the phone. It wasn't civil by any means, but the lines of communication were open, and I feel they still are. Which leads me to believe I could call her right now and she would answer."

My heart beats a little harder, the desire for forward momentum screaming at me to *move, move, move*.

"It will give you the opportunity to tell her you had nothing to do with Dad's death," Salvatore adds. "And ask where your daughter is."

I run the potential conversation over in my mind, not liking the way it sounds. "Being with Lorenzo makes me look guilty."

"That is remarkably similar to what Bishop said." There's a hint of admonishment in my uncle's tone. "Has he already discussed this with you?"

I shrug. "He mentioned something about a call. He doesn't think it's a good idea."

"Of course he wouldn't," Salvatore scoffs.

"He has a sixth sense when it comes to this shit." Matthew shifts in his chair with a wince. "If he has an opinion, we should listen."

"His judgment is clouded," Lorenzo disagrees. "It's best if we move fast. Make the call. Then deal with whatever results arise."

"The arising results could be a dead child," I state, hating how easy it is to picture my daughter murdered by my mother's hands. There are so many ways she could do it. Poison. Sleeping pills. A bullet.

"It's okay, Abri." Lorenzo meets my gaze with confidence I can't reciprocate. "Bishop has confirmed Adena is traveling with only a driver. Your daughter isn't with her."

"For now," Remy argues. "What if her next stop is the kid's house? She could be on her way there as we speak."

"She could already have ordered my daughter's death over the phone." The words claw from my throat. "She doesn't need to be present to make it happen."

"All the more reason to get moving on this." Lorenzo holds my attention. "If you truly believe your daughter's life is at risk, time is our enemy. What alternative are you waiting for?"

My stomach twists. "Bishop wanted to organize a better plan."

"Bishop is leaving in the morning. His work here is done."

"What?" Matthew snaps straighter, a small groan escaping him with the movement. "Where the fuck is he going?"

Lorenzo focuses on my oldest brother, the look sending a silent message I don't understand.

"It sounds like good news to me." Salvatore raises a glass of water in toast.

"I assure you it's not." Matthew keeps his attention on Lorenzo. "We need him."

"Especially when Matthew's in the state he's in," Layla pleads. "This is already too much. He needs to rest."

"Bishop was given the choice." Lorenzo raises his chin, imperious in his posture. "It was his decision to leave. So we move forward without him."

The squeeze of my stomach tightens with bitterness.

"I don't like this." Matthew scrubs a hand over the back of his neck. "There's gotta be a better way."

"I'm sure there is, but when a life is at stake, it's best to act quickly." Lorenzo pushes to his feet and hobbles toward me. "Call your mother." He pulls a cell from his jacket pocket and places it on the table in front of me. "If she answers, at the very least it shows she still respects me enough to talk. And if she respects me, she won't defy me."

"That's a risky assumption." Remy fixes me with a pained expression. "It's your choice, though, Bree. What do you want to do?"

I don't want to do any of this.

I don't want the choice. Or the responsibility.

I don't want Tilly's future resting in my hands… But I don't want it resting in anyone else's either.

"I'll call her." I slide a hand over the phone. "Just give me a minute."

I have to work out a story. To explain why I'm with my uncle if I had nothing to do with my father's death.

"Tell her you're trapped with us," Remy says. "That we came back to get you. To convince you what happened to Dad was for the best. But that you hate us for it."

"It's not far from the truth," Salvo mumbles under his breath.

The story isn't good enough. It will never be good enough.

"If a problem arises, I'll take over the conversation." Lorenzo places a consoling hand on my shoulder—one that brings no comfort. "My sister will listen to me. She has to."

The pace of my pulse increases, the pressure building like rolling thunder.

His fingers gently squeeze. "Whatever happens, Abri, I want you to understand that you're now mine to protect. A threat toward you or your daughter is a threat toward me and my organization. You will be kept safe."

"Even though she's your sister?" I ask.

"Even though she is my sister." His smile is kind, the gentle wrinkles of age shadowing his eyes. "I will prove myself to you, *mia cara bambina*. Your life until now may have been built on mistrust and cruelty, but the future will be a far kinder path."

I'm not convinced.

Right now, I have no other option than to see where this leads though.

"Thanks for the phone." I drag the device closer.

"You're welcome." He leans over to unlock the screen with his thumbprint, then hobbles back toward his seat.

Shit. Now I have to make the call before it locks again.

All eyes are on me as I type my mother's number, my insides waging war because although I can't stand the thought of Bishop's presence, it feels like a mistake to do this without him.

I glance to the backyard, hoping for a sign that doesn't come. The asshole isn't even in sight.

Give me more time, belladonna.

"I'll get you a glass of water." Salvatore stands and makes his way to the kitchen.

I nod, my finger hovering over the connect button, my mouth dry. I hold my breath as I plant my finger, the ring sounding through the room when I place the call on speaker.

"*Abri*." Bishop's voice carries from the yard, his bulking frame coming into view as he stalks across the overgrown lawn. He yells something else. Something I can't hear.

I hang up on instinct, wanting to trust his earlier dictate because he's the only one to ever have had my back.

"*Don't call her.*" He bounds up the stairs and yanks the door open, his eyes wild on mine. "Am I too late?"

"No. I dialed but—"

"Good." He storms toward me, holding up his cell screen. "Do you know this guy?"

I squint, not able to make out the picture on display until Bishop's standing right beside me, the hint of cigarette smoke in the air.

The photo is a close-up of a man's face, black and white, blurred and low quality. But I'd recognize the aviator sunglasses perched atop that roman nose anywhere.

"That's Aaron Geppet." I frown. "He's part of our family's security team."

"Would he answer your call?" Bishop locks his phone and shoves it in his pants pocket.

"In a heartbeat." Salvatore approaches to place a glass of water in front of me. "The asshole has been trying to get in her pants for three years. Why?"

Bishop lowers to his haunches beside me, his gaze charged as he exudes intensity. "As of yesterday afternoon, when this picture was taken, he was with Adena. *He's* her driver. *He's* who you need to contact to get through to your mother. You could pretend you're calling your way through your security team to see if anyone has heard news about her. That way she won't need to know you're here with Lorenzo or your brothers."

My head fills with static, the frantic switch in tactic leaving me disorientated.

"I told you I'd find a better way," Bishop murmurs. "You have to trust me."

I give him an incredulous look, wordlessly reminding him he's already burned that bridge.

"Where was the photo taken?" Matthew asks

"The other side of Kansas City."

My heart beats harder. "That's less than a nine-hour drive. They could already be here if they traveled through the night."

"They could." Bishop nods. "But their progress hasn't been that fast so far. If I was placing bets, I'd say they spent the night at either Topeka or Junction City."

That would make it roughly seven hours to get home.

"Don't worry. She's not here yet," he continues. "I've got men on watch around Denver. And sent more out on the road this morning. If Adena takes the direct route home, they'll cross paths. Then we'll have constant eyes on her until we decide her fate."

"But the closer she gets to home, the more comfortable and confident she will become, *mia cara*." Lorenzo stares down the table at me. "You need to make that call."

I fixate on Bishop, not realizing I'm looking to him for guidance until he nods in agreement. "Do it."

Shit.

"Okay." I pull my cell from my pocket, my pulse thudding. "But you all need to be quiet. I don't want to risk my mother listening in and hearing any of you in the background."

"Not a fucking word," Bishop reiterates, his eyes steady on mine as if he knows I need his support.

I drag in a deep breath, find Geppet's number saved in my device, then press connect.

My pulse booms louder than the ringtone on speaker, the *thud, thud, thud* punishingly heavy along my throat.

I continue to stare at Bishop through the trill sound, his hardened expression sickening in how it strengthens me.

Then the ringing stops, a whir of background noise takes over, and any chance of me confidently faking my way through the negotiation of my daughter's safety flies out the window with my sudden descent into fear.

"Hey, baby girl," Geppet croons. "What did I do to deserve your attention today?"

"Hey." I swallow over the desert drying my mouth. "I'm hoping you can help me find my mom. I'm worried she's in trouble."

"There sure seems to be a lot of that going around. Especially with what happened to your dad."

"You heard?" I add emotion to my tone, wishing I'd had more time to role-play this conversation.

"Yeah. I'm not sure if condolences are in order though with how things went down."

"Of course they are. I can't believe what's happened. That's why I'm so worried about Mom. I've been calling for days. I don't know if she's hurt or alone or—"

"Your mom is fine."

I pause for effect. "She is? You've seen her?"

He huffs a smug laugh. "I sure have. I'm the only one she's trusted with her safety."

"Oh, God." I give a dramatic exhale. "You have no idea how relieved I am to hear that. I've been beside myself. I don't even know what the hell happened. None of it makes sense. And it's not like I can trust my brothers anymore." I ramble on purpose, painting the perfect picture of concern. "I can't figure out why everyone was in Virginia Beach. What does this have to do with my Uncle Lorenzo? And why was I kept in the dark?"

"It's definitely complicated," Geppet says. "It was a shock to me, too."

I focus on my cell, the ticking seconds of the call's duration matching the thudding beat of my pulse. "Do you know where my mother is now? I went to the house after the gala on the weekend but nobody was there. Not even the guards. I've been hiding out ever since."

He falls quiet, the rumble of car noise carrying from his surroundings.

"Geppet? Are you still there?"

"Yeah, Abri, I'm still here. I'm actually right beside Adena. She's safe and sound. There's no need to worry."

My mouth works over silent words.

I'm not sure what to say. What to think.

He's not hiding the fact he's speaking to me. Or disclosing that my mother is with him. So she has to be listening in on the call. She had to have given him the green light to fill me in during the lull in conversation.

"Really?" I ask with hesitation, hoping it sounds like tightly leashed optimism. "And she's okay? Can you put her on the phone?"

"I wish I could, but there's a reason she's dodging your calls. She's not happy with you at the moment."

"She thinks I was involved?" The heavy weight of pessimism bears down on me. The hard press of everyone's attention, too. "Why? How? What could I have possibly gained—"

"It's got nothing to do with me."

"Then put my mother on the phone. Is she still with you?" I know she can hear me. "Mom? Are you there?"

The dull drone of the car carries for pained heartbeats.

"Mom? *Please*. Say something." I rest an elbow on the table, my head in my hand. "Tell me you're safe. Tell me everything is going to be okay."

"Cut the act, Abri," my mother barks with disdain, her Italian accent showing. "I know you were in on this."

Her vindictive tone becomes a noose around my throat, squeezing tight. "How could you think that? When have I ever done anything to defy you or Dad?"

"You did enough before we gained leverage. Your father and I both knew it was only a matter of time."

Leverage?

I hold in a derisive laugh at the way she describes her first and only grandchild. How she continues to hate me even now when she's all alone. No family. No support apart from whatever men she's paying.

"I was at the gala," I repeat. "Entirely defenseless, I might add. I had no protection. I could've been…"

The sentence dies on my tongue, the slow realization stealing the blood from my face.

Had my death been my father's aim? Is that why he agreed to let Gordon cross clear boundaries? Were those moments in the hotel room meant to be my last?

I raise my gaze to Bishop. Did he save my life, not just my already tattered virtue?

His eyes narrow in concern as he mouths, "*What is it?*"

I shake my head, my entire body following suit with limb-wracking trembles. "Mom, you have to tell me where Tilly is. I want to see for myself that she's safe."

"I'm not going to help a traitor, Abri. Your father always predicted you spiteful, conniving kids would come for him—"

"You know I'd never risk my daughter's life like that," I add steel to my tone. "Not once have I defied you since you took her from me. Not once have I gone against your wishes."

A shift of movement rolls around the table, but I don't look. I keep my attention on Bishop, siphoning the strength he bears down on me with hard eyes, refusing to let the approaching panic take over.

"Not once?" she muses. "Your memory must be troublesome if you've already forgotten how you let Cole Torian's sister escape our home."

My gaze snaps to Layla, her skin pale with horror.

Shit.

My mother is never going to help me. I'm never going to see Tilly again. My little girl is going to suffer because of what I've done…if she's not dead already.

Bishop's hand clamps down on my shoulder, the comforting contact tearing me apart.

"Can you at least tell me if she's alive?" I blink back the searing blur in my vision.

"For now."

The shake slams through my limbs, my whole body quaking. "*Please*, Mom." The tightness is everywhere. My throat. My chest. "I swear I wasn't involved. I was loyal to Dad. I always did everything he asked of me. Even when I disagreed with his motives. Even when it came to Tilly. I trusted he knew what was best."

They're lies, all lies. But they're all that's left to save my daughter.

"Like you had a choice," she sneers. "That kid was your biggest mistake."

No, she was my only achievement. *Is* my only achievement. The one good thing I've done.

"I have to see her," I beg. "I'll do anything."

She scoffs. "Is that so?"

The noose cinches tighter, the ability to breathe becoming harder and harder. "Mom, I—" I suck in breath after breath. "*Please.*"

Bishop grabs my arm and hauls me from my chair, his fury bearing down on me as he gets in my face.

He scowls at me. Nostrils flaring. Jaw clenched. He glares so violently I can feel his hatred against my skin. But it's not directed at me. It's meant as fuel. To strengthen and enrage.

"*Focus*," he mouths, snatching the cell off the table to hold between us. "*Breathe*."

I squeeze my eyes shut. Scrunch my nose. Fight with everything I have to maintain control. "I said I'll do anything," I repeat. "You're on your own now. I can help you. Just tell me what I have to do."

"I'm neither alone nor in need of your help."

"*Mom*," I plead. "*Please.* There has to be something."

The line falls quiet. The entire room waits on a knife's edge.

"You want to know what needs to be done, dear daughter?"

My stomach twists. I can already imagine the men she will punish me with. The scars her request will inflict. "Whatever it is, I'll do it."

"Fine. I'll make you a deal. I'll tell you exactly where your daughter is if you avenge what was done to your father. That means getting rid of your brothers. All three of them. Don't call me again until it's done."

25

BISHOP

The call disconnects.

The room erupts with sound.

Scraping chairs. Pitiful placations. Spineless threats toward Adena.

But all I hear is Abri. Her hitched breaths. The underlying approach of panic.

My gaze doesn't leave her as I dump the cell on the table.

"I've got you," I murmur close to her ear. "Just breathe."

"I, um…" She stumbles back, ghostly white, her wild eyes blindly scanning the room. "I need a minute."

She starts for the hall. I shadow her.

"*Bishop.*" Lorenzo raises his voice over the bickering. "Give her space."

"That's not what she needs." I follow on her heels.

"*Jesus, Bishop,*" Salvatore yells. "*He said give her some fucking space.*"

My volatility increases. If my focus wasn't pinpoint on Abri I'd rip that conceited piece of shit's throat out. But I keep following her, thankful she doesn't protest when I tail her into her bedroom.

She swings around as soon as we're inside, grabbing the door and pushing it shut, keeping her open palms against the wood as she hangs her head and hyperventilates.

Her shoulders rise and fall, the pain in each rasped breath slicing through me in ways it shouldn't.

"My men will find her." I step closer, not sure if she'll still welcome my touch. "I'll get the information from Adena myself. I won't stop until I do." I'll fucking murder that bitch, but not a moment before Abri has her little girl.

"She's not joking, Bishop." She struggles to speak between heaves. "She wants me to kill my own brothers. She expects me to do it."

"I know." I gently grab her hips, turning her to face me. "But we're not thinking about that right now. I need you to focus on getting air in those lungs."

Her eyes are pools of liquid as she meets my gaze. "Why is she like this?" *Gasp*. "How can she hate us so much?" *Gasp*. "Her children?" *Gasp*. "Her own flesh and blood?"

I take another step, my hips leaning into hers, caging her against the door. "I need you to look for five things in the room and tell me what they are."

She pushes at my chest, frowning. "What?"

"Find five things, Abri." I grab the scarf around her neck, loosening the material, my touch gravitating toward her scar. "Tell me what they are."

She shakes her head.

"Five things," I growl. "Just tell me five fucking things."

"Why?" she wheezes.

"Do it. Tell me."

She glances over my shoulder as my thumb strokes her throat. "The bedcovers—"

"What color are they?"

"Pink." She scowls, the heel of her palm digging into my chest in an attempt to gain space I'm not willing to give.

"What else do you see?"

"The lamp."

"What does it look like? Is it pretty?"

She scrunches her nose. "No. It's a horrible beige. It looks like it belongs in a nursing home."

"What else?"

"The chest of drawers… The vial on the carpet."

Her gaze returns to mine, the watery stare eating away at me. I hate watching her struggle, despise how she battles invisible demons that are out of my reach. It's my job to protect Lorenzo's niece, even if that's from herself. And failing in my task feels like a hot poker jabbing through my chest.

"Your eyes…" She sucks in breaths. A little slower. A little longer. "They're the darkest, deepest blue I've ever seen. A stormy sea that threatens to drown me."

She's drowning me, too. Each poetic word fills my lungs with water.

"Why am I doing this?" she rasps. "It's stupid."

I guide a stray strand of her hair behind her ear, ignoring the question. "Now tell me what you hear. Four things."

"Bishop, please." She pushes at me. "I just need—"

"You need to answer my questions. Tell me what you hear, belladonna."

She swallows. Gulps for more air. Shakes her head.

"Tell me."

"Footsteps," she says in a rush. "Behind the door."

Yeah, I hear those too. The nosy fuckers are eavesdropping.

"My pulse in my ears…" she whispers. "My mother's taunts in my head. *God*, why is she so cruel?"

I grab her chin with far more gentle fingers than I'd thought I possessed. "Don't do that. Don't listen to her. She won't beat us."

"Us?" She blinks back at me. "You're leaving in the morning."

For the love of Christ, what the fuck am I getting myself into? "But I'm not gone yet. Now keep going."

"I hear your voice. It drowns out the panic."

"Good." I trail my fingers along her jaw, noticing a little too easily how she leans into the contact before I drop my arm back to my side. "Now I want you to touch three things and tell me how they feel."

"Bishop," she begs.

I don't think she realizes she's not gasping anymore, that she's pulling herself back from the brink.

"Three things," I demand. "Come on. Don't stop now."

She rests her head back against the door, doing the same with her hands. "I feel the texture of the paint coating the wood."

"And?"

One palm rises to her neck to glide over her scarf. "The softness of silk."

"Keep going."

She drags in a deep breath, her eyes on mine as she reaches out, dragging her fingertips across my stubble that's now grown into a beard. "I feel you." Her brows furrow, as if in protest to her words. "You're abrasive. So harsh and confounding."

That seems like more of a personality assessment but I'll take it.

"What do you smell?" I ease my hips back from hers, not wanting my cock to decide it needs in on this game. "Give me two things."

"You." Her fingers run along my jaw. "The hint of cigarette smoke and—" She inhales through her nose, her brows furrowing. "—mint?"

I grin. "I stole the Altoids from your car."

"I'll add theft to your list of transgressions." Her smile is weightless, without joy as her hands fall to her sides. "Are you done with the questions?"

I should say yes. That's it. All over. Even though there's one more part to this exercise.

She's already fought back the worst of her attack. There's no need to continue.

"We're done?" she asks so softly I barely hear it, her gaze eating away at me, her lips close enough for me to decimate.

Goddamnit.

"Final question." I feel myself inching forward, no longer hearing her inhales. Is she holding her breath?

"What can you taste, belladonna?"

She gives a subtle shake of her head. "Nothing."

"Then tell me what you want to taste."

She stands taller, her expression wary.

I fucking hate myself for this. For wanting her. For craving. "Tell me how to kiss you." I'm so close I can feel her radiant warmth. Can sense her softness. "Tell me how I should have done it in the first place."

She doesn't respond. There's only the prettiest shade of blue staring back at me as I guide my hand back to her neck, my thumb grazing her scar.

Her breathing starts again, a barely audible hiss. But no words.

"You don't want a repeat?" I trail my thumb back and forth in long, slow strokes.

Still no answer.

She lowers her gaze, breaking eye contact.

"It's okay. I know I deserve to be denied."

She winces. But again, she offers no words.

It's unlike her. She usually holds the Olympic title for how fast she snaps snarky retorts.

"What is it?" I ask. "What's wrong?"

Her gaze returns to mine.

"I want you to kiss me like you don't hate me," she whispers. "And I need it to be because you want it, not because you have to shut me up."

I outstretch my hand, gently palming her throat, her rabid pulse fluttering under my fingertips as I breathe her in. "God, how I want to hate you, Abri." I lean so close our noses brush. "That would make things so much easier."

I bridge the space between us, the brush of our lips soft.

Fuck.

I've never done this. Not slow. Not tender.

It's so far out of character I feel like an imposter. A ruthless murderer playing a nauseating Prince Charming. Yet I can't quit.

My chest pounds with each velvety brush of her mouth against mine, the tiny whimper she releases sinking all the way into my bloodstream.

I want more.

More than sweet and compassionate.

More than restrained and timid.

I want to decimate this woman. To destroy her with the force of my hunger. To nip and bite and scrape. I want to break the rules I made for myself. To sink my dick inside her. To thrust so hard the feel of me never leaves her memory.

I want her screaming my name. Her fingers digging into my back. Her nails drawing blood.

She whimpers again, her hips tilting forward, her pubic bone brushing my shaft.

It takes everything I have not to haul her off the ground and throw her on the bed.

"Abri." I break the kiss, clutching the free hand at my side in a tight fist of restraint as I rest my forehead against hers. "Someone is on the other side of that door."

She swallows, her throat working in overdrive against my palm.

"I don't care. Keep distracting me. Give me something I can cling to."

"If I distract you the way I want, your brothers will kill me."

"Maybe that's my preferred outcome."

I smirk, pulling back to meet her gaze. "You want me dead, belladonna?"

"Sometimes." Her voice is solemn.

I fight to remain smug when what I've put her through has me feeling like shit. "Forgive me."

She winces again, the turmoil in her eyes a stab through my chest as she turns her head away.

"What's wrong? Forgiveness not in your skill set?" I trail my hand around the back of her neck. "It's okay. I don't deserve that either."

"That's not it." She splays a palm across my chest. "Nobody has cared enough to ask my forgiveness before. You're such a contradiction, Bishop. You confuse the hell out of me."

"The feeling's mutual."

Her gaze returns to mine, the silence lengthening, my restraint fracturing.

"Distract me," she begs.

I shouldn't.

This isn't what I'd expected when I followed her into this room. I thought she'd want to relieve her panic in other ways. Maybe she'd hit me. Plant me on my ass again. Spray me with that flamboyant rainbow of technicolor aggression she does so well.

Not once did I anticipate her wanting me back in her pants.

But that's where I need to be.

I grab the front of her jeans. Unclasp the button. The grate of her zipper is loud through the silence as I yank it down.

She snatches at my pants, starting to reciprocate.

"Not this time." I've abstained for many reasons over the years. But now I do it for penance. To make up for stabbing her in the back. I slide my hand beneath the waistband of her panties. "You wet for me, belladonna?"

"From that timid kiss?" She raises a brow.

"I guess I'm rusty." I delve deeper, wishing I had the experience with affection to give her what she needs, questioning my worth, until my hand reaches that sweet pussy and my fingertips glide through her drenching slickness.

Her lips kick at one side, her eyes slightly abashed as she whispers, "The kiss was perfect."

Fuck.

Praise has never been so fucking rewarding.

I smash my mouth on hers, stealing her gasp as my fingers glide inside her.

She grabs my shoulders. Clings tight. Kisses me back with enough heat to burn.

"Bishop," she begs.

"Shh." I clamp my free hand over her mouth. "I don't want to die today."

She whimpers, her pussy clenching around me as I begin to pump, her nails digging into my skin. I press my thumb to her clit, work my knee between her thighs for added pressure.

In seconds she's panting and gasping again, but this time it's without the panic. She blinks back at me in pleasure, her cheeks heating beneath my palm, her teeth nipping at my fingers.

I should be thankful the house is filled with fuckholes willing to kill me for my current actions. Without the looming threat, I'd have her on the floor, legs spread, throat hoarse from screaming my name. I'd throw away a decade of commitment for a temporary fix just to know what it feels like to come inside her. To have her pussy milking my cock like it's currently strangling my fingers.

I clench my teeth. Shove the temptation to the back of my mind. Lean closer. "You better come in silence." I add more pressure to her clit, rubbing back and forth. "Not one peep out of you or blood will be shed."

Her hectic exhales heat my palm, her chest thrusting forward, her head tilting back against the door.

I drop my mouth to her neck. Kissing. Biting. Sucking.

I'm so fucking hard. So fucking close to breaking.

"The things I want to do to you," I groan against her skin. "You drive me insane."

She bucks her hips closer, riding my thigh.

I kiss her scar. Trace it with my tongue. Scrape it between my teeth.

There have to be a million reasons why I shouldn't be doing this but none of them penetrate the static in my head. There's only madness, and adrenaline, and lust—so much goddamn lust—as precum seeps from my cock.

"Bishop," she whimpers beneath my hand.

I press my palm tighter across her mouth. No room for air. Or sound.

"You've got me knocking on death's door, belladonna. I hope that means you're going to come."

She nods.

I fight another groan. I fight impulse. I fight the need to storm out of here and slaughter every man who's ever done her wrong.

"Come for me," I whisper in her ear. "Come so hard you soak my hand."

Her hand finds my hair. Pulling. Tearing.

I want her. *God*, how I want her.

My balls ache through my restraint. My pulse storms.

She lets out a cry, the sound vibrating against my palm as she comes undone. All that sapphire blue, wide-eyed and blinking back at me.

I want more.

I need it.

But I push through. Breathe against the weight of insanity. Clench my teeth against the compulsion.

All too soon, her intensity retreats. The pussy flutters lessen. Her grip on my hair loosens.

I drag my hand from her mouth and she slumps against the door, her face mottled from my rough handling.

Jesus.

"What's wrong?" she whispers.

I drag a thumb over her cheek. "Did I hurt you?"

"Do you mean now or earlier?"

I wince, dropping my hand back to my side. "Women really do like to hold a grudge, don't they?"

She rolls her eyes. "It's been a few hours. If you weren't leaving in the morning, you'd get a better indication of how long we like to hold onto things."

I despise the reminder—hate how it taints the stunning picture before me. She's always profoundly beautiful in the aftermath.

When there's nothing but her bliss and my triumph for a brief slip of time before regret swoops in to steal the show.

I pull my hand from her panties and raise my fingers to my mouth, tasting her.

She watches me, her teeth dragging over her bottom lip, her chest rising and falling. What I wouldn't give to smear the slickness over those lips, to watch her eyes flare as she tastes herself.

"I'll miss this when you're gone," she whispers. "A girl could get used to coming every time she's touched."

And I could get used to doing the touching. Far too fucking easily. "Maybe steer clear of men for a while."

She chuckles. "You think I should turn to women?"

Now *that* I would happily allow. "It'll save me from killing a lot more men."

Her laughter fades, her smile vanishing along with it as she adjusts her underwear. "I can usually take care of myself just fine."

I don't doubt she's done her absolute best given the circumstances. She's fucking strong, determined, and hellbent. But her life would've been a lot easier if she'd had someone at her back. She never should've gone through all this alone.

Her eyes narrow. "You'd better not be feeling sorry for me, Butcher."

"And why is that?"

She yanks up her zipper and reclasps the button. "Your life is just as pitiful as mine."

Not true. I burned the monsters in my closet to ash a long time ago. I'm free, while she remains shackled to her demons, unable to ask for help to escape the darkness because she fears how the world will see her.

"Whatever you say." I shrug.

She glowers. "You can be such an asshole."

What the fuck? I just agreed with her. "I'm not fighting with you, belladonna."

She pushes from the door, the broken latch allowing the wood to open a crack. "No, just judging."

I clench my teeth, hating how I'm such an easy trigger around this woman. She flips my switch like a fucking toddler who's just discovered how to work the lights. "Are you ready to go back out there?"

"Are you?" She re-ties the scarf around her neck. "You're the one whose life is in danger."

Bring it on. I'd prefer to stare death in the face than deal with her animosity again. "Can't wait."

"Me either." She drags a hand over her hair, readjusts her shirt, then moves to yank open the door.

"Wait." I grab her arm. "Langston is going to ask questions."

She gives me a yeah-duh look.

"About your story," I mutter. "About your daughter. And the gala."

"And?"

"And I don't hide shit from him."

Whatever her reaction, she keeps it locked tight, hiding it under a mask of superiority. "Thanks for the forewarning."

"You're not going to chew me out? Yell at me? Demand I keep my mouth shut?"

"Would it change the outcome?"

It shouldn't. But God knows if it would.

I've already crossed a million lines for this woman. It seems all I'd need is a little push to cross a million more. "No."

She shrugs off my hold and straightens her shoulders. "Then what's the point of bringing it up in the first place? Tell him what you need to, Bishop, because he definitely won't hear it from me."

26

BISHOP

She yanks open the door and pauses, her attention moving downward to where a grey Langston sits on the floor, scowling at me over her right shoulder.

"Are you two done?" he sneers. "Because I'd like a word."

"Don't start." Abri bristles. "You gave up on being the protective brother long ago. You don't get to reclaim the title now."

"Like hell I don't. What the fuck were you two doing in there?"

"Perfecting our synchronized swimming. Now drop it." She stalks down the hall, leaving me alone with a death sentence.

He watches her, the theme song to every third act climactic scene playing in my head as I rest my shoulder against the doorframe. He keeps staring after she's gone, letting the anticipation build like a drama queen until the back door slams and the house turns deathly quiet.

"Synchronized swimming?" He glares.

"She has panic attacks."

He scoffs. "Panic attacks my fucking ass." He plants his hands on the floor beside his hips and winces as he attempts to get up. "It didn't sound like a motherfucking attack to me, you piece of shit."

I step forward, reaching out to help him to his feet. "Where do you want to do this?"

It's obvious we're about to get this out in the open. I'm surprised he hasn't already pulled his gun for a little dramatic flair.

"Bedroom." He slaps away my hand and shuffles around me to enter the room. "I need to lie the fuck down."

He continues to the bed as I attempt to close the door but the broken latch has it swinging back open.

"Leave it," he growls. "Everyone else is outside. They weren't as enthusiastic to listen to your *synchronized swimming* as I was."

"Don't go assuming things that will get you in trouble, Langston. You're not in the shape to be pissing me off right now."

He huffs a sardonic laugh. "If I was, you'd be in a headlock with my gun against your temple. So bear that in mind as we have this little chat. I'll be back on my feet soon enough." He climbs onto the bed, his face pinched as he reclines against the pillows. "We're going to try this one more time. And if you lie to me again—"

"I haven't lied to you."

"So you're sticking to the story that you haven't fucked her?"

I raise my chin. "One hundred percent."

"I guess we're playing your word games then—no lies but a million hidden truths." He scrutinizes me, his eyes narrowed. "You may not be fucking her, but something is going on."

I keep my mouth shut, unable to answer even if I wanted to. I have no idea what the hell is happening between me and his sister. One minute she's all over me, the next I'm waiting for her to slit my throat.

"Has she been sleeping in your bed?" he grates.

I remain silent, the quiet my condemnation as I stalk to the window, finding Abri seated on a bench almost overgrown by lawn.

Her hair shines in the sunlight, illuminating her like some fucking ethereal goddess. She meets my gaze from under her lashes—no emotion, no recognition, just deep blue irises that whisper to my soul.

"Have you touched her, you piece of shit?"

I grind my teeth. This asshole might be the brother I never had, but he'd want to stop throwing stones through this glass house of ours.

"Well, motherfucker?" he snaps.

My anger spikes, and I swing back to face him. "*I'm* a motherfucker?" I stab a finger at my chest. "*Me*? The one that's been by her side since the moment she cried for help?"

He bristles. "You offered—"

"What else was I going to do? You had family business with Lorenzo. And nobody else raised their goddamn hand." I shove my clenched fists into my pockets. "It was supposed to be a few hours of babysitting. I was never meant to be at that fucking gala. You should've taken over before this shit got complicated."

"Well, excuse me for getting shot. I didn't anticipate my father attempting to kill me."

"None of us anticipated any of this. I had as much control over my situation as you did over yours."

"You had fucking control over my sister being in your bed."

"Did I?" I storm closer, ready to pull him off the mattress like a rag doll. "How the fuck would you know when you haven't questioned *why* she was in my bed in the first place? Ask me how the fuck she got there, Langston. Ask me why. Because you sure as hell know me well enough to understand I'd never intentionally go out of my way to fuck around with your sister."

He raises his chin, his lips thin, his rage palpable. If he wasn't likely to die in the process, I know we'd be on the floor exchanging blows right now.

"She's been on the brink of mental collapse since I found her at that gala," I sneer. "The panic attacks aren't bullshit. I've had to save her from four of those fucking things in as many days. And do you want to know why?" I stop at the edge of the bed, glaring down my nose at him. "Because you and your self-centered brothers have no fucking clue of the nightmare she's in. *You're* the one who left her to live in hell. *You* abandoned her. *You* didn't save her from the scars she now has to contend with on a daily basis."

If looks could kill I'd be greeting the devil, but I don't fucking care.

"You have no idea what I had to save her from that first night." I stab a hand through my hair, wanting to kill Finch all over again for the memory of her half-naked on the bed as she faked enthusiasm about the prospect of being raped. "Or how that type of bullshit has become a common occurrence for her since she was a teenager."

"I'd ask what you saved her from," he mutters, "but I have a feeling you won't tell me."

My unwanted loyalty to Abri is like a choker around my neck, tightening with every breath. She needs to be answering his questions. Not me.

"You failed her." I swing an arm toward the door. "And Remy and Salvo lived under the same fucking roof and didn't pull their heads out of their asses long enough to see what she was going through."

"They've had their own shit to contend with."

"Their own shit means nothing when pitted against hers. So excuse me for comforting her in the only way that fucking worked. I've held her. I've touched her. I've done whatever it goddamn took to distract her." I let my arm fall to my side. "And I'll be damned if I apologize to the guy who left her behind all those years ago and tried to forget she existed."

He stares. Stares so hard it goes without saying that I've taken this guilt trip too far. That the decade-long brotherhood we've shared has now shifted.

"You know I never forgot her." His voice is barely audible.

I refuse to wince even though I know it's true.

I was by his side every time he travelled from D.C. to Denver to keep an eye on his siblings. I watched as his hatred for his estranged parents grew because of their traumatic parenting style.

"And you know I'd never do anything to betray you or Lorenzo." I return to the window, staring at the cause of all my problems as she clutches the bench, fixated on the grass beneath her feet. "But I've watched her for years, too."

"Does this mean I should get used to something permanent between you two?"

"No." *Hell fucking no.* "Lorenzo has me flying out first thing tomorrow."

"Right… So you're abandoning her now as well?"

The jab stings.

"What's Lorenzo got you doing that's so important?" he asks.

"Does it matter? You want me away from her and so does he."

"What does Abri want?"

"Her daughter. End of story."

He sighs, the lengthy exhale filled with regret. "I still can't believe she's got a kid. Or why she would give her away to someone else to raise."

"*Give* is the wrong verb," I mutter.

Silence hangs heavily between us for a few stagnant heartbeats. I shouldn't have opened my mouth, but being the gatekeeper to her trauma is a position I don't deserve. Once I leave, she'll need someone close who can empathize with her pain.

Even if I had a choice to stay, that person shouldn't be me.

"Emmanuel took her daughter?" he asks.

Her secrets claw at my throat. Why is it so hard to give him the truth?

"Answer me." Langston struggles to his feet. "Did he force her to give up her child?"

"He forced her to have sex," I snarl. "Forced her to carry to term. Then when she decided she wanted to keep her child, he forced her to give the baby up. He fucking stole his grandchild from his own daughter, and Abri hasn't seen the kid since."

His skin turns a more sickening shade of grey. "Is that what you meant when you said you didn't like the picture she'd painted?" He grabs the bottom bedpost, holding himself upright. "That what she was telling us wasn't true?"

"It was true enough."

"But?"

I fight against the unwanted emotions I have no business feeling. Why do I give a shit about exposing her secrets? Why the hell do I even care?

"Everything in her life is worse than she makes out," I admit.

He shuffles closer. "How much worse?"

"Put it this way—what I saved her from the night of the gala included a perverted old man, two of his henchmen, and *not* a whole lot of consent. She still has the bruises on her neck to prove it."

"Salvatore thought you might have been responsible for those bruises."

"Salvatore is a fucking idiot who deserves to be thrown in a wood chipper."

Langston paces, the slow, shuffled scrape of his feet resembling the movement of someone in a hospice center. "I guess it's safe to assume Emmanuel leveraged my niece against Abri."

I scowl at him over my shoulder. "Sit the fuck down before you fall. I'm not scraping your face off the carpet if you nosedive."

"I'm not going to nosedive." He continues to hobble. "And I can't sit. This shit has me furious."

"Welcome to the club. It's dark here with a growing kill list. I've only had the chance to cross off one name so far."

"Who?"

"The guy who left the bruises."

He nods, seeming slightly appeased. "We'll get through the list soon enough once I've recovered."

The list won't last that long.

I'll have Abri avenged the day she tells me the names of every son of a bitch who's touched her.

"What else do I need to know?" he asks as a door opens somewhere in the house, footsteps following.

I glance back outside, some fucked up part of me hoping Abri has returned even though all we do is fight, but she remains on the bench, as ethereal as ever.

"Knock, knock." Layla's voice carries from the doorway. "Just checking to make sure you two haven't killed each other."

Langston slumps back onto the mattress, patting the coverings at his side to wordlessly beckon her forward. "We've come close."

"Come close?" I raise a brow. "I don't think your damaged ass could come at all even with two hands around your dick."

Layla snickers, padding her way across the room. "Rest assured, that part of him still works just fine."

"Great." I roll my eyes. "I can stop worrying."

She smirks as she climbs onto the bed, crawling her way to Langston who welcomes her with an open arm. "You're awfully touchy today," she directs my way. "Violent, too."

"It's not surprising that you've acknowledged my hostility but lack the sense to stop taunting me."

Her smile widens. "And it's not surprising you've caught feelings for a woman and responded to it with animosity and bitterness."

"I haven't caught anything." I pin Langston with a hard stare, wordlessly warning him to tug on his woman's leash.

"You've definitely caught something," he mutters. "The most obvious being a shitty attitude. What I want to know is if you actually care about her."

"When have I ever cared about anything but myself?"

"You're not as heartless as you claim. You've always cared about our businesses. About money, and Lorenzo, and your reputation."

"And me," Layla chimes in with a chipper tone. "You know you care about me."

I glower.

Langston playfully drags her closer to his side. "You're not incapable of softness, Bishop. What I want to know is if I should be pushing back against Lorenzo's demands for you to leave."

My pulse thuds.

Langston has more sway over his uncle than I do. If I don't want to leave, this is the olive branch I need. But if I stay, all I'll do is succumb further to Abri. And she'll grow more reliant on me to stop her attacks. The blurred lines between us will become increasingly hazy and the complications will grow.

Proximity to Abri Costa isn't something that will serve either of us.

"No." I shake my head. "As much as I despise the thought of not running point on this operation, I can still pull the strings from D.C."

His eyes narrow. "But why would you need to? What does Lorenzo see that I don't?"

"Wedding bells and matrimony for a start. The old man is demanding I put a ring on it if I stay."

"Are you serious?" Layla gapes. "He wants you two to get married?"

Langston's expression hardens. "If that's his stipulation, I'll march you onto the jet myself."

That's what I thought.

Not one motherfucker who knows me would sentence any woman to a lifetime at my side. Especially the guy who understands me best.

"Like I said, I'll pull the strings from D.C." My cell vibrates in my pocket, and I pull it out of my jacket as Langston mutters what I can only safely assume is something unflattering about me.

DYKER

> Car spotted outside Burlington. Same male driver behind the wheel. No other passengers.

"What is it?" Matthew repositions himself on the bed, sitting taller.

"Dyker passed Adena's car on the highway." I type back—

ME

Don't lose him

—before meeting Langston's gaze. "She's no longer riding shotgun. Geppet was the only one in the vehicle." I scrub a rough palm over my mouth, trying to formulate the best course of action.

"Is that good news or bad?" Layla asks.

"At the very least it means we now have access to someone who's spent a lot of lonely hours with Adena." I start for the hall. "I'm going to hit the road. Get him alone. Squeeze him until he starts singing."

"Wait," Langston barks. "Abri needs to make the decision on this. It's her daughter."

I stop in the doorway, scowling at him over my shoulder. "She can barely think straight. She's too emotionally invested."

"So are you. Whatever you and my sister have gone through has you acting on impulse. And I get it. This job feels personal. But it's her choice. Her daughter's safety always has to be her choice."

"He's right." Layla gives me a pleading look.

I jab a pointed finger in her direction. "Stay the fuck out of this."

"Watch yourself," Langston snaps. "I may not be able to lay you on your ass right now, but I can certainly pay someone to do the honors."

"I'd like to see you try."

"Keep running your mouth and you will."

I tense every muscle against the invisible ties that bind me. He doesn't know what Abri needs. What's going through her mind. How hard it will be for her if she makes the wrong decision.

"You're emotional," Langston repeats, the words a slowly drawn out placation. "Let me speak to her. I won't take long."

"No, let me. Mother to mother." Layla pushes from the bed. "With what the Costas put me through with my own daughter's abduction, I'm the only one who can come close to empathizing with her right now. Trust me. I'll make her see things your way."

I clench my fists, hating that she's right, loathing that I'm already taking a back seat to Abri's situation. "Fine. But if you fuck this up, you won't like the consequences."

27

ABRI

I stare at the sky, my fingers curled around the splintered wooden bench, my limbs heavy.

How did I get here? To this random house in the middle of nowhere, where panic attacks haunt me and my backbone resembles a wet noodle?

Bishop.

He's the reason I've become soft. Weak.

He gave me a glimpse of support. Of protection. And not only did I nestle into its warmth like a petrified lamb, but I let him take over.

I lost myself under the shelter of his reliability, and I can't let that continue. Not when his help has turned me into this teary-eyed, weak-kneed little bitch. And also because he's leaving tomorrow.

Gone.

Done.

My existence no more than a memory left to fade from his mind.

The back door opens and Layla, Matthew, and Bishop walk out.

I hate that my gaze glues to the man of the moment, the one who diluted the toxicity of the so-called temptress of high society. How I try to subtly read his emotions. Gauge his commitment. Decipher whatever the hell is going on between us.

But he doesn't look my way.

He doesn't seek me out at all.

Doesn't even bother with a side-eyed glance as he moves to

Lorenzo sitting on a wooden chair and grabs the vacant seat beside him, then thrusts it in Matthew's direction.

Layla is the one who descends the porch stairs, passing Remy and Salvatore who both pace the yard, talking on their cells in muted tones and shooting me squinted looks every few seconds as if I'm likely to follow through with my mother's request and kill them without warning.

Layla continues toward me, her smile friendly as she approaches. "Whatcha doin'?"

I shrug. "Just plotting the death of my siblings."

She winces. "Do you want to talk about it?"

"Only if you have experience in getting away with murder."

She stops before me, her brows raising in contemplation. "Not personally. But I could give my brother a call. He's an expert. I'm sure he could give you a few pointers."

"Thanks for the offer, but Cole and I already have a complicated history."

"One day I'd love to hear all about it. But for now, do you mind if I sit with you for a while?"

"I won't stop you."

She takes a seat on the far side of the bench, her attention turning to the men on the porch, her smile fading. She's quiet a moment, contemplative, then finally she turns to me, her expression impassive. "Abri, I'm really sorry that helping me escape your house put you in this position."

I shake my head. "That's not what this is about. My mother only mentioned you to make me look like a traitor. More than likely to convince Geppet of all the horrible things she's been saying about me during their time together." If anything, it's a positive sign that I'm still capable of flipping him to my side. "She's never needed a reason to hate me. It's something that's always come naturally."

"I can't imagine how that feels," she speaks softly. "How much it must hurt."

It's not a question, so I don't bother responding.

"Motherhood can be the greatest gift," she continues, "but it can also be the most terrifying maze, even at the best of times. To be going through this has to be—"

"I'll figure it out." I don't want to talk feelings. Or daughters. Or my mother.

I need to rebuild the walls Bishop crumbled. To reclaim the backbone that made me the heartless bitch who waded through the muddied trenches, seducing her way to notoriety.

I glance at him again from beneath my lashes, my insides squeezing. He leans against the porch railing, holding a heated conversation with Lorenzo I can't quite make out but am certain should involve me.

"Have you worked him out yet?" Layla murmurs.

"Hmm?" I pretend I didn't hear her. I'm not overly enthusiastic to talk about the man who's driving me crazy.

"Bishop. He's very slow to warm up to people. And even then you're treading barely tepid waters if he does. But I always had this feeling he was a stand-up guy… At least until this morning."

"What changed your opinion?"

"You," she states simply. "When we first drove up to the house, it looked like you two were an item. But then he was kicking in doors and getting in your face as if the two of you are enemies." She turns her body toward mine, her gaze sympathetic. "Has he hurt you?"

"No."

"Do you feel safe around him?"

My stomach clenches. My heart follows suit. The moments I've been close to Bishop are the only times I've ever felt safe, but I don't want her to know that. I don't want anyone knowing.

"Because if you don't," she continues, "I'll return the favor you gave me last time we met and help you get away from here."

I should take her up on the offer. Should grasp it with both hands. But I'm not ready yet. I'm still flailing. "You'd betray Matthew?"

"It's not betrayal. I already spoke to him about my concerns on the flight here. He understands I owe you a debt and that it will need to be repaid."

As if sensing our conversation shift, my oldest brother stands and makes his way down the porch stairs.

"He looks like shit," I mutter.

"He really does. I'm so worried about him, but he won't listen when I tell him to rest."

"He was never one to follow orders." Growing up, he was the most headstrong of us all. The most determined. The only one capable of turning his back on our family's wealth and risking homelessness to try and make it on his own.

"Hey." He stops in front of me, his suit pristine, his face ragged.

"Hey, yourself."

"Do you feel like talking to me yet?"

"Not really."

He slides his hands into his pockets, seeming humbled. "Will you do it anyway?"

I sigh, dragging out the dreary breath as I scoot to the end of the bench to make room for him. "Only if you sit. If I'm going to be responsible for killing you I want the history books to know it was done in spectacularly violent fashion and not because you dropped dead from preexisting injuries."

"She's right." Layla stands and winks at me. "If she's going to do it, she needs to do it with flair."

"And here I was thinking you two were having a companionable conversation about motherhood." He awkwardly lowers to the bench. "Just remember, *mia dea*, you can't gain my riches unless I'm killed *after* we're married. So you'd best get started on those wedding plans."

My brows shoot skyward as Layla chuckles.

"I'll get right on it." She starts toward the house. "But first, I'm going to make myself another coffee. I'll be inside if either of you need me."

"You're getting married?" I ask once she's out of earshot.

"If you don't end me first." Dark brown eyes meet mine, my brother's stare solemn. "The engagement is new. Bishop doesn't even know yet."

I lower my attention to the lawn, trying to imagine what the marriage of a butcher and a mafia princess might look like. If it would be happy or volatile. Easy or riddled with complications destined to tear them apart. "Congratulations."

"Thanks."

We fall quiet as Layla enters the house, Remy joining Lorenzo and Bishop on the porch while Salvatore continues to mutter into his cell.

"So…" Matthew drawls. "You and Bishop…"

I wait for the conclusion to his sentence that doesn't come, then finally ask, "What about it?"

"You're going to make me say it?"

"Say what?" I frown. "I have no idea where this conversation is headed."

"You two have apparently been having a pants-off dance-off," he grumbles. "To say I'm surprised is an understatement."

"We released a little steam. It's no big deal."

"Maybe not to you, but he sure has his panties in a twist over something. My guess is that he's caught feelings that are causing some sort of allergic reaction."

My traitorous heart skips a beat before I can scoff it away. "I find that hard to believe."

"Trust me, so do I. Yet that's the only answer I can determine for his bad attitude. I've known him a long time and not once have I seen him this protective. Not even over Lorenzo. And our uncle is the only parental figure he knows."

My cell vibrates in my pocket, bringing cold dread along with it.

It has to be my mother. What outlandish demand does she have for me this time?

I push to my feet, holding up a finger to Matthew as I grab the device and check the screen.

Aaron Geppet.

The dread falters. A queasy sense of uncertainty takes its place.

"Who is it?" Matthew asks.

I open my mouth to blurt the truth then pause, questioning the pros of transparency. "A sales exec from Alleya. Give me a few minutes." I backtrack from him, from the house, from Bishop, Lorenzo, and Remy staring at me from the porch, and Salvatore, who continues to pace the lawn. I don't answer the vibration until I'm close to the far edge of the yard. "Hello?"

"Hey, baby girl. I thought I should call you back and see how you're doing after your mom dropped that bombshell."

My spine turns to dry pasta. Straight. Hard. Brittle.

"How are you holding up?" he asks.

Is he fishing for Adena? Trying to find out if I'll go ahead with the kill order? "I'm a little at odds, as I'm sure you can imagine."

He snickers. "Yeah, I get it."

Really? I've known the man for years, but I guess I never took the time to notice he was employed for brawn not brains. "Does my mother expect an update already?"

"No. Not at all. We've parted ways." He scoffs a laugh. "Could you imagine what she'd do to me if she found out I was calling you?"

Yeah, I can. And I can't think of a reason to risk that sort of backlash.

I glance over my shoulder, seeking out Bishop, wondering if he can confirm Aaron's story. His face is stony, eyes cold, lips tight, as if he can sense who I'm talking to. "So why call at all?"

"I thought maybe we could meet up tomorrow and see if we could help each other gain the upper hand on this tricky situation."

It's a trap.

A scheme at the very least.

My mother has to be right by his side, orchestrating this conversation. But why? Why not call me herself?

"Are you playing games with me, Aaron?"

"Of course not. Just trying to take advantage of a situation that can benefit us both. I've sat in a car with Adena for days, and although that woman doesn't necessarily like to talk, she does have a thing for plotting. And you and your daughter were high on her agenda."

I turn to the wooden rail fence, my stomach twisting. "She spoke to you about Tilly?"

"A little. But the conversations weren't what you'd expect from a grandmother talking about her only grandchild. There were no comments about your daughter's favorite ice cream or what piece of equipment she prefers at the park. It was all in relation to what the future holds for your kid."

My heart swells as it slowly crawls into my throat.

"Look," he continues. "I'm not far from home. Am entirely alone. And have been given the direction to take a few days off and get some sleep while your mom assembles her troops. All I want to know is—which side should I be on in this fast-approaching war? And do you want to be there with me?"

I feel myself creeping closer to his trap, wanting to inspect it, dissect it. "Where's my mom?"

"I'm not sharing that over the phone. If it hasn't already sunk in, I'm kinda putting my ass on the line by talking to you. But she's close to your daughter, if that helps."

No, it doesn't. It snags the breath in my clogged throat.

I don't want her anywhere near Tilly.

The only thing that's helpful is the knowledge that he might know the exact location I'm looking for.

"Meet me tomorrow?" Geppet asks. "We can figure this out together. Just you and me, babe."

I glance back over my shoulder. Bishop is still staring at me.

Does he know Geppet and Adena parted ways? Did he keep the information from me?

I bet he's guilty on both counts. He said he had men waiting for Aaron's approach to Denver. He'd have to be aware of the change in situation, right? Yet he's kept it to himself.

"Okay." I nod, strengthening my resolve. "When and where?"

"Eleven. I'll text you a location tomorrow."

"I'll be there."

I disconnect, pocket my cell, and return to stand in front of my brother on the bench seat, my pulse racing, my mind matching pace.

"Any problems at the label?" Matthew asks.

"No. I'm just trying to keep the staff distracted so they don't start asking about our parents' whereabouts."

"Good idea."

I nod to myself, falling quiet, too busy thinking about what tactics I can use to siphon information out of Geppet to notice my brother is equally silent.

He clears his throat. Shifts awkwardly on the bench.

I can tell an uncomfortable conversation is coming before he opens his mouth and says, "I wish I'd known what you were going through, Bree."

I fight a groan.

With my meeting with Geppet looming, now more than ever, I need to pull my head out of my ass and reclaim my tenacity. There's no more room for pitiful conversations even if I'm not the one instigating them.

He gives a sad smile. "I would've dropped everything to help—"

"Please don't. If you want to have a companionable relationship, then fine, we can have a companionable relationship. But you don't get to make apologies and pretend my daughter would be safe if only you'd been a part of our lives."

"That's not what I'm trying to say."

"But it's what you're thinking. It's what you're *all* thinking. That if only you'd known what was going on, then you could've stopped it. You could've handled our father better than I did."

"No." His voice is solemn. "I left all those years ago because I was no better at beating Emmanuel than you were. I know he would've given you no choice. Nobody blames you for this."

Nobody but me.

Footsteps crunch in the grass behind me, the sound approaching. I ache for it to be Bishop and I hate myself for it.

"Everything okay?" Salvatore asks.

I hold Matthew's gaze as our two brothers join us. Remy to my left. Salvo on my right. All four siblings reunited for the first time without the tyranny of our parents, but now we're more at odds than we've ever been.

"Yeah." I shrug. "Just trying to figure out which one of you to snuff first."

Salvatore winces. Remy's reaction is identical.

It's Matthew who smirks. "The obvious choice is Rem. Always start with the youngest and weakest."

"Very funny," Remy drawls. "If it were me, I'd pick the brother with the least brain cells."

"That's Matthew," Salvatore states at the same time Matthew says, "Salvatore."

I roll my eyes, wishing I could appreciate how they're joking about my tasked triple homicide.

"Don't worry." Remy bumps my shoulder with his. "We'll figure something out."

I want to revel in the comradery. To sink beneath its surface and let it coat me head to toe. But there's fragility in those depths. I can't start relying on anyone.

"I'm not the type to appreciate warrantless placations." I step away. "I'll take care of this on my own."

"But you don't have to." Matthew pushes to his feet with a wince. "Mom isn't with Geppet anymore. He's by himself. We can squeeze him for information."

I raise my chin, the only outward reaction to the betrayal that's gone on behind my back. "When did you find that out?"

"Not long ago."

"When?" I measure the word. The tone. My temper. "This is my daughter's life you're playing with yet somehow you think it's okay to withhold information from me? I should've been told straight away."

Matthew holds up his palms in placation. "You've got a lot to think about. We're just trying to measure that load."

"We? You and who? Remy and Salvo? Lorenzo? Bishop? Or all of the above?" I raise a condemning brow. "Who else knows more than I do?"

"Cut me some slack, Bree. I'm not the enemy."

"Well, you're proving not to be an ally either. The first and only priority here is my daughter. Yet when you received information that could lead to her whereabouts, you kept it from me."

"No, I came outside to talk to you about it even though Bishop wanted to walk out the front door and track Geppet down as soon as he got the call. I'm the one that told him you needed to decide what happens. I just didn't want to dive face-fucking-first into strategy talk when I haven't held a proper conversation with you in more than a goddamn decade."

Bishop led the betrayal?

Any lingering hesitation I had about meeting with Geppet behind their backs is gone. *Poof.* Vanished.

These people are managing me, while Geppet was telling the truth.

I shoot a glare at the main perpetrator over my shoulder, finding him still standing on the porch near a seated Lorenzo. "Did Bishop explain why he wanted to keep this from me?"

"It wasn't like that," Matthew mutters as if understanding the shit he's put his friend in. "I think he just had a one-track mind to get in the car and find Geppet as soon as possible."

"We all want to bring your daughter home, Abri." Salvatore places a hand on my upper arm.

I shrug him off. "Don't."

"I'm not trying to make this harder on you. I just want you to know that none of us will stop until we get her back. That's all that matters to any of us. It'll be our entire focus until—"

"*Stop.*" His assumption stabs through my ribs, the pointy tip puncturing my heart.

"What's going on?" Bishop's shout carries from the house.

Jesus Christ, not now.

"Here's what's going to happen." I pin Matthew with an unflinching scowl. "I'm going to leave here—"

"Fucking hell," Salvatore mutters. I pause, assuming he's cursing my plan to hightail it out of here when he follows it up with, "Why is this fucker still here?"

"What's wrong?" Bishop asks from close behind me.

I turn to face him. "You. You're what's wrong. You found out Geppet and my mother parted ways and decided to keep it from me."

His gaze travels to Matthew in lethal judgment. "Snitches should still worry about getting stitches even when they're already peppered with bullets."

Matthew rolls his eyes.

"I don't have patience for your banter." I step in front of Bishop. "You should've told me the minute you found out. *I* should've been the first person you told. Not my estranged brother. Not my uncle. Or whoever else you've mentioned it to between now and then. But *me*. The mother of the child that's lost. The one who should be calling the shots."

He straightens his shoulders. "I wanted to figure out the best course of action first."

"That's *my* job."

"I strongly disagree."

"You're not going after Geppet, Bishop. *I* will be the one speaking to him. *I* will be the only person to extract whatever information he has."

"My tactics are more effective," he snarls.

"Your tactics will get him killed, and I'm not going to risk that happening when we have no clue how much he knows. You have no restraint."

His jaw ticks. "You're the only one to tamper with said restraint, belladonna. I assure you I'm the best person to handle this."

"Okay, then tell me how many men you've successfully extracted information from without ending their life afterward."

His lethal stare hardens as Lorenzo hobbles down the porch steps toward us.

"See? You can't." I hold my chin high in victory. "So you have no experience in this, whereas I've manipulated information out of—"

"Nobody wants to know your stats, *Abri*," he sneers my name.

"This isn't just about manipulation. It's about safety. About being able to protect yourself."

"I laid you on your ass, didn't I?" I smile sweetly. "I can do it again right now if you want."

I probably couldn't.

A blindsided attack is one thing. An anticipated strike against a far bigger and stronger target is plain stupid. But my ego has climbed into the ring alongside my impatience, fear, and annoyance. I'm a volatile mix on the cusp of detonation.

"I've manipulated more men than you've interrogated, Bishop. I'm also the one who gets to call the shots. Remember?" I turn my attention to Lorenzo who stops beside the man of the moment. "That's what you said earlier, right?"

"I did." My uncle inclines his head, his expression somber. "But if I overheard correctly, this isn't something I feel you should do on your own."

"Then I'll have backup. Remy and Salvatore can be on sentry duty from the shadows."

"Not going to happen," Bishop barks.

"I assure you it is, because I've already made the arrangements to meet with Geppet tomorrow."

The few seconds of shock-filled silence are cathartic before my brothers all bark questions.

"*What?*"

"*When?*"

"*Are you serious?*"

Bishop doesn't speak. Instead, he talks to me through eyes that harden with the edge of rage yet also peer back at me with the same betrayal I felt moments ago.

"I won't let you do it," he states.

"You won't be here to stop me. You'll already be gone."

"*For fuck's sake, you're infuriating,*" he roars. "If it's me you've taken issue with then I'll organize Dyker. Or—"

"You won't do a damn thing. This is *my* situation to control. *My* daughter. *My* choice."

"You're not putting yourself at risk, Abri. I won't allow it."

My throat aches with sudden dryness. Is that what this is really about? Not control, but protection?

Don't you dare weaken again.

"I will ensure your safety." Lorenzo gives me a sad smile. "My workforce may be stretched thin after Emmanuel's impromptu culling, but I will call in a team of men to provide backup for whatever you have planned. There's more than enough time for them to arrive before tomorrow morning."

Why won't they fucking listen?

I don't want his team. I don't need additional liabilities.

If my mother is behind Geppet reaching out to meet in person, then I can't be seen with my brothers, let alone a hoard of my uncle's cronies.

And if she's not?

This is Geppet we're talking about. I've spoken to him a million times before. He's flirted with me for years, for Christ's sake. He's barely a threat compared to the capabilities of the other men I've manipulated.

"We will be with you every step of the way," Lorenzo continues, "until we get your daughter back."

That pointed knife stabs through my chest again. This time it cuts harder. Deeper.

"You all need to stop." I raise my voice, battling emotion. "You've assumed that I want Tilly back. And I assure you, that's not the case. Not once have I indicated I'm capable of being a mother."

Lorenzo stiffens.

They all do.

It hurts. Oh, *God*, it hurts.

Their confusion. Their judgment. My guilt.

"But they took her from you." Salvatore frowns. "I thought that's what all this was about—getting her back."

"They did take her." I nod over and over, my eyes searing with heat. "But I'm not a mother. All I want is Tilly's safety."

"*Mia cara nipote*," Lorenzo murmurs. "Why would you not want to raise her yourself?"

Because I don't deserve her.

Because I've already failed her.

Because no innocent little girl should be punished with the childhood she's already had to then be raised by a mother like me.

"This was never about gaining custody." I hold my head high. "It's about taking control away from Adena. What I would like to do is determine if my daughter is living with a loving and nurturing family. And if she is, I want them relocated somewhere my mother will never find them."

"And if they don't want to relocate?" Remy asks.

"With enough financial incentive I'm sure it won't be a problem." Lorenzo watches me with pity I can't stand. "It would be my honor to take care of that financial burden for you. And to fly them wherever you decide is best."

My heart breaks—a million tiny pieces scattering at my feet.

This is what I want, yet I feel nothing but sadness. Failure.

I squeeze my arms tighter around my chest, stopping the weakness from bubbling to the surface. "Thank you."

"No." Bishop shakes his head, his narrowed gaze scrutinizing me. "I call bullshit. You want your daughter. You're just scared."

My stomach bottoms, the limited contents of my gut threatening to make an introduction to everyone around me.

He's wrong.

It's not fear. It's value. And I've long since been unworthy of my little girl.

I can't tell him though. Even if I could admit to my insecurities, the tightness of my throat won't allow me to utter the words.

"Jesus Christ, Bishop," Matthew mutters. "You can't say shit like that."

"I can say whatever the damn hell I want when she's talking out her ass." He steps closer, leaning in to demand my attention.

I tilt my head away, refusing to meet his gaze, my eyes blistering, my chest restricting. "Back off."

"You heard her." Salvatore encroaches. "Back the fuck off, you arrogant piece of shit."

"You want your daughter, belladonna." Bishop remains in place, ignoring the threats, pretending nobody else exists. "Admit it so we're all on the same page when it comes to getting her back."

"Bishop," Lorenzo warns. "Leave it be."

"No." He leans his head to the side, making another attempt to get within my line of sight. "You want your daughter. Why is that so hard to admit?"

I drag a deep breath in through my nose, my teeth clenched hard, my stomach tensed to the point of pain.

He's wrong.

He's *wrong*.

He's. Wrong.

I meet his gaze with a glare. "I *don't* want her back. I will *never* want her back."

The words kill me, each syllable leaving a scar.

I fight the need to crumple. To vomit from self-loathing.

He stares me down, waiting for me to backtrack, but I don't.

Not even when the sight of him begins to blur through the heat in my eyes.

"That's enough." Remy grabs Bishop's shoulder. "Her decision is none of our business."

"Fine." Bishop's jaw ticks as he shrugs away from the hold. "Placate her. Fucking eat up her bullshit. But it's not what she needs."

I glance away again, hating him...still wanting him, too.

Salvatore mutters something under his breath.

I sense hard stares being shared between the men around me yet I keep my gaze on the lawn, biting back the self-hatred that pulls me apart from the inside out.

"I think we've all had enough revelations for one day." Lorenzo breaks the stretching silence. "And with the plan for Geppet somewhat sorted, I fear I now need to retire to the city and gain some much-needed rest. This old body doesn't bounce back from injury like it once did." He claps Salvatore on the back. "And you should return to the family home to ensure Adena doesn't send any men to claim it. You can deliver me and my driver to a hotel on the way, leaving the rental for those who remain here."

"I'll go with you." Remy's fingers touch my wrist. "Unless you want me to stay..."

"No." I find the strength to meet his gaze and shake my head. "There's no need."

"I will arrange my men for you, Abri. Just keep me updated on your plans, and I'll see you all in the morning." Lorenzo gives a sad smile in farewell, then turns his attention to Bishop. "Except you. We will catch up again at a later date. Enjoy your flight."

The lines in Bishop's jaw ripple, his animosity seeming threadbare as Lorenzo turns and hobbles toward the back of the house.

"Are you going to be okay?" Salvatore gives me a pointed look.

I nod. "I'll see you tomorrow."

"Call me if you need me."

I keep nodding even though that phone call will never happen. Even if my life was at stake.

"See you later, sis." Remy walks after Lorenzo, Salvatore following suit.

I'm left standing with a silently brooding Bishop and an equally muted Matthew. Neither one of them break the awkwardness until the back door closes behind my other siblings.

"You might want to warn that pin-dick motherfucking brother of yours that I don't like him," Bishop seethes at Matthew. "And that I have no problem killing off the things I don't like."

My brother gives a subtle smirk. "With that assumedly accurate description of my brother's anatomy, should I be worried you're sleeping with him too?"

I snicker.

Bishop glowers.

Matthew continues to smirk. "Come on, Bishop. Lighten up. That pole up your ass must feel like you're being fisted by a giant."

"I'm light as a fucking feather, *brother*," he seethes. "But it's great to see you in such good spirits despite our situation. I take it that means you and Layla are happy to share the second bedroom tonight while I spend the midnight hours punishing your sister in the other room."

He turns on his heel and stalks for the house without another word.

28

ABRI

THE LEAD-UP TO THE BEDTIME SITUATION HAS ME ON EDGE WITH BOTH annoyance and despised want.

I only ignored Bishop's taunt about sharing a bed because it works in my favor. I don't plan to let him out of my sight in case he decides to turn rogue and track Geppet down.

But the closer it gets to nightfall the more my insides buzz like busy little worker bees.

I walk inside the house as the sun begins to set, the hours I've spent alone on the porch wasted on thoughts of Bishop when I could've been strategizing about my meeting with Geppet.

I make my way to the shower, initially wishing there wasn't limited water so I could stay under the spray forever but then thinking better of it when all I can do is fixate on the things I've done with Bishop while in this tiled space.

I roughly dry myself once I get out, wrapping one towel around my body and draping another around my neck to hide my scar.

Then I pad from the bathroom and into a deathly quiet house.

"Matthew?" I call out. "Layla?"

A shiver runs down my spine, the second towel around my neck suddenly seeming heavier.

Nobody answers. There's only a shift of movement from somewhere down the hall.

I follow after it, the light from Bishop's bedroom glowing bright.

I stop in the doorway and find him seated on the closest edge of the bed, his elbows resting on his knees, his forlorn eyes meeting mine.

"Where is everyone?" I ask.

"They left to get food."

A nervous tingle skitters through my stomach at being alone with him, despite the fact we'd been that way for days.

Something is different.

He's different.

And it's not just the slump of his posture or the heartfelt way his usually intense gaze now pleads with me. It's as if all the stubbornness he previously had written into the fiber of his being is softened. Susceptible.

"Come here," he murmurs.

I raise a brow, caught off-guard by his gentle command, but I do as he asks, slowly moving forward.

He sits taller, his arms falling to his sides. He doesn't break eye contact, his stare eating me up as I approach.

For palpitating heartbeats, neither one of us speak. There's only the damage piled between us. The anger and animosity that battles with attraction and lust.

"Let your hair out."

My pulse flutters at yet another subdued demand. Is he attempting to get us back to where we were? Before my siblings arrived. Before he betrayed me.

Is that something I want?

Of course it is.

I reach for my messy bun and drag the elastic from my hair, the long lengths hitting the towel on my shoulders to shroud my chest and back. "Anything else, your highness?"

He reaches out, grabbing a handful of the towel at my waist to drag me closer, right between his parted knees. "Yes. We're not going to argue about Geppet again."

"Good. I'm glad."

"You're going to let me handle it. I'll—"

"Bishop—"

"We're not arguing, belladonna." He peers up at me with something akin to desperation. "I promised you wouldn't be used like that again and I meant it. Don't make me into a liar."

"I don't need to use my body to get the information."

"Then how will you get it?"

Good question.

"What is his incentive to forsake Adena?" he asks. "You have no money. No power."

"I've known him for years—"

"He's not going to do you any favors, Abri." His large hands cup my hips. "He'll want something in return."

I stare down at him, appreciating his concern when it isn't smothered in dictatorship. I like this almost vulnerable side of him. Maybe a little too much. But still, this is my battle—my fight. "I'll figure it out."

"No. I will."

I sigh. "Let's not discuss it then."

"We have to. Time's running out."

His time—not mine. I'm not the one who has to catch a jet tomorrow.

I break eye contact, watching through the window as the last vestiges of the sun's rays disappear from the sky. "This is a funny way to apologize for your behavior today."

He bows his head, his forehead falling to my stomach. "I won't apologize for protecting you."

My fingers itch to run through his hair, to cradle his face to my body. "What about hurting me? You've said some horrible things."

"Sometimes the truth hurts."

I attempt to take a step back but he clings to me, not letting me move.

"You want your daughter, belladonna. My guess is that you think you don't deserve her."

I fight harder to escape, pushing at his shoulders, jabbing. "Let me go."

He shoves to his feet, bringing us hip to hip. He remains calm, desperation continuing to peer back at me from those hypnotic blue eyes. "I'm not fighting with you."

"Good, then get your grabby hands off my towel."

He tugs me against him, the hardness of his erection throbbing through the layers of material between us. "I will if you promise to drop it to the floor."

Butterflies take flight in my belly like a mass of startled birds.

"Let the towel drop," he repeats.

I straighten my shoulders and drag the towel from around my neck, letting it fall to the floor.

He huffs a barely audible laugh. "I guess I should've been more specific." He raises a hand to my neck, his fingertips lightly grazing my scar before he palms my throat in a gesture so light it's barely a touch at all. "I like that you reserve your pain for me. That I get to see you without restriction when no one else does."

Those butterflies transform into vultures, the flap of massive wings ricocheting through my ribs. "And I like that showing you my pain doesn't make me feel ugly."

Only weak. So goddamn weak.

"You could never be anything other than stunning, Abri. The evidence of your trauma makes you more beautiful."

It's hard to align this man with the one who enraged me this afternoon. Or at the gala. Or almost every moment in between. He's subdued. Somehow devoid of aggression.

A part of me wants to believe it's because he's softening to me. That he *likes* me. But an even bigger part wonders if it's manipulation.

He guides his thumb along my neck. "Lay with me until Langston returns with dinner."

"Lay with you?" I frown. Not get naked? Not fool around?

"Yeah." He releases his hold and walks around me, moving to the door where he flicks off the light. The room darkens to shadow, the fading pinks and purples from the dwindling sunset the only illumination.

He returns to me, murmuring over my shoulder, "Come on. Get on the bed." He stalks around the far side and climbs onto the mattress.

It feels like another trap. One that's riddled with temptation and entirely too well thought out. But I concede, scooting onto the closest side of the bed, the towel still draped around me.

"What are you doing all the way over there?" His arm wraps around my waist, dragging me back against his chest. "Do you think I'm going to bite?"

"A girl can only hope." I wince into the darkness, hating how good it feels to be hugged by him.

I wiggle, snuggling closer, hungry for our bodies to touch everywhere when my ass grazes his dick.

"*Belladonna.*" He groans against my shoulder. "I'm struggling to keep this PG without that perfect ass increasing the torture."

I don't understand why it has to be PG at all. But I humor him, falling still in his arms. "Have you ever been tempted to sleep with me?"

"Only with every heartbeat."

The air burns in my lungs. I don't know what increases my yearning more—his admission or how he's the first man to simply lie with me. No sex, despite his body craving it. No taking advantage of every second I'm in his bed.

It's as if he knows I've been denied comfort like this all my life. That yelling and dictating to me will never work, but this…this could truly break me.

"Tell me what made you decide to quit having sex," I whisper.

He nuzzles the back of my neck, making goose bumps erupt across my skin. "I don't want to be responsible for another kid being brought into this world only to be traumatized by bad parenting."

My warmth vanishes. "Do you mean like what I've done to Tilly?"

"Not in the slightest. For starters, you've done nothing but love that little girl. The distance between you both has been out of your control." He places the softest kiss to my shoulder. "I have no doubt you would've been a far better parent than most if given the chance."

"But you wouldn't be?"

"No," he states flatly.

"Why?"

"There aren't enough hours in the day to relay all the specifics. So I'll narrow it down to the obvious—being my lifestyle choices, my sins, and my lack of compassion."

"You have compassion, Bishop." Too much of it when it comes to my safety.

"If that's true, I assure you I can turn it off without thought. If I don't want to give a shit about something, I won't."

"You give a shit about me even though you don't want to." I turn to face him, admiring his Adonis-like features through the shadows. "I'm sure you wouldn't be in here with me if given the choice."

"You're different… A fucking anomaly." He drags his fingers

along my back, light, teasing brushes through the towel as if he's an artist creating a masterpiece.

I fight a whimper, desperate to place my lips against his. "Well, you realize there's this remarkable invention called contraception, right? Have you heard of it?"

"Yeah, belladonna, I have. Had you before you fell pregnant with your daughter?"

Ouch.

He holds me tighter through the direct hit to my bad judgment. "Mistakes happen, Abri. But they won't with me. I refuse to allow it."

"Point taken." I scramble for another topic to wash away the horrid taste in my mouth. "Tell me about your parents. What are they like?"

His hand pauses its perfect touch. "They're not up for discussion."

There's coldness in his words. Trauma that could dance with mine.

"Surely they can't be worse than Emmanuel and Adena."

He doesn't respond.

"Where are they now?" I ask.

Silence.

"Do you talk to them? Do they know what you do for a living?"

"Abri—"

"Please," I beg, somehow needing answers from him more than my next breath. "I want to know you. To understand you." To see if we have anything in common.

"Not this part of me you don't."

"Yes, I do." I place a hand to his chest, my eyes on his through the darkness. "You've dragged all my secrets from me. Why can't I have some of yours?"

"We both know I've barely brushed the surface when it comes to learning all the intricacies of the profoundly secretive Abri Costa." He trails his hand from my back to my hair, running his fingers through the loose strands. "Trust me, you don't want to hear about this slice of my history. I'd prefer you kept the false assumption that I have a soul."

"Have they passed?"

"Jesus Christ," he mutters. "A long fucking time ago."

There's no compassion in his voice. It only makes me hungrier for more information.

Did he hate them? Despise them? Want them dead?

Another deep huff pushes past his lips as he drags his hand away from me and rolls onto his back. "I'm the reason they're no longer breathing. Now let's leave it at that and call it quits on story time."

"Seriously? You can't give me bread crumbs and leave my imagination to run wild." I slide my palm onto his chest, up to his neck, then his jaw, gently guiding his face back toward mine. "Tell me what happened or I'll be left thinking the worst."

"That's exactly what you need to think, Abri." He rolls away, scooting to the edge of the mattress to sit up. "I need a beer. Want me to get you one?"

"No." I scramble to grab his arm as he stands. "Stay. Talk to me. *Please*."

"As fun as that sounds—"

"I'm begging you." I tug his wrist. "And you know how much I loathe begging."

"I know you well enough to understand you'll do whatever it takes to get what you want, and it's working. I don't talk about this shit to anyone."

"I don't talk about myself to anyone either." I drag my thumb along his wrist. "Anyone but you."

"Goddamn, you're so brilliantly manipulative," he groans.

I wince, hating that he's right and how I'm not always aware of what I'm doing.

"You make me want to tell you everything." He turns back toward the bed, cupping my cheeks with his calloused palms. "You're such a fucking tempting viper."

I nod, wishing he was wrong. Wishing I was someone else.

"At least I won't judge you." I climb onto my knees, capturing his muscled waist in my hands. "You're a brutal man, Bishop. But from what I've learned, you're highly moral, too. More so than me. Whatever happened, you still believe in right and wrong."

He stares down at me, face stark, eyes hollow.

"How old were you when it happened?" I ask.

"Sixteen." His admission is softly spoken.

"You were a child."

"No. My parents' drug habit forced me to be an adult well before that. My earliest memories are of weekend benders where they'd slip something into my drink to keep me subdued. It wasn't until my uncle and aunt found out that they took me in for those nights, trying to shelter me from the abuse. But by middle school, the parties were every other night."

Sickening dread curdles in my stomach. "Did you tell your aunt that it got worse?"

"I couldn't. Not if I wanted to keep the only safe space I had. My aunt and uncle were good people, but they didn't want a little shit like me to look after at the best of times. Weekends were all they could manage, and I wasn't going to volunteer to be put into foster care." He keeps playing with my hair, his fingers slowly brushing past my cheek. "So I got used to watching my mom sell herself for crack. Or my dad pimping her out to secure his next high. There was never food in the fridge, and if there was, the electricity bill wasn't paid anyway."

I shouldn't have asked. Shouldn't have pushed.

"When they attempted to sell me to an old guy who had a taste for young boys, I knew I had to get out."

I gape. "They tried to sell you?"

"Without batting an eye. But I was a thirteen-year-old who'd hit puberty early and already looked like I was approaching adulthood. Apparently, that didn't appeal to the perverted."

I squeeze my eyes shut, hating myself for forcing this from him.

"It's okay." He strokes my jaw. "It's in the past."

No, it's not. Whatever happened to him has to be engrained in his flesh. Burrowed deep in his bones. There's no way he could get rid of it.

"I kept biding my time until I thought I could make it on my own. I got myself a job after school, saved as much money as I could, and kept my nose clean." His hand stops caressing my face, the subtle forewarning to impending doom making me anxious. "Then my mother fell pregnant."

Oh, shit.

I open my mouth, poised to apologize for being nosy. For thinking my traumatic life experiences outweigh the rest of the world's. But I can't speak.

"Both of them acted as if having a baby was a great idea. And all

I could think about was how long they'd wait until they sold that kid to a fucking pedophile."

I shake my head, not sure I can take anymore.

"My mother gave birth to a daughter," he mutters. "A tiny dark-haired, drug-addicted sweetheart, with eyes like midnight and lungs as strong as steel. She spent the first month crying, non-stop, and I was the only one with enough patience to take care of her."

My eyes burn, the heat threatening to escape onto my cheeks.

"I bought the diapers and formula. My parents only cared about the welfare check."

"Please tell me she's okay." My voice is barely audible.

"She was four months old when I came home from work to find my parents unconscious in the living room, my father still with a needle stuck between his toes." Bishop's hand falls to his side as if the memories are finally claiming him. "My sister was dead in her room, lying on her stomach in the second-hand crib I got from goodwill. Eyes wide. Skin grey. Mouth open."

I scrunch my nose, refusing to cry when he's being so strong.

"I don't know what happened." He steps back, my hands falling to my sides. "And I didn't give anyone the chance to find out. I packed my shit, torched the trailer with my parents still inside, and disappeared. I spent six months living on the street before Lorenzo found me."

I can't picture it. Can't bring sight to a heartbroken, teenage Bishop. His presence is so undeniably powerful and enduring that imagining him as anything less than impenetrable is painful.

"I'm so sorry." I reach for him, my own selfish needs demanding contact.

"Maybe next time you'll think twice about asking for my secrets." His hand finds mine in the shadows, our fingers tangling. "Little boys don't become men like me without facing demons along the way."

"I know. I just…"

The sound of a car pulling up outside carries through the house, the impending interruption increasing my guilt.

"So now you know why I despise your drug use, belladonna."
I cringe, but nod.

"And why it's important for me to help save your daughter."
Oh, God.

"Please, Bishop…" My tightening lungs make it hard to breathe. "Don't make this about your sister."

I won't be able to deny him if he does. He wouldn't have to sneak out. I'd watch him leave, my heart on my sleeve, my backbone crumpled on the floor.

"I'll go to him in the early hours," he promises. "I'll get the information. You know I will."

I know. God, *how I know.*

But if Geppet truly is just looking for a way out of the approaching war, he doesn't deserve the type of torment Bishop will inflict.

"Let me think about it," I lie.

I'm stalling, desperate to formulate a better plan we can both agree on when the front screen door opens with a screech.

"Dinner is here," Layla calls out. "I hope you're hungry."

We remain silent, staring at one another through the darkness, our shared trauma seeming to wash away all the cruelty shared between us.

"You need food." He tugs me to my feet. "You've barely eaten today."

"Wait." I cling to the towel loosening around my breasts. "Tell me why you shared all that with me."

Footsteps echo down the hall, the murmured chatter of Layla and Matthew approaching as Bishop remains quiet.

"Please," I whisper.

The footsteps stop abruptly, making me rerun how sexual I must have sounded.

Then the bedroom light flicks on, blinding me.

"Shit." I cover my eyes as Bishop presses his body into mine like some sort of shield.

"Dinner," my brother snaps. "*Now.*"

Layla chuckles, their footfalls continuing down the hall while Matthew mutters a whole heap of something under his breath.

"We weren't even doing anything." I raise my voice, blinking until my sight adjusts.

"That statement would be more convincing if you had clothes on," Matthew growls back.

I roll my eyes and meet Bishop's smirking gaze. I guess he likes pissing off my brother.

He cups my cheeks and places a chaste kiss to my nose. "You're going to let me handle Geppet because I—"

"Stop—"

"Belladonna." He gives me a pointed stare. "I'll follow your rules. Torture within your guidelines."

"I don't want him tortured at all."

"Then the two of us will just have a friendly chat." He shrugs but it's totally unconvincing. "My point is, you don't need to do this on your own."

I'm melting for him. One big, fat puddle of exposure. *Dammit*, he works me better than I've worked any man.

"I said I'd think about it." I rake my teeth over my bottom lip, unsure if I'm still lying.

"Okay." He gives a final stroke of my cheek and steps back. "I'll let you get dressed."

He leaves me staring after him, heart in my throat, soul tragically raw.

I quickly tug on a pair of loose jeans from the stockpile my brother provided, pull a cotton T-shirt over my head, and finish off the look with my usual scarf, then reunite with the others in the dining room.

The three of them are already eating their burgers and fries at the table, my food waiting at the place setting beside Bishop, a glass of wine next to my plate.

I take my seat as suspicion rears its ugly head.

Nobody else is drinking. Not alcohol anyway.

"I thought it might help you relax," Bishop says as if reading my mind.

"Thanks." I ignore the paranoia building like a threatening storm cloud. "I'm not sure I'm in the mood, though."

He shrugs and throws a French fry in his mouth, unfazed. Or at least acting that way.

But I'm not convinced he hasn't spiked my drink. It's not like he hasn't done it before to get his own way.

I unwrap my burger, the bun soggy with mayonnaise and sauce, the scent delicious. "I appreciate you two driving to get this." I force a smile on Layla.

"And I'd appreciate Bishop keeping his dick in his pants," my brother mutters. "So let's play nice for this one night while we're all stuck under the same roof, okay?"

Bishop's gleam of a smile brightens my periphery. I swear the man doesn't show any sign of happiness unless he's taunting someone.

"Now you want to play nice?" he asks around a bite of food. "I recall walking in on the two of you, not so long ago, on the dining table of the house we were sharing."

Layla's cheeks darken as Matthew scowls.

"And if memory serves," Bishop continues, "clothes were optional but apparently the use of knives weren't."

I glance between them. "You lost me at the knives part."

Layla lowers her gaze to her food, feigning intent interest on her fries.

"Are you done?" Matthew asks.

"Are you?" Bishop counters. "Because as much as I originally enjoyed the whole protective brother act, it's getting old, fast."

"Do you want to know one thing that won't get the opportunity to grow old, fast, if he keeps running his mouth?" Matthew sneers.

Bishop laughs.

I clench my stomach against how good it sounds. "Maybe we should change the subject."

"Good idea," Layla cuts in.

She attempts to keep the conversation flowing during the meal, but estranged siblings, a soon-to-be sister-in-law I barely know, and whatever the hell Bishop and I are to each other, don't make for the most companionable dialogue.

It also doesn't help that the trauma Bishop shared with me in the bedroom keeps poking at the back of my mind. Him being here may have started as a favor to my brothers and continued out of respect to Lorenzo, but I now think he not only wants to ensure my safety, but to make amends for not being able to save his sister.

And that's not fair.

It also makes him unreliable. Too prone to react due to emotion.

I can't risk it.

I won't do that to Tilly.

As soon as Bishop finishes his meal, he pushes from the table to dispose of his rubbish in the trash. "I'm going to take a shower."

My pulse increases.

Is he going to do a runner?

No, he wouldn't. If he was going to skip out of here he wouldn't hide it. His actions would be made without apology. But it doesn't lessen the urgency to make my own moves.

"I'll be outside once you're finished." I give a sad smile, already silently apologizing for what I have to do. "I need to take a walk and clear my head."

He pauses near the entry to the hall, shooting me a skeptical glance over his shoulder. "In the dark?"

"I'll stay in the yard."

His chin hitches, and I wait for him to protest. Instead, he continues into the hall and out of view.

I hang my head, my pulse thundering until a door closes in the distance and it feels like my heart stops completely.

"Everything okay?" Matthew asks.

"No." I raise my gaze and meet his eyes. "Do you want to make up for abandoning me all those years ago?"

He bristles. Layla snaps rigid.

"It's a simple question, Matthew." My heart kicks back into gear, thudding like thunder beneath my ribs. "Will you help me or not?"

He places his can of soda on the table. "What do you want me to do?"

29

BISHOP

I shove my face under the shower's spray, my hand around my dick, my thoughts fixated on Abri. I jerk off to the image of her. The sound of her voice in my head. The memory of her soft skin.

But the physical release doesn't stop the sense of impending doom from flooding my veins.

I can't let her meet with Geppet.

If she goes on her own, who knows what that asshole might do?

She could get hurt. Or worse.

And if she comes with me, it'll be a clear sign she's working with Lorenzo.

The only choice is to go without her, and it's not like she trusts me to stick around anyway.

She didn't touch her wine despite Layla being the one to prepare it. She thinks I attempted to drug her again. That I'm still capable of using underhanded tactics to get my way.

She's wrong.

Even though I'll do whatever necessary to make sure she remains safe, I have no plans to be deceitful. I'll tell her exactly what I'm going to do before marching out of here.

I kill the water and close my eyes, raising my face to the ceiling as droplets fall from my skin to the tile.

But I don't want to piss her off again, despite my addiction to her venom.

I want her to trust me. To rely on me.

And that's just a whole new fucked up problem.

I have no business wanting anything from her.

I scrub a hand down my face with a sigh and walk from the shower, taking my time to dry and dress because all that awaits me is a fucking minefield.

My cell vibrates with a text on the vanity beside my weapons. No doubt an update from my men about Geppet.

I already know he's in his suburban home. All alone. With no visible security system.

He's a sitting duck without so much as a lock on his power box to stop me from killing the electricity before I sneak in to pay him a visit.

But as I finish towel-drying my hair and reach to place the material on the rack, it's *Il vecchio* that stares back at me from the cell screen.

Lorenzo.

I snatch the device and unlock the screen to read the message.

IL VECCHIO

There's been a change of plan. You're leaving tonight. A car is on the way to take you to the airport. Unless you plan on altering your decision about my ultimatum.

I clench the cell in my fist.

Fucking Abri.

She did this. She instigated something while I was in the goddamn fucking shower.

I snatch my fresh suit pants from the hanger clinging to the side of the shower, get dressed into my suit with far too much aggression flooding my veins, then yank open the bathroom door to go in search of the conniving witch.

But Abri and Layla aren't in the living room when I storm in. There's only Langston seated alone at the dining table.

"What has she done?" I bark.

He glances up from his phone with a sigh. "I assume you mean my sister."

"Of course I mean your fucking sister." I slam my cell on the table and slide it across to him. "Apparently a car is on the way to take me to the airport."

His gaze rakes over the screen before he slides the device back to me. "What did you expect? You still don't want to let her do this her way."

She told him?

I plant my palms on the table, the image of my hands around Abri's delicate throat fueling my anger. "I'm *protecting* her. Far better than anyone in her family."

He peers back at me, exhaustion heavy in his features.

My focus should be on protecting *him*. Keeping *him* alive.

That's been my sole responsibility for years and the recent failure still stings. But Abri needs me more.

"She's a grown woman who wants to handle this on her own," he mutters.

"No. She's an isolated fucking victim who feels like she can't trust or rely on anyone to help fight her fucking battles. How can you not see that?"

He sits back in his chair. "I see it well enough. But this is her daughter and her call to make. I won't go against her wishes when the end result could be something I'm not willing to live with. And you shouldn't be able to live with it either. If Lorenzo wants you out of here, then get out of here." His eyes harden. "Unless you plan on claiming her."

I don't move. Don't react. Don't show how much the stipulation claws at my insides like a wild beast.

"Do you think someone who's been used, abused, and mistreated by men should ever be *claimed*?" I sneer.

His brows raise as if I've just proven his point. "No. And that's why you need to leave."

"So you and your perfect army can watch over her?" I shove from the table. "You, with your insides resembling a slushy. Then your brothers who not only have stab wounds—that you inflicted, I might add—but perfectly constructed incompetence. And let's not forget Lorenzo, who's older than time and can barely walk faster than a fucking toddler due to his gunshot wound."

"She says she can handle Geppet on her own. And after all the shit she's been through, I'm inclined to believe her."

"Even if she was capable," I grate through clenched teeth, "she's Lorenzo's goddamn fucking niece. She deserves to have someone handle it for her."

"And you're that guy?"

"I don't see anyone else around here with fully functioning limbs and more than two brain cells to rub together."

He rolls his eyes. "You don't think that because she's Lorenzo's niece that she should be given the chance to show her power? To be supported in her attempt to prove herself? To make her own choices regarding her offspring?"

"Save the guilt trip for someone with a conscience. We both know you'd never let Layla do anything even remotely close to what Abri has planned."

He places his hands on the table, stabilizing himself as he pushes to his feet. "Layla is my fiancée. She's mine to protect. Unless you plan on making that commitment to my sister I suggest you drop this shit before I lose my temper."

Fiancée? "When the fuck did you get engaged?"

"On my deathbed, after my father tried to kill me." He hobbles toward the kitchen, clearly not giving a shit that he's just thrown monumental information in my face like it was yesterday's news.

Jesus Christ. I sank into a black hole the night my life collided with Abri's. Everything has been turned on its head.

I scrub a hand down my face. "You barely know her."

"I know everything I need to know. And when your life flashes before your eyes and all you see is one woman, there's no stopping the outcome." He makes his way to the coffee machine. "I want a simpler life, Bishop. And I want it with Layla."

A cesspool forms in my stomach. Is this betrayal I'm feeling? Or just irritation that he wants all that white-picket-fence shit and is stupid enough to think he can obtain it?

"Then I guess congratulations are in order." I keep my petulance in check.

"Thanks." He places a fresh mug under the coffee machine. "I'll take that as high approval seeing as though you're not the type to gush emotion."

"I do approve." Somewhat at least. "You deserve each other."

His lips twitch. "Are you saying that because she's destined to turn my hair grey?"

"Probably." I walk for the windows, scanning the sea of black outside for a sign of my hellion.

"Do you want coffee?" he asks.

"Yeah." It's going to be a long night once I get my hands on his sister and start ripping her a new one. "Have you kept watch to make sure Abri hasn't left the yard? It's not safe to be walking the fields at night."

He doesn't answer. There's only the spit and hiss of the coffee machine.

"Langston," I bark, turning back to him. "Have you been watching her?"

"No." His focus remains on the machine. "Like I said, she's a grown-ass woman."

Fuck him.

I return my attention to the darkness, growing impatient.

She needs to get back here so she can reverse whatever the fuck she said to Lorenzo. Then we're going to have another chat about Geppet, and we're not going to stop chatting until she gets it through her thick head that she's not alone anymore.

"Did she walk out the back door or the front?" I ask.

Yet again, there's no answer.

"Fucking hell, Langston," I snap. "Front or back?"

He grabs the mugs and starts shuffling toward me. "I don't know."

The hairs on the back of my neck prickle, unease seeping through me. Yeah, he's tired, injured, and growing impatient with my bullshit, but he's never been unobservant.

"It's not a tough question." I scrutinize his approach. "Did she leave out the front or the back?"

He stops at the dining table, placing the mugs down slowly. "Hold up a sec. My insides are giving me hell."

Is he stalling? Attempting to keep me away from Abri until the driver shows?

"What the fuck are you playing at?" I stalk toward him.

He rolls his eyes but doesn't look at me as he clutches the table with one hand, splaying the other over his abdomen. "Just give me a goddamn second."

No. He's up to something. "Where's Layla?"

"In our bedroom."

"Call her out here." Everyone needs to take note of what I'm about to say to Abri. They all need to fucking listen.

"Bishop…"

"Call her the fuck out here." I storm for the back door and fling it wide before walking outside. "*Abri.*"

She doesn't answer.

The whole world is quiet, taunting me with its muted oblivion, the moon shining bright enough to highlight the stillness of the yard.

I stalk to the end of the porch and scan the side of the building, then farther across the fields. "*Abri.*"

There's no movement. Not even the whistle of the breeze as my pulse kicks up speed.

Something doesn't feel right.

I jog to the other end of the porch, doing the same visual sweep. "*Abri.*" This time there's anger in my voice. Livid fucking rage.

She's not out here.

"I'd learn how to run if I were you, Langston," I yell, marching back to the door to yank it open.

He's now seated at the table, coffee mug in hand, his expression bleeding with guilt.

Son of a fucking bitch.

I reach into my pocket, pull a throwing knife from its sheath, and launch it at his head.

He ducks sharply, avoiding impact but spilling his drink.

"Jesus. *Fuck.*" He slaps a hand to his abdomen. "Have you forgotten I was fucking shot?"

"You'll be fucking stabbed soon. Where is she?"

Layla runs into the room, her eyes wide. "What's going on?"

"You tell me." I march for the hall, barely a breath away from barging her shoulder as I continue to the front door and peer through the screen.

All the blood drains from my face.

We're one car short.

Hers is still here with its missing tire. But the rental is gone.

"You let her leave?" I swing around and storm back to the living room. "I'll fucking kill you."

Layla's gaze pleads with me as she stands beside Langston, her hands raised in placation. "Please calm down."

I grin, stalking to the table. "This is calm, sugarplum. Wait until I lose my shit."

Langston pushes to his feet. "Before you ask, I don't know where she is."

"Bullshit." I slam my wrist against the wood, activating the switch blade that springs out toward my palm. "Tell me." I grab his shirt and drag him to his feet.

He grimaces, one hand clamping over my wrist, the other grabbing at his abdomen.

"*Bishop, stop*," Layla screams. "You're hurting him."

I raise the blade to his throat, seeing the betrayal in his eyes that I should've noticed earlier. "I'm going to do a lot more than hurt him." I sneer in his face. "How could you let her go, you piece of shit?"

He keeps his chin steady, not tilting it away from the blade. "She gets to call the shots."

My hand shakes with the need to slit his throat. To make him pay. To ensure he suffers like I currently am.

"Where. Did she. Go?" I enunciate the words slowly even though my pulse speeds faster with every passing second.

I don't understand the fear pulsing through me. The rage. The betrayal. The hurt.

This shit is all new to me and I don't fucking like it.

"I don't know," he repeats. "I deliberately told her not to disclose the information so you couldn't get it out of me."

I grin, my teeth clenched so tight with the feral smirk I can taste blood. "At least you had foresight with the deception."

His jaw ticks. "She's my sister."

And I'd thought I was his brother.

His goddamn family.

"Please, Bishop." Layla tugs at my arm. "You don't understand. She *had* to go. It's her daughter."

I swing around to her, shoving the knife in her face. "Don't talk to me about not—"

"Don't point that at her," Langston growls. "You can threaten me all you like, but she's off-limits. You know that."

Yeah. I know.

And even with the rules of engagement firmly tattooed into my frontal lobe, I don't care. They let Abri walk out of here alone. Without protection. Without a fucking care.

"Please listen to me," Layla begs. "She'll be okay. She's going to make sure Remy and Salvatore are close by. And promised that the meeting would be held in public. Somewhere with witnesses—"

"Who will report back to Adena if they're seen together," I snap. "Why the fuck would Geppet risk that if this wasn't a setup?"

"Maybe because he's already made up his mind to change sides." She releases my arm. "Please, Bishop. You're not thinking clearly. She knows this guy."

But do they know Abri?

No.

Not like I do.

They have no clue what toll the manipulation has on her. That she gets high just to see herself through it.

"I hope you're right." I retract the blade.

"You need to go." Langston straightens his shirt with a hard tug of the collar. "Pack your shit and head back to D.C. We'll discuss this once I get home."

"Oh, I'm definitely heading out of here, asshole." I make for my bedroom to get that fucking car tire. "And if I don't return with your sister, be prepared—I'll be coming back for blood."

30

ABRI

After convincing Matthew to go against Bishop's assumed plan, I run for the front door, escaping in the slick black Lincoln.

My brother said he would contact Lorenzo. That he'd make sure Bishop had to leave the state right away. And I don't want to be anywhere near that house when the news breaks.

I can't risk caving to the man who's winning my heart. Not again.

As soon as I reach the main road leading toward the city, I dial Geppet's number, the call connecting on the third ring.

"Hey, baby girl." His voice is groggy. Sleep-riddled?

"I didn't wake you, did I?"

"Kinda. I crashed as soon as I got home. Your mom hasn't given me much chance to rest over the past few days."

Shit. "Of course. I'm so sorry."

"It's okay. What's up?"

"I need to bring the timeline for our meeting a little closer."

"How much closer?" he says through a yawn.

"Now?" I glance to the heavens with a silent prayer. "Well, in an hour or so if you're up for it."

"Babe, I'm tired as fuck."

"I understand, but this is important. I've got information you're going to want to hear."

He sighs. "The things I do for you and that pretty face of yours. Can you come to my place?"

"Not really. I'm kinda caught up in the city," I lie. I need time to get back to the hotel room I still have reserved from the nights before the gala. "Could you come to me? I'm staying at the Saffron and there's this quiet Italian restaurant around the corner that's perfect for a private conversation. I promise we won't be seen."

He falls quiet.

"Please, Gep. I need you." I let the temptress enter my voice, the first dangle of the carrot hovering in front of him.

"Fine. But call me Aaron. I like when you say my name."

I ignore the nauseating squeeze of my stomach. "Okay."

We arrange to meet in an hour—just enough time for me to freshen up and look the part. Then I disconnect and call Remy.

"You need to get your ass in the city. ASAP." This is the only stipulation Matthew demanded—that I have our brothers watch over me. "I'm meeting Geppet in an hour."

"Fuck. Okay. Where exactly?"

I relay the details, warn them not to be seen, and ignore all his concerns before ending the call.

For the first time since Tilly was taken from me, I feel like I'm making forward momentum toward my daughter. That I'll finally get to know if she's safe and well.

But the slight wave of apprehensive optimism disappears once I approach the outer edge of the city, my phone vibrating on the passenger seat. Bishop's name stares up at me, the gentle *buzz, buzz, buzz* of the incoming call seeming far more aggressive than usual.

I keep both hands on the wheel, side-eying the flashing name until the vibrations stop.

I don't answer when he calls a second time.

Or a third.

Or fourth.

By the time I pull up at the valet stand of the Saffron and hand over my keys, guilt has firmly lodged itself in my throat, making it hard to swallow.

Then the messages start, each short, sharp vibration echoing my footsteps through the hotel lobby.

BISHOP

Answer your fucking phone and tell me where you are.

My throat tightens.

BISHOP

Was that your plan all along? Get me to trust you, then stab me in the back?

My heart clenches.

BISHOP

You realize your brothers are dead if anything happens to you. I'll wear Salvo's head like a fucking crown.

I shut my walls down, blocking out any other unwanted response.

I can't let him weaken me further. I have to be focused.

I stop before the hotel elevators, my confidence regenerating enough that when the next call comes through I answer with my head held high.

"I'll find you," he warns in greeting.

"Shouldn't you already be on your way to the airport?"

"The things I should do in regards to you have never seemed to be a preference for some reason. So you'd do well to start preparing for me to make good on my promise."

"It kinda sounds more like a threat, Bishop." I slap my hand against the elevator call button and quickly check to make sure I still have the room card in my phone case. "And I rarely listen to those."

"You should when they come from me, belladonna. I don't like being ignored."

And I don't like feeling fragile, but that's exactly the effect he has on me. I always want to crawl toward his protection. To hide behind his strength. I guess neither of us are getting what we want today.

"I have no doubt you'll find me. But will it be before I meet with Geppet?" I ask. "I doubt it. And after that I won't care about your threats because I'll already have the information I need."

"You're being fucking stupid," he growls.

"And you're being a fucking dictator. Salvo and Remy will watch over me. I'm being cautious."

"Your brothers wouldn't know how to fight their way out of a preschool beat-down. Why the hell won't you trust me to do this for you?"

The elevator dings its arrival, the gleaming gold doors opening before me. "This isn't about trust. It's about me not needing to be saved."

"That's a goddamn lie. You want to be saved as much as I want to save you."

My eyes widen at his admission, my heart throbbing.

I shake my head. Denying him. Denying the way the pained organ beneath my ribs wants to agree with him.

"Look…" I swallow over the tightness taking over my throat. "I appreciate you wanting to help. And I'm grateful for all you've already done. But—"

"Shut the fuck up with that Hallmark shit and tell me where the hell you are."

And just like that, my frailty vanishes. *Poof*. Gone. "Fuck you, Bishop. I suggest you make peace with me doing this my way because I'm not changing my mind."

"I won't make peace with it, belladonna. And once I find you, you best believe I'll make you understand how much I don't enjoy being defied."

A shiver runs down my spine. One that shouldn't hold a hint of pleasure.

"You're only making this worse for yourself, Abri. Tell me where you are. Tell me when you plan to meet Geppet."

I step into the elevator. "I've gotta go. I'll call you once I'm done."

"*Wait*." There's a pause before he continues without the edge of malice. "There are easier ways. If you're adamant on going at it on your own, then fine, have it your way, but let me be the one to watch your back."

That was an Olympic backflip if ever I've heard one. Why?

"Are you tracing this call?" I accuse.

Is he trying to get me to stay on the line? *Shit*. I hang up before receiving an answer and slam my finger against my floor number.

He can't get an accurate trace from a cell tower anyway. His tactics are useless unless he's installed a tracker app on my cell.

My phone vibrates with a text.

BISHOP

I don't need to trace the call, belladonna. I already have men watching Geppet, remember? See you soon.

I stare at the screen, anger flooding my veins, but there's also the unwanted thrill of the chase, too. He's coming for me.

Son of a bitch.

I jog to my suite as soon as the elevator doors open and connect a call to Geppet.

"Hey, baby girl," he answers.

"Hey. Can you get here sooner?" I open my hotel door and start undressing one-handed. "We can't wait any longer."

"I guess... I just need to throw on some pants."

"Do it and start heading into the city now. You're already being watched."

"What? Who the hell is—"

"We'll discuss it when you get here. Just make sure you lose the tail."

"Abri, who the fuck is watching me?" Anger enters his voice.

"You don't want to know, and you won't have to find out as long as you drive like the wind."

"Jesus Christ," he mutters. "If anyone sees me with you I'm a dead man."

I wince, hating how right he is. Hating that I have to ignore it for the sake of my daughter.

"My family is going to war, Aaron. We both want to be fighting on the right side, and we need each other to figure out which side that is." I shimmy out of my jeans and rush to the closet to pull out tight black pants, a matching blazer, a white satin top with a scandalously low neckline, then a matching thin scarf. "I'll see you soon."

I disconnect and get dressed.

I'm in the bathroom, finishing the final touches on my makeup when a knock sounds at the door.

My cell vibrates with a text seconds later.

REMY

It's me.

I quickly let my brothers in, both of them taking in my borderline sultry appearance, Salvo's narrowed judgment far more scathing than my youngest brother's.

"I don't like this." Salvo stalks forward, barging past me. "I don't trust Geppet."

"You don't need to trust him." I open the door wider, giving Remy more space to walk inside. "You only have to watch him. And if that's an issue, I can do this alone. It's not like I haven't done it before."

I conveniently leave out the part where my only non-guarded scheme ended with Bishop having to save me from being beaten and raped.

"Ignore him." Remy squeezes my shoulder as he passes. "We've got your back."

"I didn't say I wouldn't have her back." Salvatore stops at the end of the king-sized bed, arms crossed over the chest of his designer suit. "I just don't like the undertones of where this could lead. How far are you willing to go to get information on your daughter?"

I ignore the sucker punch of shame and head into the bathroom. "I'll do whatever it takes." I meet my gaze in the mirror, forcing myself to become the persona staring back at me. The temptress. The belladonna. "If you have a problem with that, hurry up and get over it or leave."

I apply my lipstick and smack my lips together, ignoring Remy as he comes to stand in the doorway.

"Don't get huffy," he murmurs. "He's worried. We both are."

"I'm not huffy." I adjust my scarf so the long lengths drape down my back instead of covering my cleavage.

"You've gotta admit, this is fucked up. We're only coming to terms with what Mom and Dad made you do, and now—"

"Don't you dare do this to me." I turn to face him, his expression pinching with remorse. "I need to get my head in the game. I can't have you two judging me."

"It's not judgment—"

"Like hell it's not." I move to walk past him, but he blocks my path.

"Abri, this is guilt. We let you down and feel like shit because of it. But there's no place we'd rather be than by your side."

"You won't be by my side. You'll be hiding out of sight."

"You know what I mean." He lowers his voice. "Salvo is a fucking wreck under all that macho testosterone. A week ago, he thought he was dealing with the brunt of our father's insanity. Now he knows better and can't forgive himself. Not to mention the whole future with the mafia situation."

I cringe, my own guilt trying to dig its claws back in. "I can't talk about this now."

"I know. I just didn't want you leaving the hotel thinking we're not one hundred percent behind you." He steps out of the way. "You're stronger than I am, Bree."

It's not strength. Bishop taught me it's a lack of self-preservation. But I don't say that out loud.

I walk back into the main room where Salvatore sits on the end of my bed, frowning at his cell.

A buzz sounds from Remy's jacket and I glance to him as he retrieves the device to read the message with a matching scowl.

"Something wrong?" I grab a clutch from the wardrobe and confirm one of my mini stun guns is waiting inside.

"No." Remy locks the cell and shoves it back in his pocket.

"Is it Bishop?" I raise a brow, dropping my lipstick and phone into the clutch beside the weapon.

Salvatore flops back on the mattress, his silence telling.

"What did he say?" I demand.

"Just the same old shit he's been saying since you decided to meet with Geppet tonight."

"Elaborate or hand over your phone." I hold out a palm to Remy.

"It's nothing."

"Nothing more than a rather vivid explanation of how he's going to skin me alive," Salvatore mutters.

"Lucky you," Remy drawls. "Apparently I'm getting placed in a barrel of acid."

"He won't touch you," I say with confidence even though I have absolutely no idea how to get between a butcher and his calling. "Ignore him. I'll deal with the fallout from his tantrum later."

"No, I'll take care of him." Salvatore pushes to his feet. "It's about time me and that asshole settled our differences."

I want to protest, to tell my brother he doesn't stand a chance against someone like Bishop. But it's a discussion for another time. I don't have the bandwidth for more drama at the moment. "I need to go."

They both nod. Sullen.

"The Italian restaurant around the corner, right?" Remy clarifies.

"Yeah." I make for the door, my clutch clamped under my elbow. "Stay out of sight. If Geppet sees you—"

"He won't." Salvatore follows me. "We'll find a parking spot nearby and hide behind the tinted windows."

"Good." I pull the door wide, indicating for them to walk before me, not bothering with a farewell that could lead to an emotional avalanche. "I'll go down in the elevator after you. We can meet back here once I'm done."

They nod and comply, leaving me to gnaw on my bottom lip until my elevator arrives.

Once I reach the lobby I put my game face on, my chin held high.

I keep the guise in place as I saunter from the hotel and around the block to the meeting spot. I look inside as I approach, the romantic, dim lighting of Città Italiana making the back of the restaurant hard to see from the street but not impossible.

The perfect balance for Geppet's paranoia and my safety.

I'm about to walk inside to request a table when a hand grabs my wrist, and I almost drop my clutch.

"There's been a change of plans, baby girl." Geppet drags me away from the door. "Follow me."

"Is everything okay?" I ignore the urge to glance over my shoulder to search for my brothers and turn my eyes to Geppet. "Did you ditch the tail?"

"I did, but I want to make sure you don't have one, too." He raises my hand to tuck it around the crook of his arm. "How did you know I was being watched?"

"My brothers called and mentioned something about traffic surveillance photos of you with my mom. They told me you were already back in town. So I read between the lines and assumed they were tracking you."

He drags me across the road, dodging us through the busy traffic as I struggle to keep up in my two-inch pumps. "It sounds like they're telling you an awful lot for someone who claims to not be on their side."

"Excuse me." I pull my hand from his grip, acting offended. "I'm not going to burn a bridge that's giving me valuable information. Would you have even known you had men watching you if I hadn't mentioned it?"

"Good point." He slides a hand around my waist, pulling me back into his side. He leads me farther down the road, his touch drifting lower with each step until he's palming the curve of my ass. "Let's go in here." He stops in front of the doors to a busy diner. "We'll blend in with the crowd."

I nod, ignoring his touch. At least I try to. But it's difficult to dull the disgust when there's no coke to balm me. No liquor to stifle the taunting voices in my head.

We walk inside, being greeted by a middle-aged waitress who escorts us to a booth in the middle of the diner, the bright fluorescents making me feel like we're under a spotlight.

Geppet orders coffee. I opt for juice. My pulse is erratic enough without more caffeine.

Then once we're alone, Geppet leans his elbows on the table, taking me in like he hasn't seen me in years.

"For someone going through hell, you sure look good." One corner of his mouth lifts in appreciation. "A sight for sore eyes and all that."

Usually, this is when my confidence gains a boost. When I know my body has set the trap and all that's left is to reel my victim closer to his demise.

Tonight is different.

I've never manipulated someone with my daughter's life on the line. Never had to exude seductive perfection while my brothers watch from the shadows.

I give a half-hearted smile. "Thanks. It's been a rough week."

"Well, you always handle yourself professionally. I've rarely seen you flustered. You either don't care about much or you know how to hide your emotions perfectly."

My skin prickles.

His comment sounds like a fragment of conversation he would've had with my mother. That while they drove across country, they discussed my heartlessness or how skilled I am at hiding what's inside.

"Maybe it's a bit of both." I shrug. "But I care about my daughter and I want to make sure she's safe." My attention latches onto a couple entering the diner over his right shoulder, the woman's eyes meeting mine before she looks away. "Are you sure you weren't followed?"

"Positive." He mimics my line of sight, glancing behind him to take in the new arrivals, barely sparing them a two-second glance. "And I should thank you for the heads up about the tail. I had no clue I was being watched."

"You're welcome. Us outsiders have to stick together."

He huffs a sound, part chuckle, slight scoff. "Are you an outsider, though? Your mom is convinced you're working with your brothers."

"I'm not."

"Have you done what she asked then?"

The question is callous. Far colder than I would've expected from someone looking to work together. Then again, the conversations I've had with Geppet in the last twenty-four hours have been more than double the speaking time I've shared with him since he was employed by our family years ago. I don't know him well enough to determine if this is normal or my mother's influence.

"Do you mean, have I killed my brothers?" I lower my voice. "No. I'm not a murderer, Aaron. I can't do that, and my mom knows it."

"She seemed pretty adamant in the car."

I smile at the waitress passing by and drop my voice even further. "She's obviously still in shock after what happened. There's no way she would want me to carry out her request."

"I disagree. She spent the good part of a cross-country trip telling me it's the only thing that would make her happy. *That*, and also dealing with your daughter."

I turn cold. Fingers. Arms. Chest. "Dealing with her?"

He shrugs. "Your guess is as good as mine on what she meant. I didn't ask for specifics."

I try to remain calm. Composed. "Tell me what she said about her."

"Not as much as she said about you. I was told how you love to spread your legs to keep your father happy. And that you were practically whoring yourself out to his friends and business colleagues." He raises his hands in placation. "Those were Adena's words, not mine."

Alarm bells ring in my ears. I can't tell if he's taunting me or perhaps setting an expectation. Either way, I'm forced to swallow down the unease and keep my head high.

I can't play this game as a victim. I'll lose too much power. Egotistical men don't like damaged goods. They want to break a hard-ass, not a pathetic fool. So I smirk. "I wouldn't call it whoring. It was all a bit of fun in the name of progress."

He chuckles. "That's my dirty girl."

My dirty girl.

He's staking a claim.

At least that's a good sign.

"I've always liked you, Abri. You're my type of woman."

"You've never skipped my attention either."

"Is that so?" One brow raises. "Then why don't we stop beating around the bush and get down to why we're both here. You want information on your daughter and…"

"And you want?" I hedge.

"You." He grins. "I could keep lying and tell you how badly I want to get on the right side of this war, but the truth is, staying around here is only going to get me killed. I was a witness to the bloodbath at your uncle's house. Now I'm drinking coffee with the enemy." He grabs his mug and takes a sip. "I'm already living on borrowed time, and I knew it the entire car ride with your mother. But if I could just get a taste of the sweetness every other guy in town has already had, I could leave this place a happy man."

I still can't figure out what he's up to. I've only ever played successful, wealthy men before and those types all have the same M.O—class, subtlety, and underlying professionalism, at least in public.

Clearly, Geppet is different.

"Why don't we take this conversation back to my place and we can both get what we want?" he asks.

"Your place is compromised, Aaron. You can't go back there."

"I know. I've got another place my father left me when he bit the dust. It's quieter. More room to breathe. No neighbors in sight."

Isolated. Hidden. A billowing red flag.

Fuck. Is this seduction or an ambush?

"I don't think that's a good idea." I palm my glass of juice, the cold soothing my sweating fingers.

"You want to know where your daughter is, right? I know exactly where that is." He rakes his gaze down my chest, his eyes lingering on my cleavage before returning to my face. "I also know Adena plans to see your kid real soon."

The chill in my veins turns arctic, freezing every part of me.

"And for total transparency, I don't think her plans involve quality time with her granddaughter." He rakes his tongue over his bottom lip. "So what do you say, baby girl? Are you interested in getting out of here? Just you, me, and an exchange of favors?"

31

ABRI

I KEEP MY EXPRESSION IN CHECK WHILE MY BRAIN WORKS IN OVERDRIVE.

I need a bump. But the mere thought of coke reminds me of Bishop. And his sister. Which in return makes me wallow in guilt.

There's too much riding on this to falter now.

I have to inform my brothers of the change in location. Or do I? Maybe it's better if they don't follow. If they can't eavesdrop from nearby as I try to worm my way out of scraping the bottom of the barrel with Geppet.

"Give me a minute to freshen up." I slide from the booth, my clutch tight in my hand, only to have my wrist captured in his grip.

"Leave your phone," he states.

Those warning bells scream louder.

He doesn't trust me. And if he's smart enough not to trust me, he should be smart enough not to put his life on the line for a quick fuck. So he's either gloriously stupid or inching that trap closer. I can't tell which.

"Excuse me?" I frown, playing into the confusion.

He jerks his chin at my clutch. "I know you have one in there. Leave it on the table."

"Sure." I wait for him to release his hold, then slowly pull out my phone. "But it's concerning that you don't have faith in me, Aaron. You realize I have nobody else, right? My brothers went behind my back, my father is gone, and my mother holds me responsible. You know I have no friends. There's no other family I can trust."

He gives a smug smile. "Yeah, but I also know you're resourceful. I'm just covering my ass."

"If that's what's needed." I place my cell on the table. He can't access anything without my facial recognition anyway. But it means I can't text my brothers with an update. "After knowing each other this long I would've hoped you could trust me." I pause, hoping he'll change his mind.

He doesn't.

"But I understand." I back away, holding in a string of curses. "I won't be long."

I turn on my heels and make my way toward the bathroom sign in the far back corner pointing its way to the dim hall.

Bishop said I'd never have to use my body like this again. That no man would ever touch me. I guess a tiny part of me wanted to believe it was true because the self-loathing crawling over my skin has never felt so slimy.

And the worst part is that Geppet's touch will take away the only real pleasure I've had with a man. His hands will ruin the bliss Bishop's created.

I enter the hall, past the noisy entry to the kitchen, then shove into the ladies bathroom.

I expect panic to rain down on me as soon as I'm alone. But it doesn't hit.

There's only cold resignation. The tired realization that this is who I'm meant to be even when my father's no longer around to force my hand.

I drag my feet into a stall, lock myself inside, then breathe through the hollowness taking over my body as I wish with every ounce of my being that I was someone else.

Someone honorable.

Someone worthy.

Someone who didn't have to be a conniving, manipulative bitch.

The bathroom door swings open with a squeak and I tense, wondering if Geppet was paranoid enough to follow me in here.

Footsteps trek across the tile. Water runs from the faucet. Someone washes their hands.

I relax, exhaling with a barely audible sigh.

Come on, Abri. You've got this.

I'm so close to Tilly I can feel her. With a few perfectly phrased lines to Geppet and an inviting touch here and there, he'll tell me what I need. I'm sure he will. I can get the information without having to sleep with him.

The water cuts off. Footsteps trek back across the bathroom. The door swings open again. Then there's silence.

I'm alone.

Time to get back to work.

I suck in a breath and unlock the stall door to walk for the basins. I'm two feet from my destination when a bulking shadow enters my periphery. My adrenaline spikes. I react on instinct with a striking elbow, but a hand clamps around my mouth, the man dragging me back against his hard chest.

I'm about to drop my weight to the floor, hoping I'll catch him off-guard with the escape tactic when I shoot a frantic glance at the mirror, the familiar scent of my attacker hitting me at the same time as the sight of him.

"I told you I'd find you," Bishop snarls in my ear, his breath against my skin instantly filling the hollowness inside me.

I gasp, pushing from his hold to swing around and face him, my relief dying a quick death when I see those deep blue eyes attempting to scorch me to ash. "How?"

"My men are worth every dollar I pay them," he sneers. "Has Geppet touched you?"

I shake my head, more denying the overtly protective question than answering it.

"But something's wrong." His gaze searches mine. "What did he say to you?"

"Nothing. I can handle it."

"*Belladonna*," he warns. "I don't think you understand how close I am to becoming a man you don't want to get acquainted with. I suggest you tell me what he's done to upset you before I storm out there, blow your cover, and find out for myself." His volatility is so thick and rich it enters my lungs with each inhale.

But if I tell him what's going on he'll kill Geppet. And if he kills Geppet I may never find my daughter.

"It's just about Tilly." I shake my head to clear the building fog. "He said he knows where she is."

His eyes narrow. "Why would that upset you?"

"It doesn't. I'm overwhelmed. Relieved and apprehensive at the same time. He wants to go someplace quiet to talk. To—"

"No," he barks. "No secondary locations. No getting in his car. You're not doing any of that shit."

"He has the information I need, Bishop."

"Good. Then I can follow him home and get it for you."

"He won't go back to his house. He knows someone is watching him."

His jaw flexes with animosity. "How would he know that?"

"Because I needed to earn his trust."

He steps closer. I'm sure the proximity is meant to be threatening, but all I want to do is sink into his arms. "And did you?"

"Somewhat. Enough to work with at the very least."

He doesn't respond. Not with anything other than a flaring of his nostrils.

"I told you I can handle this," I add. "You've got a plane to catch."

"That flight has already departed, belladonna." He leans closer, his words murmured over my lips. "Unfortunately for you, me leaving is no longer an option. So now we also have to deal with the consequences of Lorenzo's ultimatum."

My skin prickles, a sheen of goose bumps skittering up my arms. "What consequences?"

"You, me, and matrimony. You're mine now, belladonna. To protect and worship as I see fit."

A laugh slips past my lips but he doesn't mimic my humor. If anything, his intensity increases as if I've doused the flames in lighter fluid.

He stalks closer to me, his hips bumping mine, his thighs pushing me backward until I stumble into the vanity.

"And let me make something clear," he growls in my face, "I will never allow my woman to place herself in danger."

I rerun his statement in my head. Over and over. He can't actually be that warped, can he?

"*My woman*?" I roll my eyes. "Really?"

I can admit some parts of me are getting a kick out of his outrageously caveman response—mainly my tumbling stomach and the tingling void between my thighs. But my life is spiraling closer toward Armageddon with every passing second, and I have no time to encourage this *Beauty and the Beast* stitch.

One minefield at a time please, Satan.

"And *I* would never allow *my man* to dictate *my life* for me." I shove at his chest, my clutch thumping his shirt. "This is *my* daughter." I shove again. "*My* responsibility." Another shove. "*My* mistake to fix. Don't back me into a corner, Bishop. You won't like how I fight my way free."

"Cute threat." One side of his lips kicks in a violent grin. "Want to slide a hand over my dick and see how hard violence makes me?"

My throat dries. And my heart—*holy hell*. The hammer of arrhythmia makes me dizzy.

This isn't the Bishop I know. This man is next level. Bishop 2.0.

Or, more accurately, the Butcher.

"I need to get back out there." I sidestep to walk around him. "Geppet is already suspicious."

"He's also a few dumb moves away from a death sentence." He grabs me by the hips, dragging me backward into him again. He places his mouth right near my ear, his nose nuzzling my hair. "Let me protect you, belladonna."

Is that a request? No longer a demand?

My heart squeezes at the slight fracture in his dictatorship. But I can't cave. "I need to do this on my own," I whisper.

"No, you only think you do." He roughly turns me to face him, the harshness of his stare holding me hostage more than those forceful hands. "Why are you so fucking stubborn?"

"Why are you?" I counter.

"Because getting the information from him will cost me nothing. Can you say the same?" He stares at me pointedly. "I see you, Abri. You're not the viper you think you are. That heart of yours is full of gold."

I force out a laugh. "You don't know me."

"I know that you want me to save you."

I shake my head, denying him. Denying the truth. Denying how the weakness threatens to seep back in.

"That you want nothing more than to be taken care of," he continues. "And I know you're well aware I'm the only man capable of doing it. I'm the only one who can calm you. Protect you." He pulls me against his hips, his crotch rubbing against my pubic bone to make me burn. "*Pleasure* you."

Oh, God. "Stop it."

"Never." He smashes his mouth to mine.

I gasp into the contact, his tongue sliding between my parted lips to deepen the kiss.

His hand grabs the back of my neck. The other is possessive on my hip. He consumes me until I'm a puddle of need, clawing at his shirt, scratching at his throat, completely and utterly immersed in him.

"Bishop…" I pull back, struggling for air. I'm about to plead my case to get back out to Geppet but that deep ocean blue staring back at me catches me off-guard.

All the anger is gone. It's not even passion that peers down at me.

It's something deeper. Something like what he shared with me in his bedroom at the safe house.

Our panted breaths mingle between us. The silence stretches.

Finally, he presses his forehead to mine, the hand on my neck tightening. "I claimed you. You're mine. Stay safe or I'll kill you myself."

I should laugh in his face. Should shoot him down in flames and tell him I'll never be claimed. Never be owned. But my chest becomes tight and achy. I swear, my heart swells.

Men have looked at me in many ways before—with lust, greed, hunger…spite, animosity, and hostility, too. Yet the way Bishop currently peers back at me is foreign.

There's fear in his eyes, glacial and unwanted. Fear he loathes. Fear for *me*.

His calloused hands cup my cheeks. "If something happens to you—"

"Nothing will happen." I force strength into my tone. "Geppet is far less intelligent than the men I've dealt with in the past. He'll give me the information I need."

His expression hardens. "I don't want you using the tricks Emmanuel—"

"Don't." I splay my palm on his chest and gently push. "You have your tricks and I have mine. Let me do what I have to do."

"Abri…" For pained heartbeats he stares at me, his thoughts loud, his battle not to argue evident in his feral stare.

"Please," I beg. "I really need to go."

"Then leave knowing I will torture, maim, and murder him if he lays hands on you."

I wince. "You're making this so much harder than it needs to be."

"Safety is hard, belladonna. If you want to do this your way, you need to go the extra mile to ensure you don't place yourself at risk."

"You sure that extra mile isn't due to jealousy?"

"You think I'm jealous of the men who've mistreated you?" He grabs my arms and yanks me closer. "What courses through my veins is a hatred so fucking deep and consuming I battle each second not to slaughter every man who lays eyes on you. Not to mention how difficult it is to watch you act as if you deserve that treatment. Don't underestimate the sacrifice I'm making in letting you do this your way."

My splintered confidence gains more cracks. "I need to go. Wait in here a few minutes. Then slip out the back. If he sees you—"

"He won't."

"Good." I take a deep breath and mentally prepare myself to back away from the security of his arms.

"But I *will* follow you, Abri. I *will* make sure you're safe."

Gratitude warms my chest, yet so much fucking fear surrounds it. Relying on him could risk Tilly's life. If he's seen… If he's heard… "You can be such an authoritative asshole, you know that, right?"

"And just think, belladonna—you've got the rest of your life to figure out how to love me for it."

My stomach gives birth to a mass of fireflies, the heat of them making me burn.

I think it's too late. I might already love him.

At the very least, I love the way he wants to protect me. The way he worships my safety.

"If you need help, use this." He reaches into his pocket and claps something into my hand.

I flip the small plastic device over in my palm with its tiny metal chain hanging from the top. "A rape alarm?"

"I would've preferred comms and listening devices, but my

woman had to go off and do shit on her own without my approval. So this is all we've got on short notice." He gives me a pointed look. "*Use it.* Once you get to wherever you're going, I doubt I'll have eyes on you. I'm going to have to trust you'll sound the alarm if something goes wrong."

"I will," I lie, placing the device in my pocket.

"Believe me, your ass will be mine if you don't." He releases me, coldness entering his eyes as his game face falls back into place. "Now go before I change my mind."

32

ABRI

The giddy fireflies remain in my stomach as I pull open the bathroom door and step into the hall.

I sense a presence to my left, the close proximity making the fireflies vanish.

A split-second glance determines it's Geppet before he yanks me in the opposite direction to the dining area.

"Keep quiet," he murmurs. "Don't say a word. I think I'm still being watched."

I press all the right buttons for the perfect response—wide eyes, parted lips, a frantic gaze scanning our surroundings. "Are you sure you're not being—"

"I said not a fucking word." He drags me farther down the dimly lit hall and through a staff-only door.

We enter the kitchen, the chefs and kitchen hands all busily marching around stainless-steel benches and cast-iron cooktops. A few of them acknowledge us with a quick glare but seem far too swamped to deal with anyone intruding on their space.

"Where are we going?" I ask.

"I parked my car out back. We'll talk at my dad's house."

What? *No*.

I need to leave out front. Where my brothers will see me. Where it'll be easier for Bishop to follow.

I cling tight to my clutch and tug my arm from Geppet's grip. "Slow down. I can't keep up."

He meets my gaze, his expression scrutinizing as if he expects me to run in the opposite direction.

"It's okay." I jerk my chin, instructing him to keep going. "I'm coming. I just need you to walk a little slower."

He frowns, and for a second I think he's going to grab me again. Instead, he turns and pushes through the screen door into the darkened alley.

"Come on." He waits for me, holding the door open.

"Why do you think you're being watched?" I shoot a glance over my shoulder, unsure if I'm hopeful one of my spies will follow or panicked at the thought of them blowing my cover.

"I don't know. Something doesn't feel right. I just want to get out of here." He grabs my hand, gently this time, reclaiming my attention. "My truck's right up there."

I step into the alley, following his line of sight to the hood of the familiar blue Ram pickup parked on the street ahead.

He moves faster.

I deliberately struggle to keep up. At least physically. The mental sluggishness is completely out of my control. I can't figure out how to stall him without drawing suspicion.

He guides me to the truck and opens the passenger door. "Get in." He waits for me to slide inside, then strides around the hood and climbs in the driver's seat. "Buckle up."

I do, but it's not without quickly building apprehension. "Why don't we go to my hotel instead?" I glance at him in hope. "It's right around the corner. We wouldn't even have to drive. I'm sure there's a staff entrance—"

"I'm not staying in the city." He starts the ignition. Revs the engine.

"Geppet, I don't want to go somewhere I'll be stuck without a car."

He pulls into traffic and takes off at speed. "You won't be stuck, baby girl. You'll have me."

That hollow resignation takes over again, boring through my limbs, settling in my belly.

I let out a weary breath.

This was what I was going to do in the first place. Meet him alone. Do this without help. The only thing that's changed is that stupid desire to rely on Bishop. The weak, pathetic reliance I always knew was a liability.

"Where are you taking me?" I ask casually, shutting the thought of any man other than the one beside me entirely from my mind.

There's only Geppet. Nothing else exists except the need to get information on Tilly.

"I already told you—out to my father's old place. It's quiet there. We'll know if we're followed."

I nod, my gaze on the cars directly in front of us.

I don't check the mirrors. Don't allow myself to hope that anyone is following.

"You seem awfully sure of yourself over there." Geppet weaves in and out of traffic, defying the speed limit. "You're not worried we've got a tail?"

"Should I be?" I shoot him a confident stare. "You would've jumped through my father's rigorous hoops to gain employment, so I assume you have the skills to win a game of hide and seek."

He smirks at the thinly veiled compliment.

"You'll lose them, Aaron." I turn my attention out my side window, watching the towering city buildings grow smaller and smaller. "I have faith in you."

He cuts down side streets. Treks back onto main roads.

We reach a less densely populated industrial area with far fewer cars where Geppet turns down a desolate street.

There's no sign of life in sight. No lights follow. There's absolutely no glow from another vehicle traveling behind us.

I'm alone with Geppet. Nobody but me, myself, and I to finish this.

"What a fuckin' rush." He twists his hands around the steering wheel. "That was close for a minute. But I lost them."

"Good." I nod, ignoring the empty chasm that grows inside me.

"You okay?"

"Yeah." I drag in a weary breath, playing my role. "I'm just trying to make sense of all this. I didn't expect car chases and secondary locations. If my brothers had their men follow you to the diner, it means they know we're working together."

He reaches over, placing a palm on my thigh and lightly squeezing. "It'll be worth it."

I know it will. Anything is worthwhile if it means I find Tilly.

What's concerning is how he's already taking liberties with my body.

His fixation on sleeping with me is building. I can hear it in his voice. Can feel it in the slight rub of his fingertips. But if he becomes solely focused it also means he can become completely blindsided.

I've always gained control with men who think with their dicks. Tonight will be no different.

Just one last time, Bree.

"I have to admit, I'm looking forward to getting you in bed." His touch moves higher on my leg. "You're so fucking gorgeous."

I paste on a smile, hiding my self-hatred behind fuck-me eyes. "Are you sure that's not the thrill of the car chase making you excited?"

He chuckles and returns his attention to the road. "No. This hard dick is all for you, baby girl."

The self-loathing increases, lathering me in a thick layer I'm sure I'll never be able to remove. He continues driving farther away from the city, taking the freeway to fast-track us toward isolation.

"So, how do we do this?" I slide my hand over his, my fingertips dancing along his knuckles, my traitorous mind comparing their size, shape and texture to the last man I touched.

"Well…" He grins. "First, I thought you'd suck me off, then I'll tell you what your mom has planned for your daughter tonight."

My pulse falters.

He's too crude. Too callous.

"Then we're going to take a ten-minute breather to let my cock regenerate before I fuck you in exchange for her location." He shoots me a wink, and I struggle to remain in character. "And after another ten-minute breather, I'm going to blow a load in that perfectly sculpted ass of yours as payment for giving you a ride back into the city."

I measure my breathing. Ignore my disgust.

He's sounding a hell of a lot like Gordon Myers and his men before they attacked me, the similarities making the scarf around my neck feel tighter.

"Three times in quick succession?" I drawl. "I'm impressed."

He laughs. "And after all the dick you've had, that's quite a compliment."

I keep my sly mask in place, my gaze sinful, my interest seeming piqued even though his continued insults set off more alarm bells.

Most men I target are enamored by me. Hypnotized. They don't know my past or the intricacies of my family. They just want something they think only the best can have.

That isn't the case with Geppet.

He sees me for what I really am—a high-class whore with nobody left to save her.

We take an offramp toward the outer edges of Denver, where homes are spread apart by massive yards half a mile apart and most of the buildings are old, unkempt, and uncared for.

"How far are we going?" I ask.

He jerks his chin up the road. "We're almost there."

Thirty seconds pass before he pulls into a cement drive, his headlights sweeping over a small weatherboard house, the paintwork around the window frames chipped and peeling, the front screen door askew and hanging on one hinge.

He kills the engine and turns to me. "You ready to exchange *info*?"

I ignore the waggle of his brows and smirk. "Actually, I'm ready to renegotiate terms."

"Your mom warned me you were slippery, but that woman has no idea how fucking hot you are." He swipes a thumb over his bottom lip. "What do you want to renegotiate, baby girl?"

I drag my attention to the house, the moonlight beaming down on the tin roof. "We go in there and talk. About us. About what you want to do to me. But also about my daughter. There will be a constant exchange of information on both sides. You'll tell me everything my mother said to you on your cross-country trip." I return my eyes to his. "While I make us both feel good."

He raises his brows and contemplates a moment. "Okay. I guess I can agree to that."

"Perfect."

He unclasps his belt and shoves open his door.

"Wait." I lick my lips as he glances over his shoulder at me. "Tell me something to get me out of the car, Aaron." I open my clutch and retrieve my lipstick, ensuring my stun gun is easily accessible as I add a new coat of color to my lips.

"Something about how I'm going to fuck you?" he asks.

"No." I fight not to roll my eyes. "Something about my daughter. Give me incentive to make your dreams come true."

"Baby girl, you're going to want to do that all on your own." He pushes from the car and rounds the hood to pull open my door.

I don't move. I blink up at him, Bambi-eyed, pouty lips. "Incentive, Geppet."

His gaze narrows slightly. "How 'bout this—I dropped your momma in the same vicinity as your girl earlier today."

My chest tightens. "How far away are they?"

"Come on, Abri." He holds out a hand. "I agreed to talk, but this isn't really the type of conversation to set the mood now, is it? Let's not lose momentum."

He's right. I can't push too hard too fast.

I scoot from my seat, my clutch tight in my grip as I reach for his hand.

I listen for cars as my heels settle on the cement drive. For a sound of life. But there's nothing. Only the chirp of crickets and the rustle of trees.

Geppet leads the way onto the darkened porch and pulls open the dilapidated screen. He grabs a key from his pocket, unlocks the front door, and shoves it wide. "Make yourself at home."

He reaches inside to flick on a light, the cheap energy-saver glow exposing an empty living room save for the ratty closed curtains and the scratched up dining table with three chairs skirting the rim. On the far side there's an entryway that I assume leads to a kitchen.

"This used to be your dad's place?" I step inside a whole new low for me.

Selling myself while drinking Cristal champagne in lavish hotel rooms under sparkling chandeliers doesn't chip away at my pride like the current scent of mold and mildew coming from threadbare carpet.

I saunter toward the table, not allowing my soul the bathroom break it craves. Not one opportunity to crumple or wade in regret. Just straightforward momentum. I grab the back of the closest chair and drag it into the middle of the room. "Take a seat."

"A seat?" He closes the front door. "What for?"

"You want me on my knees, don't you?"

If I can incentivize enough information from him before he has the chance to get between my thighs then I'm only a stun-gun trigger away from stealing his keys and getting out of here.

I drop my clutch to the floor before the chair. Within reach for when I need it. Then take my time gently guiding my hair over one shoulder as he strolls forward.

He takes his place before me, the old chair whining under his weight.

"I'm a lover of foreplay, Aaron." I discard my blazer, letting it fall to the dirty carpet. Then I reach behind my back, lowering the zipper of my top an inch. The material dips across my chest, gaping lower over my cleavage, the upward curve of his mouth my cruel prize. "How about you?"

"I just want to fuck, baby girl." He grabs for my hips.

"Nuh-uh-uh." I slip out of reach, waggling my finger at him. "Be patient. I'm worth it."

I reach for my zipper again, giving another inch. My top slips lower, the plumped curve of my breasts on display through my white La Perla lace bra. "I want this to last."

He huffs, sulking as he grabs the armrests.

"You're an attractive guy." I slink closer, skimming my touch over his shoulders as I walk around him. "But you know that, right?"

He shrugs. "Yeah, I've been told once or twice."

"I bet." I saunter around to the front of him, biting my lip as my gaze creeps down his chest to the bulge in his pants. "Have you ever imagined me going down on you?"

"Like you wouldn't believe." He grabs his crotch and squeezes. "You'd probably laugh if you knew how many times I've come thinking about my cock at the back of your throat."

Gag would be more appropriate, but let's not get nitpicky.

"I wouldn't laugh." I reach under the bottom of my top and undo the front clasp of my strapless bra, letting it fall to the floor beside my blazer. "I might get a little wet, though."

He huffs a snicker and rubs his palms back and forth along his thighs, his gaze on the large expanse of cleavage provided by my gaping top.

He's eager.

Impatient.

Perfect.

"Where did you leave my mother?" I lower to my knees before him, leisurely undo the laces on his black sneakers, then remove his shoes. Once I'm done, and still don't have an answer, I meet his gaze, my hands gliding up his thighs. "You said it was in the vicinity of my daughter. Does that mean they're together?"

"Not yet." His smirk is subtle. "She's waiting to hear what you do with your instructions. Imagine if she could see you now."

What a delightful thought.

It's a fight not to glare. To keep the sultry expression on my face. To stay in the zone.

Concentrate, Abri.

I try, but it's so much harder tonight. The disgust is thicker. My contempt impossible to ignore. And it's not just because Geppet lacks the wealth and success of my normal marks. It's because this feels like a betrayal to Bishop. Like I'm cheating on a man I don't want to admit I painfully care about.

But there he is, haunting the back of my mind.

"Where are they?" I ask, wondering if picturing Bishop in his place will help see me through. I imagine dark blue eyes peering down at me instead of light grey. Dirty blond hair sweeping a beard-covered jawline rather than the chestnut brown mullet.

I skim my touch higher, playfully grazing his hard cock beneath his jeans on my way to his belt.

It still feels wrong.

"Closer than you ever would've thought," Geppet groans. "At least that's what your mom said."

I pull the leather belt from his pants, slow, measured. "You need to tell me where."

"Not yet."

"Please, Geppet." I bite my bottom lip, sinful as I beg.

"No." His patience vanishes in the blink of an eye, my unease tightly leashed as he grabs a fistful of my hair and reefs my head back. "You need to suck my fucking dick first."

I blink up at him as animalistic rage *drip, drip, drips* into my bloodstream, dancing with the adrenaline entering my veins.

I could break his hold and have him on his back with one of the chair legs crushing his windpipe in less effort than it would take to make him climax. And I'd do it, too. Enjoy it. If I didn't need him.

"Play nice," I purr, my head awkwardly cocked, my neck straining.

"That's the problem, baby girl." He leans forward. "You think I'm playing and I'm not. Suck my fucking cock or that evil bitch mother of yours is going to hightail it overseas and disappear with your kid."

Fear places its powerful hands around my throat, squeezing tight. My sensuous mask slips.

Geppet's eyes narrow as if sensing the blow he's made, his lips kicking up at one side.

Focus.

Be calm.

"You like it rough?" I whisper, leaning into his hold on my hair, blinking back into my persona with a smile. "What a pleasant surprise."

He tugs harder and I smile broader, watching intently to see if his enjoyment comes from my fear or his show of dominance.

"I like a lot of things most women don't appreciate." He strokes the fingers of his free hand down my left cheek. "But your mom tells me you'll do anything if correctly incentivized. Is that true?"

"I enjoy sex, Geppet. Most women do if the men they're with know what they're doing."

"I told you not to call me Geppet." He grabs my chin, his fingers digging into skin as he continues to hold my head cocked at a painful angle.

"Sorry, Aaron," I croon, shuffling closer on my knees. I need to get within reach of my clutch, but can't when he has my hair held hostage.

"You deserve to be punished." He releases my chin with a grin, his arm retreating before it quickly snaps back.

I have a split second to tense before the backhanded blow lands across my cheek. Heat lashes the left side of my face, the burn consuming my eyes. I blink away tears, not of weakness or pity but of pure fucking rage.

"That's enough." I attempt to yank my head away, but he holds tight to my hair.

"Then suck my fucking cock." He drags my face close to his crotch, lowering his zipper with his free hand. "I've humored you long enough. It's time to see what Daddy taught you."

"Without my consent?" I ask.

I want to know exactly where his head is at before I lose my temper and turn the tables on this asshole. My clutch is now in reach. My claws are ready and waiting to latch onto his dick with force.

Hell, I could unleash the years of Krav Maga and MMA to re-right this approaching train wreck. But I won't do it over a pitiful slap.

"You consented, baby. You came all the way out here. You climbed into my car. You followed me into the house. Don't pretend you don't want it."

"I want the information. I *want* what you promised me."

He grabs his dick, pulling it out of his pants. "And you'll get it. After I get mine first."

"I'm warning you, Geppet. Let go of my hair."

His expression turns feral, wild eyes, clenched teeth. "And I'm warning you—call me by my fucking first name." He shoves to his feet, dragging me backward by my hair. "This is going to happen how *I* want it to happen. *I'm* the one in charge. I'm going to fuck you. Then fuck you again. Over and over until I've had enough. And when I'm finally done with you, *then* I might give you the information you're gagging for."

I struggle to keep up with his footsteps as I scramble backward like a crab. He releases me a few feet from the chair, towering over me as I fall onto my ass and elbows.

"Be a good girl and spread those legs." He shimmies his pants lower. His briefs, too. "Or don't." He shrugs. "I think I might prefer if you fight a little."

Good. I grin and kick out, my pointy pumps hitting him in the ankle, causing him to teeter forward with a curse. Then I pounce forward, launching my fist at his exposed cock, slamming my knuckles against his junk.

Air escapes him on impact, his bulking body hunching over as he clutches his crotch.

"Do you prefer that much fight?" I scramble around his legs, scampering on hands and knees to my clutch, flipping the flap open and dumping the contents on the floor.

"Stupid bitch," he groans, storming for me, his footsteps thudding close behind. "I'll fucking kill you."

I snatch the stun gun, hiding it at my side as I swing back around, expecting a blow to the face, not anticipating the shocking impact of his shoe as it makes direct impact with my stomach.

Pain slams through me. All the oxygen in my lungs escapes.

I retch. Gag.

He grabs my hair again, dragging me to my knees, his own agony etched into his watery eyes as he cups his balls with his free hand. "I should've listened to your mom when she told me to kill you straight away."

I try to yank my head against the restriction. I fight to speak. To breathe. "Wait." I hold the stun gun behind my back, needing balance to strike, the device almost slipping from my sweaty hand.

"I'm done waiting." He leans down toward me. "I waited for you to quit looking at me like I was an unworthy piece of shit for years. I guess I'll just fuck you when you're dead."

"No," I beg, stabilizing myself on my knees, blinking up at him with the fear he craves as I jab my arm forward and slam the stun gun to his upper thigh, pressing the trigger on impact.

The electrical current ticks to life. His body jolts with the voltage.

He stumbles backward, falling to his knees, one hand still cradling his junk. "*Fuck*."

I kick off my shoes and force myself to my feet, my legs heavy, my pulse deafening in my ears. I fumble after him, screaming my fury as I jab the heel of my palm against his throat. "*Tell me where she is.*"

His eyes bulge with the blow. He chokes for breath.

I grab his hair and backhand him like he did to me, my knuckles blazing, my gasps for air pained and weak. "*Tell me.*"

He snatches for my leg, wheezing.

I jump out of reach.

He snatches again, this time for my ankles, catching my left foot and reefing me off-balance.

My ass hits the floor with a thud, but I cling tight to the stun gun.

As soon as he climbs on top of me, I hit him with more voltage against his chest, knee him in the groin, gouge his eyes.

He roars, the noise vibrating in my ears.

"*Tell me,*" I shriek, slamming the stun gun against his neck, pulling the trigger. "*Tell me.*"

He jolts, rolling away with a groan.

I need a taser. A knife. Some rope or cable ties.

I can't continue this close proximity fight. I'm losing strength. I can barely breathe.

"Tell me." This time it's an exhausted plea. "Please, Aaron. Just fucking tell me where my daughter is."

He begins to laugh, the sound choked and haunting.

He's going to kill me. As soon as he gets the chance, I'm dead.

What will that mean for Tilly?

"*Please.*" My heart thuds in my chest, the sound so loud I almost mistake it for the footsteps that carry from outside.

I freeze, pure panic draining the blood from my face.

Geppet set me up. He has reinforcements.

I glance around the room, frantically trying to figure out how to escape, how to protect myself against more than one attacker when a loud crack splits the air. The front door swings open and slams into the adjoining wall.

A man stalks inside, face full of fury, fists clenched at his sides.

"*Bishop*," I gasp, slumping in relief.

I fall back onto my ass as he strides for me, those angry eyes pinning me in place. But I don't care. He's here. He found me.

He barely spares Geppet a glance as he passes, planting his foot on the guy's shoulder to shove him to the ground before continuing toward me. "Are you hurt?"

I shake my head, too overwhelmed with gratitude to complain.

"How did you find me?" I croak. "You weren't following."

"I was always following." Calloused fingers grab my chin in a delicate hold. "My men placed a tracker on his car. We kept a few miles behind. But I never should've let you fucking leave."

"I…" I don't know how to excuse my foolishness. Don't know what to say.

"Tell me you're okay," he demands.

"I am now that you're here." The vulnerable admission sears my throat, but it's the truth.

His gaze falls to my throbbing cheek, his eyes turning feral as his thumb strokes the swollen flesh.

"I'm okay," I repeat. "He's in worse shape."

"What else did he do?" His touch continues to lovingly stroke. So gentle. So sweet. "Where else are you hurt?"

I slide my palm over his hand and lean into his affection with my entire soul. "It doesn't matter. Not now. He knows where Tilly is. He said Adena is preparing to take her out of the country."

"Where else are you hurt?" he barks.

"That doesn't matter. What's important is getting the information he has on Tilly."

"The information will come. But not before I understand what happened here."

I glance around his hips, seeing Geppet crawling toward the door. "Bishop, please. He's going to run. Then all this will be for nothing."

"He's not going anywhere. Just tell me what he did."

"*Please*. He's almost at the door."

"Here's the problem we have, belladonna—*you* are my concern. *You* are my focus. So until I know *you* are okay and not sustaining any injuries that need urgent attention, I'm not dragging my eyes away from you, let alone my hands."

I could wither. Arms. Legs. Body. Soul.

This man makes me insane.

But he also makes me feel worthy. So unbelievably valuable.

"He slapped me," I blurt in a rush. "Pulled my hair. Dragged me across the floor. Then kicked me in the stomach. That's all."

His jaw ticks but he keeps his thoughts locked tight.

"I'm sore. But that's it. I promise. Nothing is life-threatening."

His fingers trail to my chin, his thumb swiping my lower lip. "I'm going to kill him, belladonna."

"I know." Geppet can rot in hell for all I care. "But not before you get the information on Tilly. Make that asshole sing."

He leans down and plants a kiss to my hairline. "With pleasure, my beautiful woman." Then he turns and stalks for the man who attacked me.

I should sigh in relief, but his words cement the air in my lungs.

My woman.

My—*beautiful*—woman.

It says a lot about my life that here, in this moment, swollen and bruised, that I find the compliment from a notorious murderer to be the most endearing thing I've ever heard.

The words reach my heart, tinkering with my resilience. I tremble, my hands shaking, my legs weak.

It's shock. Yet even with the acknowledgement, I can't help watching with admiration as Bishop approaches Geppet with such commanding confidence it strengthens the most fragile parts of me.

"Where the hell do you think you're going?" He hauls Geppet to his fumbling feet by the back of his shirt, dragging him into the middle of the room. "Now we do this shit my way."

33

ABRI

Geppet swings a wild elbow. "Get off me."

Bishop blocks the attack, then retaliates with a bone-crunching punch to the jaw.

Geppet's head jerks back while he continues to get dragged farther into the room. "You're going to regret this."

"Highly doubtful." Bishop flings him into the closest wall, catching him when he rebounds and begins to fall. "This right here is what people like to call a passion project. It's where my shit shines."

"Adena will have you killed. She'll fucking slaughter you."

"She won't even know I touched you, my friend, because you won't live to tell the tale." Bishop slams him into the wall again, this time holding him upright with a forearm across his throat while his free hand reaches behind his back and beneath his suit jacket.

He retrieves something long, sharp, and shiny, the sight there and gone before Bishop slams it into Geppet's right shoulder, the impact thudding through to the plaster.

Geppet roars, his pain ricocheting in my ears.

I stare dumbfounded by the calm callousness as Bishop steps back to admire his handiwork.

"Start talking," he demands.

Geppet tugs at the knife, whimpering in his failed attempts to dislodge himself from the wall. "Who the hell are you?"

"The man who's going to make you regret touching her."

Geppet struggles harder, shaking his head. "She agreed to fuck me. Ask her yourself."

I cringe, my cheek protesting the shame-filled response.

"I don't care what she agreed to." Bishop reaches beneath the back of his jacket again, retrieving another long blade as he retreats. "She's not yours to touch." He juggles the weapon between his hands like a master bladesmith. "She's Lorenzo Cappelletti's niece. Matthew Langston's sister. And my—"

He cuts the sentence short, my curiosity piqued for him to finish.

"You don't understand," Geppet blubbers. "This was all Adena's idea. She knew her daughter would come crawling to me for help." He holds up his left hand in surrender, the palm now smeared with blood. "She's the one who told me to take advantage. To rough Abri up a little before ending her. I was only following orders."

Bishop glances over his shoulder to meet my gaze, as if concerned the news will break me.

Am I hurt? Yes.

Am I surprised? Unfortunately not.

I'd never thought it would come to her having me raped and murdered, but it's not as if her actions are out of left field. She did challenge me to kill my brothers.

I straighten my shoulders, letting him know I'm okay.

His eyes fill with something I'd like to believe is pride, then he turns his attention back to his victim. "Just because you're following orders doesn't mean you get to skip out on the consequences."

"I get it. I fucked up." Geppet glances down his impaled arm, the blood soaking his shirt to the elbow. "But I can't even move my fingers, man. My fucking arm is dead."

"Want to know what else will be dead real soon?" Bishop gives one final juggle of the blade, then sends the shiny metal flying through the air, the pointy tip spearing Geppet's opposite shoulder but not deep enough to hit plaster.

Another roar blasts the room.

Bishop cocks his head to the side, studying his prey as he clucks his tongue. "I didn't apply enough force." He storms forward, ignoring the wails as he retrieves his knife, then rams it back into Geppet's shoulder, this time pinning the opposite side of his body to the wall.

The howls sear through my skull, deafening me.

"Let me tell you, Gep, I'm fucking delighted you picked an isolated location." Bishop grabs my attacker's right wrist, dragging his forearm upward to rest against the plaster. He retrieves a blade from his pants pocket. This one smaller. Less hilt. "Nobody can hear you scream."

"*No. No. No.*"

"Yes." Bishop smirks, impaling Geppet's hand—one succinct stab straight through the middle of the palm. "Where's the girl?"

Tears stream down Geppet's face, his pitiful blubbering growing louder. I feel no guilt for his suffering. Not the slightest sense of empathy. In fact, I appreciate Bishop's brutality. The judgment he inflicts upon my tormentor is the sweetest gift after years of mistreatment.

"Where's the girl?" Bishop repeats.

I find the strength to push to my feet, eager for a front-row view to the answer.

Geppet shies his head away, sniffing back whimpers.

"Do you know how many places I can stab a man before he dies, Gep?" Bishop crowds closer. "My high score is thirty-eight. But he was a hard-ass motherfucker. I don't think you've got the balls for that."

"I don't know." Geppet sobs as snot streams from his nose. "I promise I don't."

"He's lying." I step closer, the metallic scent of blood filling my lungs. "He said he dropped my mother in the vicinity of Tilly. How would he know the vicinity unless he knew her location?"

"She told me the kid was close by," he pleads. "That's all she said."

"You know what?" Bishop grabs another knife from his pocket. "I'm going to go with the pretty lady on this one and agree that you're full of shit." He raises the blade to Geppet's face as the coward whimpers, slowly dragging it along his eye socket, a slim trail of blood following in its wake. "All that's left of life for you is pain. Whatever loyalty you think you have for Adena is pointless. She won't mourn the death you've earned. She won't care how long it took you to break."

"You can't kill me," he cries. "I was just doing my job."

"And I'm just doing mine." Bishop draws back the blade,

lowering it to his side as he leans close, right in Geppet's face. "Where's the kid?"

"I don't—"

Bishop stabs the knife into Geppet's abdomen.

I gasp as my attacker's eyes widen, the shock or maybe the pain rendering him speechless.

"Getting stabbed in an organ doesn't feel the same as a limb, does it, Gep?" Bishop claims another blade. "I'm told it's a pulsing, throbbing pain unlike no other. One with the potential to render you unconscious. And maybe you're too amped for it to feel like that just yet. But it'll eventually hit, and you'll wish you were dead."

Geppet's eyes remain wide, his mouth gaping like a fish.

"You might even feel like you've pissed yourself," Bishop informs clinically. "And hell, maybe you have. Lord knows most do. But it's also likely that the warm sensation traveling from your groin all the way down your leg is the blood seeping from your gut."

"Sh-she's…" Geppet struggles for air.

Bishop cocks his head. "She's?"

"Sh-she's this side of H-hudson."

I straighten, devastation rendering me rigid. "That close?"

My daughter has been living a few short miles from me this entire time? All her life? Where I could've watched her grow?

"Give me an exact location," Bishop demands.

"I-I don't know." Geppet shivers. "Somewhere in W-weld County. I can't remember the name of the s-street."

"Try harder."

Aaron shakes his head, his eyes losing their wideness. "I…" His breaths grow shallow and sharp. "I…"

"I what?" Bishop snarls.

I stalk closer, my anger renewed, savagery taking me by force. My daughter has been within reach for years, right under my nose while my parents acted as if she was a world away.

I snatch the knife from Bishop's hand, livid. "Where in Weld County?" I lower the weapon, positioning the tip of the blade against Geppet's crotch.

He winces, turning his head away. "I-it's in my phone. In the maps app."

I fumble for his pants, retrieving the cell sticking out of his pocket. But it's my phone, not his. "Where's yours?" I dig the knife deeper.

He tenses against the blade, whimpering. "In my b-back pocket."

"Let me, belladonna." Bishop grabs my shoulders, leading me a few steps back as if this macabre art piece pinned to the wall could hurt me.

I let him claim my prize and hold up the device to Geppet's face to unlock the screen.

Bishop scrolls silently until he pauses and looks at his victim. "Does Bayvis Street ring a bell?"

My heart kicks up pace, the location I've wanted for so long humming in my ears.

"Yeah." Geppet hangs limp against the wall. "That's it. Now can you let me g-go?"

Bishop turns to me, posture stiff, eyes questioning. "Is there anything else you want to know from this piece of shit?"

I open my mouth only to be rendered speechless by indecision.

I have Tilly's location. That's all I need. She's who I risked my life for. The only reason I deceived Bishop.

But Geppet was in a car with my mother for days. Do I want to know why she hated me so much? Why she tortured me with my daughter's absence for years? Why she stole the only thing I've ever cared about?

"Belladonna?" Bishop steps closer, placing a soothing hand to my cheek.

I swallow. Shake my head. "No." I hold his gaze. "I don't need anything else."

The reasons for Adena's hatred don't matter. They won't change who she is. What she's done.

"Are you sure?" His brow furrows. "I've still got a lot of skills left to use."

"Of that I have no doubt, but there's nothing else."

He strokes his thumb over my cheek. "Alright." He swings back to face his craftsmanship on the wall, fluidly grabbing a blade from his pocket and raising it to his victim.

Geppet's mouth opens. Before he can protest, the knife is embedded in the side of his neck, then quickly retrieved, the gush of blood spraying from his carotid like a broken faucet.

I stand stunned, watching the river of crimson arc the air as Geppet remains pinned to the wall, unable to clutch the wound.

The shock of approaching death haunts his face, his stare fixed on me in a silent plea. I drag in a shaky breath, knowing I should look away while being powerless to comply.

"Come with me." Bishop grabs my hand, dragging my stunned ass from the horror, my gaze not leaving the gruesomeness until I'm tugged around the corner. "Are you okay?"

I blink the new room into view in a daze. The eighties-style kitchen with its bright orange countertops and old wooden cupboards, the curtain-less window giving sight to the moon. But all I see is Geppet. All I can picture is the stream of life rushing from his body. How long will it take for him to die?

"Abri?" Bishop closes in on me, his hands sliding up my arms. "Come back to me."

I lick my drying lips and focus, peering into the soul of a brutal murderer. Every stab wound he inflicted replays in my mind. Every fierce demand echoes through my head.

There's not even an ounce of blood on him, his brutality so efficient he's left without a stain.

Yet those eyes sing to me in a melody of concern and fear.

He confuses me with his savage violence that's equally potent to his fierce protection. He's strong and sure and unfathomably confident. He's also damaged and pained and heartbreakingly vulnerable.

All his conflicting attributes meld together in a dance of wild savagery that's so mesmerizingly beautiful it almost hurts trying to understand him.

But I *do* understand him.

I appreciate the violence that stems from a tormented childhood. His commanding need to protect after the loss of his sister. The loyalty he learned from the men who finally showed him what it was like to have a family.

I shake my head, trying to remember where I am and why we're here, because those intense eyes make the rest of the world disappear.

"Now I understand why they call you the Butcher," I whisper.

He winces, releasing my arms.

"It's not criticism." I quickly grab his lapels, reconnecting the tether between us. "I'm thankful."

"Don't mention it." He retreats, my arms falling to my sides.

"Then don't go cold on me. What's wrong?"

"Nothing." He rubs a rough hand over his beard. "I need you to remove your top."

I blink at the sudden change in topic, my insides instinctively warming without my permission. "Excuse me?"

"To check your injuries."

I shake my head, trying to keep my thoughts clear even though the riotous emotions from what I've been through begin to shift to desire. "I have nothing on underneath it."

"That much is clear," he mutters. "But we're not leaving until I get a visual on that kick to your stomach. And anything else Geppet might have inflicted."

I open my mouth to protest.

"Don't," he warns. "I'm just as loath to do this as you are, but it needs to be done."

"Loath?" I whisper.

"You heard me. Now stop dragging this out, belladonna. The adrenaline currently poisoning my veins has me hard as stone."

I'm so confused. My body is too, all my erogenous zones thrumming for attention despite a man dying in the next room. "Then why say you're loath to look at me?"

His eyes harden. "Because my foolishness in letting you do this your way is the reason I have to inspect injuries that never should've been inflicted." He leans closer, trying to intimidate me into compliance. "I'm loath because even though I know you're hurting, and after what you just witnessed, I still can't stop myself from picturing how I want to turn you over, plaster you to that fucking countertop, and sink into you from behind."

My throat dries, the yearning for what he described overwhelming me. Is it due to the stress hormones currently flooding my system? Obviously.

Does understanding that make me want him any less due to the inopportune timing and location? Not one little bit.

"I'm not in pain." I can't feel anything other than quickly surging lust.

"Then hurry up and take your top off to prove it."

"Do you think that's a good idea?" It can't be when my breasts are now aching for his touch. I want him. I'm dying to have his hands back on me. His fingers stoking the fire crackling to life in my veins.

But that's not what he wants or needs.

The stress-hormone high is the only reason he's thinking about sex, and I don't want this moment to be the catalyst that breaks his years of abstinence.

I really, really don't…even though my body really, really does.

"Are you worried I'll force you after what I just did?" He scowls. "I'm not a monster. Not that type at least."

"I'm not worried you'll take me, Bishop. My fear is that you won't."

34

ABRI

His nostrils flare. "We're not doing this here."

He's right. It's ridiculous to even contemplate. So why can't I quit longing for him to touch me? To wipe all the destruction from my mind with his possessive grip?

"Abri, we're not fucking at a crime scene with blood still on my goddamn hands."

"I know." I nod.

"Then quit looking at me like that and get your fucking top off so we can leave."

I swallow, my heart thunderous as I lean back against the counter and obey, pulling the material over my scarf and head to let it hang limp at my side.

He turns rigid, his chin arrogantly high, his jaw tense as he blatantly ignores my breasts and lowers his attention to my stomach.

My skin comes alive under his gaze, every inch of me breaking out in feverish goosebumps.

"That son of a fucking bitch." He reaches out, running his fingertips over the reddened shoe print marking my abdomen. "I should've made him suffer."

"You did."

"Not nearly enough." His touch grazes the outline of the injury, gentle enough to make me shiver.

"I'm fine. I can barely feel it." My problem is the deep throb between my thighs.

"That's the adrenaline." He gently prods my stomach. "Tell me how much this hurts."

I shake my head. "It doesn't hurt at all."

His eyes raise to mine. "You're breathing heavy."

"I think we both know that has nothing to do with pain."

He straightens. "Put your top back on."

I should. It's in both our best interests to take the instruction and run. And I would, if only my body would listen. But it's all caught up in wanting to kiss him. To drown in him. To lick and bite and moan my way out of this adrenaline whirlwind until we're both sweat-slicked and sated.

"Your top, Abri," he growls. "Before I do something we both regret."

Yes. We'd regret it.

It would be distasteful and shameless. Animalistic and wild. Hungered and so goddamn fulfilling.

"I want you," I murmur.

His lips thin. "You taunt the wrong man, belladonna."

"I'm not taunting." My top falls from my fingers, flittering to the floor. "If you're worried about my suffering, you're the only cause."

His jaw ticks. The way he battles with restraint only makes me hotter.

"All I want is a kiss." Just one touch of his lips. One bite of relief against the slickness building between my thighs. "To hold you against me. You make me feel safe."

"Fuck, woman. Why do you do this to me?" He palms my ribs, his grip wonderfully harsh.

He infuses me with fire, destructive and uncontainable. "Because I've never needed anyone before."

He breathes through his nose, long, deep, those eyes incredibly stony through his palpable silence.

He's so handsome. So determined, and vigilant, and merciless.

I want to be consumed by all that power. To be chewed up and spat out in the most delicious way. "Please."

"Goddamn you." His mouth smashes down on mine.

I gasp into the contact, his tongue delving deep. He grinds his hips into me, his cock thick and hard against my pubic bone.

"You'll regret me," he snarls against my lips.

"No." I cling to his shoulders, pulling him closer, kissing him with everything I have. "Never."

"Why does it fucking kill me to deny you?" He clings to me, his calloused hands seeming crazed as they roam my blazing skin. "You're an affliction."

"A toxin," I agree as his fingertips skate over my hips. His palms cup my breasts. His claws dig into my ass.

He groans. *Oh, God,* how he groans.

"Take off the scarf," he demands.

I obey, tugging and yanking at the material until it slides from my neck into the ether.

"I always want your scars bared to me." He leans in and nuzzles my neck. Licks. Bites. "Your trauma is mine to tame."

I whimper.

It *is* his to tame. He's proven that every time he's drawn me back from the height of anxiety. My wounds are his to own.

"And your body is mine to savor." He says it like a threat, cold and vicious as he pulls back and roughly turns me toward the kitchen counter. His hand reaches around my waist, grabbing my zipper, tugging it down. "Are you sure you want this, belladonna?"

I nod. Pant.

"Say the words, Abri. Tell me you want me to fuck you."

Oh, God, yes. "Please fuck me, Bishop."

He yanks down my pants. Pulls at my lace underwear.

My breaths come hard and fast as another zipper grates. Then he shoves down his trousers.

He leans into me, his chest covering my back, his weight manipulating my breasts toward the counter, his low, husky growl tickling my neck as he positions the head of his cock against my slick entrance. *"Sarai la mia morte belladonna. Ma morirò volentieri."*

I want to know what he said, but I'm too busy holding my breath, waiting for him to give me what I need. To fill me. To complete this hedonistic ritual.

"You're the sweetest damnation." He thrusts deep.

I cry out, feeling him everywhere, his length stretching me.

"My precious, poisonous flower." His arm snakes around me, nestling in my cleavage, his hand grabbing one breast as he fucks me, the other hand viciously gripping my hip.

My back aches with pleasure and I cry out, "*Yes*." I hold onto the counter, taking each punishing entry, clenching my core around his dick. "Don't stop."

"There's no stopping until your pretty pussy comes all over my cock." He digs his fingers into my flesh. "I want you screaming my name."

"I'm not going to last long." My mind is too wild. My pulse too fevered.

"You'll last until I let you come." He releases my breast, his hand latching onto my throat in a restrictive grip as we continue to fuck. "Do you hear me?"

I shake my head, trying to wordlessly tell him I have no control. Absolutely no restraint even though I'm a slave to his commands. "Bishop."

"Jesus fucking Christ."

I freeze at the outraged male shout. One that didn't come from Bishop. One that distinctly carried from outside.

I glance toward the kitchen window. "Was that Salvatore?"

"Ignore him." Bishop keeps fucking me, keeps thrusting his cock so deep I can barely breathe. "Don't stop squeezing your sweet little cunt, belladonna. It's fucking heaven."

I struggle to determine what to focus on. My brother. Bishop's compliment. The harsh slap of our thighs through the quiet house.

It takes a split second for hypnotizing pleasure to claim victory, dragging me back into the clutches of thriving mindlessness.

I moan, arching my neck against Bishop's grip.

"Good girl." He snakes his hand from my hip to my sex. "You're so damn wet, Abri."

I jolt with the direct contact to my clit, the explosion of tingles blazing through my limbs. "I'm going to come."

"Not yet," he growls.

"I can't help it. I'm close."

He bites my shoulder. "You'll wait."

I mewl. In pain. In pleasure. In mindlessness. "I can't. You feel so good. It's right there." I keep grinding, searching for the peak, almost finding it.

He clutches my breast tighter, his grip sure to leave marks. And that hand on my clit... I moan. He squeezes the bundle of nerves between two fingers and I begin to gush. "Bishop," I pant. "Bishop, I'm coming."

He keeps his rhythm, not deviating from the perfect pleasure. His fingers still on my clit. His mouth on my neck. "*God*, you undo me."

He groans, coming with me, his touch everywhere. His lips, too.

I close my eyes to the euphoria, the two of us the only people in existence, our fulfillment all that's right and good in this world as my core slows its rampant pulse and I fall into a chasm of boneless bliss.

He holds me in the aftermath, his chest plastered to my back, his head pressed to my shoulder. Slowly, his hands lose their possessive grip, falling from my body to leave me frantic for their return.

When he pulls out of me, I feel the loss on more than a physical level. The grate of his zipper is a sterile end to the heated passion.

Something in the air changes.

It skitters over my skin like a bad omen.

Regret.

Not mine. I sense it emanating from him.

"Give me a sec," he mutters while I remain frozen, unsure how to act. "Here." He places something between my thighs. Something soft. A material of some sort. "A clean handkerchief is all I've got unless you want my shirt."

"Thank you." I slide my hand between my thighs, cleaning the mess we created, before righting my pants.

When I turn to face him, he doesn't look at me.

There's no lingering pleasure in his features. No post-orgasm superiority.

All I see is remorse. And of course that's how he should feel. He abstained for over a decade only to succumb to my selfishness.

"I need to get you to Hudson." He rakes a hand through his hair. "I'm assuming you want to go there straight away."

I nod through the shame, wanting to talk to him, *needing* to apologize... But words fail me.

He snatches my scarf and top from the floor and hands them over. "You might want to get dressed before we walk outside."

Shit. "Are my brothers here?"

He nods. "Among others."

Oh, God.

I tug my top over my head, then wrap my scarf around my neck, the euphoria well and truly evaporated. I want to rewind and start over. To crawl into a hole and die.

"I'll get your shoes." He turns and walks from the room.

I follow, watching as he stops to scoop up my bra and blazer, then holds them out for me to take.

"You might want to put these on, too." He hands over the lace underwear first and I make quick work of dragging it on beneath my top, my gaze straying toward Geppet.

"Don't look," Bishop warns, his eyes pinning me. "You can forget a lot of things in life, but the sight of death isn't one of them."

"What will happen to him?"

Bishop steps closer, helping me into my blazer. "My men will take care of it."

"Meaning they'll dispose of his body?"

He starts across the room toward the door. "Yes, Abri."

"Wait." I hustle after him, hating the sterility he's directing at me as I slide my feet into my high heels. "I need to use the bathroom."

What I really need are a few seconds to regain my equilibrium. To take a breath and rationalize why his cold demeanor should mean nothing in this whole fucked up scheme.

He stops near the open door. "Do you want me to help you find it?"

Although he asks in kindness, I can see how he's praying for me to decline the offer. He needs space as much as I do.

"No," I murmur. "I won't be long."

He inclines his head. "I'll stay here until you're done."

I take the opportunity to escape down the hall, finding the dilapidated bathroom easily. I use the facilities, because a UTI is the last thing I need, then wash my hands in the basin, refusing to meet my gaze in the mirror.

I've done a lot of horrible things over the years, but not once have I had an issue staring at my own reflection. Until now. Until after I seduced an abstinent man into sleeping with me moments after he finished saving my life.

"You okay in there?" Bishop calls in the distance.

"Yeah. Give me a sec." I drag in a deep breath and force myself to stand tall. Tilly is all that matters. Everything else means nothing. At least until she's safe.

I return down the hall, not making eye contact with Bishop who waits in the doorway as I quickly divert into the living room to grab my clutch and all the scattered items off the floor. But I follow his instructions and keep my gaze from Geppet, only pausing for a moment to stare at the asshole's blood-soaked shoes. "I hope you enjoy dancing with the devil."

I walk to Bishop, who leads the way onto the porch toward the three men waiting in the dark. They're crowding the few steps to the yard where Remy stands, leaning against Geppet's pickup while Salvatore paces in front of him.

Were they all here this whole time? Through the torture? During the sex?

I guess that explains why Bishop wasn't concerned about Geppet fleeing when he first arrived.

"Dispose of the body and torch the house," Bishop instructs the men as he approaches. "But don't lose my knives. I want them back."

The bald man in front jerks his chin, the moonlight gleaming off his head. "Do you want the body to be found?"

"No. Make him disappear. I want Adena thinking he's still alive to spill her secrets."

The men move aside as we descend the stairs.

I give an awkward smile of greeting as I pass, wishing their first impressions of me weren't moans of pleasure from a murdered man's kitchen.

Salvatore storms up to us, stopping an inch in front of Bishop, his face scrunched with fury. "You slimy prick. You tell your men to keep us outside, then make us wait while you fuck our sister?"

Jesus Christ. I look away, unwilling to risk eye contact.

"You were warned that what I was doing wasn't fit for public consumption." Bishop grows taller with the straightening of his posture. "You shouldn't have snooped."

"You think I would've chanced glancing through that window if I'd known what you were doing, motherfucker?"

"*Sister* fucker," Remy corrects.

I clear my throat to stop a groan escaping.

"She's hurt, by the way," Bishop snarls. "Not that her wellbeing ever seems high on your list of priorities."

Remy pushes from the pickup. "Geppet hurt you?"

"What the fuck did he do?" Salvatore turns to me.

"I'm fine." I focus on my Aston Martin parked on the road. Bishop must've put the tire back on and driven it from the safe house.

"Like hell you are." Salvo reaches for my jaw. "What happened to your face?"

I slap his hand away. "It's nothing."

"I'm serious," he warns. "Did Geppet hit you?"

"I'm *fine*," I repeat.

"He kicked her in the stomach, too." Bishop crosses his arms over his chest. "She's going to be sore tom—"

"That fucking piece of shit." Salvatore glares toward the house. "I'm going to—"

"Sit on your ass and do absolutely nothing," Bishop drawls. "Unless you plan on giving a few swift uppercuts to a warm corpse with those girlie hands of yours."

Salvatore's lips curve in a vicious smile. "That's not an appropriate way to speak to your future boss."

Bishop stiffens. "You need to earn respect before you claim that title. And you haven't acquired any of mine. Following us to Hudson to help find your niece would be a good start."

"You act as if I wouldn't do everything I could to support my goddamn fucking sister."

"Probably because it's hard to imagine, seeing as though you did everything you could to ignore her suffering."

"Stop." I wince, turning pained eyes to Bishop. "That's enough. Both of you. We don't have time for this."

"Time didn't seem to be an issue while you two were fucking," Salvatore mutters.

"In her defense, it's not like the big guy took very long." Remy shoves his hands into his pockets, feigning innocence. "Seemed to me that he was trying to break a time trial."

The men on the porch snicker. Bishop snarls.

I sigh, the dwindling adrenaline making way for exhaustion. "I'm going to do this on my own if all of you can't grow up." I head toward my car, but the sound of an approaching vehicle has me pausing in the drive.

I glance over my shoulder, eyeing Bishop to gauge whether the noise could be an oncoming threat as the advancing headlights brighten the road.

"Come here, belladonna." He beckons me back to him. "It should be Lorenzo and his driver, but I'm not taking any chances."

We meet in a few short steps, his large frame gliding in front of mine to block my body from the road as a black SUV pulls up, the passenger side window descending.

My uncle's face comes into view, the wrinkles of age heavier than they were this morning. "What's the update?"

"Geppet's been dealt with, and we have the location of Abri's daughter. There's word Adena could be preparing to take her out of the country." Bishop turns to me, placing a hand on the low of my back, directing me to continue toward my car. "We're going there now."

Lorenzo nods. "I'll follow."

"No. Follow them." Bishop jerks his head at my brothers. "I'll text the address. But all of you need to stay out of sight. I don't want to see even a glimmer of a fucking headlight. Do you hear me?"

Nobody bothers to answer as I reach my passenger door and climb inside.

There are more murmurs of conversation. A subdued argument maybe.

But in seconds Bishop climbs in behind the wheel, starts the ignition, and takes off down the road, silently tapping the Hudson address into the GPS.

I itch to talk about what happened. All of it. The things Geppet said. The things he did. And everything that happened afterward.

Instead, I clasp my hands in my lap and squeeze my fingers until they ache.

Bishop doesn't want to talk. He probably doesn't even want to be in this car with me. I need to be thankful he's still by my side.

"How's your cheek?" he asks five minutes later as we speed along the highway.

"Aching a little."

"It'll hurt like a bitch tomorrow."

"As long as I make it to tomorrow I'll be happy." I focus out the windshield, my heel tapping against the floor, nervous anticipation fueling my pulse.

He doesn't placate me. Doesn't make grand statements of positivity.

He does something far more punishing by reaching over to glide his palm over my clamped hands.

The warmth of his skin seeps into me. The affection delves deep.

I lower my gaze, my attention affixed on the point where we touch, my body feeling the contact right through to my heart.

But all too soon the GPS announces the upcoming corner, and he steals his hand away to change gears.

I try not to let the absence of his touch affect me. I try so fucking hard. I'm sure it's the weight of what I have to soon face that makes it impossible to bear.

"What if we're too late?" I scrunch my nose against the emotional ache climbing its way into my throat. "What if my mother has already left the country with Tilly?"

"Then we keep searching. I've got eyes watching from inside the airport. If she flies out of Denver we'll know where she's going. And Najeeb is still on top of traffic surveillance. If we don't find her tonight, we'll find her eventually."

Eventually.

That could be weeks. Months. Years.

"I know trust isn't something you give willingly," he adds, "and I give promises with equal enthusiasm. But I promise you this, belladonna—I won't stop until your daughter is found."

"Take the next left." The GPS cuts off my response.

I slump into my seat, the world passing by in road signs, darkened houses, and oncoming traffic. I obsessively glance at the navigation screen to fixate on the length of our trip.

Eighteen minutes until arrival.

I clench my palms together as we drive onto I-76. Nibble my bottom lip. Watch the train tracks beside the road.

Fifteen minutes until arrival.

We pass Brighton in silence. Then Lochbuie.

Eight minutes until arrival.

I tug at my scarf, loosening it from around my neck.

We turn off the highway and head onto bleak, bare streets leading to hobby farms and vacant fields.

Does Tilly like it out here? Will she be upset having to start over or is she too young to understand?

I know nothing about kids her age, just the brief information from childhood development books I've read in an attempt to understand my daughter's milestones.

The only thing that's certain about her future is the necessary location change that will take her farther away from me. Her adoptive parents will have to go somewhere Adena will never find them. Somewhere I won't be able to take a thirty-minute car ride so I can visit.

Bishop retrieves his cell from his suit jacket and dials a number, the call connecting to the car speakers as it starts to ring.

"What?" Salvatore barks.

"Pull over and stay where you are. After the next turn, the roads become more isolated. I don't want to draw attention with our convoy. Call Lorenzo and tell him to do the same."

"Fine. But if I don't hear from either of you in ten, I'm following regardless."

Bishop's hands squeak against the steering wheel before he growls, "I'll text you when we arrive."

He disconnects the call, the finality leaving me chilled.

This is it. I'm about to meet my daughter and the people who raised her, and I have no clue what to say.

Hi, I'm Tilly's biological mother and you need to pack your worldly belongings and relocate somewhere far, far away, doesn't seem like the best first impression—not that I've been great in making those tonight.

Bishop takes a left turn, then a final right onto Bayvis Street, and my heart lurches. The only glow of illumination comes from a mile or so up ahead, the house lights marrying up with the final destination dot on the GPS.

Bishop turns off the headlights and slows our approach. "There it is."

I nod, my palms sweating as Tilly's life takes shape in front of me.

She lives in what looks to be a quaint red-brick home with a wraparound porch and a tiny attic window above the front door. The yard is lush and green, the red rose bushes coming into view as the car slithers closer. When I squint, I can make out a metal swing set alongside a small pink slide.

My daughter grew from a baby into a toddler here. She sits on those swings. Slides down that slide.

I lower my window, wanting to experience more of Tilly's surroundings, needing to inhale the air she breathes as we inch closer, the road crunching beneath the car tires.

Bishop stops a few hundred feet away from the dirt drive, quiet as he scrubs a hand over his mouth.

I glance at him, sensing his unease. "What is it?"

"The car. The lights."

I frown, glancing back at the property, taking note of the black vehicle parked in front of the garage. My heart sinks. "You think that's my mom's car?"

"Maybe. But with the porch lights on when it's close to midnight, it's a safe bet they have visitors."

The tremble returns to my hands, the adrenaline making a comeback. "What do we do?"

He pulls to the side of the road, turns off the interior light, then cuts the ignition. "I'm going to check it out and see what we're up against. I want you to get in the driver's seat while I'm gone. Just in case."

"In case what? I'm not leaving without my daughter. Or you for that matter."

"You'll vow to leave at the first sign of danger or I'll restart this car right now and dump you with your brothers, you hear me?" His tone brooks no argument. His narrowed, lethal stare, too.

"Bishop, you can't expect—"

"I don't just expect it, I fucking demand it. You're not putting yourself in danger again, Abri. I won't allow it."

My stomach twists. "But what if—"

"You either trust me to handle this or you get babysat. What's it going to be?"

I want to curse at him. To protest and fight. But I'm too wrecked, my confidence flittering in and out of stable currents like a feather in the wind. "Okay."

He stares at me a moment. Reading me. *Scrutinizing* me.

Until finally he gets out of the car, walks around the hood, and silently pulls my door open. "The key." He holds out the fob, grasping my hand when I reach to take it. "Promise me you won't do anything stupid."

I stare into his eyes, my heart aching.

"Promise me, belladonna."

I sigh. "What happens if my mom leaves the house with Tilly?"

"Then you need to have faith I'll take appropriate measures to make sure she doesn't escape."

"But what if—"

"Abri, you know we don't have time for twenty questions." He crouches before me. "You have to trust me."

"I'm scared."

"You wouldn't be sane if you weren't." He kisses my knuckles and releases my hand. "As soon as I'm gone, climb into the driver's seat and turn your phone to silent. I'll text you as soon as I can confirm whether or not it's Adena."

"Will you text my brothers?"

"You can. Tell them to stay where they are until further notice." He stands, towering above me, making me feel so incredibly small.

He reaches out, gripping my chin.

I ache for him to kiss me again. To whisper against my lips that everything will be okay. But all too soon his fingers leave my skin and he retreats to grab the door handle, quietly closing it between us.

I watch through the moonlight as he jumps the wire fence with effortless efficiency, his shadowed form melting into the darkness of the empty field until I can't see him anymore.

I do as he instructs, climbing into the driver's seat, texting Salvatore with an update and letting him know I'll keep him posted. After that, all that's left to do is wait as time ticks by in agonizingly sluggish seconds.

Crickets chirp. The faint breeze rustles through grass in the distance. The world continues to spin while I bite at the quicks on my fingernails until a muted *pop, pop, pop* makes me stiffen.

My heart stops.

Then a far-off wail from a child has me frantically reaching for the ignition.

35

ABRI

I plant my foot against the accelerator, the car jerking to life before speeding down the road.

Those pops had to be gunshots.

And that wail...

Oh, God, Tilly.

I struggle not to burst into tears as I slam my foot against the brake, the tires screeching with my abrupt stop in front of the house's dirt drive.

I kick off my heels, shove open my door, then run.

"*Abri, wait,*" Bishop shouts from the darkness, but not even a broken promise to my savior can stop me from sprinting toward my little girl's continued cries inside that house.

She's still alive. While she's screaming, there's still air in her lungs.

I skid onto the drive and continue across the lawn. The front door opens and a man rushes out.

One of my family guards.

My steps skitter to a stop.

He clutches a silenced gun, holding the door open to allow those innocent screams to pierce the night.

I struggle to breathe. To think. To figure out what to do as my mother follows behind him, carrying the owner of that petrified voice—my little girl, kicking and flailing in her arms.

I'd know her anywhere. The beautiful blonde hair. Those ruddy cheeks.

She's in pretty pink pajamas, her little toes covered in fluffy purple socks as she fights the bitch holding her.

"*Freeze*," Bishop shouts from somewhere to my left.

My mother's gaze snaps to the yard. The guard's gun swings in the same direction.

Evil eyes narrow on me.

"Kill them," Adena commands.

I struggle for breath. Frozen. In shock.

After years thinking on my feet, I'm lost in a sea of desolation, unable to flee when my daughter is so close and in trouble. I can't even move to escape the aim of the pistol as the barrel claims me in its sights.

"*Abri*," Bishop roars, the crunch of his rampant footsteps approaching. "*Get down.*"

Pops blast the air, the sound ringing through my malfunctioning brain.

I wait for impact. For pain.

It's the guard who jolts, blood splattering from his chest as he stumbles on the porch. Another bullet hits his face, sending his head flying backward, his body following the momentum to hit the ground with a thud.

"*You bastard*," my mom screeches.

Bishop clambers in front of me, shoving me behind him as he points his gun at my mother. "Put the girl down, Adena."

I peer around his shoulder, watching my mother scowl, her chin high with superiority.

Tilly no longer fights for freedom. She stares. Skin ashen. Eyes wide. Expression pure horror.

"It's okay, sweetheart." My voice waivers. "You're going to be okay."

She doesn't acknowledge my words. She's too young or too frightened to understand.

"Put her down," Bishop repeats, cautiously approaching the porch.

"Stay where you are." My mom wraps a tight arm around Tilly's neck, reigniting the little girl's fight for freedom, her tiny hands gripping the forearm strangling her.

"Stop. She can't breathe." I make to run around Bishop, to claw my daughter from my mother's hands, but he slings an arm around my waist, hauling me backward.

"Don't, belladonna." He shoves me behind him, one hand remaining tight on my thigh as he continues to aim his gun at my mother. "You're on your own, Adena." He steps forward, his touch leaving me. "This isn't going to end well for you."

"Fine," she snaps. "I'll put her down. But the two of you need to back away from the drive. I want access to my car."

"No." I shake my head.

She wouldn't give up this easily. She plans to leave with my daughter. To disappear.

"Just put the girl down and we can talk." Bishop inches closer, so slowly I can't stand it.

My mother removes her arm from around Tilly's neck, my daughter's body losing the rigidity, the bright red seeping from her face as she wheezes for air between hysterical hiccupped sobs.

She's so frail. So scared.

"I already said I was putting her down." Adena leisurely crouches beside the lifeless guard, Tilly's feet hitting the wooden porch floor. "See." But instead of releasing her victim, my mother reaches for the guard's gun.

"*Stop*," I gasp as Bishop runs for them.

I follow. The weapon is jabbed against the back of my child's head before we even reach the porch steps.

Bishop stills.

I do the same, my eyes burning. "Please, Mom. Don't do this."

My mother straightens again, hitching Tilly in her arms.

She's going to kill my daughter. Going to make me watch.

"There's no way out." Bishop creeps forward.

"Who says I'm looking for a way out?" she drawls. "Maybe all I want is retribution for my husband's murder."

"Then take it up with your sons. Abri and the child have nothing to do with Emmanuel's death."

Tilly blubbers. Shaking. Wheezing.

I can't stand it. Everything inside me aches for her—my chest unbearably tight, my stomach painfully hollow.

"*Please*." I fall to my knees, struggling to breathe through the agony. "Mom, take me instead. I'll help you set up a new life. I'll do whatever—"

"Put your gun down." My mother ignores me, talking directly to Bishop.

"You know I can't do that. If I lower my weapon Abri and I are both dead."

"And if you don't the girl will be."

"You're going to kill your own granddaughter, Adena?" Bishop takes another slow step.

"If I have to." She jabs the gun against the back of Tilly's head again, causing more anguished cries. "The kid is no loss to me. I've despised her existence since birth."

"But if you kill her, then I'll kill you." He inches closer to the porch, the space between us feeling like a chasm as I remain on the cold lawn, panicking over how I can cause a diversion. "It doesn't seem like a great plan if you're both dead."

"My death will mean I'm reunited with my husband." Her response is spoken through a taunting smile. "Either way I get what I want, which is my daughter's suffering."

"Have I not suffered enough?" I choke out. "You stole my child."

"A child you never could've raised on your own. Now tell him to put his gun down or watch your bastard kid die."

There's no winning this. If Bishop doesn't drop his gun, Tilly's life is over. And if he does we're both dead.

"*Now*," she roars.

Tilly screams, every second of her fear scarring me, never to be healed.

"Mom, listen." I clasp my hands in front of me, praying to a god who never saw me. Who never acknowledged my existence in this living hell. "You don't want me to suffer because every moment I remain alive I'll be constantly at the back of your mind. Haunting you. Stopping you from moving on." I climb to shaky feet. "End me now. Get this over with."

"Abri," Bishop warns.

"No, this is what she really wants." I don't have a death wish. More than anything, I want to see tomorrow and what it holds for Tilly. All I'm striving for is enough of a distraction to keep Adena occupied until my brothers question why I haven't sent another update and rush onto the scene. Hopefully then my daughter won't be the center of attention. "If you hate me so much, kill me now."

"Abri, stop." Bishop raises his hands in surrender, the gun falling limp in his pinched grip on the hilt.

"What are you doing?" I whisper. "She'll shoot you."

The briefest hint of crunching asphalt carries in the distance, the sound of cars approaching bringing the barest dose of hope.

"You're targeting the wrong person." Bishop stands tall, his back to me. "I'm more to blame for your husband's death than Abri. Who do you think got in Matthew's ear and told him Emmanuel needed to die? For years I nagged your son to kill the asshole who murdered his childhood sweetheart just so he could get some closure, let alone karma."

That's not true.

He's lying.

For me.

"He's been by my side for years," he continues, "earning a brutal moniker, yet his father's actions haunted him. It's no surprise he took the chance when he could."

"Bishop, don't," I beg.

My mother's gaze narrows, his admission clearly getting to her even though skepticism wrinkles her features. "That girl died a lifetime ago."

"She did." He nods. "And it took fucking baby steps to get him to retaliate. At first I convinced him to skim a few thousand from your accounts. Do you remember that? The banks blamed it on an international scam. Then there was the fire at your Seattle warehouse that reporters quoted you blaming on a competitor. News flash—it was us. And more recently, Emmanuel had a slight mishap with the brakes on his Bentley."

I suck in a breath. Maybe he's not lying.

"Bishop." I shake my head, unable to look away from my mother's murderous face.

"Matthew never had my taste for revenge," he continues, "but I wore him down."

My pulse grows frantic. My hands tremble.

"Don't do this." I don't want him to die, yet I can't bring myself to protest more. I don't know what else to do other than wait for those cars. Play along with his charade. Let him risk his life while the guilt slaughters me.

"I'm going to put my gun down." Bishop crouches.

No. No. No.

My mother grins, her weapon leaving the back of Tilly's head, her chin high with superiority as the slow arc of the barrel moves to pin him in its sights. "You're a stupid man. Do you think I won't kill you?"

"I know you'll at least try. But I suggest you make it quick. You're about to be surrounded."

She stiffens, her gaze snapping to the darkened street.

Bishop charges, rushing the porch.

I gasp as my mother's attention swings back to him, her eyes widening as a scream pummels my throat.

She glares. Realigns the gun's aim. Then shoots.

36

ABRI

Bishop doesn't stop. He bounds up the stairs.

"*No.*" My mom backtracks, firing again as she holds Tilly like a rag doll.

Bishop's head violently lashes to the left while he barrels forward, his feet stumbling. He strikes out with a fist. Knocks the gun from Adena's hand. His momentum continues as he rams her with his shoulder, grabbing Tilly from mid-air as my mother drops her.

I scramble for his gun, intent on snatching the weapon from the grass even though I can't drag my gaze from Bishop as he crashes to his knees with my daughter in his arms, then falls face-first to the floor.

Tilly's cries stop abruptly. Bishop doesn't move.

My mother scrambles to escape the porch as I point the weapon at her.

"Stop." My demand is fractured. Broken.

She doesn't listen.

"*I said stop.*" I fire three shots in her vicinity. Quick succession. Threatening yet loosely aimed.

She freezes on the bottom step, her attention narrowing on me with a scowl. "You won't kill me."

I want to. My head screams at me to pull the trigger, but my fingers won't comply. "Move another inch and you'll see how wrong you are." I approach, my legs weak, my heart on fire at the silence that comes from Bishop and Tilly.

I can't see my little girl because of his bulking frame. Can't understand where she is. If she's trapped beneath his body.

There's only the sound of running footsteps carrying from the road.

"Tilly?" I raise my voice. "Bishop?"

I keep the gun trained on my mother as my brothers rush the yard, weapons drawn.

"What the fuck?" Salvatore comes up beside me, panting. "Where's…" The question fades as his attention falls to the porch. "Are they dead?"

I open my mouth but can't answer. I can't do anything as Remy rushes up to my other side.

"Are you okay?" he asks.

No. I'm the farthest from okay I've ever been.

I can't understand what's happening. To Tilly. To Bishop. To me.

My body wages war, pulling me apart from the inside out. I'm shaking. My heart trembling. My stomach hollow. My chest tight.

I feel like I'm racing against the clock while stuck firmly in place. Still but frantic. Alert yet so goddamn cloudy.

I want to rush the porch but I can't move. Want to kill my mother yet can't bring myself to do it.

She squares her shoulders, a look of authority bearing down on me. "You should have let me leave." She takes a step.

I squeeze the trigger, the bullet passing her right shoulder to hit the house with a *thwack*.

"*Fuck.*" Salvatore flinches. "Goddamnit, Abri. I've got her in my sights, okay? She's not going anywhere."

"Neither are they." My mother grins at Bishop and Tilly. "I shot him in the head and your daughter no longer cries to be saved, Abri. I think the son of a bitch may have crushed her."

My vision blurs, my worst fears hitting my ears.

Remy hesitantly reaches for my gun. "You should go to the car. We'll take it from here."

"No." I find the strength to step away but let him take the weapon. "I need to see for myself."

"Abri, don't." He grabs my wrist. "I'll do it for you."

I ignore him, my feet moving of their own accord, tears blurring my vision.

My brothers follow me forward, stopping in front of our mother.

I barely take notice of how they grab her, lowering her to her knees. My attention is too focused on Bishop, lifeless as he lays face-down against the blood-splattered porch.

My pulse pounds in my ears. In my throat.

I can't make out the muffled words of my brothers as they sneer at my mother. There's only my deafening pulse as I approach certain heartbreak.

Tilly's torso pokes out from under the large arm that's wrapped around her, one that tried so hard to keep her safe. Her face remains hidden beneath Bishop's shoulder, the top of her head barely visible. Her pink pajamas are splattered with blood. Gruesome little polka dots I'll never forget the sight of.

He tried to save her. He put his life on the line, risked everything, and now…

I suck in a shaky sob and fall to my knees beside them, my hands numb as I grab Bishop's shoulder to haul him off of her. I close my eyes as I lift, silently begging for mercy. For hope. For a second chance.

But as soon as I get Bishop onto his side, gravity takes over and he tumbles onto his back. Lifeless.

I squeeze my eyes tighter.

I can't open them.

I don't want to.

"Abri?" Remy asks. "Are they dead?"

I suck in breath after breath, my eyes burning beneath shut lids, my heart on fire. "Give me a sec."

Come on. Where is your strength?

It's lying on the floor with the man who made me weak.

I force myself to look, to stare down at the little girl who peers back at me, eyes wide, Bishop's hand cradled under the back of her head like he used his final moments to make sure she hit the floor as softly as possible.

I stiffen. Hold my breath.

She's looking directly at me but…she's not moving. I can't hear her inhales. I can't hear anything through the pounding in my ears.

She blinks, and all the air rushes from my lungs.

"Tilly?" I gasp, reaching for her.

She keeps blinking. Stunned. Motionless.

"It's okay, sweetheart." I place a frantic palm to her chest, feeling the rampant rise and fall of her lungs. "Are you hurt? Can you move?"

"She's alive?" Salvo calls out.

"Yes," I wheeze. "You're safe now, beautiful girl. You're going to be all right. I promise." I gently guide her to sit, my hands skimming her limbs for injuries while I try to ignore how Bishop doesn't move. How his arm remains limp on the floor. "You're so brave."

I paste on a calming smile even though my heart breaks and soars and melts all at once.

I've never touched her before. Never felt her skin. Now here she is, traumatized, robbed of speech, and covered in blood, but warm and soft beneath my fingertips.

"My name is Abri." I guide her onto her feet, slowly dragging her toward me. "I'm going to help you. Is that all right?"

Her eyes are fathomless pools of fear, her gaze darting from me, to Adena, then back again. "Momma," she cries.

For a second I'm caught up in a fairytale where my sweet little girl recognizes me as her mother. That her heart knows me on instinct. Then reality hits like a bus and I realize she's calling for the woman inside the quiet house. The one who hasn't come to save her.

"Momma," she sobs.

"It's okay." I pull her into my arms, nestling her against my chest, holding her with so much love. But rage enters the mix, nipping at the edges of my tenderness, swirling with the sorrow.

I shuffle on my knees, turning to face my mother. "What did you do to her parents?"

She gives me a haughty look. "Their services were no longer needed."

I slowly rock back and forth, unsure if the comfort is for me or Tilly. Unsure how I'm going to climb to my feet and walk this innocent girl away from her dead parents.

"You fucking killed them?" Remy leans down to snarl in her face. "Who the fuck are you?"

"She's the product of loveless parenting," Lorenzo's voice calls from the darkness, the light *thud*, *thud*, *thud* of his walking stick approaching. "Aren't you, Adena?"

My mother spits on the ground before her, releasing a slew of Italian I can't understand.

Lorenzo limps from the shadows onto the lawn, his driver by his side. He glances between us, searching for something, his gaze finally landing on Bishop's limp body.

He stops. Frozen.

My bottom lip trembles as understanding dawns on his aged features.

"Is he dead?" His attention turns to me, his eyes pained.

"I…" I shake my head, cradling Tilly close to my chest. "I don't know. I can't look."

His face softens, pity staring back at me as he continues toward us. But I don't want him here. Don't want anyone else to enter my bubble of misery.

"Wait." I pull in a shuddering breath.

I don't want to be told Bishop is dead. I need to be the one to break the news.

He risked his life for me. The least I can do is confirm his sacrifice.

I cradle Tilly's head, just like Bishop must have when he hit the floor, and slowly lower my gaze to his body. I stare at his hands, the strong fingers, the calloused palms.

My mother chuckles.

It takes everything inside me not to climb to my feet and scratch her heart out.

I drag my gaze up the sleeve of his trademark suit, along his broad shoulder, and press my lips tight as I reach his face.

His eyes are closed. Mouth parted. Skin pale.

I scrunch my nose against renewed tears as I stare at him.

He might almost seem at peace if it weren't for the sickening gash on the right side of his face, a bullet wound tearing through his cheek, the seeping blood covering his nose and trailing to his jaw.

Dark, deep scratches mar his forehead, the skin already bruising from where he must have collided with the wooden floor.

I look away, instead reaching for his outstretched arm, sliding my palm over his to guide his hand back to his side. Even now, destroyed and mutilated, he's beautiful. His strength. His sacrifice.

I've never been more devoted. More destroyed.

I wish I could tell him how thankful I am. How important he became to me in such a short space of time.

A storm of grief threatens to overwhelm me, and I can't break down in front of Tilly, not when she's already suffered enough.

I squeeze his fingers. They squeeze back.

I snap my gaze to his face.

His eyes remain closed, his mouth still open. But that hand continues to hold me in a fragile grip.

"Bishop?" I scamper closer on my knees, Tilly glancing over her shoulder at him. "Don't look, sweetheart." I tilt my shoulders, trying to avert her gaze. "Bishop, can you hear me?"

I place a hand to his sternum, the thudding beat of his heart pounding beneath my palm.

I shake my head in disbelief, not trusting that I'm not hallucinating. "Bishop, talk to me."

"Belladonna," he croaks.

Oh, my God.

I glance to Remy and Salvo standing over our mother, still kneeling in the yard. "He needs an ambulance."

"No." The grip on my hand tightens. "No ambulance."

I return my attention to Bishop, my entire heart consumed by the piercing blue that blinks back at me.

"You've been shot in the face," I whisper.

"Is it a graze or do I have the misfortune of having a bullet in my head?"

I quickly scrutinize his wound, noting the elongated gash, the flesh around his cheekbone swelling. "I-I don't know. A graze, I think."

Remy bounds up the stairs, his frown pinning Bishop. "Holy shit. Your face looks like ground beef."

"Graze or direct hit?" Bishop grates.

"Graze. Definitely a graze. You're one lucky son of a bitch."

"Then I'll live." Bishop releases my hand and winces as he pushes to a seated position.

I want to believe him. *God*, how I do. But luck has never been on my side.

"Please," I beg. "You need medical attention."

"Belladonna, we're in the middle of a crime scene. My injuries can wait."

"But your head… Doesn't it hurt?"

"Like a motherfucker."

Tilly's head snaps around, her fragile stare eating up the gory sight of him as she shrinks into me, her fear renewed.

"I'm scaring her." He winces, concern etching his brow before he glances away. "You need to get her out of here. Take her to the safe house."

"I'm not leaving you."

"Momma." Tilly attempts to wiggle from my hold. "I need Momma."

"Shh. It's okay." I soothe, gliding a hand through her hair, rocking us gently back and forth.

"Leave, Abri." Bishop struggles to his feet. "You need to get somewhere safe before the cops show, and I don't want the kid close when Adena gets what she deserves."

37

BISHOP

The girl looks at me like I'm a waking nightmare, her blue eyes so astonishingly similar to Abri's that it fucking kills me to have her peering back at me with vivid terror.

"Go." I push to my feet, my head throbbing as if I'm living on borrowed time, blood slowly oozing along my jaw to drip onto my clothes. "Now, belladonna. The kid is petrified."

Abri frowns. "Are you sure?"

"I don't want you here."

She bristles. Cringes.

Fuck.

I didn't mean it like that. Or maybe I did. Maybe I don't give a shit how I get the two of them away from here as long as they're gone.

She stands, cautiously eyeing me, hesitant as she clutches her daughter to her chest. "I'll wait in the car." She sidesteps Remy and starts down the stairs, meeting Salvatore's gaze once she reaches the lawn. "Look after him. And do the opposite with our mother."

She doesn't wait for a response. Doesn't even acknowledge Adena's conniving scoff. Instead, she tilts her head toward the little girl. "You're shivering, sweetheart. Are you cold? Or just overwhelmed? You've been through so much. But you're incredibly brave. I promise you're going to be okay now. We're going to work this out together."

She continues to reaffirm and coo to the child while she walks down the gravel drive on bare feet.

I don't look away, not even once they disappear into the shadows of the road. Everyone else remains quiet, as if biding time until hell inevitably breaks loose once the child is out of earshot.

But although they're no longer in sight, I can't blink those pretty horror-filled eyes out of my mind. Can't quit hearing Abri beg for her daughter's life. Can't stop remembering how it felt to listen to them suffer.

Lorenzo clears his throat. "Are you sure you're all right, *figlio*?"

I drag my attention to him, despising the unfamiliar weakness that follows every thought of Abri.

"Why the fuck is she still alive?" I snap, descending the stairs on weak knees, snatching my gun from Remy as he holds it out for me. I stride up to the smirking woman knelt on the lawn, her tenacity making my blood toxic. "Are you ready to die, bitch?" I shove the barrel of my Sig against her forehead, her smile sneering up at me.

"*Stop*," Lorenzo warns. "She's to remain alive."

"Like hell she is." I jab the metal harder. "She deserves death."

"*Bishop*," he warns again. "She is still my sister. She *will* remain alive."

"You've gotta be fucking kidding me," I snarl

"You heard him." Adena bats her lashes. "I'm his sister. I remain alive."

I clench my teeth, my finger itching to pull the trigger, consequences be damned.

"How's the face?" she taunts. "That's going to be some scar. I have a funny feeling you're going to think of me every time you look in the mirror for the rest of your life."

"Shut your goddamn mouth," Salvatore snaps. "Or I'll shut it for you."

She continues to beam up at me, eyes bright with delight while screams of revenge ring in my ears.

She needs to pay for what she's done.

Abri and Tilly deserve to be avenged.

I press the barrel harder against her forehead, pushing her backward as she laughs.

"You will not defy me, *figlio*," Lorenzo demands, grabbing the sleeve of my suit. "She can still be of use."

"No *use* is worth the weakness you will show by letting her live," I seethe. "She tried to have you killed."

"And failed." He lowers his voice, reining in his anger while I remain a slave to mine. "She holds the key to the Costa fortune, and her kids are entitled to their inheritance."

"Fuck the money."

"I agree," Remy murmurs. "I want her dead."

"She *will not* die tonight," Lorenzo warns. "Stand down."

I can't do it. Can't step away from this fucking bitch. Can't let her get away with the nightmares she's inflicted upon the two females I've grown to worship.

"Stand. Down," he repeats slowly. Viciously.

Fuck.

I swing around to glare at him, my head protesting the sudden movement. "You're making a mistake, old man. One that can't be forgiven."

"In time you will understand."

"In time I will only resent you more." I hold his stare and coldcock Adena across the side of the face, making her drop to her hands and knees with a cry. "At least now the anger will be reciprocated."

He scowls at me, nostrils flaring, fury bubbling.

I storm for the house, hauling myself up the porch stairs by the railing, careful of the vertigo fucking with my head and giving me shitty balance as I lean over the dead guy with the head-shot and drag him inside the front door.

I dump him in the hall and continue toward an open archway beaming with light, a pink bunny laying on the floor in front of me, blood splatter covering its fur. Tilly must have dropped it.

Poor fucking kid. A lifetime of nightmares awaits her, half of them no doubt inspired by the shit show currently known as my face.

I leave the bunny and continue into the living room, not surprised by the carnage greeting me.

Two bodies. A man and woman. Both Caucasian. Roughly in their mid-thirties.

The female is face-down on the floor a few feet in front of me, a stream of crimson trailed along the cream carpet behind her as if she attempted to crawl for help.

The male is on the sofa, head lulled back, blindly staring at the ceiling. Mouth wide. Skin pale.

Nothing else seems to be touched.

The muted television plays in the corner, some kid's cartoon flashing across the screen.

Family pictures hang on the walls. Bright smiles and affectionate embraces. Infant artwork is framed alongside the images, the paintings treated like precious mementos. That little girl was loved by these people. Adored.

Fucking Adena Costa.

I walk to the woman and kneel beside her, flipping her onto her back. "If Abri were here, I know she'd thank you for raising her daughter." I pull a blade from my pocket and dig into the wound on her abdomen, retrieving the bullet that killed her. "Here's hoping you're in a better place."

I stand and perform the same ritual with the male. Pay respects on behalf of Abri. Retrieve the bullet from his chest. Then stand to enter the kitchen.

I turn on the gas stove, all four burners hissing to life as claret drips down my cheek.

I don't have the time to properly cover up this bloodbath. The house might not burn completely before the fire brigade arrives. The bodies may only get charred not cremated. But heavy-handed payments to certain government officials will get this case labelled as an accidental house fire.

Not that it's my ass on the line.

I'm doing this for Abri.

For her daughter, who doesn't deserve to live with the guilt that could come from finding out her existence was the cause of these people dying.

Hopefully her little kiddie brain will enable some of those useful defense mechanisms and block tonight's events from her memory. And if it does, I want Abri to have the choice of deciding whether or not her child knows how her life started.

I search through the drawers, scattering utensils and silverware. I don't stop until I find an old-school box of matches.

I snatch the candle from the wooden dining table and walk back through the slaughter scene, lighting the wick and leaving the flickering torch on the TV cabinet to buy some time before detonation.

Then I make for the front door, picking up the blood-splattered bunny as I pass.

Adena is already on her feet when I reach the porch, her arms held behind her back by Remy, a gun trained on her by Salvatore.

"I'm done," I say as I descend the stairs, my scowl directed at Lorenzo. "Don't call. Don't text. Don't even think about me, old man. Until that bitch is dead, you can act like I'm the same."

He raises his chin. "You will forgive me, *figlio*. You will understand my decision in time."

"Fuck that." I continue across the yard toward the drive. "Lose my number. And get the hell out of here before the place blows."

Salvatore mutters a curse while I storm for the road, not slowing my approach toward Abri's car until she comes into view, the front passenger seat slightly reclined as she cuddles her daughter to her chest.

They look good together—her daughter's cheek resting on her shoulder, Abri's chin leaning against Tilly's head. And that sound…

I slow my steps, taking in more of Abri's soft, sweet lullaby, her voice melodic and soothing despite how it hits me like a fucking truck.

I shouldn't interrupt.

I should turn on my heel and leave them the fuck alone. But Abri catches sight of me through the darkness, her gaze pinning me, her expression falling. My face must be a fucking sight.

I stop a few feet away from her window.

"Is everything okay?" she asks quietly.

I don't want to ruin their peace. Can't stand the thought of fucking this up for her.

"Bishop?" Her gaze implores. "Talk to me."

I take another step but can't bring myself to move any closer once Tilly raises her head and turns to face me.

The little girl shrinks back into Abri, her frightened whimper piercing my chest like a fucking poisoned arrow.

"Don't be scared," Abri whispers. "He's a good man. He won't hurt you."

The kid isn't convinced. She stares at me in silence for long seconds, then finally buries her face into the scarf around Abri's neck.

I've never felt more monstrous. More fucking ashamed to be me.

"You need to get out of here." I jerk my chin toward the road, all casual and shit when I feel anything but.

I want to make sure they're safe. To keep them protected. Yet there's no way I'm putting that little girl through a car ride with me when I look like a Halloween special.

"You're not coming?" Abri's eyes widen in panic.

"No. I've got shit to take care of." I wince when Tilly flinches, as if despising my bad language, or maybe just my tone. "Here." I quickly step closer and hold the fluffy bunny through the window. "The house is about to blow. There's no time to argue."

The little girl bunches her shoulders and snuggles tighter against Abri, sending another poisoned arrow straight through my chest.

I can't fucking take it. Can't stand being the cause of more of the little girl's pain.

Abri takes the toy, her lips parting as if she's about to say something.

I don't stick around to hear it. I force myself to turn on my heel and walk.

"Bishop," she calls after me.

I keep marching toward Remy who approaches the road, ignoring the anger building inside me, the thunderous storm of need that roars for me to be the one to bring them to safety.

"*Bishop*," she begs, the pained arrows now piercing my back.

"Take your sister to the safe house." I glare at her brother as I pass. "Langston and Layla will be waiting."

"Where are you going?" he asks.

"None of your goddamn business." I continue down the road, not caring where I'm going, only cursing where I've been. "Just make sure they get to safety. Or I'll come for you."

38

ABRI

My eyes burn as I sit helpless, Tilly's frantic breathing choppy against my neck while Bishop walks away.

He says something to Remy. My brother then jogs toward us to pull the driver's door open.

"What's wrong?" I ask. "Where's he going?"

"I don't know." He slides in and buckles his belt. "Have you got the keys to this thing?"

"They're in the console. But I'm not leaving without him."

"I'm going to politely request you change your mind so that scary mofo doesn't kill me for my disobedience." He presses the ignition, the engine humming to life. "Hold onto her. I need to get us out of here before the house blows."

My heart skips a beat, the fear, panic, and confusion overwhelming. "But what about Bishop?"

"I'm pretty sure that guy makes the devil shit his pants, so I'm sure he'll be fine." He shifts into drive and takes off.

I quickly pull the belt around Tilly, clasping us tighter together, her arms clinging to my neck. "It's okay, sweetheart. We're going somewhere safe."

At least I hope we are.

I just don't want to go there without the only man who's ever fought to protect me. To protect *us*.

I try to catch sight of him through the darkness, to gain just a glimpse in the hopes of deciphering what his abrupt rejection means. Is he concussed? Confused?

The pained beat in my chest says it's neither of those things. That Bishop's dismissal has everything to do with my actions tonight. How I betrayed him by fleeing the safe house. How I broke my promise to stay in the car and almost got him killed.

And worst of all—how I dared to seduce him. How I *begged* him to turn a blind eye to his abstinence despite knowing how much it meant to him.

"Seriously, Abri, don't worry about him," Remy murmurs. "He'll be fine."

I nod, hoping he's right, praying I get a chance to apologize, when an explosion thunders through the silence, the bright glow of flames illuminating the sky.

I flinch. Tilly whimpers.

"It's just fireworks, little one." Remy smiles at her. "Someone must be having a party."

My heart hurts. For his compassion through the carnage. For Bishop's absence in the midst of my growing anxiety. For the beautiful girl who trembles in a stranger's arms.

I glance to the side mirror. Fire smothers the house.

"What about our uncle and Salvatore?" I whisper. "Where are they?"

"Right behind us." Remy takes the next corner, heading back toward Denver.

"And what about *her*?" I stare at him, attempting to read anything he might try to hide. "Was she left behind?"

"No." He keeps his attention on the road. "She's in the car with Lorenzo and his driver."

I stiffen. "I thought Bishop..."

I don't finish the sentence. I can't. Not in front of Tilly.

"Lorenzo forbid it." My brother shoots me a pitying glance. "To say Bishop was unhappy about the instruction is an understatement. And I don't blame him. With that bullet wound, the poor guy isn't going to need to dress up for Halloween for the rest of his life."

Remorse twists at my gut.

I drag my stare out the window, the whirlpool inside me

spinning faster and faster as I cling to my little girl. Anger mixes with devastation. Anxiety with regret.

I wish my mother was dead, but that yearning also comes with guilt. And the heavy agony where I'm left to mourn something I never had—a maternal nurturer. Someone who should've been everything good, kind, and comforting. Instead, she was cruel, mean, and heartless.

A soft hum of vibration drags my attention back to Remy. He pulls his cell from his pants pocket and answers a call.

"Pull over," Salvatore says loud enough for me to hear. "Lorenzo needs to talk to Abri."

"Why?" I ask. "What's going on?"

"Just pull over."

The call dies and Remy slows the car, giving me a sympathetic glance while he pulls to a stop in the middle of the desolate road.

Headlights close in behind us. One car. Then another.

I stalk the side mirror as a figure approaches in the moonlight. The cane. The hobbled footsteps.

I lower my window when Lorenzo stops beside my door.

He stares down at the child in my arms, his face grim. "I can take her from here."

"What?" My heart lurches, my arms instinctively tightening around my daughter.

"I will make sure she's safe." Lorenzo's face softens. "I already made the necessary calls this afternoon. I never expected this, but I didn't trust my brother-in-law to have given this precious girl the parents she deserves."

I sit stunned. Frantic.

Lorenzo opens my door, his kind eyes taking in my daughter who inches away from him. "It's best to make the transition now. Before more attachments are made. I will go straight to the airport and deliver her to friends of mine in Florence."

Florence?

"No." I need more time.

Lorenzo reaches out, his wrinkled fingers gently touching Tilly's arm. She whimpers, her fear slicing through me with serrated edges.

"Don't." I tilt her away. "Let me think."

"Momma," Tilly cries. "Want Momma."

"I know, sweetheart." I rock her in the seat, the two of us

swaying while I fight panic. I'm not ready to let her go. I want to get to know her. To understand her. To mother her.

Even just for a little while.

"It's going to be hard regardless," Remy murmurs. "Now or later, it's all the same, but the aftermath will be easier on her if she doesn't get attached to you in the meantime."

Does he think I don't know that? That I'm not well aware every second she clings to me will cause more damage later?

"The Bernardis are good people." Lorenzo places a hand to my wrist. "They're childless despite their best efforts and will cherish Tilly like the gift she is."

My rampant pulse chokes me. The beat too fast. Too hard.

"They will love her as if she's their own."

"But she's not their own." My voice breaks. "She's mine. My daughter. Mine to protect."

Lorenzo pulls back, his expression filled with concern. "Only if you're willing to take on the responsibility."

Willing?

My will has never been the issue. It's always been my worth. My ability. The likelihood that I'll make Tilly's life worse merely by being a part of it.

"You could be a good mother, Abri," Remy whispers. "Hell, just look at you. You already are."

No. I suck in a breath and Tilly's arms tighten around me. Clinging. Grappling.

I don't know the first thing about being a mom. I wouldn't even know where to start. And right now, this beautiful child needs the best.

"I'll help however I can," Remy adds. "We all will. Salvo and Matthew, too. You're not alone in this."

Heat licks at my eyes, the burn increasing.

Tilly deserves so much better than me. Better than the sleazy 'temptress of high society' as her mother. Better than this family. Than the blood in her veins.

But the thought of letting her go tears at me, ripping at the walls of my heart and hollowing my chest.

Lorenzo glances toward the back of the car, his lips thinning. "Abri, the police are on the way to the fire. You have to make a decision."

I can't. I need time.

"Momma." Tilly cries against my chest, her tears soaking my satin top.

"If we get arrested, even momentarily, she will be taken from you." Lorenzo's gaze returns to mine, now hardened with concern. "The investigation will be brutal and public. It could take time to find where she ends up."

"I know." Tears spill down my cheeks.

But I can't let her go.

I can't be her mother either.

"Abri, we're running out of time." Remy shifts in his seat, eyeing the rearview mirror.

The threat of an anxiety attack squeezes at my head, tighter and tighter, until it feels like my brain will explode.

"The Bernardis will love her," Lorenzo vows. "I swear it to you."

"*Momma*," Tilly wails. Sniffles. "*Pease, Momma*."

I can't decide. Can't figure out what's best.

I cling to my daughter so tight I fear I might hurt her. But no matter how much I hug that little girl, it's not enough. It will never be enough.

"Decide, *mia cara nipote*." Lorenzo's gaze hardens. "Do it now."

My heart climbs to my throat, the frantic beats making it hard to breathe.

"What do you want to do, Abri?" Remy asks. "I'm here for you either way."

I believe him. After everything we've been through. After all the secrets. Despite all the betrayal. There's no doubt in my mind he'll stand by me.

I just don't know how to make this choice.

"Abri?" Remy repeats, his attention panicked as he stalks the rearview. "What's it going to be?"

"I…" I swallow over the bile threatening to flood my mouth, tears trailing down my cheeks like rain. "I need to do what's right."

39

ABRI

I take the first step out of the jet, pausing at the top of the staircase leading to the tarmac, the chilly air hitting my face to steal my breath.

Tilly clings tighter to my chest, her monkey grip growing more intense as her darting gaze looks over the sprawling private airport.

"This is Washington D.C., sweetheart," I murmur into her hair. "We're going to stay here a little while."

She doesn't respond. She never does.

I've spent two days talking to her despite her silence. She doesn't even acknowledge when I call her name, but Layla keeps encouraging my patience. She tells me not to fret. To give my daughter time.

I'm trying, *oh, God*, how I'm trying. Yet all I do is worry.

Is Tilly still thinking about what happened? Does she understand that the only mother and father she knew are now dead? Does she trust me? Is she eating enough? Will she always cry herself to sleep?

"I'm sure she'll love it here." Matthew slides a hand across my back as he slowly passes.

"We all will." Layla follows close behind, her concerned stare fixed on my brother while he hesitantly descends the steps onto the tarmac.

"Do you hear that?" I whisper in Tilly's ear. "We're all going to love it here."

The last forty-eight hours have been a crazed minefield of emotion.

We stayed in the safe house the entire time—me, Tilly, Matthew, and Layla, with nothing but the peace of isolation and the confinements of my parental ignorance while Remy and Salvatore took our mother God knows where under our uncle's guidance.

The heartache during those days was the heaviest I've ever felt—not only while I questioned if I'd made the right choice to burden Tilly with me as a mother, but also the pain of not knowing what happened to Bishop.

Hours were spent staring at the tire tracks trailing down the hill toward the safe house, waiting for him to show.

He hasn't called.

Not even a text has been sent.

I was told of his fight with Lorenzo. How he walked away from the only family he's ever known. And it's all my fault.

I dragged him into a battle he never should've been a part of. I would've sickened him with my seduction when his adrenaline was high and his morals low. I didn't even stay in the car when I promised I would, and now he's disfigured, or scarred, or maybe even dying of infection.

Between the long hours Matthew spent resting to recover from his bullet wound, he assured me Bishop would be okay. Layla did, too. But I could hear the worry in their voices. Could see it in their eyes.

Everyone is as concerned as I am.

"Come on, Bree," Matthew calls from the tarmac, jerking his head toward a waiting limousine. "There's a lot to do."

I nod, then quickly fumble to catch Tilly's bunny as it slips from her hands. "Hold tight, cutie-pie. You don't want to drop him."

I descend the stairs, my heart squeezing at the thought of her losing the only thing she has from her past.

She cried the entire time Layla had the plush toy in the washer. Then didn't seem to notice that half the color had bleached from its fur when it was returned, the blood no longer visible.

Layla tells me it's normal. That kids don't care about their favorite things being torn or scuffed or disfigured, just as long as they know they're there to cling to.

The comfort of familiarity is all they need.

"Become that familiar comfort," she'd told me. *"Love her. Let her rely on that love. And someday soon, she'll give hers in return."*

I'm not holding my breath for that moment to arrive, but each morning my chest grows tighter.

Everything has changed in such a short space of time.

Was it a week? Ten days? I can't even remember how much time has passed since the gala. It's all a blur of memories, each one filled with Bishop. How he changed my life. How he saved me from everything—my father's plans, from Gordon and his men, from myself.

I went from barely knowing him to not wanting to know life without him, all in the blink of an eye.

But I guess I'm destined to live with one part of my heart always missing.

Matthew holds the limo door open, his free hand gently pressing to the top of my daughter's head as I climb inside to slide against the far seat next to Layla.

"Are you ready to see your new penthouse?" Layla beams at Tilly. "I'm told it's absolutely beautiful. You can even see Capitol Hill."

I wince as Tilly shrugs into me, her cheek resting against the scarf at my neck.

"Thank you for everything you've done," I murmur awkwardly as Matthew slides into the opposite seat, closing the door behind him. "I don't know how you found a furnished place for us so quickly, but I'll repay you as soon as I can."

"There's nothing to repay." Matthew scowls at the cell in his hand, aggressively typing on screen. "I called in a few favors and we were fortunate enough that things panned out. Grasp the good luck while you can."

I nod, taking the hint that he's just as uncomfortable talking about me being indebted to him as I am.

Originally, the plan was that Tilly and I would move in with him and Layla. He'd order a child's bed, some sheets and kiddie things, too, and we'd make do living together for a while.

I'd actually preferred it that way, with another mother close by to whisper words of encouragement and guide me toward easier solutions when necessary.

Now I'm going to be on my own, and it's scary as hell.

"You'll be fine." Layla places a hand on my thigh and squeezes. "I'm told you'll only be living a few short blocks away."

"I know." I lean my face closer to the tinted window, pretending to take in the sun.

The drive takes a while, the busy city streets full of honking cars, while every sidewalk teems with people in business suits.

It's entirely different to Denver. More green. Entirely prestigious.

I can't get my head around the influx of change.

A child psychologist has already been arranged for Tilly. Daily appointments are scheduled as of tomorrow. I'm told I already have my own bank account filled with a generous amount of my uncle's money. A payoff, it seems, in an attempt to distract me from the air that still fills my mother's lungs.

Then there are all my worldly possessions back at the family home that strangers are now packing to bring to D.C.

I couldn't stand the thought of stepping foot inside that house again. I wouldn't care if it was torched to the ground. If it weren't for my father's paperwork and any potential secrets hidden amongst the pages, maybe I would've set the house to flame.

Perhaps I still will.

The limousine stops in front of a towering skyscraper, the cement pillars reaching farther than the vehicle's window will allow me to see.

"We're here." Matthew opens the door and shuffles out, a protective hand over his stomach.

I follow on numb legs, taking in the marble lobby, the leather furniture, the opulence, all without letting it fully digest.

It isn't until I'm in the hall of the twenty-ninth floor, watching movers haul boxes out of the penthouse to place beside the elevator, that confusion takes over.

"Are someone's belongings still inside?" I ask.

"Apparently," Matthew growls. "Everything was meant to be out an hour ago."

Annoyance pinches his face as he does more aggressive typing into his cell, Tilly bouncing in my arms while she watches the movers.

I want to ask if this place is legitimate. If it was secured through professional channels and not by an alternate route paved by my brother's brutal moniker. But I keep my mouth shut, knowing I'm too tired to protest even if underhanded tactics were used.

"Feel free to go inside," a bulky man with a box states on his way to the elevator. "We're done now."

"All personal items have been removed?" Matthew raises a disapproving brow.

The guy nods. "They sure have."

My brother stalks inside, but I wait in the hall as hollowness hits. It feels like something is missing. *Someone.*

"Thinking about Bishop again?" Layla asks, quietly inching toward the door.

I wince and drag my hand through Tilly's hair, delicately trying to untangle the knots she wouldn't let me brush this morning. "I think I just need to see for myself that he's okay."

"Are you sure that's all it is?"

No. It's so much more.

I'm wallowing in heartache. Gorging on sorrow.

"I barely know him." I sigh. "Yet it doesn't feel that way."

"Some people spend years together and never get dragged through the events you two had to face in such a small stretch of time. You would've learned more about each other in those days than most couples figure out by the time they get married."

That's exactly what it seems like. That the intense moments we shared fast-tracked us through so many emotional checkpoints but exposed a wealth of vulnerabilities, too.

He knows the worst of me. He's experienced it firsthand.

Now all I want is the ability to apologize.

"I feel guilty." I keep my voice low. "He didn't even say goodbye. And after everything that happened, I don't want him to hate me."

"He doesn't hate you," Matthew mutters from a few feet inside the penthouse.

"How do you know?" I scrutinize him. "How could you possibly have any idea how he feels unless you've lied about speaking to him?"

He doesn't respond, only readjusts his suit jacket in silence.

"Have you spoken to him?" I frown.

Layla awkwardly clears her throat.

"Have you?" I repeat louder.

"No. We haven't spoken a damn word, but I fuck—" Matthew cuts off the curse too late, his attention snapping to Tilly in apology. "But I know him. You don't need to worry about any sort of ill feelings toward you."

I wish I believed him.

I wish any sort of other motivation made sense. But for Bishop to vanish from my life after what we went through screams of animosity and anger. I can't imagine doing the same to him.

"I'll leave you two to talk." Layla walks into the penthouse, passing Matthew. "I'm going to do some snooping and make sure the cleaners I contracted did a good job."

I follow a few steps after her, entering my new home to be greeted by high ceilings, polished floorboards, an immaculate kitchen, and a breathtaking view from the massive wall of glass.

It looks like the front cover of a house magazine—perfectly curated, loads of style, and absolutely no heart.

Matthew remains quiet, staring across the open living area, his mind seeming elsewhere as Tilly's cheek nestles into my neck, the little bunny tight in her hands.

I'm not sure I'm going to like it here. Not when my thoughts, before and after crossing the threshold, are smothered with memories of Bishop.

He's tainting my fresh start. I'm so haunted I swear I can smell him in the air.

"It's a serious thing, him walking away." Matthew turns to me, his face solemn. "He's turned his back on Lorenzo. On his responsibilities. On the organization."

All because of me, I add silently.

"I never would've thought it possible," he continues. "He's the most loyal man I know. But that's why I'm certain his disappearance is temporary. He has to come back. Leaving isn't an option."

"I don't blame him for staying away." I turn in a slow circle, noting the expensive leather sofas, the thick, wooden dining table. "One of the last things he said was how Lorenzo demanded we get married. I would've run for the hills, too."

"He doesn't run from responsibility, Abri."

He did this time.

Not that I want to get married. I wouldn't burden the insanity of my life onto anyone, let alone the man who risked death to save me and my daughter. I just need to see him. To know I'm forgiven.

"I guess my actions have changed the very foundation of the man you once knew." I huff a sardonic laugh. "I was always efficient at breaking the good ones."

"You didn't break him."

"No?" I swing back around to face my brother, wanting to tell him I know exactly what broken looks like because I've stared at its reflection in the mirror for years. Instead, I say, "So why hasn't he called? Why isn't he here?"

He winces. "I wish I knew."

We fall silent, nothing but the far off squeak of door hinges carrying from down the hall.

"I should find Layla and start making a shopping list." He focuses on Tilly with a sad smile. "I don't have the first idea of where to begin when it comes to buying things for children."

"That makes two of us." I place Tilly on her feet, my arms aching from constantly holding her. "But I can order everything once you're gone. You need to rest."

"That's all I've done for days." He starts across the room.

"Wait. There's something that's been playing on my mind since the other night that I need you to clarify."

He stops. Turns. "What is it?"

I swallow, reliving the memories and the horror that comes with them. "Bishop took the blame when Mom was condemning me for our father's death. He mentioned the warehouse fire and the recent brake issue on Dad's car. He said he manipulated you into gaining revenge. That he'd been pushing you toward taking action for years. Is that true?"

A part of me begs for him to say yes. To place some sort of accountability on Bishop's shoulders so that his injuries aren't entirely my fault.

But Matthew's face sobers. "No. He hated Emmanuel for what he did to me, but I was never in a place where I wanted to take action that could affect you or our brothers, and he respected that. I assume he was only saying whatever he could to protect you."

To protect Tilly, I want to clarify. But I don't even know if that's true.

The more I think about it, and after the way he left, the more I believe Bishop's actions had nothing to do with caring for me or my daughter at all.

He wanted to make up for his past. To right the wrongs that caused his sister's death. And he achieved that.

Now he's gone.

"Is that the answer you wanted?" Matthew asks.

I swallow. Nod. "Yeah. I'm just trying to understand him. That's all."

"I know. But sometimes there's no making sense of Bishop."

I disagree.

After everything I've learned, he makes nothing but sense.

He protected me fiercely because he thought he was making up for failing his sister. He cared for me during my panic attacks because that's one of the only loving lessons he was taught from parental figures as a child.

None of it was about me.

It was all based on his past. On his trauma.

"You'll hear from him soon." Matthew gives a sad smile. "I have faith."

I don't.

I'm convinced I mean nothing to Bishop. I never did.

As far as I'm concerned, he's never coming back… At least, not for me.

40

BISHOP
ONE WEEK LATER

I stand at the front doors of Lorenzo's Virginia Beach property, my mouth set in a sneer, the expression pulling at the stitches in my cheek.

This was a mistake. One I should turn around and walk away from. But it's not like the fucker inside doesn't know I'm here. The exotic birds caged in his backyard announced my presence long before I jumped his front gates and stalked my ass across the drive.

On cue, the door opens without me having to knock, the face of my mentor staring back at me, his attention briefly fixating on the sickening wound on the right side of my face before he meets my gaze.

"*Figlio*," he greets, schooling his expression.

I keep my mouth shut and glare.

He inclines his head as if my silence is answer enough. "I appreciate you coming."

"We both know Adena is the only reason I responded to your constant messages. Your promise better not have been for nothing."

He sighs. "It was a peace offering. One that comes with stipulations."

"Of course." I scoff. "I should've fucking known."

"I won't apologize for doing what I could to get you to return to the family—"

"I haven't returned. I told you I'm done."

"You were angry."

"Nothing has changed," I seethe.

"Then maybe what I offered is best left for another day."

"Like hell." I barge past him and enter the house. "Is she downstairs?"

"Wait." He slams the door and turns to me. "I haven't changed my stance on her punishment. She's to remain alive."

I clench my hands at my sides, my rage not having lessened in nine days.

"You need to stick to the plan," he continues. "Remain professional. Be the man I taught you to be."

I smile. All teeth. Loads of aggression. "The man you taught me to be wants to bathe in her blood."

"There will be no bathing today."

I shake my head in disgust. "That bitch shot me in the fucking face."

"Is that why you're still angry?"

"An inch to the left and I'd be dead," I snap.

"Yes. But you didn't answer my question."

I shove my hands into my pockets, clenching my fists harder. I'm sure he's well aware my injury isn't why I crave Adena's death. He knows it's because of Abri. Because of my unwanted attachment to a woman now stuck under my skin.

But I refuse to confirm his assumptions. I don't dare to speak her name out loud from fear she'll take more of a hold over me.

"My anger is not your concern." I force myself to relax, to release the tension in my jaw. "Is Adena downstairs or not?"

"She is." He inclines his head. "But I will remind you there's to be no bloodshed. She's to remain alive."

"Whatever you say." I turn on my heel and stalk to the door leading downstairs.

I take the steps two at a time, descending to the sterile open space mainly used for emergency surgical procedures, and stop before the metal medicine cabinet to drag it forward.

The bottles inside the heavy piece of furniture rattle with the movement, the wheels on the bottom making it easy to shift away from the hidden door behind.

My pulse thrums as I enter the pin code into the security panel on the wall and wait for the steel door to slide open. Then I continue into the secret bunker, the florescent glow from the lights illuminating the windowless room.

I've waited nine long fucking days for this.

Over a week, praying the opportunity would come.

And now here it is—Adena in the barred cell I helped build eight years ago, the clothes she wore the last time we met now stained and filthy as she sits on a stool a few feet in front of the portable cot in the corner.

The room smells of piss and shit, the rusted bucket on the floor a fun reminder that there's no bathroom facilities in her new home.

What I don't approve of is the fucking hobby Lorenzo allowed her—the big ball of pink wool on the floor beside her feet dancing as she knits like a weathered grandma.

The soundproof door automatically closes behind me, locking us in together.

"How many times do I have to tell you I'm not handing over the financial information, brother?" She doesn't raise her gaze from the project in her lap. "I don't care if you keep me here forever."

"Your brother tapped out," I drawl, stepping farther into the room. "You've got me now."

Her attention lifts, her eyes sparkling with delight as she eyes the damage she caused to my face. "My, don't you look a treat?"

I smirk, my stitches pulling taut with the movement. The bullet grazed my cheek, slicing all the way to my jaw. Almost three inches worth of damage that itches like a motherfucker and will probably leave me looking like a Wish version of the Joker. "I can't wait to return the favor."

She laughs, the chuckle of a maniacal bitch grating my last nerve, the *click, click, click* of her knitting needles chipping away at my control.

"Let me tell you how this is going to work." I drag a spare stool from the corner of the room and approach her cell, entering the pin for the barred door to release and open. "I'm going to ask you for the same information Lorenzo has failed to acquire for more than a week. But this time, you're going to spill the details."

I plant my stool a few feet away, sit, then hunch forward, resting my elbows on my knees, gifting her with my full attention. "I want the code for the house safe. The specifics for all your crypto. And any other financial particulars you might have hidden."

She raises a derisive brow and continues *click, click, clicking* those knitting needles.

"Your children are going to clean you out, Adena. If you're ever lucky enough to leave this cell, you'll be nothing but a financial prisoner for the rest of your life, just like they once were. No more Luis Vuitton. No more Prada. You'll be the failed widower of a designer label now stuck wearing the latest fashion from Walmart." I give a subtle grin. "When was the last time that old skin of yours was draped in nylon?"

She rolls her eyes. "Lorenzo will look after me."

"The same Lorenzo who locked you in a basement and deprived you of food for three days? How's that chamber pot working for you? You also realize every square inch of this room is being recorded, right? I'm sure watching you hover over a bucket has become a favored pastime for your brother's men."

The knitting needles pause.

"You think you can provoke me into caving?" She glares. "I attempted to kill my brother, yet here I am, in his home, without so much as a scratch." She returns her attention to her wool. "Lorenzo has always had a soft heart toward me. Eventually, he'll give up and have someone send me a meal. Then new clothes. Then I'll get proper bathroom breaks. And eventually freedom. All I need is patience."

"You'll need a lot more than that now that I'm here."

She scoffs. "Have you grown sick of Abri already? Why am I not surprised?"

That name on her lips turns my vision red.

"I wouldn't leave her unsupervised for too long." She drags up the string of wool, continuing her knitting. "She doesn't know how to live without a man. Once a whore, always a—"

I shove to my feet, the stool clattering to the floor behind me. "I'm not here to discuss her. What I want is the money."

I measure my breathing, my teeth clenched. Interrogations have always been my forte. What I excel at.

Today is different.

I feel like a fucking novice, my calm nowhere to be found.

My cell vibrates in my suit jacket, and I use the excuse to look away from the bitch, biding my time to slowly take it out and read the message from Lorenzo.

IL VECCHIO

> She's baiting you. Don't fall for it. I will not condone more family bloodshed.

I shoot a glower to the surveillance camera in the corner to my left and return my phone to my pocket.

"You seem tense." Adena places her knitting needles in her lap, the attached wool piled beneath it. "Don't tell me you're still under my daughter's spell." She clucks her tongue. "It was obvious you'd fallen for her when you fought so hard at that girl's house."

"That little girl is your granddaughter."

"No," she says sweetly. "That illegitimate child is no kin of mine. She was a decent money pot though. Her father never ceased to give in to our increasing financial demands. But I suppose he had no choice when all we had to do was wave a picture of the kid in his face and threaten to show his wife. We didn't even have to tell him about the explicit video we had of him with Abri." Her smile fades. "I'm afraid that was a wasted opportunity. But you could hold it over him if you like. The things he did to my daughter were quite—"

"That's enough," I snarl through the jealousy. Through the disgust and anger and need to carve the flesh from Adena's bones.

She sits straighter, her enjoyment beaming back at me as she sighs. "Dear boy. How could such an intelligent man fall victim to the manipulations of a tramp? I would've thought you smarter than that."

My pulse throbs in my temples. My throat. My chest. "What's the code for the house safe, Adena?"

She chuckles. "Was it her eyes? Men always get ensnared by those lying baby blues." She cocks her head to the side, scrutinizing me. "Or maybe you thought you were different. That she actually had feelings for you and you weren't just another mark to get what she needed. Because with no money, no contacts, and no idea where her daughter was, she would've needed a lot."

"The code, Adena." I picture myself grabbing those knitting needles and stabbing them through her neck. The shock would be enough to knock her senseless. That I'd dare hurt Lorenzo's own sister. Her fear would be more delightful than her screams of pain, the acknowledgement of her precarious situation a deliciously heady thrill.

"Please tell me you didn't sleep with her. If the fear of STDs weren't enough, you must realize you're probably going to father her next child. Without family funds she needs to get her money from somewhere."

My nostrils flare because, yes, the thought had crossed my mind. Not the STDs. But the offspring that could eventuate after what I did to Abri in that fucking dilapidated kitchen.

I'd been so goddamn mindless for her I hadn't spared a thought to protection.

"Oh, Bishop. You pathetic fool."

"That's enough." I inch closer, towering above her. "I'll ask one more time, Adena—what's the code to the family safe?"

She clutches the knitting needles like a weapon. "You know my daughter would fuck anything if it meant—"

I lunge, wrapping my fingers around her throat, dragging her backward off the stool to the cot.

She gasps, jabbing those knitting needles into my ribs, my stomach, my chest. The punctures don't penetrate, the material of my suit too thick as my cell vibrates in my pocket with what I'm certain is another warning from Lorenzo.

"How long do you think it will take your brother to hobble down here to save you?" I sneer in her face. "To descend those stairs with his cane. To get through that fucking door."

She drops the needles and grabs at my wrists, her face turning red as she scratches and claws.

"Did you know your daughter suffered like this the night of the gala?" I squeeze her throat tighter. "Her beautiful skin left bruised and sore by a man your husband knew would take advantage."

My cell vibrates again, and again, and again, each jolt a warning I'm meant to adhere to.

This isn't bloodshed, old man.

"You deserve death, Adena."

Her hands lose the viciousness. Her eyes roll.

I release my grip, dumping her on the bed, leaving her to gasp and sputter on the thin mattress as I stand tall.

"And see…" I glance around the room. "No brother here to save you."

She retches, gagging as she coughs and hacks.

"Now what's the code for the safe?"

She glares through her suffering, heaving to fill her lungs. "Fuck you."

I grab a fistful of her hair, yanking her into a seated position. "Don't mistake me for a patient man. I have better things to do with my day."

"And don't mistake me for someone stupid enough to believe my own brother would sanction my death. You may be allowed to hurt me. But I'll survive."

"You're right. He still wants you alive. We wouldn't appreciate those bank accounts frozen before we had a chance to clean them out. But your mistake is thinking death is a worse option than what I have planned for you."

"I'll never tell."

"I was hoping you'd say that." I clamp my hands around her throat again, adding pressure to the carotid on either side of her neck—not too hard. Just enough for her to know unconsciousness is inevitable as she scratches at my face. "How many times do you think you can withstand being choked, Costa? Three times? Four? Because I could do this shit all day."

Her nails find the stitches on my cheek, my cell buzzing as she tears open the healing wound. But all too soon, her fight dissipates. Those eyes roll again.

I dump her back on the bed, limp yet still breathing.

The vibration in my pocket continues. No longer text messages but a phone call.

"You said no bloodshed." I raise my voice, speaking to Lorenzo through the surveillance camera. "I'm adhering to your rules. So grow a set and watch quietly or step away from the fucking video feed."

The buzzing stops. I don't kid myself that the lack of vibration is for positive reasons.

Lorenzo could be hobbling his way down the stairs to the basement. Or calling his guards to storm the room.

If that's the case, they best be ready to put a gun to my head, because I'm not leaving until I'm finished getting what I came for.

I reclaim my stool, waiting as Adena blinks in a daze. I reach into my pocket, pull out the small plastic vial of smelling salts, and open the lid to wave it under her nose.

She gasps in shock, her eyes flaring wide, her cough hacking. She sits up, one hand to her throat, her shoulders hunched.

"Ready for round three?" I ask.

She spears me with a spite-filled gaze. "I won't break."

"Neither will I." I push to my feet, surprised when she scrambles backward, cowering.

Victory heats my blood. Pure, euphoric triumph.

"The code to the safe, Adena." I look down my nose at her.

"Go fuck yourself."

I incline my head and lunge again.

"*Stop*," she screams, plastering herself to the metal bars of the cell.

"The code."

She shakes her head. "There's nothing in the safe. A few hundred thousand dollars and some jewelry. That's all."

"Tell me the numbers."

She glowers with the feistiness of a broken dog—all rigid backbone, but no fight left to give as she hangs her head in shame. "Five-eight-seven-nine."

"See? That wasn't so hard. And I bet it took a lot less convincing than you thought it would."

She sniffs. Heaves for more breath.

Don't tell me this bitch is about to cry.

"It's okay." I take in the glorious sight of her downfall, enjoying it for all those who deserve to bear witness. "We still have a long way to go. You might gain your second wind and have the balls to withstand a round of waterboarding. I will admit it's a specialty though."

She bounds forward to her hands and knees and spits, the saliva hitting my jacket lapel to dribble down my chest.

I stand tall, giving her a few moments to deal with her humiliation, simply staring at her with superiority. "I'm a man on the verge of breaking, Adena. So keep that in mind if you have the urge to disrespect me again."

"You're nothing but Lorenzo's dog on a leash," she mutters.

"Maybe." At least I was a week ago. "But the ties meant to hold violent animals tend to wither and fray over time. Especially when those beasts have been left to feast on the atrocities of their enemies." I smile, slight, not enough to tweak the now broken stitches in my cheek. "I want nothing more than to kill you. I've dreamt about it every day since I found out you were responsible for your daughter's trauma—"

"You mean nothing to her. No man ever will."

"Believe me, I've told myself the same thing. But funnily enough, it doesn't stop me wanting to avenge her suffering." I reach out, enjoying the way Adena flinches when I drag my knuckles over the dark red marks I've created on her wrinkled neck. "Now are you going to tell me the password to your online bank account, or do I get to have more fun?"

Her sneer returns, her animosity short-lived.

It takes another nine minutes to break her completely. Then her secrets flow like a stream, matching the tears cascading down her cheeks.

I make sure she verbalizes every password, every pin code, every secret so Lorenzo has it recorded on his surveillance for future reference.

Then I leave her there, sobbing on the flimsy bed, the room smelling like sweat and desperation.

I'm not surprised to hear Lorenzo's walking stick thudding against the tile from the kitchen as I stalk toward the front door.

He doesn't deserve a goodbye. As far as I'm concerned, we're still at odds even though he kept to his end of the bargain and allowed me to torment Adena without intervention.

"Wait." He enters the hall through the archway to the open living area and blocks my path. "Was that necessary?"

"I've never been in the business of leniency. But I followed your rules. I didn't draw blood."

He scowls, the hard eyes of the only father I've known staring back at me with disappointment. "You made it personal."

"Of course I made it fucking personal. She dragged your niece through hell and attempted to kill her own grandchild. She deserves to suffer."

He raises his chin, a brow hiking along with it. "It's confusing to me that you refer to her as my niece and not your future bride. It's also telling that your ferocity downstairs seemed entirely on Abri's behalf and not because of the gunshot wound to your face.

Yet I'm told you've made no attempt to speak to *my niece* since Denver."

Fucking Langston and his big fucking mouth.

I step forward, giving him a derisive clap on the upper arm. "I'm not talking about her with you."

"Yes, you will. We need to discuss your marriage."

I drop my hold and walk around him. "Abri is her own woman. She will choose her own fate. And I'm a man now fully grasping my freedom. If you have a problem with that I suggest you train your fledglings a little longer before you plan my punishment because none of the men you currently have stand a chance against me."

"Bishop," he growls. "I know you've been watching her."

Motherfucking Langston.

"Bishop," he snaps.

"*What*?" I stop before the towering front doors and shoot him a glare.

He drags in a tired breath, his shoulders slumping with the exhale. "You deserve to be happy, *figlio*."

I scoff. "We both know that's not true. But even if it was, I don't deserve it at her expense." I yank open one side of the heavy wooden doors. "I won't force her into marriage. Not for you. Not for me. And definitely not now that she's got that kid hanging around."

41

ABRI

THREE WEEKS LATER

"It's been another great session, Abri. You should be encouraged by the progress you and Tabatha are making." The child psychologist pushes from the elegantly carved dining table with a smile.

"Thanks, Kim." I wince through the words, hating the use of my daughter's real name.

With all the things I've had to get used to in my new role as a fully functioning mother, trying to accept Tilly isn't actually Tilly has been near the top of the list.

What made the painful discovery worse was that I wasn't the one to figure out the problem. It was Dr. Pentacost. On our very first in-home consultation.

Me, with my ignorance and complete lack of parental experience, had thought it was normal for my daughter to ignore me when I addressed her by name. I'd assumed it was due to trauma. And when every second had been so hectic with tears, pleas, and hiccupped cries, it hadn't seemed out of place for Tilly not to acknowledge that one simple word.

Then Dr. Kim Pentacost arrived.

She was so incredibly good with Tilly—patient, compassionate, understanding. I fell in love with her straight away... Until she began bonding with my daughter, asking to be introduced to Tilly's stuffed rabbit, then later discreetly telling me what she'd found.

"The label on her toy says, 'Property of Tabatha Marks.'"

I hadn't wanted to believe it. That my parents would not only steal my child but also hate me enough to give her a name other than the one I'd chosen.

But the doctor was right.

On the flimsy, tattered slip of material poking out of the bunny's thigh was all the evidence I needed in faded, barely visible writing.

"I'm sorry." Kim places a hand on my shoulder, gently squeezing. "I'll start calling her Tilly from now on if you'd prefer. As we discussed, she's young enough to accept the name change. Just use the steps I wrote down. Make it gradual and fun. I'm sure it will take her no time at all to understand that's her new normal."

I nod. Force a smile.

"And I don't think we need another session tomorrow either." The doctor grabs her thick binder off the table, dragging the heavy weight to her chest. "You can handle a long weekend without me."

My stomach plummets.

"You've got this, Abri. You really do."

I swallow back the nerves and turn to watch my little girl playing in the sunshine streaming in through the living room window, her tiny hands building a tower of clunky plastic blocks. "I'm not sure you're right, but I'll trust your expert opinion."

Life is nothing like what it used to be.

Before Tilly, I used to wake up empty and soulless. There was no hope. No joy.

Now, my mornings start with my heart open and my faith restored. I spend every day dedicated to making Tilly's life better. To being a good mother. A patient caregiver. A strong role model.

We play. We learn. We sing. A *lot*. And not just nursery rhymes. Taylor Swift is our jam. Then there are the television jingles, and our own silly mashed up sentences to remember important hygiene routines.

Where once all I thought about was manipulating powerful people, now the only thing I set out to achieve is creating little patches of light in Tilly's life to cover up the holes of darkness my parents created.

And it's working. Slowly.

Tilly still breaks my heart whenever she's startled, scared, or scrapes her knee. Her instinctive response is to call for her momma. And that momma isn't me. But the more often I come running, the quicker she accepts my love, opening those tiny arms to me so I can hug her tight.

"I'll see you Monday." Kim starts toward the front door, her heels clapping along the polished wooden floorboards. "But my cell is always on if you need me."

"Okay."

"And you don't have to keep relying on Layla for backup either. You know what you're doing. You're one of the most natural mothers I've met, and those skills don't come easily."

"Thank you." I push to my feet, making my way toward Tilly. "I'll try not to call her so much."

"Good. Enjoy your weekend." She slips into the hall, the automatic lock engaging as soon as she pulls the door shut.

"Well, sweetheart, strap in for a wild weekend without the good doc. Things could get crazy." I settle myself on the rug beside my daughter as she concentrates on the towering construction in front of her. "Are you getting hungry?"

Tiny hands pause on large plastic blocks as bright blue eyes peer up at me. She nods. Energetic. Enthusiastic.

Pride consumes me. "Would you like to help me pick a snack?"

Would you like to help Momma *pick a snack*?—Kim would correct if she was still here. *Get those subtle changes in place, Abri. Get her used to you being her momma.*

But I can't.

Not yet.

I may hold the title—now not just maternally, but in practice—but it's too soon. My soul would shatter into a million pieces if Tilly sat straighter and glanced around as if the slain woman who'd raised her was suddenly alive again.

We need to take baby steps when possible since everything else around us has moved in leaps and bounds.

We're still climatizing to the D.C. move, and even though I grew up in luxury, this lush penthouse has taken getting used to. All the appliances are brand new and above my technical knowledge. The security system alone is a minefield of buttons I refuse to press. One that wasn't installed until after we arrived.

I'd begged Matthew not to worry about it.

He hadn't listened.

In fact, he doesn't listen to much of anything when it comes to the safety and security of me and Tilly. He just gets grouchy and refuses to humor the conversation.

What's more hurtful is how Bishop has become a taboo topic. Nobody speaks about him. Not Matthew. Or Lorenzo, who calls to check up on me every few days.

There hasn't even been word from the man himself.

There's been nothing but radio silence after he demanded I marry him the last night we spoke. So it's safe to assume that unprotected sex was a deal-breaker.

I'd laugh if it didn't make me want to cry.

"Froot?" Tilly pushes to her feet, picking up her tattered rabbit by the ears.

"We can definitely have fruit." I reach out a hand for her to take, her soft fingers sliding over mine. "Or honey on toast. There's also the sandwiches those nice ladies delivered this morning. I think there were some of the cheese ones you like so much."

"Cheese pease." She beams.

My heart damn near melts.

"Okay. Cheese it is." I make my way to the fridge, unbelievably thankful for the support network I now have. Meals are brought to my door each morning. Cleaners come every few days. Toys and clothes and books are delivered without notice.

It's as if Matthew is trying to make up for all those lost years between us. And whenever I try to thank him he becomes this awkward, macho man who doesn't want to discuss the millions of ways he's enriched my life.

"Why don't you get your special *Bluey* plate out of the cupboard and I'll see if there's a juice box in the fridge with your name on it?" I squeeze Tilly's fingers and release her hand.

She nods and runs ahead to the kitchen.

We're both seated at the dining table a few minutes later, my daughter nibbling her sandwich while I sip on instant coffee because I can't figure out how to work the expensive coffee machine, when my cell buzzes in my pocket.

I smile, knowing it's Layla. I bet she's already on her way here.

LAYLA

How was the visit with the doc?

The warmth in my chest grows.

ME

Good. Slow progress as always. But progress, nonetheless.

LAYLA

How long until Tilly's nap?

ME

About twenty minutes. She's just having something to eat.

Layla replies with a thumbs up two seconds before a knock sounds at the door, startling me.

She was messaging me from the hall?

The concierge never lets her up without approval. Then again, she's been here every day for weeks, so it's safe to assume she's welcome.

Tilly continues to munch on her sandwich as I stand, her tiny jaw working overtime, her cute little lips smooshed.

"Do you think that's Aunty Layla coming to check on us?" I ask as I cross the room.

Tilly ignores me, too engrossed by her cheese and bread.

I fling the door wide. "Fancy seeing—"

The greeting dies on my lips.

My heart stops.

It's not Layla.

The person standing before me is tall, broad, bearded, handsome, and wearing his trademark perfectly fitting black suit as he strangles a plush blue bunny in a one-handed grip at his side.

"Bishop." I swallow over my drying throat. "What are you doing here?"

His brows knit in an expression I can't decipher. It's not anger. Not even frustration. If anything, the awkward furrow makes him look sheepish. "I needed to see you."

I don't know what to say.

In all honesty, his fragility makes me itch to close the door in his face and forget his existence. To shut out a complication I don't need. A hurt that's still fresh. Yet I can't. Not with my stomach twisting in knots and my pulse picking up pace as if I'm reaching the finish line of a marathon.

"How are you?" he asks.

I drag in a deep breath, wishing I could give him a placating response. But this man owns more of my truth than anyone, and lying doesn't feel right.

"I'm okay," I admit. "Most days."

"I hear you're taking motherhood in your stride."

"You've been checking up on me?" Why does my heart skip a beat at the thought? "I hope whoever's feeding you information described my stride as that of a newborn foal."

One side of his lips quirk up, reminding me how rare his smiles are. "I'm sure you're doing just fine."

I swallow over my erratic pulse. Nod. Shrug. "And how about you?" My attention falls to his cheek where a nasty red scar is partially hidden behind his thick beard. "You've recovered better than I imagined."

"I'm a tough nut to crack." His expression sobers. "I would've come to see you sooner, but I've been biding my time, waiting for the facial scruff to cover the wound. I didn't want to scare Tilly or remind her of what happened."

He's been biding his time? For Tilly?

My stomach does a sweeping roll, my insides entirely enamored by his thoughtfulness while my head defiantly rebuilds walls around my heart.

He could've called.

Instead, I've lived in fear for his well-being, constantly haunted by what could've happened. How he was maimed. If he even survived.

"That was nice of you," I murmur.

He huffs a laugh. "You lying to me, belladonna?"

That word. The endearment. *Damn him.* It sinks under my skin, warming my insides.

"No. I'm not lying." I cement a friendly expression in place, not wanting him to see how hard this is for me. "It was nice of you to think of Tilly."

"But not nice that I left you in the dark?"

I square my shoulders, floundering for a response he won't see through.

I don't want to be annoyed. I'm still yet to apologize for my wrongdoings. It just hurts, that's all.

"I couldn't call, Abri. Not when I couldn't visit." He lowers his gaze to the bunny in his hand. "I've kept tabs on you though. I made sure you didn't need me."

But I *did* need him.

I needed his confidence every time I fumbled my way through important decisions for my daughter. I needed his calm when the panic stopped hovering in the shadows and attacked like a pack of rabid wolves.

I needed his strength.

His protection.

His touch.

His eyes narrow as if he can hear my thoughts. "You've had everything you needed, right?"

"Yes." I scrunch my nose. "Of course. Matthew took control of everything. He's been great."

The patter of tiny feet approach behind me, Tilly's hands clasping my thighs as she peers around my legs to spy our visitor.

He straightens. Stiffens. I swear he holds his breath.

"Do you remember Bishop?" I run a comforting hand through my daughter's hair. "He came to say hello."

She nods, clinging tighter to my legs.

Neither one of them speak, creating an awkward ravine between us.

"I think he might have a gift for you," I hedge.

Bishop's gaze snaps to mine before understanding dawns. "Shit," he mutters, the word barely leaving his mouth before his eyes flare. "I shouldn't have said that."

I smile. "It's okay. Just give her the bunny."

Hesitance takes over his features as he lowers to his haunches and raises the toy for Tilly to take. "I thought this little guy could be best friends with the one you already have."

She slinks behind my legs, hiding.

She reacted the same way with Layla and Matthew the first few times they visited even though we'd spent the previous days together. She still does with Remy and Salvatore when they call to video chat, wanting to form their own long-distance bond with their niece while they set up their new lives on the East Coast with Lorenzo.

"You don't need to be shy, sweetheart." I reach behind me, gently brushing her arm. "Bishop's a good guy."

He winces, this big, merciless man crestfallen by the rejection of a child. "It's okay. She doesn't have to take it."

She scampers away without a response, her pattered footsteps crossing the room behind me, the clatter of plastic blocks announcing she's gone back to play.

He pushes to his feet. "I should go."

"Why?" I ask too quickly. With too much need.

"Because I hate scaring her. The memory of how she looked at me that night still fucking kills me. And I'm sure your days are difficult enough without—"

"She's shy, Bishop." I glance behind me, finding my daughter back on the rug, content as she concentrates on what blocks to pile on top of her tower. "If she was scared, she'd be hiding in her room." I open the door wider, letting him see for himself. "Instead, she's playing."

He steps closer, his gaze seeking her out as the scent of his aftershave assaults my senses in intoxicating hints of citrus and sandalwood.

I fight the urge to close my eyes and breathe him deep but notice he doesn't smell the same. There's no longer a smoky undertone. He's lost the underlying tinge of tobacco.

"You don't smell like cigarettes," I whisper.

His gaze remains on Tilly. "You told me to quit."

I blink through the bewilderment. I don't understand what he's doing here. What the impromptu visit means. Why he brought Tilly a gift. What drove him to end a habit just because I asked.

I know what I want it to mean, but that's not what this is.

Not when he left me in the dark for weeks.

"How are things with you and Lorenzo?" I change the subject before my heart fixates on unrealistic daydreams. "Are the two of you talking again?"

"Not really. He calls. I answer."

"And then?"

"He questions how I'm doing and I respond by asking if Adena is still alive, and when he confirms the bad news, I hang up."

I wince. "I'm sorry she hurt you the way she did. That she almost killed you."

"I'm not. The alternative would've been worse. If you or Tilly had been shot…" His jaw ticks. "I wouldn't have appreciated that."

I give a half-hearted chuckle at his understated concern. "I'm told she's practically living in her own private prison."

"She is. The only freedom she's tasted since that night was when the news of your father's death broke. She was under strict guard while making the necessary public statements."

My brows knit. "You were a part of her security team?"

"No. I was watching." He turns to me, those brilliant blue eyes holding me captive. "I've kept tabs on you both."

My body shivers under his attention.

I want to reach out. To touch him. To cup his cheek. To trail my fingers over his scar. I want to hold him. Be *held* by him. But…

"Why did you disappear?" I whisper.

He looks away, staring blankly over my shoulder. "You want to do this now?"

"It's been a month. Have I not waited long enough?"

He stands taller, almost defensive.

"I already know it's because of the things I did," I admit. "But I want to hear it from—"

"What could you have possibly done?" His gaze snaps to mine.

I swallow, not wanting to state my crimes out loud. It's been hard enough having them run through my head non-stop.

His eyes narrow. "What actions make you think you're responsible for my behavior?"

It's my turn to look away, lowering my focus to the top two open buttons of his white dress shirt.

"Why don't we go inside where we can talk properly?" I backtrack, buying time until he grabs my wrist, halting my escape.

"What about Tilly? I don't want to step into her safe space. She's been through enough."

The squeezing and aching inside my chest intensifies. For a man who doesn't want anything to do with children, he sure seems to care about them.

"You won't upset her. We can keep our distance and sit at the dining table while she plays. I'll make you a coffee." I gently twist my arm from his grip, hating how a mere touch has made my skin ignite. "I can only offer instant because I don't know how to work the coffee machine, but—"

"What's wrong with the machine?" he asks.

"I can't figure it out."

He pauses long enough for me to take in the hesitance in his features, his gaze cautiously watching Tilly before he strides inside. "What's to figure out?"

I close the door behind him and follow toward the kitchen. "Only every button and lever. It's got me stumped." I stop beside him at the shiny stainless-steel machine that taunts me from the appliance nook. "It's been weeks, and I still haven't had a chance to look up the online instructions."

"Let me do it." He dumps the blue bunny on the island counter, then opens the drawer beneath the machine. He retrieves two coffee mugs, then places them on the dripper tray, his confidence in what should be an unfamiliar kitchen catching me off-guard. "How strong do you want it?"

I frown while he opens a nearby cupboard, grabs the necessary coffee pods left by the previous tenant, then dumps one in the machine. "Just regular, I guess."

A few pressed buttons later and the machine whirs to life.

I stare dumbfounded as he hands a filled mug over, not sure if I should be embarrassed at my lack of coffee-making skills or impressed by his. "How do you know your way around the machine?"

He palms his drink and leans back against the cupboards to take a lazy sip. "It's not exactly rocket science."

"It was to me."

He shrugs, his attention diverting to Tilly over my shoulder as he takes another mouthful. "If you've used one machine, you've used them all."

"I guess your instincts must be crazy accurate, especially when you found the mugs and pods without thought."

"Is it really that surprising to find the mugs in the drawer below the coffee machine?"

Maybe not. What is surprising is how different he is. How he struggles to hold my gaze. How things between us seem so far from where they once were.

I don't like it.

"How did you get past the concierge?" I ask. "Usually he calls to get approval before allowing any visitors an elevator pass."

He pushes from the cupboards and stalks toward the dining table. "People love me."

"People do *not* love you, Bishop."

"Maybe not, but I have a way with words."

Oh, God. Did he threaten the staff? Am I going to be kicked out of the building?

Bishop shoots me a glance over his shoulder. "Don't panic. I know the guy."

I release a relieved breath, the respite only lasting a second before more confusion floods my brain.

After weeks of Layla arriving like clockwork, it's safe to say she knows the concierge too, but not once has she been allowed access without my daily approval.

"Have you been here before?" I trail after him. "Matthew said he found this place through a realtor friend, but I didn't have the mental capacity to ask questions when we first arrived."

"Langston has friends?" He places his coffee at the end of the table and grasps the back of a chair instead of taking a seat. "That's news to me."

I ignore his attempt at humor, the hairs on my nape rising.

Not only did he slay the coffee machine, Bishop hasn't even taken in his surroundings since he arrived. There was no awe at the view. No pause as he attempted to gain his bearings. Even now, he doesn't look around as if the penthouse interior is foreign.

Instead, he stands at the head of the table as if he owns it.

"Have you been here before?" I repeat.

He sighs. "What's with the interrogation, belladonna?"

What's with the deflection?

"You're hiding something from me." I scrutinize him. "I don't like it."

He holds my gaze, his expression unreadable as he falls quiet.

Each second of silence makes my pulse pound harder. Louder.

"Yes, I've been here before," he states simply.

My throat tightens, the clogs in my brain moving faster. Puzzle pieces I didn't realize were out of place start to show themselves, huge holes being carved into the memories of the past few weeks. "Did you organize for us to stay here?"

That would explain my brother's awkward refusal to accept my gratitude over our new home. But that would mean the two of them have spoken. That they've communicated over the last month, even back during those excruciatingly painful first days when worry left me breathless.

Bishop leans over to reclaim his coffee and takes a gulp.

"Answer me." I step closer.

"Yes, I arranged it," he admits. "I wanted you somewhere safe, and this building has the best security."

The blood drains from my face. My brother lied to me. Was Layla in on it, too?

All this time they've been in contact, and not once did they ease my concerns.

Fucking bastards.

I turn on my heel and stalk back to the kitchen, dumping the contents of my mug to the sink in a subtle childish tantrum.

How could they have done this to me? Left me in the dark when all I wanted was to know Bishop was all right. That he was alive. That he didn't despise me.

His footsteps carry forward as I scowl at the mug in the sink, my anger rising.

"You didn't like the coffee?" he asks.

"I waited for you to call," I whisper, loathing his ignorance. "Every day, Bishop. Every night. Wondering why you didn't want to speak to me has torn me apart. Do you have any idea how worried I've been?"

"It's not that I didn't want to speak to you. It's that I couldn't."

"Couldn't how?" I snap under my breath, not wanting to alert Tilly to our argument while I glare at him. "You obviously spoke to Matthew."

"I messaged him. Relayed information. And only in those first few days. I made sure he brought you here. Nothing more."

"Did you also make him take credit for this place? Because he did."

He raises his chin. "Yes."

"Yes? That's all you have to say? My brother lied to my face for you. Over and over."

"He had no choice, Abri. My actions have been less than exemplary these past few weeks. He knew I was off the rails and that the threats I made for him to hold his tongue were real."

I stare at him—stare so hard my eyes burn. "Threats?"

"I got creative. I was willing to say and do anything to keep my actions toward you under wraps."

There's so much to unpack in those short sentences. So much that I don't know where to start.

"Don't worry," Bishop murmurs. "I wouldn't have hurt him. The asshole knows it, too. I think the reason he kept quiet was because he held the same fears I did."

"Fears?" I'm down to one-word questions, my vocabulary nonexistent.

"I didn't know if you'd stay here if you knew this was my penthouse. I was worried you'd take off, and then I wouldn't be able to keep you safe."

My eyes widen. "This is your home?"

"It used to be. It's yours now."

I step back, mouth gaping, pulse erratic.

From my peripheral vision I catch Tilly pause her building game to sit straighter, watching me.

I'm forced to school my expression. Be calm. Smile. I look to her with bright eyes. "Hey, cutie-pie. It's time for your nap."

I need her away from here. Out of earshot from my building meltdown.

She pushes to her feet, eying Bishop as she approaches the kitchen. The murderous, manipulative bastard has the audacity to straighten with her proximity, like a lion frightened by the approach of a timid lamb.

He remains rigid as she reaches the counter, raises her arm above her head, and quickly retrieves the bunny he brought for her, snagging it to her chest before running for the hall.

He glances at me in confusion.

Goddamn motherfucking shit.

"It's a good thing," I mutter. "She trusts you enough to accept your gift."

"Right…" He wipes a hand over the back of his neck. "Do you need to—"

"Help put her to bed? Yes."

"Want me to leave?"

Yes. No.

Fucking hell. I hate this.

I want to tell him to get out of here. To give me time to straighten my thoughts and figure out what the heck has been going on.

But what if he disappears for another month?

What if he never comes back?

"Wait here. I won't be long." I follow Tilly, trying to decompress while I read her a quick book and tuck her in to bed. But all I can think about are all the things I thought my brother had spoiled me with over the past month.

The cleaning staff. An endless supply of food and gifts.

Girlie sheets. Princess quilts. Toiletries.

I'd assumed Matthew and Layla had overindulged us. Now I wonder if it was Bishop the entire time.

When I return to the open living area he's standing near the floor-to-ceiling windows, his body turned toward the view. Tall. Quiet. Commanding.

I close the hall door behind me. The latch clicks. He pivots to face me.

"Did you organize all the deliveries?" I make my way to the kitchen to turn on the baby monitor near the fridge, Tilly's soft mumbles murmuring into the room. "The food. The clothes. The toys."

"Yes," he admits.

My heart lurches in anger. In traitorous reverence, too.

"And all my belongings from Denver—did you have something to do with them being packed and sent here?" Because they smelled like him.

I thought I'd been sinking into madness. That when I arrived here and all the rooms held his scent, that I'd started to lose my mind, the psychosis only increasing when my boxed belongings arrived from Colorado.

"Yes."

Shit. Shit. *Shit*.

He's been fucking with me this entire time. While I grieved his loss. While I struggled with guilt.

"Why?" I beg. "Why do all that yet not speak to me?"

He opens his mouth to reply but I cut him off.

"And don't you dare blame my daughter." I cross my arms over my chest, squeezing against the pain. "I get that you didn't want her to see you while you recovered, but that didn't stop you from calling. Or sending a text to let me know you were still alive. I've been worried sick, Bishop. I haven't slept. I've barely eaten—"

"I can see that." His gaze fills with remorse.

"I've hated myself for what I did to you. For dragging you into my drama. For almost getting you killed."

"Don't you fucking dare blame yourself." He strides toward me, expression menacing. "That was *my* fault. *Entirely* all mine."

"No." I shake my head, my body trembling along with it as he stops bare inches in front of me. "I seduced you out of your abstinence."

"You'd just been assaulted, Abri. You'd watched me kill a man. You were out of your fucking mind." He grabs my chin, the contact jolting through me. "*I'm* the one who messed with you. *I'm* the asshole who lacked the restraint to stop myself from rutting on you like a goddamn fucking animal."

"You didn't want to. I—"

"Like hell I didn't. I've never wanted anything more, and I hate myself for taking what should've been given in a far better location under better fucking circumstances." His hand slides to my waist as he pulls me closer. "I didn't even use protection, but I know you're well aware of that."

I stiffen, sensing a pointed meaning behind his words yet not comprehending what it is.

"That's part of the reason why I'm here." His breath brushes my lips as he closes his eyes. "I know you're pregnant."

"Excuse me?" I shove at his chest. "You *know* I'm pregnant? Just how closely have you been watching me?"

He winces, that stern face looking back at me in pained apology. "You don't want to know."

"Guess again."

He scrubs a rough hand over his mouth.

"*Spill*, Butcher."

He glowers, his nostrils flaring. "I had the cameras installed the day after you came to D.C. I've watched every time you left the building. Every visitor you received. Every delivery that arrived."

Okay, so when he said he was keeping an eye on me, what he meant was spying. Stalking. Why the hell am I not disgusted?

"The bank account Langston told you was arranged by Lorenzo is actually managed by me," he continues. "I gave you that money.

I've kept track of your expenses. And the laptop you've been using to place grocery orders sends me detailed activity reports. I get copies of your emails. I've taken note of every pharmacy purchase you've made."

Holy hell.

"I know you haven't purchased any pads or girlie shit in a month. And from going through the medical records your father kept in Denver, I'm well aware you're not on the pill or any other contraception."

"So that's why you're here." I backtrack. "You waited a month—one full menstrual cycle—to see if your worst fears had become a reality?"

"No. I waited a fucking month for this shit to be covered." He indicates his face with a wave of his hand. "So that I wouldn't scare the ever-loving crap out of your daughter when I turned up at your door. So we could have this conversation in person. So I could look you in the eye when I said what I needed to say."

"*Your* door," I correct. "This is *your* home. Not mine."

"Abri," he warns. "Don't get feisty with me. I haven't seen you in weeks and God knows I still lack the restraint to keep from repeating the same mistake I made the last time we were together."

My blood runs hot.

Stupid fucking blood.

"I'm not pregnant, Bishop. I *can't get* pregnant. I made sure my father couldn't hurt another child through me long ago."

He frowns.

"I had an endometrial ablation." I shake my head at the absurdity of this conversation. "I deliberately destroyed the lining of my uterus. I don't bleed every month. That's why I don't need *girlie shit*. And although I can technically get pregnant because I still ovulate, I can assure you that hasn't been the case. I'm not carrying your child."

I wait for relief to cross his face.

It doesn't come.

Instead, he looks angry. Hostile and livid. "How did you get the procedure with no money?" he asks. "Without your father knowing?"

I raise my chin, hating myself. "I blackmailed Tilly's father into paying for it."

"Jesus fucking Christ," he snarls. "If Emmanuel was still alive…"

My eyes burn. My throat, too.

I sigh, no longer trying to fight the confusion. I let it wash over me. Consume me. It's far better than the agony I suffered when wondering if he was dead.

"You should leave." I walk for the door. "I appreciate everything you've done. But I'm not pregnant. You're free to crawl back into whatever hole you came from."

I open the door, keeping my back to him while I wait for his footsteps to follow.

And wait some more.

After agonizing seconds of silence I turn to face him, my limbs heavy, my heart hurt. "Bishop, please. I don't know what you want from me."

He stands taller, his shoulders tense, his jaw tightening.

"Everything," he admits. One word. Three fierce syllables. "I want everything, Abri."

"I told you I'm not pregnant."

"And I'm telling you I don't give a fuck. I'm here because you're mine."

I want to laugh at the ownership. To turn my nose up at the absolute absurdity.

But my entire body aches with how much I want his claim, too.

"Is this about Lorenzo's ultimatum?" I ask. "I'm not your responsibility or obligation."

"Lorenzo can go to hell. Me being here has nothing to do with him. I swear that to you. I know staying away was a shitty move, but I had a million reasons to keep my distance. Not only because of my face and the pregnancy scare, but because I hated myself for what I'd done. For treating you like shit the night of the gala. For lacking sympathy during our time together. For allowing Geppet to hurt you. Then for how I disrespected your body after I killed him."

"You didn't—"

"I fucking did." He raises his voice. "I've done some messed up shit in my time but never have I struggled with disgust over my actions like I have with the things I've done to you."

"Then why come back at all, even if I was pregnant?"

"Turns out I'm also a selfish prick." He walks toward me,

stopping a foot away, hands at his sides, expression intense. "I figured I could make do keeping an eye on you. Ensuring you were safe."

"But?" I backtrack, bumping into the door, the heavy wood clapping shut behind me.

"But then I thought about you moving on and convinced myself you wouldn't appreciate every man who touched you going missing."

I choke out a laugh. One filled with sarcasm…and fear…and soul-crushing need.

A million butterflies awaken inside my chest, their wings rabidly flapping. What is it about this man that makes me so nauseatingly clingy?

"Every single man for the rest of your life, belladonna."

I am not going to swoon over his bloodthirsty nature. Nope. Not going to happen.

My betraying knees turn weak.

"I wouldn't be able to stop myself." He inches closer, increasing my pulse, making it harder to breathe.

"No." I place my hands on his chest, wanting to push him away, but those big, strong hands clamp around my wrists, holding my palms in place. "Things are different now. I have a daughter. I'll never stop being a mother. And I know how you feel about child—"

"You know how I *felt*," he corrects. "That little girl changed everything. I can't fucking sleep because I'm so tied up worrying I've caused her nightmares. How I wish I could make her life easier. How the only thing I've ever been proud of is saving her from Adena. I know Pentacost has helped but—"

"You arranged her psychologist, too?"

He nods, solemn. "I'm told she's the best there is… Well, the best in a clinical sense. When it comes to the firewall protection of her patient files, she's highly lacking, but Najeeb would've got into those documents one way or another."

"You're insane."

"I am. But I had to know what Tilly was going through. And how you were handling it. So I've kept myself up-to-date with the session notes. I'm aware the caregivers who died used to call her Tabatha, and how you're making slower-than-necessary steps to get her to recognize Tilly as her name, because you don't want to make her life harder." He gives a sad smile. "And I fucking wish I would've been here to help get you through it but…"

"But you weren't." I accuse, letting out some of the pain he's caused.

He winces. "I knew the start of your new life together was important. I had no business being a part of it. You needed to find your way on your own, to learn how to be a mother without me complicating things or being crazy fucking protective. So I did what I could from a distance."

I stare at him. Stare so long my need for air increases, my breaths becoming ragged.

I love this man.

I love his craziness. His security. His intense eyes as they peer down at me. His warm grip on my wrists.

I don't love that he stayed away. In fact, the amount I hate it sickens me. But I ache at his reasoning. That he battled with the space between us as much as I did.

"Let me be a part of your lives, Abri. I'm not too proud to beg."

"Oh, God." I heave for air, each inhale coming up short.

"Don't panic." He cups my cheeks. "Please don't fucking panic."

It's not anxiety that overwhelms me. The frantic gasps are something else.

Hope.

Happiness.

So much unfathomable, earthshaking adoration. "I can't breathe."

"I'll get ice." He drops my arms, turns, and walks for the kitchen.

"No. I don't need it." I grab his hand and pull him back. "I just need you to kiss me."

42

ABRI

TWO MONTHS LATER

I stare down at the street below. Bishop is in his immaculately tailored suit as he walks from the park, lifting Tilly to sit on his shoulders.

It took her eight daily visits to lose the shyness around the formidable man. Ten more to become obsessed with him.

Now she follows Bishop around like a puppy, climbing over him like he's a jungle gym when he's on the sofa, listening intently when he reads her a bedtime story.

His patience is remarkable. His adoration outstanding. His overprotective nature definitely needs to be dialed down a notch, but I'm working on it.

"Obviously Bishop and Tilly are on their way back from the park," Remy says from the dining table.

I keep staring as the two people who own my heart cross the street below, walking toward the lobby of our building. "Lucky guess?"

"No. The huge smile on your face is telling."

"I can't help it." I turn to face my brother. "They make me happy."

"And so they should." He stands hovering over the table, shuffling the scattered legal pages into a pile. "When are you going to take the plunge and let the homicidal maniac spend the night?"

"He can do that whenever he likes." I walk for the kitchen,

grabbing a bottle of water from the fridge. "He's the one who's made all the stipulations."

He places the stack of papers into an envelope and leaves it on the table. "Do I want to know?"

I shrug and crack open the lid of my bottle. "Probably not."

He pauses, scrutinizing me. "But you've slept together since…"

"Yes, Remy." I cringe. "I've slept with him since that night. Thanks for your concern."

The first time was the day he returned.

One kiss multiplied into a million more as he consumed me, taking his time to make up for past mistakes while Tilly napped. He stripped the scarf from around my neck to pay homage to his favorite scar, his hands everywhere, his grip possessive as if I'd somehow float away if he let go.

My brother holds up his palms in surrender. "Just doing my brotherly duties to make sure everything between you two is—"

"Everything is great." I speak over him, then take a sip of water.

Everything in absolutely every aspect of my life is almost perfect.

Tilly has found her feet here. She's now sleeping and eating well. She's even made a few friends at the park.

When times are tough, she continues to call for her momma, and I know that's still not me, but it's my arms she runs to for comfort. It's me she looks to for support.

"So he's treating you right?" Remy asks.

I smirk, cocking my hip against the kitchen counter. "Would you do something about it if he wasn't?"

"Of course." Remy rolls his eyes. "I'd pack your bags and disappear with you, because I sure as shit wouldn't approach that scary motherfucker about it."

I chuckle. "He's not scary." Even his scar is beautiful. A heroic reminder of the risk he took. "If Tilly doesn't fear him then—"

"Tilly has been through a lot. Let's not do a deep dive into why her judgment of character might not be at its best."

I screw the lid back on the bottle of water and playfully throw it at him. He dodges the projectile, laughing as it hits the ground to skitter along the floorboards.

"Her judgment of character is just fine," I grumble.

Even the bond with my brothers has changed into something I

adore. Where once we all fought our own private demons, not having enough time or energy to pay attention to what was going on in each other's lives, we now have the peace and security to maintain a healthy relationship.

Remy and Salvatore might live in another state, and have limited spare time with their new roles in our uncle's organization, but now they take notice when I've had a trying day. Or I'm exhausted. Or resentful of the past.

They visit often.

They send Tilly gifts all the damn time.

And they video call almost daily.

Matthew pays us the same attention, but in person, having explained how hard it was for him to keep Bishop's communication to himself. He hadn't even told Layla.

Since then, he's groveled a lot. Bribed, too. Layla, Tilly, and I take full advantage, enjoying spa days and shopping sprees at his expense without remorse.

"Are we done here?" I tilt my chin at the envelope on the dining table that contains the mass of paperwork we spent the morning going over.

"Yeah." Remy continues to chuckle. "As long as you're still happy for us to go ahead with the sale of Alleya."

"I am." I don't want the distraction the fashion label provides. I no longer want any ties to my parents either. "The sooner it's gone the better."

"In that case, everything is signed and initialed. Now, all I have to do is submit the documents to the legal team for them to—"

The front door opens, cutting off my brother's words, and the two most important people in my life walk inside, hand in hand.

My chest warms like it always does when I see them bonding, the heat quickly vanishing when I notice the stern look on Bishop's face.

"What happened?" I ask.

Tilly releases his fingers and rushes for the dollhouse in the corner of the open living room, oblivious to whatever has made Bishop seethe.

He stalks toward me, his face a mask of animosity as he drags me in and plants a kiss to my temple, muttering, "I killed two snotty-nosed assholes."

All the blood drains from my face, my stomach free falling. "You did what?" I whisper.

"What the fuck?" Remy rasps nearby.

"In my head." Bishop releases me and continues to the coffee machine, grabbing coffee mugs from the drawer below. "Snapped their necks like fucking toothpicks."

"So you didn't kill them?" I gape. "Are you trying to scare the life out of me?"

"Jesus Christ, Bishop." Remy drags a hand through his hair. "I thought you were serious."

"I was. I *am*. I'm itching to go back to the park and finish the job." Bishop shoves pods into the machine and presses a button to make it gurgle and spit. "One of them pushed in front of Tilly on the slide. The other dared to kiss her." He glares at my brother as he enunciates under his breath, "*He. Fucking. Kissed. Her.* Can you believe it? Right on the cheek. Those two little shitbags need a lesson in who they're dealing with."

I shoot Remy a what-the-fuck glance.

He gives me one in return.

"Okay, for starters, you can't walk in here after being on a play date and say—I killed two snotty-nosed A-holes. *Pause*. In my head." I walk up to him. "You say, *in my head*, I killed two snotty-nosed A-holes. In that order. There's no other acceptable way to relay that information."

"Your way is far less dramatic."

"*Exactly*," Remy and I say in unison.

Bishop grabs a filled mug and shoves it toward my brother, then hands another to me before claiming his own. "Do you seriously think I could've snuffed two ugly-ass twerps while at the park with Tilly?"

Would I have thought it likely? No.

Is he capable? When it comes to my daughter's honor and protection, I wouldn't put anything past him.

"You are psychotically protective," Remy mutters around a sip of coffee.

"True." Bishop inclines his head. "And it would serve you well to remember that."

"I'm not likely to forget."

Bishop takes a gulp from his mug and places it down on the

counter, then grabs mine from my cupped hands before I can even taste it. "Are you two finished doing what needs to be done?" He pulls me against his chest, his lips finding my hairline, his palms hot against my waist.

"Yeah." Remy nods as I sigh, unable to withstand the charms of Bishop's possessive hold. "All the family assets have been equally divided and once the financial institutions do their thing, my sister will be a very rich woman."

"They were far from equal." I stare up at Bishop, trying to relay my annoyance with the unfair distribution of wealth.

"You're ripping her off?" He releases me and takes a threatening step toward Remy.

"No." I grab his hand, threading our fingers. "It's the opposite. Matthew declined any financial compensation from the family trust. Then Salvatore and Remy decided Tilly deserved an equal share. So I'm receiving half of everything. Mine and hers combined."

"Tilly is part of the family." Remy glances to his niece. "And after what she went through…"

Bishop relaxes, his gaze returning to mine. "Good. How long will it take for the money to come through?"

"We're not sure, but as soon as it does I can repay you for everything you've done." I snuggle into him, sliding my arms around his neck.

"I suggest you retract that insult, belladonna. Otherwise my response won't be kind."

"But will it be dirty?" I tease, tugging the hair at the back of his nape.

Remy groans.

"Not this time." Bishop's eyes smolder as he palms my ass, roughly dragging me closer for a quick kiss. "I provide for you, end of story."

"What if I don't want to be provided for?"

He grabs my wrists, dragging them away from his shoulders. "Then you learn to deal with it."

I keep my smile in place, even though his show of old-school chivalry hurts.

I know he generously provides for me and Tilly because he still feels guilt over what happened. That he thinks he needs to buy my love.

"What if having financial independence means I'm now ready for you to move in?" I ask.

Bishop's gaze narrows as he slowly returns my wrists to his shoulders. "I'm listening."

"I feel like this is a private moment…" Remy says awkwardly. "Should I take Till to get some ice cream?"

"Ice cream?" My daughter jumps to her feet and runs for her uncle. "We get ice cream?"

Bishop ignores the commotion, his eyes not leaving mine. "I told you the stipulations of me moving back here. Are you saying you're ready to concede?"

"What I'm saying is that I want you to move in."

"But you know my terms," he counters. "We've gone over this. If I return, I'm never leaving. You'll be my wife. We'll become a family. Are you ready for that?"

No. I'm not ready. I'm not sure I ever will be. I'm still petrified I'm not good enough. That Bishop will finally realize I'm severely used merchandise and regret being stuck with me.

But there's no denying how the three of us fit together perfectly.

All our damaged, broken pieces join to create a remarkably happy picture. One I could never turn my back on.

"Ice cream," Tilly begs. "Pease, Unkie Remy,"

Remy clears his throat. "Can someone give me a heads-up to what I should be doing here? Am I leaving with the princess or do I keep standing here like a—"

"I'll move in tonight." Bishop grips my waist tighter. "We'll get married tomorrow."

My stomach fills with butterflies. My chest, too. "We're *not* getting married tomorrow."

"Ice cream. Ice cream. Ice cream," Tilly singsongs.

"Why?" Bishop leans in, his mouth a bare breath from mine. "Tilly is already excited."

I scoff. "She's excited for ice cream."

"This feels really awkward," Remy mutters. "You two are talking marriage and I'm standing here like a spare dick."

"Ice cream." Tilly grabs her uncle's hand and twirls like a ballerina. "Pease, ice cream."

"Marriage doesn't happen overnight, Bishop." I rake my teeth over my bottom lip, nervous energy filling my limbs. "There's paperwork and hoops to jump through."

"Is that a challenge?" he counters.

"Okay, we're leaving." Remy leads Tilly to the door. "We'll be back in twenty, even though past experience dictates the big guy needs less than five to seal the deal."

"Get the hell out of here, Costa, before I destroy you." Bishop leans in, his nose nuzzling mine as the front door opens.

"Tilly, wait." I pull away and turn toward my daughter as she stops and glances over her shoulder.

My chest is on fire at how she acknowledges her name. It's not the first time, but it's becoming more and more common. "Aren't you forgetting something?"

I crouch and open my arms wide. She giggles and rushes me, her face bright with happiness as she returns for a quick hug.

"Make sure Uncle Remy buys you two scoops, okay?" My heart thuds with pride. "Sprinkles, too."

My eyes burn as she nods and wiggles to escape my embrace, then impatiently scrambles back to her uncle. I stand, my insides all gooey and warm as her little hand takes his.

"Two scoops it is." Remy leads her into the hall, closing the door behind them.

The latch has barely clicked shut before Bishop's hand is on my chin, dragging my gaze back to his. "Are you done barking orders?"

I scowl. "I do *not* bark orders."

"Well, you sure as shit don't follow commands, otherwise we'd be married already."

"We have our reasons."

"No." He leans close, his mouth a breath from mine. "You have excuses."

"It's only been a few months. Don't you want more time to know what you're committing yourself to?"

"Belladonna, I knew you were the one the moment you laid me on my ass the night of the gala. There will never be anyone else."

My lips curve upward at the memory—the good that came from the incredibly bad. "How can I marry you when I still don't know your last name?"

He stiffens, growing tense like he always does with this

conversation. "I've told you I don't have a last name. I disowned my family a long time ago."

Yes, he's told me. We've spent hours talking about his past, and he's spent days getting to know mine. We've exchanged weaknesses and exposed flaws. No skeletons have remained hidden in either of our closets.

But through it all, he's refused to acknowledge the people who created him, which I understand. The problem is, it leaves an empty space on the marriage certificate he's trying to get me to sign. Especially when I no longer want to harbor the reminder of my parents with my surname either.

"You can pick a surname for us both," he offers. "And I'll bear it with pride."

My breath catches at the way this conversation is going exactly how I anticipated. My eagerness to fix broken bridges increases my pulse.

"Pick a name," he repeats, his mouth closing in on mine, his hands sliding to the waistband of my pants

"Any name?" I ask, already breathless.

He lowers the zipper at my crotch, one palm delving beneath my panties, his deft fingertips eagerly finding my clit. "Any fucking name, belladonna. I don't care as long as you're mine."

"Cappelletti." I gasp, our noses nuzzling as I drag my lips over his for a teasing kiss.

He freezes. Pulls back.

He looks at me with narrowed eyes, as if understanding he's just fallen into a trap.

"That's the name I want," I whisper.

His tattered relationship with my uncle is the only thing left to fix.

My parents have been dealt with. My brothers are safe. The wealth I'm owed will soon be mine. And I have my beautiful daughter, her past without me now never having existed as far as the authorities are concerned due to a mass of illegal paperwork and database tampering by Najeeb.

Bishop and Lorenzo's relationship is the only thing left to repair, despite Bishop's unwillingness to move on from the betrayal.

He doesn't know how to forgive and forget. He's never been taught.

"He's your family." I cup his cheek, my thumb brushing the scar hidden beneath his beard. "You need him in your life."

His chin hitches. "You'll marry me if I take his name?"

With or without the name, it doesn't matter. But I want this for him. To help him mend something he's too stubborn to fix.

"Yes." I nod. "I will."

"From a Costa to a Cappelletti?" He raises a brow, his fingers sliding back and forth over my clit. "You realize people might think you've married a relative."

I chuckle, tilting my hips to gain more friction, grabbing his shoulders for leverage. "I don't care."

His mouth dives toward my neck as he tugs at my scarf, dragging it off my shoulder, while his other hand continues enslaving my sex. "Why am I not surprised at this trickery?"

"Because you know me." I kiss his cheek, moaning against his stunning scar while two fingers plunge inside me. "And you know I want nothing more than to make you happy."

"You do make me happy." He grinds into me. Kissing. Licking. Grappling. "Now get to work taking off those clothes. You've got less than twenty minutes to fuck me like you're single, belladonna. Because come tomorrow, you'll be fucking me as my wife."

I hope you enjoyed Bishop.

A bonus epilogue from Bishop's point of view is now available in the bonus section of www.edensummers.com

ALSO BY EDEN SUMMERS

Hunting Her World

Hunter

Decker

Torian

Savior

Luca

Cole

Seeking Vengeance

Ruthless Redemption

Bishop

Start the Reckless Beat series

Blind Attraction (Reckless Beat #1)

Start the Vault series

A Shot of Sin (The Vault #1)

Information on more of Eden's titles can be found at www.edensummers.com or your online book retailer.

ABOUT THE AUTHOR

Eden Summers is a bestselling author of contemporary romance with a side of sizzle and sarcasm.

She lives in Australia with her own sarcastic, dark-eyed hero and two equally sarcastic teenage boys who are well aware she's circling the drain of insanity.

If you'd like access to exclusive information and giveaways, join Eden Summers' newsletter via the link on her website.

For more information:
www.edensummers.com
eden@edensummers.com

Made in the USA
Coppell, TX
26 July 2024